WORLD'S COLLIDER

A Shared-World Anthology

Edited by
Richard
Salter

First Edition

ISBN: 1-938644-02-6
ISBN-13: 978-1-938644-02-3

Nightscape Press, LLP
http://www.nightscapepress.com

CONTENTS

THE CONSTRUCTION
OF WORLD'S COLLIDER

This book is unique. Before you roll your eyes and skip this introduction, hear me out. Plenty of intros start by claiming something similar, but this time I really mean it. This anthology isn't like most others.

There have been shared-world collections before, where all the stories take place in the same universe and share some common elements. There have been so-called mosaic novels before like Robert Asprin's Thieves' World or Paul Cornell's Life During Wartime. But I think World's Collider separates itself from its predecessors by assuming the characteristics of a novel. Told by multiple writers, with their own unique styles and ideas, they will each thrill and unnerve you. Some stories will make you think and a few will make you cry. Each story in this collection could stand alone as an individual, apocalyptic tale. But taken as whole, read in order, one after the other, a story emerges. A 21-part story with twists and surprises, themes and recurring characters, and most importantly, a common narrative.

An anthology posing as a novel? Or possibly a novel posing as an anthology.

When I was commissioning stories, I chose a mix of those that could be adapted to fit a larger narrative; and some that were so delicious in their own right, I just had to include them. Some stories had to be edited quite a bit to make them fit; others were specially commissioned to fill a gap in the narrative. All are just great stories.

You might be wondering why I didn't just write a novel about a big rift that opens in the middle of Europe, and all the terrible things that emerge from it. I do plan to write a novel next, now that this anthology is delivered, but I didn't want to impose my ideas on other writers in this case. What made putting together World's Collider such a thrill was the melting pot of ideas. So many concepts and characters, and places for the storyline to go. There's no way I could have come up with all this cool stuff on my own. Most of the story elements in this book came from the contributors, not from me. The result, and the overall storyline, really is completely unique, because with a different set of writers involved you'd be reading a radically different book. I wasn't interested in mapping out a plot line and assigning chapters to different writers. Instead, World's Collider grew from the elements of the stories.

I want to take this opportunity to thank a number of folks, without whom I wouldn't have had a hope of completing this project. Firstly to all the writers, you are a talented bunch and highly entertaining to be around. The writers' Facebook group was often overflowing with good humor, terrible puns, and double entendres. Just ask them about the mustard.

I don't want to single any of them out, but I will anyway. A special thanks to Elise Hattersley for volunteering to beta read the manuscript and helping out with the writer interviews for my website, (http://www.richardsalter.com). I also want to thank Dave Hutchinson for stepping in to fill a gap with a specially commissioned story, which he wrote and turned in within two weeks — astonishing! To James Moran for introducing our main protagonist in just 2,000 words. And lastly (for the writers) to the class acts that are Steven Savile and Steve Lockley. Mr Savile was commissioned to write the final story some time back, but due to being a busy bee he couldn't start until quite late in the day. He was given an impenetrable brief by an editor who kept changing his mind and moving the playing pieces around, and had the Herculean task of making sense of all the plot threads while telling an exciting story. He stuck with the project even after breaking his arm(!), whereupon he enlisted the help of Mr Lockley to complete what I think is an excellent and exciting finale. Thanks to you guys and all the amazing writers who worked so hard to blow an enormous hole in the centre of Europe.

Many thanks to the gracious Carolyn Edwards, who produced the gorgeous "Tower" image that adorns the cover page and the promotional postcards. Thanks to Lukas Thelin of Foxrain for the cover—a real beauty, and to Steven Savile (again) for hooking us up. Huge thanks go to Robert Shane Wilson, Jennifer Wilson, and Mark Scioneaux of Nightscape Press. As a new publisher, they went to bat for World's Collider as soon as it was available, and they won me over with their personal commitment, their great ideas, and their respect for the writers. Thanks guys and may Nightscape live a long and healthy life.

A heart-felt thanks to you, the reader, who may just be sampling this anthology or perhaps you've already bought it. I hope we won't let you down.

And lastly thanks to Jennifer, my long-suffering wife, who wondered if I would finish editing this infernal manuscript so I could pay her some attention, or at least take the kids to the park so she could have a lie down. It's all done now, my love.

Now, about that novel…

Richard Salter, June 2012

WRAITH LIGHTS
by Jonathan Green

*S*he doesn't know what's worse; the screaming howls or the sound *of pounding footsteps echoing along the passageway behind her.*

She doesn't dare look round. She already knows what she'll see, and it's nothing good. She daren't look down either, even though she can feel her feet slipping from under her, so she keeps going, half-running and half-sliding on the blood-slick tiles.

And then there's the lab door in front of her.

Suzie's at the door, screaming, the look on her face one of blind panic and abject horror. And seeing that, even though she knows she shouldn't — that nothing good can possibly come of it — she looks round...

"Jackson, take a look at this, will you?"

Penny glances up from scanning the reams of dot matrix print-out and puts her polystyrene cup of coffee on the counter in front of her. "What?"

"Just come and have a look," Bosley says.

Penny unfolds her legs and gets up from her chair. Crossing the lab she peers over her team-member's shoulder at the digitized data display on the screen in front of him. He doesn't need to tell her what she should be paying particular attention to; the spike is obvious. The results speak for themselves.

"What is that? Electromagnetic?"

"It shouldn't be," Bosley huffs in annoyance. "I mean how could it be?"

Penny gasps. "Not gravitational, surely?"

The rumble of plastic wheels on the tiled floor tells them they've got the attention of the third person in the lab now.

"What are you looking at?" Suzie asks bringing her chair rolling to a halt with judicious application of her feet against the floor.

"I don't know. I mean I really don't know what to make of it," Bosley says, clearly bewildered. "And what's more, we haven't even run the experiment yet."

"Charles needs to see this," Penny says, turning to Suzie. The Chinese-American programmer is painfully beautiful, with her silk-smooth hair and perfect complexion. She may only be wearing jeans, Converse and a Harvard hoodie but she still looks far more stylish than Penny feels about herself.

The lab door opens and a man with a shock of blond hair shoulders his way into the room, his hands full of bag-wrapped sandwiches.

"Okay, so I've got salami on rye, tuna salad on wholemeal and"—he checks the scrunched greaseproof packages in his hands—"one blueberry muffin. Sorry, Bosley, they were right out of chocolate."

"Never mind that, Brunner," Bosley says, beckoning the blond man over. "Take a look at this."

Brunner plonks the food down on a desk and joins the others at Bosley's terminal.

"*Scheiße!*" Brunner swears, momentarily reverting to his native tongue.

"You could say that," Bosley agrees, steepling his fingers together in front of his face and touching his fingertips to his lips.

"Is that" — Brunner peers more closely at the data-diagram on the screen — "gravitational?"

"We haven't even run the test yet!" Penny interjects.

"Where's Stockwell?" Brunner asks. "He needs to see this."

"I know," Penny agrees. "Suzie Q?"

"He was still checking the Collider last I heard," Suzie replies. "I'll buzz him."

"No, it's all right," Penny says, already halfway to the door. "I'll go. I could do with the exercise. Besides, knowing Charles, he probably hasn't even got his phone on him."

Seeing Bosley again, like that — more beast than man now — is more than she can bear and a ragged scream escapes her own tortured lungs.

She turns back to Suzie and the lab door. She can see others behind it — security guards, engineers and other CERN staff — but she can't tell if they're trying to push the door shut or holding it open for her.

The sight of Bosley and the fear-fuelled adrenaline rush send her careening onwards. But in that moment she loses purchase and her trainers slip on the smeared tiles. Her lurching flight sends her to the floor in a sprawl.

Her grasping hands try to get a grip, as if she intends to pull herself along the floor, but cannot. And behind her the animalistic snarls and pounding footfalls are only getting closer with every passing second…

Penny finds Charles Stockwell, the project's team leader, atop an extendable platform before the gaping mouth of the Super Collider's solenoid.

Every time she sees it like this, Penny can understand why the uninitiated call it the black hole machine.

"Charles!" she calls over the thrum of magnets and machinery that fills the vast, man-made cavern.

The middle-aged physicist continues with what he's doing, apparently lost in his work.

Tilting her head back, one hand on the dome of her plastic hard hat to stop it falling off—her dyed auburn locks spilling out from beneath it around her shoulders—she calls again. "Charles!"

The man frowns and peers closer through the dark aperture at the open heart of the immense machine.

"Charles!"

He turns and sees her then, looking like he's waking from some unsettling dream. He appears old; older than she has ever seen him look before, old and grey. His skin has acquired an unpleasant waxy pallor. He doesn't look well.

There is a faraway look in his unfocused eyes.

"I…"

"What is it, Charles? You look like you've seen a ghost." She laughs humourlessly.

"It's just that I..." He hesitates. "I thought I saw someone."

It suddenly feels uncomfortably cold in the Collider chamber. It's May in the world above but down here it suddenly feels like winter. Cold sweat prickles on the skin at the base of her spine.

"Saw someone? Where?"

The man glances at the aperture in the machine again. "There."

"But, Charles," she says with forced laughter, "that's impossible. It was probably just your reflection."

He stares at her blankly, like some geriatric pensioner suffering from dementia.

There's something unnerving about the vacant look on his face. The man's highly regarded in his field, the proud owner of three doctorates.

For a moment she forgets why she's there, and then, "Charles, there's something you should see."

"Huh?"

"In the lab."

"The lab?"

And then the fog of confusion suddenly clears, as if he has just had a Road to Damascus moment.

"Oh yes, the lab. Of course." He puts a hand to the platform controls. "I'll come down."

Hands close around her ankles, her calves, her thighs, fingers that feel like clawed talons digging into the taut flesh of tensed muscles.

She kicks and screams, raging against the dying of the light. And then her furiously pin-wheeling legs are free again and she catches the thing in the mouth — she can't think of it as Bosley anymore, she won't let herself — breaking teeth and caving in its nose to boot.

She feels hands on her shoulders and screams again.

Only it's not one of the infected, it's Suzie.

And then she's on her feet somehow, and racing for the door, screams of encouragement drowning out the savage baying of the things behind her…

"It's happened again," Bosley says as Penny re-enters the lab, Charles traipsing after her like a lost puppy, a hangdog expression on his crumpled face.

"What?" Penny can't believe what she's hearing. "But we haven't even—"

"Run the test," Bosley finishes. "Tell me about it."

He breathes out loudly through his nose, resting his closed mouth on his steepled fingers once more.

"What has?" Stockwell asks.

They show him. What little colour is left in the old man's face drains from his cheeks. He looks ill, like death barely warmed up.

"Charles, are you all right?"

Penny finds the team leader a chair and guides him towards it. He mutters something in reply and sits down. With all that's going on, it is a few moments before Penny's subconscious processes what it *thinks* she heard him say.

She takes an uncomfortable step back from the old man. Is she imagining things or did he really say—

"Look, we need to run a diagnostic check," Brunner says vehemently, his voice rising in pitch and interrupting her barely conscious thoughts.

"Way ahead of you," Suzie replies from her terminal. "I've run the diagnostic twice. The software's fine. Those results are genuine. Those fluctuations are what the sensors are picking up."

"But we haven't even run the test yet!" Penny cries, exasperated, as if simple repetition of the facts will help solve the mystery.

"And yet there's nothing wrong with the software," Suzie insists.

"What about the hardware?" Brunner asks.

"I don't think so." Everyone turns to look at Stockwell. "And once you eliminate the impossible, whatever remains, no matter how improbable…"

"Must be the truth," Penny finishes for him. "But *what* truth? What are we witnessing here?" She points an accusing finger at Bosley's terminal screen.

The Large Hadron Collider was always about making the big discoveries, things no one had ever seen before—perhaps never even contemplated. She feels she should be feeling excited by this, but instead, rather than joyful elation, she is unnerved, unsettled.

She feels scared.

The others do too. She can see it in their faces.

"So," she says, ever the pragmatist, "what do we do now?" All eyes turn to their distant team leader once more. "Charles?"

"Hm?" The old man appears distracted. And his complexion isn't any better.

"Charles, what's the matter?" Penny demands. "Try to stay focused. What do we do now?"

Usually she'd have a few ideas herself, but not this time.

"Look, I say we run the diagnostic test again," Bosley says, waving away Suzie's protests, "and get back down to the Collider and check the hardware for ourselves, just to be sure. Is that all right with you, Charles?"

"I saw something moving," Stockwell mutters as he stares vacantly into space.

"What? *Where?*"

"In the heart of the machine," Stockwell replies, not once making eye-contact with Bosley. His voice has acquired an eerie, almost sing-song quality that suits the distant look in his misty eyes. "As through a glass darkly."

"What's he saying?" Brunner asks. The German's English might be good, but his knowledge of English Literature isn't. He's a scientist, not a scholar.

Bosley's the same. "Mumbling bullshit," the American fumes, sounding even tetchier than Brunner.

"It's from the Bible," Penny explains.

"I know where it's from! So now he's getting all Revelations on us, predicting the end of the world and all that crap!"

"It's from Corinthians," Penny said before she could stop herself.

"Whatever," Bosley snaps. Then he adds, not so under his breath, "The guy needs a psych test, if you ask me."

"He's sitting *right there*!" Penny hisses, furious now.

Bosley glowers at her and then turns his attention to Stockwell, who doesn't seem to have noticed the comments.

"Charles, you've been working damn hard, we all have," Bosley says. "When was the last time you slept?"

"I…"

Stockwell suddenly shakes his head again, as if still trying to dispel his waking reverie. He stares at Bosley, and then at Penny, as if seeing them for the first time.

"Charles, please. Get yourself back to your dorm, get some rest. We'll monitor things here," Bosley says, his calm air having reasserted itself, fingers steepled before his face.

And then the fog of otherworldly confusion descends on Stockwell again.

"Just don't look into the light."

Penny and Bosley exchange anxious glances.

"What was that he said?" Brunner asks, perturbed.

"Nothing. It was nothing," Penny says, understanding the fierce look Bosley's giving her.

"Come on, Charles," her co-conspirator says, helping the old man up from the chair.

Stockwell doesn't resist as Bosley directs him towards the door. "Get some sleep. Maybe grab a bite to eat first. We'll let you know if we need you."

Penny watches Bosley intently. She knows that some sort of line has been crossed. Whether she likes it or not, she's complicit in his conspiracy to oust the old man now.

As Stockwell shuffles out the door, Bosley turns to address the rest of them. "Jackson, you and Suzie Q stay here, keep an eye on those readings, see if there are any more fluctuations. Karl and I will go downstairs and take another look at the Collider, get a couple of engineers to help us while we're at it. Give Lauren a call, see if she's available."

As Bosley and Brunner leave, Penny slumps down in her chair again.

"What's up with Stockwell?" Suzie asks, although she hardly sounds concerned.

"I don't know," Penny says, preoccupied.

And then she hears the old man's strange proclamation again inside her head, and now there's no doubt in her mind as to what she had heard him say. The hairs on the back of her neck rise again as agitation crackles throughout her, down her spine and right to her fingertips.

The Wraith Lights are waiting.

And then they're through, and Penny tumbling into the lab, landing hard on her knees, as the others slam the door shut. A split second later she hears the thud of something colliding with the door.

More shouts from inside the lab followed by the scrape of furniture and crash of instruments falling to the floor — a table being dragged across the door as a makeshift barricade.

Penny stays where she is, hunched up in a ball, sobbing, gasping for breath, feeling the clawing fingers of the dead upon her still. A ragged scream escapes her in a moment of blessed release.

Suzie sits with her back to a terminal, hugging her knees, whimpering softly.

Her scream exhausted, lungs empty of air, Penny finally unfolds herself and sits up.

She watches the desperate movements of the others in the room as if viewing a film running at half speed. One of the security guards appears to have taken charge of the situation, directing the others to lug whatever heavy objects they can over to the barricade to increase its durability.

Only, as she watches them work, Penny can't help thinking that as much as the barricade will keep the infected out, it will just as effectively keep them trapped inside...

"Jackson, are we good to go?" Bosley's voice comes a second time over the intercom, irritation and the crackle of static underlining his words.

"Yes. Sorry. Yes, we're good to go."

"All right then, firing it up now."

Penny watches them via the camera feed from the Collider chamber. Bosley and Brunner poring over the laser scanner they've set up to allow them to take readings from the Collider's core; Lauren and the other technicians doing whatever it is technicians do…

All five of those working on the platform suddenly step back from the machine and over the com Penny hears Lauren intone, "In three… two… one…"

There is a bright flash that blurs the screen, causing Penny to look away for a moment, turning her gaze to the monitor screen, so that she sees the spike occur in real-time. She gasps.

"It's happened again!"

Suzie's at her side in an instant.

"And it's still happening."

The readings have never shown anything like this before. It would take a team of scientists months, if not years, to make sense of them. But her surprise at the sudden fluctuation in the readings the computer's picking up from the myriad sensors inside the machine is soon forgotten in the light of what she hears Bosley say next.

"Sweet Moses! The old bastard was right!"

She feels the tingle of anxiety at the base of her skull once more and asks the question, even though she already knows the answer. "Bosley, what do you mean?"

"There's something moving in there," comes his reply over the com.

Her eyes are back on the camera feed now, as are Suzie's. The scanner's been switched off. Bosley's hunched over — steepled fingers to his lips once more — peering into the guts of the machine. Like Stockwell before him.

"What is it? What can you see?" Penny persists.

"It's... It looks like a dark aperture."

As through a glass darkly.

"It's like some kind of... rift." Bosley breaks off again and turns to Brunner. Penny hears him say, "You don't think it could be... temporal, do you?"

And that's when it happens, even though afterwards Penny can't quite be sure what "it" actually was.

There is a flash of light — like the laser firing up — and the screen glare causes her to half-close her eyes. But through the blurred bars of her lashes she sees... *thinks* she sees...

It looks like the beam, or whatever it is, is projecting from the heart of the Collider and not the scanning equipment.

And then there's the noise; a snapshot of sound, like the death-scream of a planet.

It only lasts a moment — mere nanoseconds — put Penny still chucks her guts all over her jeans, and the sudden clogging ammonia stink in the room tells her that Suzie's pissed herself.

Staring dumbly at the screen, strings of vomit-thickened saliva drooling from her chin, she sees the five bodies now lying on the platform, unmoving.

And somehow — something about the way they're lying — she knows they're dead.

They're clawing at the door now, Bosley, Brunner and the others — Penny brings herself up sharply.

No! They're not Bosley and Brunner any more. The two men, her colleagues, are dead. They died in the…

What's she to call it? The accident? The disaster? The beginning of the end?

That's what it feels like for those trapped in the lab, 574 feet below the Swiss mountains. Ten thousand people work within the CERN complex. How many of them are already infected? And how long before the infection spreads beyond CERN?

She feels sick; sick with fear. Sick with the realization of the finality of their fate. She's feverish too. Sweat beads her brow and her skin prickles with heat.

Surely it is only a matter of time now…

She just sits there, inside the cubicle, on the closed loo seat, a wodge of paper in her hand, sobbing.

Bosley, Brunner, Lauren, the other two engineers whose names she doesn't know. All five of them, dead.

The Wraith Lights are waiting.

The dim lighting in the restroom flickers and then goes out altogether. The constant hum of the air vents goes quiet.

A sob catches in her throat. Silence permeates the darkness.

Penny stares at the cubicle door in the darkness, hoping that, as her eyes adjust to the gloom, she might see some gradation to the black that will at least help her find her way out. But there is no such differentiation to the darkness.

Her ears strain to pick up any sound.

"Hello?" she calls, self-consciously. "Is there anybody there?"

The silent darkness offers no response. She isn't even rewarded with an echo in the acoustic-deadening cubicle.

She tries again, louder now: "Hello?"

She gets up and carefully pulls back the bolt, suddenly worried about making any kind of sound at all, and opens the door.

She hears nothing but the gurgle of water in the pipes and the rustling sound of her own movements.

Taking small steps, and sticking to the edges of the room, using her hands to guide her, she eventually finds her way to the door. Grasping the handle she pulls it open, only to be met by more darkness; silent and total.

"Is there anybody there?"

With a *plink* the neon lights flick on above her head and she's blinking at their sudden brightness, eyes stinging with fresh tears at the intensity.

The corridor is empty, the only sound the hum of the strip lights, but it's better than the silent darkness that went before.

She's about to set off for the lab again when she pauses. She must look a state, she thinks, but she doesn't go back into the restroom to use the mirrors there. Instead she turns right, heading for the vending machines. She needs a coffee.

As she makes her way along the empty corridor she wonders at the blackout. She's never known anything like it before and she can't help wondering if it's connected to the... the problems—that's it, the problems—they've been experiencing.

And then she's playing back the images on the monitor screen inside her head once more: the bright flash; the five bodies, motionless on the platform, all since transferred to the morgue.

When five people die at precisely the same moment whilst working on the Collider, nobody is going to be allowed to leave the complex until all five autopsies have been completed and a thorough investigation carried out. None of them are going anywhere any time soon, the living or the dead.

And that's when she hears the sound that sets her teeth on edge, like nails on a blackboard, and she rounds a corner.

She can hear them scratching at the door — like a cat wanting to be let in — fingernails scrabbling at the lock, the squeak of bloodied fingers on glass.

She can't bear it any longer. Scrambling across the floor on all fours she drags herself under a desk. Above her streams of impossible data continue to scroll across the screens of computer terminals — the end of the world spelled out in zeroes and ones.

Suzie is rocking backwards and forwards where she sits, still hugging her legs, her whimpers a constant monotonous drone now.

Penny throws her hands over her ears to drown out the doomsday sounds. How long can it be before they're all either dead or… changed?

Sitting there, under the desk, rocking herself now, la-la-la-ing away the end of the world, the stinging salt-sweat trickling into her eyes, she becomes aware of the itching inflammation at the back of her left leg.

It's no good, she can't ignore it anymore.

Taking her hands from her ears she pulls up the leg of her jeans…

Bright red graffiti covers the walls of the corridor.

Wraith Lights.

The Wraith lights are waiting.

Waiting and watching.

Beware the watchers.

The Wraith Lights are waiting.

Like the pronouncements of some mad prophet, the words have been inscribed over and over, the dripping red letters running into one another again and again.

The mad prophet in question is lying against the wall, feebly writing out yet another prediction.

He doesn't have any fingernails left. Judging by the blood on his lips and the gory lumps of keratin on the floor, the lunatic's chewed them off.

The lights flicker and threaten to go out again, but even this isn't enough to distract her from the sight of the wretch scrawling doom-laden warnings on the wall with the bloody stumps of his fingertips.

Penny gasps in horror. "Charles! What are you doing?"

"The Wraith Lights," the man mumbles. "The Wraith Lights are waiting."

He suddenly turns his wildly staring eyes on her then, eyes that blaze with the sanity that only the truly insane possess, making her start.

"I told you, didn't I? I told you they were waiting."

They both hear the crash and turn together in the direction of the sound, looking back down the corridor behind Penny.

"And now they're here."

The lights flicker and for a moment Penny fears they're going to be plunged into darkness again. The burst of fitful whimpering and coarse swearing tells her she's not the only one.

The lifts are already out of action, she knows that, so surely it can only be a matter of time.

Twisting her leg, she looks at the exposed calf.

The others are arguing over what they should do. Some are suggesting somehow blowing up the Collider and destroying the entire complex to keep the infection from spreading. Others claim it would be impossible, this isn't a military base with a self-destruct system.

Someone else suggests sealing all the exits to the outside world.

The resulting flurry of activity is accompanied by a cacophony of raised voices and hysterical sobs as the desperate plan is put into operation.

But Penny doesn't take in any of it, the screams, the barked instructions or the howls of premature grief. She's too busy staring at her leg.

In the adrenaline-flooded moment of panic and racing emotions she didn't realize that she had been hurt – that she had been...

The skin is inflamed around the injury, the bite marks themselves already black with coagulated blood.

A seismic shudder shakes the room, and the lights fail again, to a chorus of desperate screams.

Feeling suddenly so alone in the darkness, Penny wonders if this is the beginning of the end or merely the end of the beginning...

INNERVISIONS
by James Moran

My name is Scott Fletcher, and I'm losing my mind. I know I'm losing my mind, because the giant talking insect in my kitchen told me I would. That was before I blew it up, obviously.

I'm jumping ahead, sorry, I keep doing that. That's why I'm writing everything down, so I can get the details clear in my head. Things keep getting mixed up, I forget what order they happened in and lose an hour trying to rearrange them. Writing this should help. If I can finish it in time.

It all started when my doctor told me I had a brain tumour. Well, that's when it started for me, the rest of it must have started before that. Doesn't matter. Can only put down what I know for certain. Like the fact that there's a tumour the size of an apple in my brain. The doctor pointed it out on the scan, as if I wouldn't believe him otherwise. But I knew he was telling the truth. You don't get a tumour that big without side effects. It explained a lot.

Like the hallucinations. He said they'd get worse. Along with everything else. The list of symptoms meant my life would swiftly become unbearable. Headaches, vomiting, seizures, personality changes, possible paralysis, and many more classic hits, not available in the shops, call now for your chance to go crazy and die. At least it seemed to be benign. Silver lining, and all that.

He got me straight into radiotherapy, said it was my best option. Surgery was out, as the tumour was in an awkward place, and seemed to have moved between scans. Not sure how that was possible without my head exploding. The doctor was pretty baffled, too. Benign my arse. I think I scared him. To be honest, I scared myself sometimes, I was so calm about it. Must be the personality changes he warned me about. Or maybe some things are just so fucking huge and terrifying, you can't see enough of them to be properly afraid.

That night, I got pretty drunk. Wouldn't you?? I watched TV, fascinated by how the newsreaders could say so much about so little. The Large Hadron Collider had been sealed from the inside for two months, the military had been trying to get in since then. No change in the story for weeks, the desperate reporters were starting to sound like they were on a home shopping channel, filling time and talking endless shit about what *might* be happening.

I passed out around 2am. Had weird nightmares about monsters inside the LHC, flesh-eating horrors, roaming the corridors, looking for victims. Don't drink and watch the news, kids. At least, at the time, I thought it was the booze's fault. Now I know better.

Woke up the next morning, hung over and covered in tiny, scaly insects. Jumped off the sofa, freaking out, brushing them off. Then calmed down. I was good at calming down, back when I thought there was no point in worrying about anything. The doctor said I'd be seeing more stuff like this.

What was more likely: hallucinations, or an infestation of weird, scaly creatures out of nowhere?? Yeah. Hindsight, and all that shit.

Despite the hangover, I managed to drag myself out of the house and go for my usual jog. Didn't see much point staying healthy when I had an inoperable brain tumour rapidly killing me. But hey, healthy body, healthy mind. And there was still a chance the radiotherapy would do its stuff. No point giving up, or you may as well just throw yourself under a bus.

The park was pretty empty, surprisingly for a weekday morning in London. Normally it was full of commuters, striding to work, always in a hurry. I used to be one of them, until recently. The side effects of the brain tumour had stopped all that; you can't focus on tech support when your head feels like someone's hitting it with a sledgehammer every hour or so. Never thought headaches could be that bad, even migraines would have been more manageable. One of them stopped me in my tracks that morning, bringing the jog to a sudden halt. I had to collapse onto a bench, gasping, barely able to stay upright. I puked, splattering the grass around me.

A jogger came over to see if I was all right. She kept her distance, warily, in case I was a nutcase. I didn't blame her, I must have looked a total mess. I managed a smile, and said I'd be okay. The headaches were mercifully brief, I'd probably have cut my head open by then if they were any longer. She nodded, then recoiled, pointing at me. Told me I was "covered in them". I didn't know what she meant, the clothes were fresh out of the dryer, the only thing I could see were the hallucinatory insect things crawling all over me —

That's when I realized they were real. She could see them

too.

I may have shrieked like a six year old girl. Okay, I did. Really loudly.

The jogger ran away as I brushed the things off me, panicking. The insects were real. What the hell were they? I had no idea. I still don't. So I headed for the nearest place I could find that sold pest control supplies.

Back at the flat, I took each room in turn, spraying, squashing, trapping, hitting, swearing, advancing through each stage like a Roman battalion. The insects were everywhere, but as I cleared more territory, they retreated until they were concentrated in the kitchen. I followed them in, closed the door, and kept spraying.

The insects gathered together in the centre of the room, seemingly to protect themselves. But then they started forming into a shape, a larger, humanoid figure, a horrible approximation of my appearance. To mock me? Put me at ease? No idea. And then it spoke, using fake vocal cords formed from insects, the sound chittering and echoing through its insect lips.

hello Scott. we like your world. it's nice. much better than ours. shame it's going to end, very soon. lucky for you the invader in your brain means you won't see it happen. enjoy the last drops of sanity before your world starts to burn.

Surprisingly well spoken for a bunch of insects. And then it laughed, a terrible, crackling laugh.

So I did what any reasonable person would have done. I blew up the building.

Obviously I cleared the building first, pulled the fire alarm, and waited until everyone was outside. Then I turned the gas on full, waited ten minutes, and threw in a sheaf of burning newspaper. I slightly miscalculated the timing, and the door came flying off, knocking me out. I woke up in here. They call it a hospital, but it's a loony bin. They don't like me saying that. They think it upsets the patients. They're not patients, I tell them. They're loonies. Like me. Or they wouldn't be here. They don't like me saying that either.

There were interviews, police, doctors, psychiatrists, even Special Branch (in case I was a "home grown" terrorist). I tried to tell them that an alien insect gestalt had warned me that the world was about to end. That went down about as well as you'd imagine.

In the meantime, the headaches got worse. When they came, I'd see an afterimage in front of my eyes for several minutes, like someone had just taken a flash photo. This one was like a large black ball of swirling nothingness, inky black, making it difficult to see where I was going. I was obsessed with it, started drawing it to try and work out what it was. What did it mean?

The answer came while watching TV one day. It was getting hard to concentrate on anything else, so I preferred to just sit and stare at the news for hours. There'd been some developments at the LHC, the military were breaching the facility and seemed to be making progress. A news helicopter hovered high above the building, all the action happening out of sight somewhere. It looked like it was going to be another uneventful report, until the building exploded—followed by the whole collider itself, under the ground, in a sequence of explosions travelling around the entire 26 kilometre circumference of the main tunnel. And then it got weird.

Everything inside the circle of the collider seemed to implode, falling downwards into the Earth. But not *into* the

Earth, more through it, a hole in reality sucking away that section of ground. It kept getting wider, not stopping at the limit of the explosions. The news helicopter was pulled down too, so I only got to see a few seconds of it before the screen went black, and they cut back to the two shocked newsreaders, speechless for once.

I had to check with the others in the TV room that they'd seen it too, that I wasn't just hallucinating. But no, it was real. Whatever the hell just happened, it had really happened. The news readers were equally baffled, until more reports started coming in. There was a massive hole in the planet, destroying large chunks of Switzerland and France. Casualties were estimated at between a hundred thousand and twenty-two million, depending on who you asked. And nobody knew what to do.

The damage was massive, a circle seven or eight hundred miles wide around the initial explosion. Nobody was sure how that was possible, but any time they sent aircraft in to investigate, they got pulled into a black nothingness and destroyed. What they did know was that a huge cloud of debris was heading west across Europe, towards the UK. It wasn't quite clear what kind of debris, so just in case, they said it'd be safer if everyone stayed indoors for the next 24 hours or so. The tried and tested, head in the sand defence.

They may not have known what was in the debris cloud, but they could at least show us a picture and talk about it for ages, and so a satellite image was hastily rustled up. The cloud was drifting right across France.

And beneath it, where a huge chunk of Europe used to be, was a massive, inky black ball of nothingness.

Just like the image I'd been seeing lately, during my

headaches. I'd seen this coming, I'd seen an image from the future, I had somehow known this would happen. I stood up to say something, but another crippling headache hit me, worse than any of them so far.

I screamed in agony, seeing the debris cloud shape again, but this time, there was more. I was in the middle of the strange implosion, hearing and feeling the pain of the millions who had died so far, their bodies torn apart as they were pulled into the darkness. The hole in reality led to another universe like ours — but not like ours. Somewhere much, much worse. Filled with terrible things, things that were angry, and hungry, and despicable, things that now knew there was a way through to our world. I saw them all, too many to remember, flashes of horror and death and pain.

And then I saw a young couple flee through the streets of Paris, carrying a newborn wrapped in a coat. He was desperate and terrified. She was tired and blood soaked. The fish-with-no-water that swam through the air smelled the blood and swarmed. I saw it all from their point of view. Saw the man tear the stained skirt from his ailing wife and yell at her to take the baby and run. Saw the mother carry her baby through a gap in a fence. Saw the swarm descend on the man holding the bloody fabric aloft.

And later I saw another man, this one with one green eye and one blue eye, who looked normal, but wasn't, not by a long shot. And he liked the smell of our world.

So now I know what's coming. But I'm locked away in a loony bin, babbling nonsense, with nobody who'll listen to me, and a brain tumour that'll probably kill me in a month. And that's why I'm writing all this down. In the faint hope that someone will believe me.

My name is Scott Fletcher, and I'm losing my mind, because I'm the only person who knows that the Collision is just the beginning and that the world is going to end. And there's nothing I can do to stop it.

KEEP CALM AND CARRY ON
PART ONE
by David N. Smith and Violet Addison

Jess
Monday, 3rd August, 2015
21:30pm

The sky is burning.

Have you looked out of your window tonight? The horizon to the south-east is glowing red. Even now, the sun is going down, but it's not getting dark; everything is bathed in this eerie reddish glow, as if the world itself has caught fire.

I turned on the TV to try and find out what was going on, and the first thing you notice is that half the channels have gone off air, their programmes replaced with emergency fault cards or just silent static.

The BBC, CNN and Al Jazeera are still on air, but none of them has a clue what has happened. All contact has been lost with a great swathe of Europe; France, Germany, Austria and Switzerland have all gone silent.

There's just thirty seconds of video footage, being looped repeatedly, underneath a commentary of wild theories from baffled experts. The shot, taken from a news helicopter, shows a line of fire exploding upwards, even as the ground on the other side of the flames begins to fall downward, caving into an impossibly deep darkness.

It doesn't look real; it looks like a really cool special effect from a multi-million dollar Hollywood movie. The way the news helicopter plunges into the void, glass shattering and pilot screaming, feels incredibly real. Then you remember that this is real; this is the news.

An early satellite image shows this massive black ball, crashing into the Earth—or so the newsreader said. We've been calling it "The Collision" ever since, but the helicopter video shows the ground collapsing before the satellite image was taken, so how does that work then?

There's a lot of speculation; much of it focusing on the Large Hadron Collider, which is located at the heart of the explosion. The British Government is telling the public to keep calm, saying that there's no immediate danger to us here in the UK, and people here seem content enough with this reassurance for now.

My mom phoned from the States, telling me to come home immediately. I told her to stop being ridiculous. I've built a life here in the UK and I'm not going to abandon it just because of some event hundreds of miles away.

So, the world knows something terrible has happened, but it doesn't really know what; so life inevitably goes on. I have to be at work at 7am in the morning, so I'm off to bed now. I wonder what kind of world I will wake up to tomorrow.

Sleep should be impossible, and yet I'm tired and craving my pillow. I think perhaps I haven't really understood what I've seen on TV; right now it's all just pictures of faraway, foreign places.

If any of my friends out there in mainland Europe are reading this, then get in touch and tell us what the hell is happening over there.

Paulo, are you still working in Switzerland? If so, tell us what you can see out of your window.

Naomi, you're back-packing your way around Europe, are you close to this? Hope not!

Mike, weren't you coming back from the fashion show in Paris today, did you make it home?

My thoughts are with you all.

Michael
Tuesday, 4th August, 2015
1:45am

Hey! I'm alive! But only just! We were on the Eurostar when it happened. The lights went out and then the train ground to a halt. I've just spent hours walking through dark tunnels with hundreds of other terrified people. My suit is ruined! Now I'm stranded on the wrong side of the channel, in Calais. Nobody has a clue what has happened. There's no power here, so once my phone battery runs out, I'll be incommunicado! Don't suppose you know anyone with a boat, do you?

Jess
Tuesday, 4ᵗʰ August, 2015
7:17am

Woke up at 5am and immediately turned on the news.

That's what we do these days when there's a massive disaster, right? We make straight for the news channels to watch people speculate.

They now have footage from an RAF helicopter, showing an unfeasibly large black void where once there were mountains, fields and towns. It makes you feel nauseous just looking at that impossible image. The big black ball is gone. They flew an unmanned drone plane into the void but it burned up as soon as it touched the surface of the rift, so they've decided not to send anything else in. Drone planes are apparently quite expensive. People are apparently cheap, because some brave soldier "volunteered" to put a hand into the rift. I can still hear his screams. I hope he wasn't right-handed.

The news people have been busy overnight.

They have satellite photos and graphics now, all indicating that the Collision — yes they're still calling it that — covers everything from Southern France to Northern Italy.

It took me several minutes to realize that this includes the whole of Switzerland, which means that my friend Paulo is in there too. They were talking about a possible death toll on the BBC. Could be thirty million, could be more! And yet I can't even get my head around the fact that my friend might be gone. I have to get to work. That's all I can really think about right now. It's much easier not to think about what's happened, rather than to try to comprehend it, the scale of it is just overwhelming. For now at least, my brain is parked in neutral.

On the plus side, I have heard from one friend on the continent; Michael is fine, although he is stranded in Calais (Sorry Mike, I don't know anyone with a boat!). I've still got no idea where Naomi is, but I'm choosing not to think about that either. She's a force of nature, and I know I've not heard the last of her; she'll be out there somewhere, getting herself into trouble as usual.

If all this wasn't surreal enough, I then opened my front door to discover that it had snowed overnight; In August!

It didn't take long to work out that it isn't snow; it's ash and dust. Everything is covered in it, and it's still falling. It's beautiful, strange and incredibly inconvenient.

The tube is down. Obviously.

This shouldn't be a surprise. If a bit of snow or a handful of leaves can close the London tube network, then a bucket-load of ash is probably going to knock it out for weeks.

I went in search of a bus, but most of them are full.

I've already had three angry calls from work. A&E is swamped and they need me, but I just can't get there. Not sure how they can blame me for that; the chaos is hardly my fault!

I've finally got on a bus, my face wedged into the window, and I'm making this post from my phone, as I watch the world go by.

I just saw a car that had been crushed by a boulder.

That's not something you see very often in London.

There's flashing blue lights everywhere. Police Cars, Fire Engines and Ambulances; they are all speeding through the traffic, often heading in opposite directions.

Today is going to be mad. I know it. Everyone knows it.

Arriving at Hammersmith now, should be at work in 15 minutes.

Stay safe.

Sheena
Tuesday, 4th August, 2015
7:30am

Would you stop writing your blog and get yourself to work! Sorry for shouting earlier, but nobody else has made it in either, and I've been on shift for the last twelve hours! I'm a wee bit tired and stressed!

Jess
Tuesday, 4th August, 2015
7:32am

Almost there, hun x

Michael
Tuesday, 4th August, 2015
10:45am

You'd be surprised at how few people have boats! I've just been totally ripped off by some French bloke who's charged me 250 quid for a trip on his yacht. They're all clearly expecting the worst. Hell, most of the passengers on the boat were French. There's no Dunkirk spirit, just people fighting to get out, or trying to cream a profit off the back of it.

Everyone knows that whatever's happened, it isn't just bad, it's really bad.

I'll be glad to get home! Drink tonight?

Jess
Tuesday 4ᵗʰ August, 2015
16:52pm

Yes! Worst day ever!

Michael
Tuesday, 4ᵗʰ August, 2015
17:30pm

You're saying this to a man who got stuck in the Chunnel, forced to walk to France, and then mugged by an opportunistic sailor?!!

Jess
Tuesday, 4ᵗʰ August, 2015
17:35pm

You haven't seen the things I have today. x

Michael
Tuesday, 4ᵗʰ August, 2015
17:38pm

And you haven't seen the things *I* have today. I'm just not posting it here, because I don't want people thinking I've gone nuts. I've seen *things*. I've got so much to tell you.

***

Jess
Saturday, 8ᵗʰ August, 2015
18:03pm

The world has changed.

The life I used to lead only five days ago, now feels like a distant memory.

All vacation at the hospital has been cancelled and we're working sixteen hour shifts. NHS resources were already at breaking point, but when something this big happens, they're suddenly stretched impossibly thin; there's just not the capacity for us to cope.

I've seen almost four times the usual number of heart attacks, brought on by stress and shock of recent events. The stock market has crashed, rolling black outs have swept across the UK and London is being flooded by immigrants fleeing the continent. Just watching the news is enough to give anyone palpitations. I'd never realized before just how precariously balanced our world was, but now it feels like it was always just teetering on the brink of the abyss, just waiting for something to nudge it in.

Lots of people were killed by falling chunks of France. There was a rumour about a man in Canterbury who was impaled by a piece of the Eiffel Tower. Sounds like bullshit to me, but who knows what's true these days?

The number of respiratory cases seems to have peaked. They say this is because most of the dust and debris from the explosion has fallen back into the Collision. They say it very uncertainly, and it's very clear that nobody expected this to happen. Apparently it's a good thing though, as otherwise the dust alone would have blocked out the sunlight, caused an ice age and wiped out humanity in days. I'm a little unnerved that nobody mentioned this earlier, but perhaps I should just be grateful, as the resulting panic and alarm would undoubtedly have trebled our workload. The resulting earthquake from such a huge explosion should have killed us all too, but nobody felt so much as a brief tremor. How weird is that?

There's been an increase in the number of physical injuries we're seeing coming through the doors, mainly due to drunken assaults. Typical, isn't it? The world goes to hell, and all people do is go out, get drunk and turn on each other.

Suicide attempts are at a record low. I guess every apocalyptic disaster has a silver lining. Perhaps life suddenly seems more valuable? Or perhaps everyone just wants to see what's going to happen next?

I'm very sure that in years to come, they'll write text books about the way people dealt with this crisis.

For now, all we're really doing is patching people up, turfing them out on the street, and letting the next batch roll through the doors. We don't stand a chance of keeping up. The army will be opening up a field hospital on Ealing

Common soon, which should ease some of the burden down here in Hammersmith, it's just a shame they didn't do it days ago!

According to the news, they are sending help from home, but that's going to take more than a week to arrive. God bless America. As ever, we're painfully slow reacting to events beyond our own borders; we're always happy to help, provided you can wait until a week next Thursday, which is not much use to anyone whose house is already on fire...

The help can't come soon enough. At first, the hospital managers threw every resource they had at the various problems, but now — only a few days later — they're rationing supplies and keeping a close eye on their budgets. Everyone knows this event is going to have a long term impact, and that we're going to be dealing with the aftermath for months, not just weeks.

My mom called again, now begging me to come home.

But how can I leave now?

I'm needed here.

Michael
Saturday, 8th August, 2015
18:32pm

Have you seen the footage leaked on internet? Freakin' Zombies running around the Large Hadron Collider (before it blew up). I have a feeling it's going to be a long time before things go back to feeling normal!

Sheena
Saturday 8th, August, 2015
18:55pm

They're not Zombies. They're not supernatural. They're reanimated cadavers, acting on basic primal instincts. Which is completely different, right?

We got an order directly from Department Of Health, giving us clear guidance regarding the on-going situation. Item no.17 covers this story. Nobody in the public sector is supposed to use the word 'Zombie', as apparently the word scares the hell out of people.

I'd argue that it's the Zombies that actually scare the hell out of people.

Michael
Saturday, 8th August, 2015
19:14pm

Trust me; I saw much scarier things when I was in France! I reckon it's only a matter of time before they find a way over here....

Ben
Monday, 9th August, 2015
10:14am EST

Yo, Sis! Mom reads this blog, you know. You are scarin' the bejesus outta her. Hang on in there though, only come home if it gets really crazy! You know you've always got my support, even if you are doin' something really stupid!

Jess
Monday, 9th August, 2015
08:01am

Thanks, Ben, but no matter how crazy things get, I've got to stay. I just hope you and Mom understand why. Hopefully it's a decision I won't regret.

Perhaps I've actually learnt something from my time in Britain.

They have a motto over here: KEEP CALM and CARRY ON.

It was a phrase originally devised during World War II, to be used in the event of a NAZI invasion, but only now is it seeing its first official use. It's considered a very British thing to do… but given a crisis like this, what else can you do?

***

Jess
Friday 23rd October, 2015
19:45pm

Naomi Gorman is alive.

I've just been on the phone to her for the last two hours, which in itself is not unusual, but this time she really does have a story to tell.

She was in Austria when the Collision happened and apparently has video footage of entire mountains sliding into the rift. She saw things come out too. Monsters and worse. Things that we don't even have words for.

Normally I wouldn't believe such a wild story, but it's coming from my most trusted friend, and Michael has already confided in me about similar experiences he had whilst he was in France.

Ever the opportunist, Naomi is selling her story and photos to the papers, so I am guessing that by tomorrow the world may yet again be waking up to worry about new truths.

I'm just glad to have her back

I'm so glad I stayed in England, just so I can see her again.

Even in these terrible times, good things do still happen.

Naomi
Friday 23rd October, 2015
20:01pm

Also on the plus side, given that I've been surviving on scraps for the last month, I've actually managed to lose some weight. So naturally, with some of the money I made from the papers, I've treated myself to a whole new wardrobe, including a couple of pairs of Ricky Soza jeans. Hell, if a girl survives an apocalypse, she can treat herself, right?

Come on guys, the world hasn't ended and I'm not dead, who's up for some serious dancing?

Naomi
Sunday 25th October, 2015
14:20pm

Oh, forgot to ask you last night, any word on Paulo?

Jess
Sunday 25th October, 2015
18:30pm

No. There's been no memorial for him, as his entire family were in the Collision zone, so there's nobody around to organize it. :-(

Following your return, we just live in hope.

Michael
Sunday 25th October, 2015
18:32pm

Welcome back to Blighty! And to being alive! So glad you're ok, Naomi.

I haven't dared even talk about what I saw, and look at you, you've been through hell but you can just immediately go out and sell it all to the papers. You don't care what you they think. Wish I had that kind of nerve.

Naomi
Sunday 25th October, 2015
18:40pm

Mike, trust me, there's no point being shy anymore. You've seen some of what I've seen.

Do you really think that we're going to get to grow old and retire?

Live fast, because most of us are going to die young.

THE RISE AND FALL OF THE HOUSE OF RICKY
by Kelly Hale

A nd, of course, still no freaking GPS.

He can't drive this car for shit. Why do they keep sending him out on these emergency missions that require navigation *and* driving?

Oh hell no. NO! No no no, shift god damn it, get into gear for the love of—

"I *am* trying to move, jerkwad! What the fuck do you think I'm doing?" Christ. Every cab driver in Manhattan must have his picture on their dash by now. Please, please you expensive piece of crap, just get through this light without dying. Please, please, please—

He can practically hear Ricky's voice in his head, "*Cooper, sweetie, it's not the Jag's fault you can't drive a stick. Clearly you need a boyfriend. Right, everyone? Am I right? Cooper can't drive a stick shift because he's never had a boyfriend. Laugh at my hoary old double entendres, minions, laugh I say!*" Dick.

Ricky Soza couldn't find a sense of humor if it got out of a clown car in front of him and bashed him over the head with a funny hammer. Then again, Ricky doesn't exactly need a sense of humor. He's got talent and looks.

Cooper glances in the rearview mirror and sees some Gramercy Park estate agent wannabe in a Porsche, gunning his engine and looking pissed off. Yeah, got news for you, Brotox, a Jaguar can totally kick Porsche ass. Probably. Anyway, your hair is stupid.

"Incoming call from Trusova Creative Management."

No GPS but the freaking phones work just fine.

"We need shoes," Svetlana says. As usual, there isn't any sort of preamble or hello or acknowledgment of his humanity.

"I know," Cooper replies. "I'm almost there." The singsong, kiss-ass cheeriness in his voice is so automatic it doesn't even fill him with shame anymore. He awkwardly flips off Porsche-guy in the rearview.

"How almost?"

"Really, really pretty close almost—shit, I missed the turn—"

"I hear the gears making that noise He doesn't like."

"Then perhaps He should send one of the many interns on these errands. This would be the highlight of any sad little life destined to an eternity of pattern-making for Jones New York. Why do we bother having interns anyway? I mean, if we're not going to use them for stuff like this?"

"Oh, poor Cooper, driving around Manhattan in a Jaguar with thousands and thousands of dollars worth of shoes in it."

"Seriously, Sweaty, I'm seconds away."

"Do you know how much it's costing us for tech and talent *per second* because we are waiting on shoes and handbags? Did you just call me 'sweetie'?"

"You know the sooner you hang up the sooner I'll be there."

In the background, Cooper hears Ricky's squeaky little mournful sounds, the precursor to complete meltdown. Whenever things fail to go according to plan Ricky tends to collapse like an over-watered orchid. Or a cheap umbrella.

"Oh my God," Sweaty mutters, "seriously *minutes* away from losing the whole day. I am hemorrhaging money here. It's like a bank loan miscarriage. What are you laughing at?" she hisses furiously. "How funny is no paycheck, asshole?"

"Wait. Oh, hey! I see it. Turning now. Bye."

The photo shoot is in an abandoned warehouse with an ancient loading dock and other vestiges of bygone industrialism. It's kind of last decade as an artistic choice, but hey, he's not the artistic director, is he? No. That'd be Amish beard guy in the Nike cycling gear. Yeah. Hey, buddy, Portlandia called and wants its look back.

As soon as the bins of accessories hit the floor, stylists descend upon them like crows on a discarded Taco Bell wrapper. While hair and make-up fairies add finishing touches to the talent, Cooper settles back with his trusty tablet to run the daily Ricky Soza-search. This is one of those things an intern *could* actually do, and one of the things he chooses to keep all to himself. Sure, part of the problem with delegating tasks is *his* problem, but, really, what else does he have besides the promise of a little schadenfreude? There have been some bad reviews. Some questions about sourcing and sustainability. Jealous rivals talking smack. Some days just knowing that not everyone loves Ricky is the only thing that keeps Cooper going.

GPS service might be spotty and unreliable since the LHC disaster, but internet search engines are even more luminous and transcendent, like a 21st century Book of Kells — the more you look the shinier it is. Sometimes you get answers before you even ask the questions.

An intern from Parsons hands him an extra-foamy, non-fat, double shot decaf, one shot regular latte with a half pump of vanilla. He takes a sip while she waits anxiously to see if she got it right. Not that he could tell if the ratio between decaf and regular is correct, he just likes to make his coffee orders really *really* complicated. It gives the interns focus, motivation, purpose, a sense of accomplishment. A reason for being here.

This one is wearing those new hair thingies from Japan. She's Chinese though, like lots of art school kids these days. China's about the only country left that can afford to send their kids away to study frivolous crap like fashion design. And oh my god isn't she excited to be here. Jesus. Take it down a notch, *mei mei*.

Little China Girl is *so* not going to last. She's too bouncy. Too enthusiastic. Too…curious. Why no interns in the workroom she may be wondering. What's that all about? They all wonder it. They've all been told not to ask. If they ask, they're gone.

They'd had a spy in once. Well more than once, but this guy claimed to be from Anna Sui, which pissed Ricky off more than the spying part. "Anna Sui? Anna Sui? Seriously? I mean, sure she did that 1940's revival collection in 2012 but no red carpet looks at all. You know who should be worried about me? Those twats at Alexander McQueen. Badgley Mischka at the very least. Anna Sui? Pulleeze. Pathetic." Of course later it turned out the guy wasn't from Anna Sui at all, but the *government*. And what the fuck was *that* about, anyway? Cooper never found out. Anna Sui faker disappeared pretty fast—accelerated particle fast, ha ha. Gone in a blink. Ricky probably bribed him with jeans or a scarf or some shit.

Speaking of scarves…

"What's with the turban, Svetlana? Bad hair day?" Turbans haven't been on trend since before Milan went away. Kind of thing you only see on trailer park dwellers these days.

Sweaty's hand goes to her scalp as if she's forgotten she has a head let alone a turban on it. The turban is actually a Ricky Soza scarf she's wrapped over her hair. Svetlana loves her scarves—Ascher, Hermes, that sort of thing. Until Ricky gave her one of his own designs. Ricky doesn't usually bestow his designs upon those he employs. It's a thing. He feels it sets a bad precedent. But he gave Sweaty this scarf a couple of months ago and she's worn it practically every day since. It's been migrating slowly from her throat to her head.

She gives Cooper a sudden, sour look, what he calls her fermented cabbage look. All the aging Russian models have that look. "I'm busy," she says pointedly, implying that he's not.

He shakes his tablet like an old timey etch-a-sketch. "Search is sluggish today," he lies.

Her eyes go squinty and there's the hint of a furrow trying to work its way out of the smooth expanse of her Botoxed forehead. But then she pats her turban absently and after a moment, a magenta fingernail deigns to point out something wrong with the lighting—to the annoyance of the photographer. Whatever unusual emotion she was about to have is gone, just like that.

Cooper doesn't ponder long though. With a gulp from his needlessly complicated beverage, he begins his journey through the Ricky-hits. He's just supposed to flag and file the stuff Sweaty might want to use (or expunge), but he's always on the hunt for anything fun or scandalous or anything ANY THING that doesn't play into Ricky's self-created mystique because that shit is so done. But, as always, it's mostly stuff he's seen a zillion times already.

He starts with *Women's Wear Daily* which is simply the first place anyone who wants to know anything about the fashion industry starts. Mergers and acquisitions, yeah, yeah, Suri Cruise's new K-Mart kids collection oh my freaking god, seriously? Those Japanese hair thingies, what the hell are they? Cotton crop recovery impeded by the Disaster, blah blah, and, of course, the usual lamentations about the tragic loss of the great couture houses—Chanel, Dior, Valentino, Yves Saint Laurent. It's like they can't get over it, even though they've still got Stella McCartney and Marc Jacobs. Yeah it's sad, but Cooper agrees with Ricky Soza on this one. Those people have had their time and now their time is over. Hell, their *century* is over. It's a brand new world in the wake of catastrophe and Ricky Soza crawled up out of the hole it left and got busy. And he's busier than ever. A regular busy little crazy-fucker bee.

Yup, Ricky is some kind of terrible genius.

Cooper had never seen anyone look more haunted or vulnerable than Ricky Soza back from the disaster zone in Europe—kind of the way he'd looked on Project Runway Season 11, except times infinity. So few people could claim any sort of escape, let alone a harrowing one; a repatriated refugee with tousled hair and vintage Olympian Ray Bans hit all the right media kinks. He was fragile, gifted, and looked *great* on camera. He'd been studying bio-engineering before he dropped out of Carnegie Mellon and went off to pursue fashion design, so he was also really smart. That little personal revelation was in one of the Project Runway backstage interviews. It's why Cooper fell in love with him. He never dreamed he'd someday be working for him, hating his guts.

Nowadays, nobody goes in the workroom but Ricky. He's got no stitcher, no cutter, no finisher, does all the dyeing, draping and sewing himself. Just him and his trusty Juki industrial sewing machine. All the fabric he'll ever want or need too: super high tech, high performance, developed by his own hand. He practically sleeps with it.

Cooper's only seen the fabric in its raw form once, stored in giant hammocks suspended from the ceiling of the loft—a rich, luxuriant cascade of no discernible color, something between silk and leather, spilling over rafters and pooling on the floor. The kind of luxurious you want to lie down in, roll around in, cover up with and fall asleep inside of forever. But of course Cooper has never gotten closer to touching the stuff than that one long gaze before Ricky shut the door in his face.

Ricky's "process" is not a business model of which Sweaty approves however. It's time consuming and not cost effective. They had a huge fight about it a while back, so bad that he'd locked himself in the loft for a week. She had to promise not to question his methods again—he actually made her *sign* something he slipped under the door—and when he came out he gave her the scarf as a peace offering. The way she's wearing it right now should have him cringing in horror. But

Ricky doesn't seem to notice. He's all fixated on his creations at the mo'.

Women's Wear Daily is a bust except for a tiny blurb about the Soza collection launch next month. Cooper flags it to send to Sweaty later. He turns to the world of online magazines, magazine blogs, blogs *about* magazines, fashion blogs, and trend blogs. *Nylon, Lucky, V, BUST, Vogue Nippon, LULA, Lola, High Snobiety* —

"A master of draping!" declares an editor at *Elle*. She's the one Cooper tried to give his portfolio to once upon a time. She'd been coming out of a clinic on East 66th that does those vampire face lifts. She probably bathes in the blood of virgins these days.

"It's so versatile, I never take it off." Pippa LeFavre tells *InTouch* magazine. He's almost as sick of the LeFavres as he was of the Kardashians. Honey, it's an *evening gown*. It's not for popping out to the bodega for vodka and Advil.

A sound has him turning from the screen. He's heard it before, only now, for some reason, (maybe because he's reading about reality TV celebrities) it gets right under his skin. Or maybe it's just this particular model that's making it. She's got a weird flat face, fat baby lips, and the vaguely Down's syndrome eyes that all the fashion mags love right now. Her overly muscular Madonna arms are above her head as the stylist helps her into the dress with a pair of padded tongs. Ricky has started making everyone use tongs so the fabric is handled as little as possible. Cooper watches the gown slither over and down, thinking how fucking hideous it all looks from this angle. Is that even a color?

As it settles in around her form she makes the sound again, the sound they all make. Everyone who puts on a Ricky

Soza creation makes that sound: an involuntary shuddering "ooh" followed by a soft keening sigh, kind of like an orgasm jerked off in front of the television while your mom's asleep in the next room. It's creepy and weird and embarrassing. But then the dress is on her. She steps into a pair of Giuseppe Zanotti heels and suddenly he sees, hey, not so bad really. In fact, pretty spectacular. I'd come too if I'd just put on that dress.

His tablet pings softly for his attention and there it is, *The Daily Truffle*, blog of blogs, all lit up for him like a palm tree at Christmas. Buried in the party posts and coffeehouse/micro-distillery/hookah bar reviews is an appeal for prayers and good wishes sent out to Rose Bush (daughter of film producer Acker Bush) who suffered a seizure, and is now in a coma at Cedars-Sinai Medical Center. The entire thread is flagged for his attention and he can't figure out why until he comes to this:

incamummygirl: She was still wearing the dress she wore at the GG's. Housekeeper said she wore it two weeks straight, every day.

vintagedior120: Two weeks?

zeebus-n-bentleyIII: This one?

Cooper taps the link. Red carpet. Golden Globes. Rose Bush in a Ricky Soza halter dress. Marc Jacobs shoes. Cartier necklace and earrings.

incamummygirl: That's the one. Wouldn't let paramedics cut it off to put those monitor things on. She punched one in the face or something.

Vintagedior120: Dress IS amazing. I love Soza. Shoes don't work though.

HouseofHouse: Anyone know where she got what she took? Want to avoid whatever it was.

Zebus-n-bentleyIII: Liar!

veganesque: She looks totally anorexic in that GG shot.

theotherson: Two weeks in the same outfit? That's effed up.

Scooterhiggs: Good vibes and prayers people!

Cooper goes back to the photo. Another link takes him to "who are they wearing?" and a quick search gets him three other Soza's at the Golden Globes — one A-lister in the russet banded bodice, one WB actress in the candy striped pleated drape, and a B-list comedian-slash-actress wearing the bronze-green, cowl-draped bodice with hip sash and fish-tail train. He can't tell whose shoes she's got on, and the jewelry, spectacular as it is, doesn't scream its maker, so he figures it's not borrowed but her own. She looks vaguely familiar, in a BBC television sort of way. He heads for her IMDb page but he never gets there. Or rather, something else gets him first.

Ooma Kauser has died of what is suspected to be a ruptured brain aneurysm. Dead, as of yesterday, at twenty-two years old. As he's reading, news of it starts popping up everywhere, on the BBC news feeds and Huffington Post and a bunch of other sites. There's a YouTube video of her being loaded into the ambulance, the bronze green fish-tail train of her gown spilling over the side of the gurney.

Her life, as told and created and recreated over and over, becomes far more interesting than it probably was. The loss to the world is greater and more tragic as a result. Already there are interviews with actors that worked with her. Microphones thrust into the faces of stunned family members. Experts have begun weighing in about brain aneurysms, and there will be much speculation on whether or not it could happen to YOU and what to do to assure it doesn't happen to YOU, and then in a week, two, a month, she'll be forgotten—

She was still in the fucking dress!

He's busy not quite absorbing what this means when his tablet chirps a text message at him — **Two down. More to follow.**

What? What? What the fuck?

Do I know you? — he shoots back, but his message is returned undeliverable.

"Cooper?" He looks up suddenly but can't see the speaker. He sees something else and there is no parallel in nature for what he sees—not moss on trees, or tiny fish on sharks, or birds on hippos. Nothing looks like this. Nothing in the world looks like this.

The gowns are *wearing* the models.

"*Cooper.*" It's Ricky. Ricky is saying his name. Ricky is looking at him. Normally it'd be hard to tell because the Ray Bans lenses are almost black. But Ricky is looking directly at him now, Cooper *knows*, and there is nothing behind those dark lenses but more dark—a great dark rift as shifting and impenetrable as the one in Europe.

"What's the matter, Cooper?" The voice still has that tremulous breathy uncertainty, like it's about to fall onto a fainting couch with the vapors. Bullshit. All lies. "Is it a bad review?"

Another chirrup from the tablet. Again, no number, but this time there's a name attached: **Deepthroat.**

Seriously? Deepthroat?

Svetlana laughs. "Christ. You look terrified. Did you get porn-spammed again?"

Then everyone laughs. Cuz it's a joke, right?

Days later, photo shoot drama over, he's running around solving more life or death fashion emergencies. The comas and aneurysms and the—the other *thing* he's not thinking about, well, just when everything seems normal-ish again, that's when he gets another message from Deepthroat. The name alone makes him want to block the asshole, but he doesn't. He ends up following where the hyperlinks lead despite his best intentions to just mind his own business. But he can't help himself. It's so compelling.

Cooper is the spy now and nobody has a freaking clue. It's so easy it almost makes him giddy. He's kept his real feelings shoved down so hard for so long that he hardly remembers he has them anymore. Smile, blush at their jokes, run errands, do what they want but not too well, then do everything wrong, but still get everything *done* – he's got it all down to a science.

Tuesday he takes off early for a dental appointment, and thirty minutes later he gets off at Clark Street Station in Brooklyn.

Deepthroat's basement apartment is in a pretty nice building—which is kind of disappointing in a way, now that he knows the history of Deepthroat and alleys and parking garages and Dustin Hoffman and Robert Redford when they were young and hot. He presses the button and a moment later he gets buzzed through to the lobby. He knocks on the door marked "A" and someone says, "Come in."

His contact is sitting at a desk facing the main door, facing whoever enters. There's an open laptop on the desk. Empty water bottles litter the parquet floor. Half empties stand sentinel between the man and a wall of prescription bottles.

There's the soft hiss and clunk of an oxygen tank somewhere beside the desk where he can't see. Not that he'd need to see it. The breathing tube in the guy's nose says it all.

Grayish skin drapes loosely over sunken cheekbones, eyes ringed with dark circles, sores around the mouth, on those skeletal hands—

Cooper doesn't realize he's trying to escape until his butt hits the door. One hand gropes blindly for the doorknob while the other flaps in the direction of the spectral man as if waving away cigarette smoke.

"It's not what you think," the man says. He has an accent Cooper can't quite place and the voice is surprisingly... soothing. Considering he looks like death.

"I wasn't thinking anything." But he is. He turns the knob, getting ready to pull the door open and flee.

"It isn't AIDS."

"Ookay." Right. Like he hasn't *seen* the photos or the public service videos or the sex-ed films. The horrors of HIV filled his tiny middle school boy brain with epic anxiety, hammered in hard by a germ-obsessed mother, and his Evangelical grandfather. *Philadelphia* on Netflix hadn't helped one bit. All the "it gets better" videos, condoms, and antiretroviral drugs in the world are not enough to overcome his crippling panic when it comes to the dangers of sex. That's why he's twenty-seven and, still, a terrified virgin.

"There are scarier things than AIDS."

Cooper stops fumbling with the doorknob. Yes. The world is much scarier now. "Who are you?" he sputters out. "And don't say Deepthroat because I looked it up and it's not just from a movie about Nixon."

"I'm Julien Gallus." The man pauses significantly.

"Uh huh," Cooper prompts.

"Ricky has never mentioned me?"

"No. Why would he?"

"I thought you were close to him."

"To Ricky?" Cooper laughs. "Nobody's close to Ricky."

"I am. Or...I was. We're still married. Technically."

Ricky is married! He doesn't know why and it's really awful, but it strikes him as hilarious. Autistic paranoid genius boy is married to a guy with AIDS.

"He was so very talented," Julien says wistfully. Like Ricky's dead or something.

"Um, yeah. He still is. Technically."

The man snorts. "Yes. I suppose. They couldn't be so beautiful if he didn't coax them to be."

Julien isn't talking about the models. Or the actresses, or rich girls, or the rich girls' Chihuahuas. "Shit. Oh shit, oh my god."

"You *have* seen it then? What the clothes — what they do?"

"I-I don't know what I saw, exactly. It was just that one time anyway and I was —" He tried sucking in a breath but couldn't fill his lungs. The air sparkled and his hands were tingly. Crap. "I need to sit down."

"I'm so sorry, yes, yes, of course." Julien gestured to the chair across and a little left of him. It was a Barcelona lounge chair. A nice one. Maybe even a real Mies van der Rohe. Cooper was a little afraid to sit in it, mostly that he wouldn't be able to get out of it fast should the need arise.

"I'd offer you refreshment but it's difficult for me to move about."

"What's wrong with you?" Rude, but if he was sitting this close he wanted to be sure he couldn't catch it.

"Nothing that I haven't done to myself. I'll probably live forever, as long as I keep my trousers on." He pushes away from the desk, rolling the chair back far enough so Cooper can see his pants.

Pants was a not a word fit to describe these jeans. They look like something angels would wear, pulsing with an aura of glory, each cross-dyed fiber glowing with vitality, and cut in such a way that they could never possibly, *not ever*, go out of fashion. The Soza insignia is embroidered by hand just below the pocket rivets—A and Z superimposed to suggest a pentagram surrounded by the O, with the S like a squiggled halo just above. It was one of Ricky's very first pieces, had to be. These were the most beautiful jeans Cooper had ever seen in his life and he'd paid eleven hundred dollars for a pair of mint condition 2002 True Religion jeans on eBay. Still...

"They're killing you?"

"Only if I try to take them off."

"But what about—" He flaps his hands at the pharmaceutical array on the desk.

"I've been experimenting with various compounds. I'm a chemist you see. All this—" he picks up a white plastic bottle and shakes it in the direction of all the other bottles and foil covered pill packs— "this is just me, trying to kill the pants without killing myself. You may have noticed it isn't working."

"What the hell kind of fabric did Ricky engineer anyway?"

"Oh, he didn't make it himself. He found it. Or rather, it found him."

Then Julien told him the story of Ricky—strange, brilliant, autistic Ricky and what he picked up at the edge of the hole in the world.

Everyone forgets he has the keys to everything. He's the one who gets sent to make the fucking copies. He knows all the alarm codes because he's always the first one in. Even so, he's surprised at how easy it is getting into the actual workroom. He'd expected booby traps, some vestiges of Ricky's ever-growing paranoid psychosis. There's none of that.

Ricky's at an LHC Disaster charity event for survivors—all two thousand or so of them. Cooper has plenty of time to get in and get out. He can afford to look around a bit.

The bluish glow from the safety lights guides his feet as he maneuvers around dress forms and storage bins. The cutting tables are covered with butcher paper, a stack of pattern weights and a single magnetic pin holder in one corner. Scissors and rulers hang from pegs mounted on one end of the table. The Juki sewing machine is all by its lonesome under the tiny skylight. Tag board patterns hang suspended from hooks and marked with the names of the clients on a rolling rack. Another rack has jackets, dresses and other pieces made up in muslin. Or so he thinks until he brushes up against one—

"Jesus! Fuck!"

The muslin uncurls like a baby's fist, briefly resolving into a color and shape before settling back into its blank state, which, for the record, is decidedly *not* cotton muslin. He remembers that he hasn't ordered muslin for Ricky in quite a while. None of these are muslins. He can see that pretty clearly now. In fact he can see the whole room pretty clearly despite the fact that he hasn't turned on any of the overhead lights. He looks up and there they are, or *it* is—the stuff, the things, the creature from out of the rift, folded into hammocks above his head like taffy, pulsating with a soft pink glow as if very happy to see him.

The thing is, he's not scared of it at all. Cooper had anticipated being scared shitless after talking with Julien. But it's giving off a nice, mildly energizing vibe, kind of feels like sunshine through the kitchen window on a Saturday morning in May. His mom's making pancakes—

His heart clenches suddenly, remembering what he's here to do. The smell of gasoline hits him like a hammer.

"Cooper?"

It's Ricky standing in the open door. Cooper brandishes his Zippo candle-lighter. "Stay right where you are or I'll burn this place to the ground."

"But the gas-can is out here."

"I know where it is! I fucking brought it here. I'm the one who fills the Jaguar's tank, not you!"

"Okay. Well, we can get someone else to do it, no need for all this drama."

"Oh my God? You really think that's why I'm here?"

"Hush now. You're upsetting the fabric."

He tries not to look up despite the soft shifting noise above his head. Ricky takes a step into the room, then another. Cooper grips the lighter harder in a shaking hand.

"That stuff came out of the rift," he tells him. "It's dangerous. I'm not going to let you destroy the world—"

"Me? How am I responsible for global destruction? All I did was pick up a specimen. I barely knew what a Large

Hadron Collider *was* until Julien told me—" Ricky pauses, an aha look on his face. "You've seen Julien."

"Your *husband*. That you're killing."

"He chooses to poison himself."

"That's because it's the only way to kill the—" He can't bring himself to say "pants" it sounds so stupid. Instead he gestures with the Zippo indicating what hangs above his head. "That—whatever it is—it's not natural."

"Of course it is, don't be silly. Just because it didn't originate on Earth doesn't mean it isn't natural. Look at it. It's a living organism."

Compelled, Cooper looks up at the hammocks in the rafters. The glow is much brighter, a bit warmer now, and the folded layers ripple enticingly. Ricky's presence is the cause. The fabric loves him. *Loves* him.

"People love how my clothes make them look." Ricky's voice is suddenly closer. He's on the other side of the cutting table now, stance earnest, but as always, the dark glasses hide most of his expression. "More than that, Cooper, they love how we make them *feel*."

"Problem is they feel so good nobody wants to take them off. Ever. People have died, Ricky. You're killing people."

"Really? Like who?"

Cooper names names. Rose Bush. Ooma Kauser.

Ricky's lips take on a pensive moue. "So…that's what? Two or three people out of—how many pieces have I sold now? Seventy? Eighty?"

"Seventy-eight," Cooper mutters sullenly.

"Some people have trouble letting go, that's all."

"Like Julien? I mean, you don't make a lot of casual wear, but you made him a pair of jeans he can't seem to let go of."

"So?"

"You've never made a pair of jeans for yourself, or even a shirt. In fact you don't wear anything made from your special fabric. Why is that? If it's not dangerous like you say."

Ricky chuckles, soft and breathy, "I don't have to wear the fabric, Cooper."

Of course he doesn't. He's the designer. People wear him.

And suddenly, all of Cooper's long repressed ambitions come surging to the fore, a tidal wave of want. He wants to make the beautiful things. He wants to be the one everyone's talking about in Nylon and Lucky and Vogue Nippon. He wants people to want to wear him—

A quick sprint and he's out in the reception area. He picks up the gas can. The liquid sloshes around; super heavy, it almost throws him off balance. He takes a deep breath, not minding the fumes, and faces Ricky with resolve. "I want my own line under your label!"

Ricky seems startled. "Eeeesh, that's, that's…you don't…"

Cooper dribbles gasoline over the threshold and starts working his way along the walls. "Nothing big at first," he shouts out. "Belts and bags maybe. T-shirts. Just until I prove myself." He comes back to the door with lighter in hand, wiping his hands awkwardly on the Zegna grey plaid trousers he paid way too much money for. It doesn't matter now. "I know you weren't impressed with my portfolio before, but I've been doing a lot of sketching and I think you'll be pleasantly surprised."

Ricky stands over his stalwart Juki. "It seems I won't have much choice."

Cooper glances up at the hammocks in the rafters. It's the first time in forever that he's felt anything besides apathy.

Excitement beats a near forgotten rhythm in his chest. "How do you communicate with them? Get them to become what you envision?"

Ricky has his hand on the sewing machine's flywheel. He rolls the flywheel back and forth. "How many times did you audition for Project Runway?"

"What? Why?"

"Three times was it?"

"I was really young. They said I needed seasoning."

"I was nineteen and I made it to the final four."

"Yeah, and then you didn't *win*."

"Fate watched out for me. All the winners faded into obscurity. I've actually made a name for myself."

"Oh please. You're the luckiest person in the entire world. You ran off to Italy. Met a guy who loved you enough to marry you and take care of all the hard stuff while you got to fuck around with your *art*."

"I take care of him now. Did he tell you that?"

But Cooper is on a roll and isn't about to argue piddly details. "Then, not only do you survive the biggest catastrophe in the history of the planet, you also happen to find the only cool thing in the mess that was left. You have it all. I just want a little piece. That's all I'm asking."

"All right," Ricky says. He turns the flywheel hard and the needle goes up and down frantically a few times as he moves away from it. He slaps a pen onto the paper-covered cutting table. "Show me what you can do."

Cooper sucks in a breath. This is it! Oh God, this is it. He walks back into the workroom, wipes his hands on his trousers one more time to stop the trembling before setting down the lighter. He picks up the pen and starts to sketch.

Can the fabric make itself look like python because he has an idea for a bright yellow python clutch—

Ricky grabs a fistful of hair and bangs Cooper's face into the table.

A trick, of course a trick! Fucking fucker. Stunned, he gropes blindly for the lighter. Hears it fall. And then they grapple, two desperate people who never learned to fight with fists, kicking and punching and falling and crawling—

Ricky is on top of him now, bashing his head into the old oak floor over and over. Rage is the only thing keeping him conscious. His fingers find a grip over the rims of the stupid fucking Ray Bans, and he pulls, pulls until they snap right off. Ricky reels back and Cooper shoves him hard. Ricky crashes into the bins under the table. Cooper rolls over and crawls to his feet. He sees the Zippo and snatches it up, flicking the flame to life as he stumbles towards reception.

He doesn't make it. He hears the creak above his head before the blanket of creature comes down on him smothering him into the ground.

When he comes to again, Ricky is looking at him. He gets it then, understands completely what Ricky was trying to tell him. He sees it in his eyes, sees it moving around inside his skull.

Ricky doesn't have to wear the fabric. The fabric is wearing him.

"Did you reschedule Katie's fitting?" Sweaty asks, not looking up from her notebook.

"Yup."

She makes a check mark with her finger. "What about the venue for the show in May?"

"Deposit made."

Another check. "Did we decide to go with Wilhelmina or IMG for models this time?"

"Ricky wants to try Next. They have Shu Pei." Ricky's become obsessed with Chinese models.

"Okay then, all I need you to do now is run down to Fine's and try to talk Hershel into loaning us the di Massima chunky pearls. He likes you better." She makes a sad face and Cooper laughs. Sweaty knows he can charm the pants off anyone when he's wearing his lucky jacket.

He checks the crispness of his pocket square and pats the Soza emblem embroidered on the breast before grabbing the keys to the Jaguar.

KEEP CALM AND CARRY ON
PART TWO
by David N. Smith and Violet Addison

Jess
CHRISTMAS DAY, Friday 25th December, 2015
18:03pm

I made a Christmas wish.

Just for Christmas Day, I tried really hard to believe that life had returned to normal.

I was at work. There's nothing unusual about that, I worked Christmas Day last year too. Someone has to do it and I really don't care; after all, my family are all on the other side of the Atlantic, safely out of the reach of all the weirdness that's coming out of Europe.

I avoided watching any television, particularly the news, as they are always covering some new freakish incident on the other side of the channel, discovering something monstrous and potentially lethal to us all. It doesn't really add to the festive cheer.

The first wave of patients on Christmas Day are always those who have had too much to drink the night before. Then, after lunch, you get a handful of extreme food poisoning cases. By early evening one or two people come in with physical injuries; the result of rows that get out of hand, or older people trying to keep up with their much younger relatives.

To me, that's a traditional Christmas.

So, just for one day, everything seemed to be normal, just like it was in the days before the Collision.

There was a trio of young children huddled around a frosted window, talking excitedly and pointing out at the sky, and just for a moment I assumed that they were talking about Santa Claus; so I joined in their fun, peering up at the sky, half expecting to see a sleigh pulled by magical flying reindeer. You just never know these days.

It was not Santa. Obviously.

It was a Toothfish. I recognized it as I've seen countless documentaries about them on the National Geographic Channel. They're hovering little balls of hate, made up of little more than eyes and teeth, which are timid on their own but downright lethal when you encounter more than about a dozen of them.

I've seen footage of hundreds of them flowing through the streets of Berlin, devouring anything and anyone in their path. We were assured that they were not capable of crossing the Channel. We were told we were safe.

The Toothfish blinks at me and swims away, disappearing behind the bins in the parking lot.

I convince the three children to move away from the window.

The evening shift arrives and I'm supposed to leave, but it doesn't feel safe outside, so I've bunked down at work for the night. I'll leave tomorrow because it feels safer travelling in daylight when there are other people around.

I feel stupid.

I wished for things to be normal, but they are normal, this is normal now; to be living with a permanent low-level of fear, always half expecting something to lurch at you from out of the shadows, in a world where the monsters from your worst nightmares are all very real.

It just doesn't feel like Christmas.

Michael
Friday 25th December, 2015
18:32pm

You are not sleeping at that hospital. Answer your phone. I'm coming to get you.

Naomi
Friday 25th December, 2015
18:40pm

I'm at the flat with Teresa. We're bored. If you've both got nowhere better to be, then get yourselves round here. We've got tasteless mince pies and lame crackers.

Ben
Friday 25th December, 2015
13:50pm EST

This is not how you should be spending Christmas! Mom is upset. Dad says he'll send you the money for your air ticket. It's time to come home, sis.

Jess
Friday 25th December, 2015
18:55pm

It's ok, bro. I have the best friends in the world. They're looking after me.

Mike's just pulling up in his car. I'll be at Naomi's flat in 20 mins x

Jess
Friday 25th December, 2015
18:52pm

I think we just ran over the Toothfish! Oops! Naomi, we might be a bit late. Puncture! x

Ben
Friday 25th December, 2015
15:50pm EST

Please come home, before it's too late.

***

Jess
Tuesday, 10th March, 2016
14:00pm

There's a man stood in the doorway of A&E—and he's laughing.

It's been a long time since I've seen someone laugh this hard.

Despite the odd times we live in, this is without a doubt one of the most disturbing things I've seen so far. When the paramedics wheel in a five-year-old girl, covered head-to-foot in tooth fish bites, this wild-haired Chinese maniac is just standing there pointing and guffawing.

So I call down a couple of the orderlies; otherwise known as Stuart and Hasan.

They're both big blokes. Stuart used to be a soldier and Hasan is a semi-professional boxer. They're both hard as nails. They've had my back on a couple of night shifts, and I trust them absolutely.

They grab the weirdo, carry him through the parking lot and dump him on the sidewalk.

He continues laughing, harder than ever.

Thirty minutes later he's back at our door, wiping the tears of hysterical laughter from his eyes. Hasan tells him to leave, in no uncertain terms, using language I won't repeat here; but the madman tries to push past him. Hasan hits him. There's a smattering of shocked exclamations and a little light applause from the motley assembly of injured people in A&E.

All very English! The man is left sitting on the floor, cradling a broken nose, blood seeping through his fingers, giggling. Yes, even then, giggling.

It was then that I realized that I'd completely misunderstood the situation.

It was his eyes that gave it away. Despite his laughter, there was no humour there, no joy. Instead, there was something you often see in a patient's eyes, something that I'm seeing more and more these days: fear.

He had spent hours trying to get to a hospital, looking for help, and we'd just picked him up and ditched him at the end of the road. He was so over-powered by his own laughter, that it had taken him half an hour to walk the short distance back to the doors.

I ask him what's wrong and he puts his head in his hands and just laughs, his shoulders shaking like a person crying. He can't even talk.

Stuart and Hasan apologize, pick him up and carry him in to be examined. I ask Sheena to get Doctor Ogundana, our toxicologist, and they all disappear behind closed doors.

They find nothing that would normally induce anything like this; no drugs or alcohol. However, his dopamine and serotonin levels are off the chart, causing his euphoric high; but they can't identify the cause. They dose him up with anti-psychotic drugs, and bring his mood under control long enough to get some answers out of him; but he knows nothing, he hasn't been bitten, or stung, or encountered anything that could provide an explanation for his condition. He was just sitting on the tube, reading a paper when he was struck by a giggling fit. Our first, most horrific thought, was that this was a viral infection, but we've run his blood work and found nothing out of the ordinary.

Twelve hours later, he seems fine, and his body chemistry appears to have returned to normal. He signs the consent forms and we discharge him.

We're at a total loss to explain what it was. Given the times we live in, I'm assuming whatever the cause, it probably had its origins in the Collision.

Has anyone else encountered anything like this before?

Sheena
Wednesday, 11ᵗʰ March, 2016
16:30pm

Please don't post medical cases on-line. It's a violation of the patient's privacy.

Jess
Wednesday, 11ᵗʰ March, 2016
16:45pm

Sorry, but I think it's important to discuss these things. Too many of our cases these days are hidden and forgotten. I've not mentioned the patient's name. I'm not taking this down.

Sheena
Wednesday, 11th March, 2016
16:51pm

I'm not discussing this on-line. Take this post down, now.
    Come and see me as soon as you get in to work tomorrow.

Pang
Wednesday, 11th March, 2016
16:54pm

I have no objection to my case being discussed online. I would quite like to know what happened to me! I have always found silence to be the enemy of hope and reason.

Jess
Thursday, 12th March, 2016
9:15am

Thanks, Mister Xeu. Your consent really took the wind out of their sails. They were about to reprimand me. They can't now!

Laura
Monday, 16th March, 2016
14:15pm

My name is Laura Lynn. I'm a doctor at the new walk-in centre at Kings Cross. I have a case very similar to this. Could you let me know what combination of drugs and dosages you used to treat your patient?

Jess
Monday, 16th March, 2016
14:41pm

I'll get Doctor Ogundana to contact you directly. PM me your contact details.

Laura
Tuesday, 17th March, 2016
14:45pm

Our patient has stabilized. Thank you for your assistance today. Perhaps we should learn a lesson here, and try to be much more open and honest with our information? After all, we are facing new challenges every day. Interestingly, our patient was also taken, for want of a better word, *ill* on the tube.

Naomi
Tuesday, 17th March, 2016
15:01pm

I think I may stop using the tube!

Laura
Friday, 1ˢᵗ April, 2016
9:05am

THIS IS NOT AN APRIL FOOL'S JOKE!

I've just had one hundred and three patients enter the centre showing these symptoms (i.e. suffering uncontrollable laughter). It's very disconcerting having that many people laughing at you. The noise is terrifying.

They all came off three tube trains, running in close succession on the Northern Line. If that doesn't prove there's something down there, I don't know what does!

They've suspended the line.

We're getting more drugs requisitioned, but right now we're completely out of anything with a haloperidol and clozapine base, so we are now trying some of the alternatives.

We're beyond our capacity, so expect some of these patients to start heading your way, just as soon as we can organize some transport!

Naomi
Friday, 1ˢᵗ April, 2016
9:15am

I'm definitely staying off the tube!

Jess
Friday, 1st April, 2016
17:02pm

The first coach has just arrived. We've got thirty-five of them. Should have enough supplies to treat that many. Good luck, I think we're going to need it!

Naomi
Friday, 1st April, 2016
18:11pm

They've suspended the whole tube network! The buses are crammed. I reckon I'm going to have to sleep at work tonight! Then again, the clubs will still be open… May just pop out and buy myself a change of clothes and hit the dance floor later. Like I need an excuse to buy more Ricky Soza! Well the cheap knock-offs anyways. I might as well make the best of a bad situation! Come join me when you finish your shift!

Jess
Friday, 1st April, 2016
18:32pm

Wish I could, hon. But I can't leave work, even if my shift has finished. It's chaos here.

Enjoy yourself x

Laura
Friday, 1st April, 2016
18:40pm

We've had more arrive. These ones aren't from the tube. Whatever it is, it's spreading, fast. We've got about thirty-odd additional patients, all of them from a river boat restaurant on the Thames. They're sitting in A&E while we try and figure out what to do. Suggestions? How many can we send your way?

Jess
Friday, 1st April, 2016
18:50pm

We've got the same situation here. We've taken in about fifty people, all of them from houses along the Thames. We've had to start turning people away. We just can't take in any more.

Stuart and Hasan are guarding the front door. It's horrible. There are people lying in the car park, laughing, but there's nothing we can do to help them.

Laura
Friday, 1st April, 2016
18:59pm

The police have arrived.

Riot gear, water cannons, horses. The works.

I've even seen guns.

Jess
Friday, 1st April, 2016
19:10pm

Same here. They're arresting the people outside, I'm not sure what for!

Laura
Friday, 1st April, 2016
19:15pm

Public disorder/breach of the peace, apparently!

Jess
Friday, 1st April, 2016
19:29pm

The police just pulled out! They've abandoned us! Not sure where they are going.

There are still people turning up here, laughing at us through the doors. Almost every TV channel we can get is showing the story, as it appears to be happening across most of south-east England. They're telling people to stay in their homes. They're telling people to keep calm.

They're talking about implementing martial law, and as much as I disapprove, I'm inclined to agree that it might be necessary.

Michael
Friday, 1st April, 2016
19:40pm

If you need a lift home, you just have to ask, I'll be there in a shot.

Jess
Friday, 1st April, 2016
19:55pm

I don't think I can leave. There's people here suffering. I'm not sure what good I can do, particularly now we're out of supplies, but I don't think I should leave. How can I? These people came here for help, and it's my job to provide that help.

    If I go, where does that leave them?

***

Jess
Saturday, 2nd April, 2016
5:15am

Glass shattering.

    That's the sound that woke me up.

I've worked here long enough to know exactly what the sound was; it was at least three large windows in A&E being smashed in.

I can hear shouting. I can make out Stuart and Hasan's voices. Calming, but confrontational. They're trying to maintain order. A fight starts. I can hear things breaking downstairs. Stuart and Hasan's voices are drowned out by the mob, seeming by turns to be both angry and wailing with grief.

Nobody is laughing anymore.

I glance out of the window.

There are cars on fire in the parking lot.

There are people fighting in the street.

Some guy hurls himself off the four story building opposite. He plummets. The world around him does not react.

I'm hearing hurried footsteps coming up the stairs so I've locked the door.

Now someone is rattling the handle!

I've scuttled under the bed and curled up in the corner, like some terrified child; but that's how pathetically terrified I am.

It's Hasan at the door. He's scared and frantic, tones I've *never* heard in his voice before. He's begging me to let him in.

It's been a minute, maybe more and I'm still here, somehow hoping that everything will just go away. I can't bring myself to move.

So I went and opened the door. I'm back here, under the bed now. Oh God. It was awful. I found myself clambering out from under the bed. I'd like to claim that I'd thought things through and decided to help him, but I was just acting on instinct. I think I just don't want to be alone.

I got as far as the door. Then he started laughing.

A shiver swept through me.

Dozens of footsteps thundered up the stairs, a mob jeering and hollering insults and threats. They swept past the door and carried off Hasan. I could hear his laughter fade away.

I opened the door a crack, enough to see the mob storm the fire door at the end of the hall, push Hasan outside and over the edge of the building. He was still laughing as he fell.

So I locked the door and here I am, back under the bed, crying.

I'm not proud of any of this, but I want you all to understand what it's like.

About fifteen minutes pass. I regain enough of my senses to phone my friend, Mike.

He's on his way now in his car, my knight in shining armour. My cavalry.

I'm posting this now from my phone.

I'm still under the bed, which is a bit dumb as it's the first place anyone is going to look. But it feels safe, so screw logic. I'm staying here until Mike arrives.

I'm worried to hell about everyone else.

Sheena and Doctor Ogundana were still here last night, long after their shifts had finished, but Sheena is not answering her phone, and I don't know Doctor Ogundana's number.

No word from Naomi either, but hopefully she's just somewhere with a hangover, or a bloke, or knowing her, both. But part of me knows I'm being optimistic.

The worst thing is, I don't know how far this thing has spread. I'm so used to having all the information at my fingertips, but now it's difficult to find out even the most basic facts.

I checked BBC news on my phone but it's not been updated since yesterday. Mike says all the main TV channels are off the air.

Any news would be welcome! I need to work out what to do next!

In the meantime, there's nothing to stop the mob coming back to my door.

Why did they change? What's going on?

Anyone?

Ben
Saturday, 2nd April, 2016
0:30am EST

CNN say that Britain is now under martial law, but that all official channels of communication have now gone quiet, which means they have no idea who is in charge over there… if anyone.

I've wired you some money.

Please: Get. On. A. Plane.

Michael
Saturday, 2nd April, 2016
7:14am

Funny.

Jess
Saturday, 2nd April, 2016
7:21am

Sorry? What? You are coming to get me right, Mike? I'm not joking. It's not 'funny'. I've never been so scared in my entire life.

Mike
Saturday, 2nd April, 2016
7:33am

Funny. Ha, ha, ha!

Jess
Saturday, 2nd April, 2016
7:36am

Mike. Just called you. Was that you laughing at me? Has it got you too?

Michael
Saturday 2nd April, 2016
7:46am

It's too funny. Sorry, this is ridiculous. This is hilarious. I can't help laughing. I can't stop laughing! So, yes, I think it got me. But where's the harm in that? I've never been this happy. It feels brilliant. Don't think I can actually drive though. You're on your own. Sorry ;-)

Jess
Saturday 2nd April
7:47am
****!!!!

***

Jess
Saturday, 2nd April, 2016
11:00am

I want to run.

I want to go home.

I've been speaking with my family on the phone and they all want me to leave.

I have to find somewhere safe.

The noise from downstairs has calmed down a little.

So, even though I'm terrified, I am going to open the door.

I've been planning it.

I'll go downstairs to the ambulance bays and 'borrow' some transport. I'm driving straight to Heathrow. Mom is trying to book me a flight home as I can't get the web on my phone to work.

I'm leaving this God-forsaken country.

I can't keep calm. I can't carry on. Maybe I'm just not British enough.

Dear friends, if you're out there, wish me luck.

Sheena
Saturday, 2nd April, 2016
12:45pm

Honey, we're up on third, over the reception wing.

I've lost my phone, so we're using a patient's laptop. Doctor Ogundana is here too. If you've not gone already, wait for us, we'll go together. It's not safe for you to go on your own, the people down there have gone mad. They're smashing everything! Wait for us. Let me know you got this message.

Laura
Saturday, 2nd April, 2016
13:13pm

We're in much the same position over here in King's Cross.

We're trapped on the fifth floor.

I find it interesting that we've all found safety on higher ground.

Could this condition somehow be influenced by altitude?

Sheena
Saturday, 2nd April, 2016
13:16pm

Well, it started in the underground...

Laura
Friday, 2nd April, 2016
13:22pm

Or accumulated there…

It's a bloody gas, isn't it!

The concentration thins out as you go up, the same way a mountaineer will find the oxygen level diminishing as he climbs higher.

If I'm right, then if any of us try and go downstairs, we'll be overpowered by it.

We're trapped.

Sheena
Saturday, 2nd April, 2016
13:30pm

Doctor Ogundana respectfully disagrees.

His words, not mine.

He's suggesting the gas could act as intoxicant, so that much like alcohol or any other drug, it depends on the quantity in your system. In the initial stage it creates an overpowering sense of euphoria, which in turn leads to an emotional crash as the body attempts to stabilize.

Uncontrollable laughter is replaced by anger, violence or depression, it would then repeat in a never-ending cycle as the victim goes through repeated highs and lows, never able to properly stabilize because they are constantly exposed.

This means we could spend a limited amount of time at a lower level, before we succumb.

Not sure what use this knowledge is to us!

If this is the end, that we're all going to be drugged and mad for the rest of our lives, I think I would rather not have known.

Laura
Saturday, 2nd April, 2016
13:28pm

Any sign of Jess?

Sheena,
Saturday, 2nd April, 2016
13:32pm

None. I'm going to go and look for her. Might as well test our theory.

Ben
Saturday 2nd April, 2016
08:02am EST

Please find her.

***

Jess
Saturday, 2nd April, 2016
15:50pm

London is beautiful.

So beautiful, that I cannot help smiling. I cannot help laughing.

I've stolen an ambulance but I don't think anyone will mind. The world has stopped caring about such things. The world has stopped caring about everything. We're finally free to do whatever we want. I want to go home but now I'm confused, and I'm not sure what I'm doing anymore.

I only made it a few metres down the road. The street is filled with abandoned cars, doors left wide open, people wandering aimlessly around.

I accidently hit one of them with the ambulance.

I know that's not funny, but for some reason I just can't stop laughing about it.

I'm crying too.

I know what this means. I really do.

Did I really think I could outrun the end of the world? The very idea! It's hilarious!

Laura
Saturday, 2nd April, 2016
15:52pm

Your friend Sheena is out looking for you. Turn on the siren.

Jess
Saturday, 2nd April, 2016
15:54pm

She's not my friend. She's my boss.

Can't stand her. She's always so serious and grumpy. She's ridiculous.

Laura
Saturday, 2nd April, 2016
15:55pm

Turn on the siren, Jess.

Jess
Saturday, 2nd April, 2016
15:58pm

I've turned on the woo-woo. I like the woo-woo.

Sheena's here, she's banging on the window and shouting at me.

Typical. Bet I've done something wrong.

She's all red-faced and out of breath. Don't think she found it funny when I pointed and laughed at her, but she looks a complete state.

I think if I ignore her, she'll go away.

Laura
Saturday, 2nd April, 2016
15:59pm

Let her in, Jess.

Ben
Saturday 2nd April, 2016
11:02am EST

Let her in now, or you'll be in trouble with me.

Sheena
Saturday, 5th April, 2016
17:32pm

We've got her. I had to smash the window and haul her out.

She's giggling like a loon.

We've got her up on 3rd.

I've read what she wrote, but I'm not taking offence.

She's ill. Out of her mind. And also, the things she wrote weren't entirely untrue. You've got to laugh, right? Maybe not.

Ben
Saturday 2nd April, 2016
12:33pm EST

Thank you. I am grateful beyond words.

My sister is lucky to have you looking out for her. I'm sure she knows that.

Sheena
Saturday, 2nd April, 2016
17:35pm

No problem. My nurses are my responsibility, even if the organization we work for has stopped functioning, they are still *my* people.

If I didn't believe that, I'd have nothing right now…

Laura
Saturday, 2nd April, 2016
17:37pm

Give her oxygen. If our theory is right, reducing her exposure to the natural atmosphere should help her body recover. Clean air will be a much more effective mood stabilizer than any anti-psychotic drug. She'll still crash, have the worst hang-over of her life, but she should eventually stabilize. I hope.

Sheena
Saturday, 2nd April, 2016
17:52pm

We've got her on a ventilator in one of the operating theatres.

It feels good to win one.

For a moment I even hoped we could beat this thing, but we can't, can we?

Laura
Saturday, 5th April, 2016
18:30pm

We've been doing some lab work over here, and we've identified at least seven organic compound trace-gases in the air. We should consider ourselves lucky, a handful of minor variations in the molecular structures and we'd be breathing poison. We'd all be dead by now.

However, the levels of the gas are noticeably increasing. In a couple of days' time it won't be safe even on the fifth floor, which is as high as this building goes.

Sheena
Saturday, 2nd April, 2016
18:52pm

So, you've got all the answers, what can we do?!!

Laura
Saturday, 2nd April, 2016
19:10pm

Against this? I've absolutely no idea.

DISPLACEMENT
by Aaron Rosenberg

"Joseph Tern! Open up!"

Joseph didn't look up at the sudden pounding. He'd been expecting it. In fact, it had taken them almost two hours longer than he'd estimated to figure out what he was up to, find out who he was, track him down, and surround his house. European cops were so slow! Not that he was complaining—that extra time had let him just about finish his preparations. Still, there wasn't much fun in competing if it was completely one-sided. The challenge was in outsmarting a real opponent, not some chumps with badges and beer guts.

"Open up!" Someone hollered again, accompanied by more banging at the door. "This is the police!" Well, of course it is, Joseph thought as he tied off the last knot, wiped his brow, and stood to admire his handiwork, careful not to breathe too deeply. Who else would be hammering like that at this hour? And in such a nice, quiet neighborhood, too. They should be ashamed!

Part of him considered staying to teach those officers some manners. But he wasn't stupid enough to indulge that notion. Not right now. Later. For now he needed to get out of here, preferably without a lovely pair of stainless steel cuffs as fashion accessories.

Well, no time like the present. He flicked open the lighter, sparked it into a flame, and tossed it onto the knotted, twisted bed sheets he'd laid out in a long, winding curve from right beside the apartment's front door—to the doorway into the kitchen.

Then he ran like hell.

The explosion blew out the front door and presumably any cops foolish enough to stand right in front of it—hadn't they watched movies? You always stood to one side in case the crazed killer within decided to shoot at you!—and ignited most of the apartment at the same time. Including what was left of poor Mr. Trumble, stashed in the coat closet. He really shouldn't have complained about the noise.

Joseph was in the back bedroom by this point, however, having scooped up his duffle bag on the way down the hall. The apartment had a fire escape but that was on the other side, off the main bedroom. This room looked out onto the complex's postage stamp-sized central yard, and across it to the wing beyond. He'd already removed the window from its frame to avoid the risk of glass shards, and now he swung his upper body out through the opening, twisting around so he was sitting on the ledge and facing back into the room. He tossed the duffle up onto the roof—he'd been pleased to snag a top-floor apartment when he'd first moved in, though he'd rarely made use of the flat roof to barbeque or tan the way some of his neighbors had—and then pulled himself out and up, getting a good solid grip on the roof's low rim and hoisting himself over. He'd left the bedroom's curtains in place, just brushing them aside, and they swung back as his feet cleared the frame. That would keep the cops from noticing the open window for at least a few minutes, and that was after they managed to make their way into the apartment at all. By then he should be long gone.

As he loped across the roof to the next wing, Joseph allowed a healthy sense of reality to tamp down some of his pleasure at having so easily eluded the authorities. Yes, they were putzes and klutzes and fools. Yes, he'd have snuck down the stairs on the back wing and out the rear door and be a ghost by the time they even realized he hadn't died in the explosion. Yes, he'd get away clean.

But where would he go?

And he couldn't ignore the fact that they'd come after him. He'd given them the slip this time, but it meant the word was out. The authorities now had him flagged. He would show up in their system no matter where he went. And that was no way to live.

So what was he going to do? He thought about that as he pulled the roof-access door open and made his way down the long, spottily lit stairwell, his sneakers scuffing against the rough concrete. He had to lay low, somewhere the cops couldn't find him or couldn't touch him if they did. But where? He could get out of the country, of course, but with the EU there was a lot of international cooperation, so simply crossing a border might not be enough. Leaving Europe itself would be tricky, since his passport had no doubt been flagged as well. They might have reached out to people back in the States, too, so even running back to the good ol' U.S. of A.

might not help him evade the long arm of the law. So what did that leave him?

Then he remembered something. He'd worked as a security guard two years ago, on a project at the Large Hadron Collider near Geneva. He'd witnessed some of their experiments—they were messing with reality and telling the outside world it was all perfectly safe! Joseph had admired that. He'd overheard some of the scientists talking about a huge discovery, some sort of gateway to other worlds. Or other versions of this world. They were trying to break through to other realities.

He wondered if they'd succeeded. And if the cops in that other reality were as stupid and slow as they were in this one.

"Joseph? Hey, man, long time! How're you doing?" Ernie slid into the seat across from him, resting heavy forearms on the scarred table. He looked the same, still borderline overweight, still pale and freckled, still prone to sweat like a sprinkler system.

"I'm good," Joseph answered, leaning back, one arm draped over the back of the booth, the other resting along the table's inner edge, both legs extended before him and crossed at the ankles. "How about you? How's the wife?" He vaguely remembered Ernie having a wife, as tiny as he was bulky, as dark as he was pale, as quiet as he was outgoing. They were a textbook case of "opposites attract."

"May's good, thanks." Ernie beamed with pride. "And we've got a kid now! Ernie Junior, I call him, though the name on his birth certificate's actually Daniel. Ernie's his middle name, Daniel Ernest Sagat." He nodded thanks to the waitress as she poured a stream of dark, steaming coffee into his upturned cup. "So, what's the news, man? You disappeared two years ago, right after the boss ran off, and this is the first I've heard from you since."

Joseph had disappeared because of their boss, an odious little man named Alan Kurtz. Kurtz had the audacity to accuse them of slacking and wasting his time and money, and had threatened to not pay them if they didn't shape up. They were guards, for Christ's sake! They watched the gates and the parking lots and all that, checked IDs, called in any suspicious activity. In between, there wasn't much to do. But were they slacking, or just taking advantage of the downtime built into the job?

He'd gone in and tried to reason with Kurtz, but to no avail. The man was slime. So Joseph hit him in the temple with a marble ashtray. Kurtz had dropped like a sack of potatoes, and Joseph had decided it was probably time to move on. He'd been nice enough to take Kurtz with him, though, and had dumped the body into a school furnace on his way out of town. He was glad to hear that the Geneva police had never figured out that it was murder, and also to note that, if word of his more recent activities had spread here, they hadn't reached all the way down to Ernie's level yet. He still had time to make this work.

"I need a favor, Ernie," he told his old co-worker now. "I need to see the Collider, up close and personal. Can you get me in?"

Ernie rubbed at his face, the gesture continuing on up to his forehead and then his thinning red hair. "You want to see the damn thing? I mean, yeah, I suppose, but why?" A grin split his broad face. "What'd you do, leave some money stashed in your locker or something?"

Joseph feigned a sheepish smile. After all these years, it wasn't hard to fake the friendly gesture. "Yeah, you got me. When Kurtz lit into us like that, I figured pink slips weren't far behind and decided I'd rather leave on my own terms— you know, beat the holiday rush and all that. But I left in such a hurry I didn't clean out my emergency stash... if you know what I mean."

Ernie and a few of the other guards had often given him trouble for keeping so calm all the time, even hinting now and then that maybe he had a little pharmaceutical help to steady his nerves, and the grin his friend gave him now was knowingly smug. "I hear ya. Sure, I can get you in, no problem. When's good?"

Joseph drained his cup and set it down with a clatter on the damp saucer. "How about now?"

"You go ahead," Ernie told him after they'd cleared the main gate and the initial checkpoint on the building's service entrance. "I'm gonna check in with Charlie, let him know I'm here and warn him you're picking up some stuff so he don't get spooked and hit an alarm when he sees you on the monitors. You still remember how to get to the lockers?" Joseph nodded. "And from there to the security station?" Another nod. "Okay, so just meet me there when you're done. We'll go grab some dinner, maybe a few brews, and catch up more." His smirk said that he expected to share in whatever goodies Joseph retrieved.

"Sounds like a plan," Joseph agreed easily, clapping the bigger man on the back. "I'm buying." He walked away without a second glance, the smile dropping from his lips as soon as he was out of view. He had no problem promising all of that, though. It wasn't like he intended to make good on any of it. And it was definitely a plan, all right. It just wasn't the one he had in mind. He glanced down at the ID card he'd palmed off his former co-worker, and this time the fleeting smile was more genuine. No, not his plan at all.

Finding the changing room was easy enough, and he opened his old locker and rummaged around in it for a minute just for appearance's sake, for the cameras. After a few minutes he straightened up, shoved his hand into his pants pocket like he was stashing something he'd found, and shut the locker door. Now for the real deal. The locker next to his proved to have someone's uniform in it, and whoever owned it was about Joseph's size. He tugged the shirt on over his T-shirt, grabbed the cap and heavily laden belt. He'd deliberately worn dark pants instead of jeans tonight—at a glance, it looked like he was in full uniform. Perfect.

Next he made his way toward the door. Instead of turning right out of the changing room and pacing the short hall to the security station, he turned left. That hall led to a heavy and securely locked door but his new security card worked like a charm, gliding through the card slot and setting off a cascade of little green lights, followed by a hefty click. Joseph pulled the door open and slipped through.

He still remembered this place's layout from all those nights walking it, and he didn't pause or slow down as he made his way through the maze of hallways, doors, and rooms. At this hour the only people here were the guards, and the two he saw from a distance Joseph merely waved to as if he were still one of them. The second one startled and shouted something, but a courtyard and two walls separated them, and he'd disappeared through another door a second later. By this point Ernie and Charlie had certainly noticed him wandering around in the borrowed shirt, and had probably warned the other guards, but unless one got directly in his way there wasn't much they could do to stop him. And that would only slow him down. They could sound the alarm, of course, go into full lockdown, call in the local police, and so on, but then Ernie would have to explain why someone who'd quit two years ago was walking around unescorted using his ID. No, they'd try to catch him on their own.

He was counting on it.

Finally he reached a thick portal that looked more like an airlock than a regular door. His borrowed card still worked — they hadn't thought to shut it down yet — and Joseph hauled on the door and swung it open.

Beyond was a small chamber lined completely in silvery metal. The far side had something like a giant spout sticking out of it. That was the tail end of the collider, the end point for whatever it spat out.

And hanging there in mid-air was a shimmering curtain of light.

Joseph stopped dead. He'd never seen anything so beautiful, or so eerie. Though the air in this chamber was perfectly still, the curtain shifted and swayed as if dancing on an invisible breeze. It cast strange, flickering shadows that didn't match its form at all, and he thought he could hear a faint hum and behind that a murmuring, as if from many voices all at once. The lights in this chamber were off, but still he could see the curtain perfectly, every glimmer of color undulating within it, the way it faded along the edges like a Technicolor cloud brought to earth. It was amazing. The sight of it was almost enough to make him forget his intentions.

Almost.

Tearing his gaze from the curtain and looking around the small room, Joseph spotted the one security camera. He drew his newly appropriated pistol and put a bullet through the lens with a single shot. He'd always had good aim. The noise of the report should have echoed to deafening levels, but instead it was only a sharp crack, like the rest of the sound had been . . . stolen away somewhere. His eyes drifted back to the curtain, and he experienced a strange twinge in his chest. Was this what fear felt like?

Not that it mattered. He was out of other choices.

So, taking a deep breath, Joseph Tern stepped forward, right into the shimmering curtain — and disappeared.

Agony. That was Joseph's entire existence. His body arched and convulsed, thrashing as pain shot through him in white-hot spikes that lanced him from every side and then dug deep, until he thought his very insides would explode. Bursts of light exploded behind his eyes, a roaring filled his ears, the very air burned his lungs and his nose and mouth and eyes. He felt as if he'd been torn apart, ripped into tiny shreds, and then shoved through a cheese grater for good measure. He couldn't think, couldn't breathe, couldn't move — but he'd been in the act of walking when he'd entered this nightmarish place, and now his own momentum carried him forward, cutting through the pain and the strangeness. He staggered a step, the pain lessening, then another.

And then there was a blinding flash of light, and a noise like someone ripping the world in half, and he half-walked, half-fell out of this increasingly strange and distorted space and into one that was calm and quiet. He leaned against the wall, catching his breath, trying to restore the feeling to his extremities but at the same time studying his surroundings. It all looked almost the same as what he was used to, with subtle differences he might not have noticed if he hadn't been warned—a slightly different shape to the door frames, a shift in tint in the light bulbs, a different smell to the air, a different pitch in the subsurface hum of reality and daily life.

He'd made it.

He was in a new world.

"Hey! You! Stop right there!"

With a sigh, Joseph stopped. He'd stepped out of that little room, relieved to get away from the memories of that curtain and the feelings that billowed off it, sensations of despair and dismay wafting loose and filling the small chamber until he could barely breathe. So he'd stumbled out into the corridor beyond, closing and locking the door behind him, and had wandered away, taking deep breaths and waiting for the spots to fade from his eyes and the gasping to work its way out of his lungs and the whole world to stop spinning. And now someone was ordering that he stop. He didn't expect that to prove a good thing, and his hand dropped to the pistol he'd automatically reholstered, just as a precaution.

"Who the hell are—" the voice demanded, rapidly approaching along with the clomp of heavy feet and the smell of greasy fries and thick coffee, but it cut off abruptly when it was close, causing Joseph to look up finally. His pursuer was a tall, skinny fellow, all joints and limbs but not enough to hold him together tightly so he wound up waving everything about every time he moved. Atop this skeletal assembly sat an equally tall and narrow face that suited the rest and which probably held a generally pleasant expression most of the time, judging by the wrinkles and laugh lines, but right now was frozen in shock.

Then he spoke—or rather, then he slapped Joseph on the back with a big grin.

"Joe! Sorry, man!" the skeleton chuckled. "Thought you had the day off, bud? What're you doing here so early?"

"Oh, I—" Joseph thought fast. "Yeah, I had some forms to fill out, you know how it is. I left a few of 'em here when I clocked out, so I figured I'd better grab 'em while I can."

The scarecrow nodded. "Got it. Well, I'll let Barry know you're here so he doesn't panic when he sees you. Later, man." And the scarecrow turned and ambled away.

This is too good, Joseph thought as he regathered his wits and continued on his way in the happy quiet of no alarms going off. Not only was he in another world, but this one already had a Joseph—or Joe, apparently—Tern, and he still worked security here! Talk about a built-in escape route! Sure enough, there were a lot more guards here than on his side, and they were both more alert and more heavily armed, but the ones he passed as he fumbled through unfamiliar corridors toward a way out just waved him through, calling out greetings and good-natured ribbing through the reinforced glass. The guards at the front entrance told him to have a good one as they were letting him out, and then he was on the outside—and received a completely new shock, one that froze him in his tracks.

This wasn't the Collider!

In fact, it didn't even look like Geneva.

Glancing behind him, Joseph realized his mistake. The building he'd exited was clearly a research facility of some sort, as evidenced by the labs he'd passed, and the lab techs and scientists everywhere. But it was a long, low building with lots of windows, an older concrete structure as much like an old parking garage or a college classroom building as anything else. The Collider had been housed in much more modern digs, all steel and chrome and glass. It was only because he'd been inside, with nothing to look at but halls and doors, and because he'd still been recovering from the pain of the transition itself, that he hadn't realized sooner.

So where was he, then? And, if this wasn't the Collider, or Geneva, then how had he stumbled upon the one place in all the world where his double already worked?

It couldn't be a coincidence, Joseph realized as he resumed walking, moving slowly to give himself time to think but briskly enough that anyone watching would hopefully not guess he had no idea where he was going next. Somehow, upon passing through to this world, he'd been drawn to his other self. That's why he had emerged here. But where was here?

He'd reached the end of the sidewalk and stepped out into a mostly empty parking lot. Anyone watching from the building wouldn't be able to make out what he was doing anymore, so he allowed himself to slow and look around.

Beyond the building he'd left behind, the sky shimmered astonishing colors in a constantly shifting vortex of light. The swirling spectacle stretched in either direction as far as he could see. A day ago, Joseph would have been struck dumb by the sight. Now, however he knew he was simply on the edge of this world's curtain, but one immeasurably larger than what he had stepped into.

And, seeing a certain distinctively skeletal steel tower rising gracefully on the horizon, Joseph also knew exactly where he was.

He was in Paris. And his other self — this Joe — was here somewhere as well. An other self who either didn't share his... interests or was better at covering them up. One who apparently related better to those around him, and was content to stay in one place for far longer than his own restlessness had ever allowed. One who might prove... useful. Only one way to find out for certain, Joseph decided. And he went off in search of a phone and a phonebook, assuming this world still had such things.

Ultimately he had no luck finding a phone — there was something strange going on, the few people he saw looked frightened, defensive, and the streets were mostly empty, many of the buildings showing damage as if from an explosion — but it didn't matter. Because as he roamed the nearly deserted city Joseph began to get a vague, nagging sense of where to go. Almost like a tugging in the back of his mind, which grew stronger when he faced the right direction. He had to assume it was guiding him toward his other self, and since he didn't have any other idea, he let it.

The bong of a heavy bell tolling startled him, and Joseph glanced around. He'd been to Paris before, and recognized the outline of the Basilique du Sacré Coeur, the Sacred Heart, off in the distance. It sounded like the bell was ringing from there. He wondered what that meant, that someone would be tolling the bells when clearly a massive disaster had struck Europe and all but depopulated Paris, and considered detouring to check it out. In the end, though, he decided it was more important to locate his other self first. He could always go there later.

Eventually, after numerous tolls that didn't seem to correspond to the time, the strange sensation guided Joseph to a quiet little street that looked far less damaged than most of what he'd seen. The building he honed in on was an actual house, albeit a small one, but very quaint, with a sense of quiet age about its sturdy little frame and a homey feel to its brightly painted wooden shutters and flower-filled window beds. A sudden concern floated through him. What if this world's Joseph Tern had—he shuddered to even think it—a relationship? What if he had actually allowed someone to form a permanent attachment to him? But after a second's worry he shook off the thought. It was simply ridiculous. He was a loner, through and through. Surely that would be the same on every world. And if not, well, he would deal with it then. Deliberately whistling a jaunty tune he strolled up to the door and rapped on it once, twice, three times.

"Coming!" a voice called out from within, and the sound of it sent chills through Joseph because it was the same voice he used to hear on his answering machine, a strange, distorted version of what normally came out of his mouth. An instant later the door creaked, then slid aside, revealing a slender, average-height man with short dark hair, a lean face, one blue eye and one green eye, and a ready smile. Except for the smile it was like looking in a mirror, and that expression dropped quickly anyway, to be replaced by wide-eyed shock.

"What—how—who—?" his other self managed to stutter at last. Joseph couldn't really blame him.

"Maybe we should talk inside," he suggested, keeping his tone neutral-to-friendly, and his other self nodded.

"Sure, sure—come on in." He stepped aside so Joseph could slide past, then shut the door behind him and locked it securely. "This way." Joseph didn't miss the pistol his other self had kept out of sight behind the door and now set in a little alcove beside it. Interesting.

Inside the house was just as nice, warm and homey but still neat and tidy, not a lot of personal items to clutter it but with obvious care given to the gleaming hardwood floors and the diamond-paned windows and the arching doorways. The other Tern—Joseph decided to simply call him "Joe" in his head to keep things straight—led the way into the living room and promptly dropped onto one of the two couches there. Joseph settled himself on the one opposite it.

"You're—who are you, exactly?" Joe asked after staring again. "You're me, aren't you? I can actually feel some sort of . . . connection between us."

Joseph nodded and tipped an imaginary hat. "Got it in one. Nice place you've got here. But what happened to the rest of the city? And why're you in Paris and not Geneva?" He didn't want to set up shop here if there was radiation all around. No point in that! He'd noted the oxygen tank and mask standing in the corner, always a bad sign. Plus he wanted to know why the two of their lives weren't perfectly parallel, and find out where the discrepancies lay.

"There was an explosion," Joe explained, leaning back into the cushions. "At the LHC, in fact. Took out the collider array itself, and a lot of the surrounding countryside, big chunks of Switzerland and France and Italy." He looked vaguely sick, or maybe just guilty. "I'd have been blown apart with all the rest but I'd been letting my vacation days pile up too much and they all but sent me packing, so I'd figured what the hell and bopped over to Scotland to do some hiking. I didn't even hear about the accident until a week or two later, when I wandered into a town."

Joseph nodded. He'd never had much use for vacations, either. He preferred to keep busy. "Why come here, though?" he asked.

Joe leaned forward. "Paris is right on the edge of the Collision—that's what they've named the great big gaping hole taking up most of Central Europe now. The scientists are trying to figure out what happened. A lot of 'em came here so they could take readings and all that jazz." He shrugged. "I know some of 'em from before—the lucky ones who were off on holiday or whatever when the accident occurred. I heard they were setting up shop here, and I didn't want to just sit around freaking out like the rest of the world, so I convinced one of the relief organizations to squeeze me in with the next shipment of emergency supplies. They needed guards on the facility, and like I said I already knew some of the scientists, so that was that." He waved a hand at their surroundings. "I found this house—there are a ton of empty places, you can pretty much pick and choose—and they pay me in food and basic supplies, nobody has money anymore, but I feel like I'm making a difference, or at least protecting the people who could."

"And the oxygen?" Joseph asked, indicating the tank.

"Oh, well there was this gas, it was making everyone crazy. It's gone now, but for a few weeks we had to wear the masks at all times."

Joseph nodded. "There are looters," he guessed, rubbing at his chin. "Street gangs, opportunists, probably shell-shocked loonies, too. That's why everyone was so well-armed and so on edge at your work." He grinned at the look on his double's face. "Yeah, I was there. That's how I knew about you—I came through that weird curtain in the collider's end chamber and that's where I wound up. It sent me straight to you."

"The Collision." Joe stared at him again, curiosity and confusion starting to give way to horror. "You came through the rift. Oh, God." He hunched forward, hands going to his face.

"Relax." Joseph demonstrated, lounging comfortably. This was a really nice couch, exactly the kind he'd buy himself if he could. Which only made sense. "It's all good."

"What do you want?" Joe demanded through his fingers.

"Want?" Joseph frowned at that. He glanced around, studying the nice big windows, the way the sun filled the room, the bookcase against one wall. "How about a place to crash, for starters? I need to get my sea legs, take the lay of the land, figure out my next step. And we're basically brothers, right? Twins, even! You wouldn't turn your twin brother away, now would you?"

"No, of course not." Joe straightened and let his hands drop. "Of course you can stay. You can have the guest bedroom."

"Thanks." Joseph unfolded his legs and pushed himself to his feet. "Mind if I go wash up a bit? It's been a long day. And then maybe we can get a bite, chat, catch up."

As he strode toward the hallway he'd spotted beyond this room, assuming it led to the master bedroom, the guest room, and the bathroom, he struggled not to sigh or snarl or spit or even roll his eyes. But it was a challenge. This world's him was turning out to be a whiny, weak little twit.

"So why did you leave your own world behind?" Joe asked. He'd thrown together some food—lightly seared tuna steaks, a spinach and artichoke salad, some crescent rolls hot from the oven—and they were eating at the dining room table like civilized folk. He'd even opened a bottle of wine, and Joseph sipped at the deep burgundy liquid a few times to be polite, though he'd never cared for the stuff. Or for how it took away his control. He took a sip now and shrugged, setting the glass back down gently.

"I needed a fresh start," he admitted, cutting off a piece of tuna and forking it into his mouth. Whatever else this world's him was, he was a pretty decent cook. "Too many people over there knew me and had certain preconceptions about me. It was stifling me. So I left."

Joe wasn't stupid, though. He frowned, swirling his wine in its glass. "People knew you so you left? I don't buy that. You must've had a real reason for going through the rift, especially if your world is still normal and you had no idea what you'd find on the other side." He paused. "Did it hurt, passing through it?"

"Like crazy," Joseph answered. He studied his other self and decided to see just what he was made of. "But yeah, you're right, I had reason to go. The cops were after me."

"What? Why?" He genuinely didn't seem to know.

Joseph shrugged and ate the last of his salad. "I may have killed someone," he answered slowly, chewing. "Or a few someones."

"You killed people? Why? What happened?" He wasn't faking that surprise and dismay, not if his sudden pallor was any indication. That was a shame. Joseph had thought they might be kindred spirits—they were versions of the same person, after all. But it looked like this version didn't share his tastes, which could be a problem. Time to move on to Plan B.

"Nothing happened," he answered. He cut another piece of tuna steak—it was really good—and guided the fork to his mouth, still holding the steak knife in his other hand. "I just— sometimes you just have to, you know? Someone's in your way, or has something you want, or keeps pestering you about the mail and the music and bagging your trash properly, and so you just have to take care of it. Understand?"

Joe shook his head. "No. No, I don't understand." He was clenching his jaw, and his hands were starting to knead the tablecloth, bunching and unbunching it in long, strong fingers. His eyes flicked towards his gun and back again.

Joseph sighed. "That's a shame." Then he struck, the knife blade gleaming as it arced through the air between them. There was a tiny bit of resistance and the faintest of *thunk*s as the blade's serrated edge caught his other self in the throat, slicing easily through the flesh there, severing the carotid and the jugular in rapid succession before continuing on its way. Joe reeled, half-rising from his chair as he clutched his neck, blood already beginning to bubble up between his fingers as he slumped back down, eyes bulging and starting to go glassy. Joseph watched as this other him choked on his own blood, eyes rolling back as he bled out, and he reached across the table and lifted Joe's almost empty dinner plate and salad plate out of the way before he could topple onto them and across the table itself. He set the dishes down off to one side— he'd rinse them later—and finished his own food, ignoring the body across the table and the pool of blood creeping steadily toward him. Anyone as clearly obsessive-compulsive as this

Joe would definitely have a mop and a bucket and a whole host of cleaning supplies. He just hoped none of it would seep through the tablecloth and stain the table itself.

Joseph studied his other self, whose body was now jerking out its last gasps. "What's for dessert?" he asked.

The next morning, "Joe" Tern reported for duty as usual. This uniform fit a lot better than the one he'd stolen on the other side—it had been tailored to him, after all—and it wasn't too hard to bluff his way through every encounter. Everyone at this research facility apparently knew him, and he exchanged pleasantries with most of the other guards and even a few scientists and researchers during the course of the day. One in particular, an attractive young Swiss woman named Hildy, made it a point to linger whenever she passed by, and smiled a lot when she talked to him. Joseph made a mental note of that. She intrigued him.

It felt strange to be working a regular day job again, and he spent the first day glancing over his shoulder, expecting someone to grab him at any minute, to make him answer for his crimes. They couldn't possibly know about Joe—he'd taken care of that, cleaning the table and the surrounding walls and floor thoroughly, and disposing of the body by chopping it up, carrying it out back, and tossing it bit by bit into the steel-drum firepit he'd discovered back there. When he'd finished there'd been nothing but ash and bone. He buried the bones and scattered the ashes across the backyard, in the front yard, and in those neglected little window boxes. Bye bye, Joe. Still he felt like he was wearing a large sign saying "Imposter," and he was careful and jumpy the whole day long. It was a relief to return home afterward, make something quick to eat, and just relax, staring out the window as the sun went down, the clouds of smoke and ash and dust and gas from the collider accident giving the sunset a wilder, more frenetic feel that felt completely at odds with this more sedate, more protected life he seemed to have adopted.

The second day he was more relaxed. And the third, even more so. With each passing day he felt less concern about the possibility of anyone coming through the rift after him, and no one here seemed to suspect him of anything except cheating on a hand at the last poker game, swiping a cookie or a soda from the staff fridge, and hitting on Hildy every chance he got. After a week he finally accepted the idea that he was safe here. After two, he really believed it.

And after three, he was thoroughly bored. This life was safe, yes. But it was so bland! How had "Joe" managed to live like this, with no excitement, no danger, nothing to shake him out of his quiet, comfortable little cocoon? Maybe he'd been content with that, but Joseph was made for stronger stuff. He needed to do something that would make him feel alive again. And he knew exactly what. And whom.

"I can't believe it's taken you this long to invite me to dinner," Hildy teased as he answered the door. She looked particularly lovely, too, out of her white lab coat and with her golden hair loose around her shoulders instead of pulled back in a tight braid, and the simple but well-fitted blue dress showed off her curves and her long legs and played up the color of her eyes. Joseph imagined that to most men, and many women, she would be all but irresistible. He liked what he saw as well, but perhaps not for the same reason as most.

"I clearly wasn't thinking straight," he said now, playing along as he held the door open and ushered her in. The sun was near setting, his favorite time of day, but it was a Sunday so he'd had all day to prepare. Now he shut the door behind her and followed her as she glided through the foyer and into the living room.

"This place is gorgeous," she exclaimed softly, setting her gun and her pocketbook down on the little table against the wall, next to his keys and ID. She glanced over her shoulder at him, unconsciously seductive or perhaps intentionally so, and held up the bottle she'd been carrying in her other hand. "I managed to locate a bottle of wine, the least I could do since you prepared dinner. Would you like to pop the cork or shall I?" The twinkle in her eyes confirmed that the last, at least, had been deliberate, and he grinned to let her know he appreciated the double entendre.

"Oh, I'd much rather you did," he replied, raising a soft blush to her tanned cheeks and an extra sway to her hips as she slid past him into the kitchen. He followed her in there, and they made more flirtatious small talk as she uncorked the bottle and poured two glasses. Dinner was basically ready, so he had her bring the wine out to the table while he plated the food. It was a nice meal, simple and fresh and tasty, and Hildy was more vivacious outside of work, more playful, and inclined to reach out and touch his hand or rub her foot against his leg while laughing or telling a story. He had to steel himself not to flinch each time.

"This is nice," she commented as they were finishing the main course. "And I don't just mean the meal, and the company — though both of those are excellent." She grinned at him, but then her smile faltered and she loosed a small, sad sigh. "It's just nice to do something normal, you know? Like maybe we can get back to the way things used to be, at least a little bit."

"I agree," Joseph told her. "I'd like to get back to that, too." And he smiled at his own little joke.

Finally dinner was over. "Would you like to sit for a bit?" Joseph asked as he rose to take the empty plates.

"Not really." Hildy stood as he reached around her, so that she wound up standing within his arms, and with a single small step she was nestled up against him, her breasts pressing into his chest, her cheek against his. "I'd rather do something else." Her voice had gone husky with arousal, and he tilted his head down to hers as she reached up, grabbing his hair and pulling his mouth to hers for a fierce, hungry kiss that tasted of fruit and cream and wine.

"I guess the dishes can wait," he breathed after they'd pulled apart for air, and her answering smile was slow and sultry, her cheeks flushed, her lips parted and full. He took her hand and led her through the living room to the guest room, which he'd gotten ready for just such an occasion. As they approached the door he felt his own pulse begin to race, excitement making his blood sing. A smile of anticipation creased his own face, and Hildy smiled back at him, clearly eager as well.

But when he turned on the light and guided her inside, her smile began to falter. Taking in the plastic covering the bed, the heavy panels along the walls, she stopped, staring. And when Joseph shut the door behind her and she half-turned, then glimpsed the implements he'd laid out atop the dresser, her knees went weak and she almost toppled, falling against him with a small whimper.

"Why?" was all she said, which impressed him. No cries, no screams, no pleading. Those would come later, he knew.

For now, however, he merely shrugged as he reached down and scooped her off her feet to carry her over to the bed. "Because I'm hungry too," he answered honestly. And the fear shining out of her lovely blue eyes as he set her down was a thousand times more satisfying than the dinner they'd eaten just before, or the conversation they'd shared. This was what life was all about. This was living.

And when she started screaming, later, he felt better than he had in ages.

"Morning, Joe!"

"Hey, Joe!"

"How was your weekend, man?"

"What's up, big guy?"

"Bonjour, Joe!"

"Hey Joe, where's your girlfriend?"

Joseph smiled and nodded and laughed in response to each of these greetings, and to the last one he added a shrug. "Must be running late," he answered. "You know how women are." That got laughs and nods of agreement. Then he was off to patrol the perimeter with the others who'd been assigned that duty today. No one asked him about Hildy again—he'd been careful to ask her out late on Friday so there hadn't been time for anyone else to hear about their plans—though a few of the guys teased him about "scaring her off" when she still hadn't shown by lunch time. Joseph joined in the general merriment with good grace, joking about how now he'd never know what she really looked like under that lab coat.

Which was a lie, of course. He knew exactly what she looked like. Inside and out. But no one else knew that. No one was the wiser. No one suspected a thing.

He smiled to himself as he finished his lunch, packed his lunchbox away, and went back to work, whistling under his breath. It was good here. He felt like he'd finally found a place where he belonged.

KEEP CALM AND CARRY ON
PART THREE
by David N. Smith and Violet Addison

Jess
Monday, 4th April, 2016
14:00pm

I want to die. Every inch of me hurts.

The world has never looked bleaker.

They've finally taken the oxygen mask off my face. I've made it as far as the window, and the sights outside are soul-destroying.

There's an old man lying on the road, between the abandoned cars, laughing himself raw. There's a sullen-eyed woman watching him, silently. He starts spasming, his old heart clearly giving out, only metres from the open gates of the hospital. She turns and walks away, not lifting a finger to help him. I close the blinds and go back to bed, wheeling my IV drip behind me.

I'd feel terrible, if I could, but I don't think it's humanly possible to feel worse than I do right now. We can't risk going downstairs or outside, as it would increase the chance of intoxication, so we are all prisoners inside these 'safe' white, air-conditioned walls.

We can only look after ourselves and our own. That's it. I don't have the strength for anything more. I don't even really have the strength for that.

I'm on the third floor, and there's a fire door at the end of the hall that leads out onto the roof. It would be the work of a minute to walk out there and step off the edge. End the suffering. Go the same way as Hasan. End the confusion. End everything.

I won't though, because I know the facts. The chemicals in my brain are out of whack. I'm not myself.

This is not the time to be making life altering decisions.

But I wonder how many people have?

I'm also wondering what happened to my friends. Where is Mike? Where is Naomi? Neither is answering their phone. Answer me if you're out there.

I've spoken to my mother who is back in Atlanta, and she's been unable to get me a flight home. All planes are grounded.

There's nowhere left to run.

I've cried until my eyes are red-raw and dry.

I have no more tears left to shed.

I can't even find the energy to be afraid anymore.

Ben
Monday 2nd April, 2016
13:03pm EST

Hang in there, Sis.
>   We love you.
>   Find a way home to us.

Pang
Thursday 5th April, 2016
8:00am CST

Many thanks for the help you provided when I was struck with this infliction. If only we had resolved my case, perhaps you would not be suffering now. I regret more heavily than ever my decision to leave the country, and not partake in the follow up examinations.

Instead, I returned to China on one of the last flights out of Gatwick, and discovered that Beijing is swarming with soldiers and Toothfish. The Toothfish have evolved. The Toothfish are winning.

Don't fool yourself, nowhere is safe.

I made my way west to Lanzhou, which seems so far to have avoided the spread of the Toothfish, or the 'Fanged Dragon' as they are known here.

But even here, there are oddities at work. Mei-su, my grandmother, has been experiencing visions and hallucinations. At first I wrote these off as the ramblings of an old woman, but I have come to believe they are something else entirely.

She has talked of a child being trapped in an underground tunnel, laughing as he was ripped apart by Toothfish.

There is no way she could know of events like this, as she has no access to the Western media. She knows nothing of the gas, or the plight of England.

She is becoming increasingly pre-occupied with these visions, rather than the world around her. This morning I found her wandering naked in the garden, convinced she'd had her throat slit by someone called Joseph, and that she was now just a wandering spirit.

I'm struggling to get medical help here.

What can I do to help her?

Laura
Thursday 5th April, 2016
10:05am

If you had access to the resources, I'd suggest running an MRI, just to rule out any physiological cause. I'd then be able to tell you how to deal with a blood-clot or a tumour, but if it is something rift related, then I'm not sure what I could do to help. What can any of us do? Maybe the most important thing right now is just to give her some TLC, at least that's something you can do, that will make a difference.

Ben
Thursday, 5th April, 2016
3:03pm EST

Am sure I read a news story about something like this. That guy ended up burning down his apartment block and got thrown into a loony bin. You need to look after her.

Pang
Friday, 6th April, 2016
8:00am CST

What is this TLC? Is it a drug? Where can I get it?

Laura
Friday, 6th April, 2016
7:00am

T.L.C.
    Tender Love and Care.

***

Jess
Thursday, 7th April, 2016
7:15am

We have a plan.
    In the emergency response unit there are a number of bio-hazard suits, which have been gathering dust for the best part

of a decade, that were designed for use in the event of a biological or nuclear terrorist attack. Naturally, this never happened, but they're perfect for the situation we now find ourselves in. I've even been trained in their use, so thank goodness for ridiculous HR courses!

These give us much more freedom to move about at ground level.

We're heading out of London.

We'll stock up on the way.

We'll spend the nights on higher ground, so tonight we should hopefully be in the emergency response centre at Harrow Hill, which should be high enough to protect us from the gases. The plan is to rendezvous there with Laura and the staff from King's Cross.

I've had news of Naomi, but it's not good. She was checked into King's Cross four nights ago. She died of exhaustion. According to her records, an eye witness claimed that she danced herself to death in the reception area of the Emergency Centre.

Nothing surprises me anymore.

Laura has known for days but was struggling to find a way to tell me. I don't blame her. In some ways I'm glad that I know before we leave, as I'd have hated to have left thinking I was leaving my friend behind, possibly in pain and trouble.

However, I have grieved for her before. Right now, I have no tears left. I have to concentrate on the living, on supporting the people who support me.

Sheena and Doctor Ogundana are both suited and booted in their bio-hazard suits, and I'm sure you can imagine just how ridiculous they look, so it's time for me to get a move on.

Time to go.

I'm going to stop at Michael's house on the way.

Ben, my cell network is getting erratic, so if we don't get a chance to talk again, please know that I'm ok. Love to you, Mom and Dad. Got to go.

Laura
Thursday, 5th April, 2016
19:30pm

We've reached Harrow Hill and found a dozen more bio-hazard suits.

We're attempting to use the oxygen supplies here to restore some of the staff to normal. I think we can make this work.

My mobile has finally given up the ghost. I'm posting this from the reception PC.

When will you reach here? Any luck with your friend?

Laura
Thursday, 5th April, 2016
22:21pm

It's late. You should be here by now.

I dialled your number from a landline, but it doesn't even ring. I'm hoping you've just been delayed and that it's just that your mobile network has finally gone down too; in many ways I'm surprised they lasted as long as they did.

I can't bear the idea that something may have happened to you. I'm suddenly aware of how much we need you, Jess. If you, Sheena and Doctor Ogundana don't make it here, then I'm going to be faced with a terrible choice: How long do I wait for you?

I'm not ready for a decision like that.

Please, tell me you're all right. Tell me that you're still on the way.

Let me know that you're alive.

Ben
Thursday 5th April, 2016
20:03pm EST

Please don't let it end like this. Call me.

***

Jess
Saturday, 7th April, 2016
08:59pm

I'm alive.

As Naomi once said, the rumours of my death have been very much exaggerated. Michael is alive too.

All the UK cell networks are now down. I'm making this post from a PC at the Harrow Hill Emergency Centre, which is running on power from an emergency back-up generator, probably making it one of the last working internet connections in the entire country. The rest of London has been plunged into darkness; the electricity went off around forty-eight hours ago.

If the gas does ever stop coming out of the rift then perhaps one day the power will go back on, but for now we're cutting and running, giving up on London and heading to the hills.

We're going to take four ambulances and head west on the M4, with the hope of finding some higher ground that we can make secure. Our main objective is to get out of London. It's just too dangerous here, with random outbreaks of violence and rioting, with absolutely no trace of any attempt to enforce law or order.

Michael is in the back of one of the ambulances, high as a kite on oxygen, recovering from the poisons that he inhaled. We'll treat him as we travel.

Laura waited two days for us to arrive, as we struggled to make our way through the blocked streets. I think she would have waited forever. She wouldn't give up on us...

I can only imagine that this will be my last ever on-line post, so this is perhaps the moment I should say goodbye. I doubt we'll ever get to talk to each other again. I shall miss my friends and family in the States. I can't believe I was ever stupid enough to move away from you all. I love you and I miss you. I'm glad you are all still safe, but don't expect that to last forever.

We blew a hole in the side of our planet, through reality itself, and we were arrogant enough to think we could just ignore it and carry on with our mundane, selfish, little lives. We were wrong. Don't make the same mistake that we did.

Decide what is important to you, hold on to it and protect it, because you and it are in very real danger. We have a plan. We have supplies. We are standing shoulder to shoulder. We are keeping calm and carrying on, because in the end, that's all you can ever do.

That's living.

Our old lives are gone, but we're still kicking.

Goodbye and Good Luck.

Jess x

Ben
Saturday, 7th April, 2016
08:02pm EST

As ever, I suspect my words will arrive too late.

CNN have obtained satellite images that show that the gas stopped emanating from the rift nearly a week ago and that Paris has been clear for a few days. The levels are decreasing across Europe. It should have dissipated entirely by the end of the week.

However, nobody knows what will be coming through next. I don't think anywhere is safe.

We love you. We miss you. I'll look after Mom and Dad.

Goodbye and Good Luck.

THE COMING SCREAM
by Simon Kurt Unsworth

I: The Ward

When Collister's eyes burst, it was almost a relief.

Not a relief for Collister, of course, but for everyone else on the ward. Collister was a kinetic little runt of a man, a constant blur of twitching motion wearing pyjamas and a ratty dressing gown, and he'd been moaning for days. It had started with gripes about a headache that wouldn't go despite the medications given him by the nurses, and then quickly escalated to near-permanent muttering and demands that someone help him, *help* him. It had become first annoying and then frustrating and eventually wearing, and all of them had, Scott suspected, prayed for him to shut up.

Collister finally reached a fever pitch, shouting "Something's coming, something's coming!" and sitting at one of the scarred tables in the television lounge, holding his head and rocking back and forth and groaning. Some of the other patients shouted at him; the nurses in the glass-walled station were watching him with concern on their faces and with their mouths stretched thin and taut. Scott tried to ignore him.

The problem was that it seemed to be contagious. Not long after Collister started, the usually silent Gerteux started moaning out loud and rubbing at his temples and then Bernard the ex-policeman began as well. Soon, most of the ward's residents appeared to be afflicted to some degree by headaches and, in the case of Borden and Gillen, by pains in their eyes and ears that made them rub at themselves near-constantly, moaning. It was, Scott thought, like being in a fucking nuthouse. The first time he'd said that to himself, not long after his admittance here, it made him smile; now, it didn't.

Scott Fletcher, whose memories of blowing up his own apartment and his entire building in the process were fragmented and had the feel to him of badly spliced film, at first thought the other patients were catching their afflictions from him. After all, the tumour in his head ensured a running supply of blinding headaches, hallucinations, dizzy spells and vomiting. But the symptoms displayed by Collister, Gerteux and the others weren't the same; not quite.

Late in the afternoon, Collister came and sat next to Scott. It was the first time Scott had left his room for more than a few minutes in days; his headaches had lessened in the last couple of days, and his dreams the previous night had been almost normal. Almost. He could even cope, he felt, with Collister.

The man looked terrible; he was sweating, muttering, his head shaking back and forth as though trying to dislodge bubbles of water from his ears. His hands fluttered about, clutching each other in his lap and then rising to scratch at his ears and his temples and across the top of his head. "Why can't you hear it, Fletcher?" he said. "You can't, can you? You can't."

"Hear what?" Scott suddenly realized that he didn't know Collister's first name, didn't know the first name of anyone else on the ward. Sometimes, they didn't seem like real people to him at all but were more like ghosts drifting through his days. Hell, sometimes he felt like his own ghost, a shadow of the person he used to be; maybe it *was* catching. Collister gripped his upper arm, his fingers digging into Scott's bicep.

"Tell me how you can't hear it," he said, leaning in. Veins bulged in his forehead and spittle flecked his lips. His breath smelled rotten, of old meat and stagnant water. It was the medications, Scott knew, that made them smell, the medications and sometimes the psychoses sweating out of their pores. He wondered if he smelled and hoped he didn't.

"I don't know," he said, humouring him.

"Someone's coming," said Collister, "and they're screaming. Can't you hear them?"

"No," said Scott, trying not to think of insects emerging through cracks and the thing in the kitchen and flames sucking hungrily at his home. The doctors had explained it, that it was all in his head, and he had learned to nod and agree and swallow the little white and blue and pink pills, and sometimes he even believed it himself. Of course, it was as if everyone had visions now. They only had to look out of their door to see the end of the world happening about them. It was no longer a madman's dream, he thought, it was a sane man's nightmare.

"I can hear it," said Collister. "Please, tell me you can hear it. You've seen things, I can tell. You know what I'm talking about."

"No," repeated Scott and peeled Collister's fingers from his arm. The smaller man hunched over in his chair, rocking to and fro, fro and to, his arms wrapped up around his head.

"Someone's coming! Please," said Collister, "make them go away!" He began to scream, wretched, and then his eyes exploded.

They went with a noise like thin fabric ripping. Blood sprayed in thin arcs from the punctured eyeballs, spattering across Scott even as he cried out in disgust and launched himself backwards over his chair. Collister rose, twisting, his hands coming down from the top of his head in clawed desperation and clamping against his ruined eyes as though to force them back in. Blood burst from between his fingers, rolling down them in thick strings and meeting at his wrists, soaking into the thin towelling of his robe. He took an unsteady step, caught his foot around a chair leg and stumbled. He flailed, one hand leaving his face and trying to find support, droplets of blood leaping from his fingers.

Around the ward people were screaming as Collister took another couple of lurching steps and then fell to his knees. His cries had descended into a series of yelps, each on the exhale like a rutting dog, as staff ran towards him. Goffin, that bastard orderly who'd taken great delight in putting the restraints on Scott until he'd learned to keep his head down and nod and be polite, was in the lead. *Figures*, thought Scott, *he wouldn't want to miss the action.*

Collister held out his hands, tried to call out but his jaws went sharply rigid and snapped shut, his muscles standing out in thick cords. His teeth clamped around the tip of his tongue and a moment later a pink nubbin fell to the floor and fresh blood began to pour from his mouth. He stiffened as Goffin reached him and then pitched sideways, starting to spasm. Goffin jammed a needle into Collister's arm as the other nurses arrived and the alarms wailed and people screamed, but even Scott could see it was hopeless.

It took Collister a long time to die; even after they'd managed to get him onto a gurney and into one of the treatment rooms, he screamed for hours. Sometimes, he'd try to form words but they reached Scott on distorted waves, mutated by the man's battered throat and incomplete tongue and constant howls. Even for this place, where screams were usual, Collister was setting everyone's nerves on edge and there were several arguments during the course of the evening. Even the chemically coshed Benoit, normally so calm, snapped at people if they came too near him saying, "Mine!" and holding his arms to indicate a space around him.

When Doctor Rhodes finally announced Collister's death, not long after the last scream had faded away, there was an almost palpable drop in tension. People shuffled off to bed, went to get night-time medications or painkillers; got back to normal, as far as there *was* a normal in a place where two sets of locked doors separated them from the outside world and the windows were unbreakable glass and every resident saw things or heard things or believed things that weren't real.

The story was that Collister had suffered a major and rapid deterioration and had clawed his own eyes out whilst in the grip of some new and catastrophic psychosis. No one asked Scott what he'd seen, and he didn't say; it was none of his business. The story, which gained new details as it travelled up and back along the ward as a hermit crabs picks up new pieces for its shell, retained its currency for just over twelve hours.

Until the precise moment, in fact, when Gillen drove the pencil into his own ear.

It was Rhodes's idea; a communal discussion about Collister's actions to help the patients deal with their feelings. Seeing as most of the ward's inhabitants, even those who were aware enough to come to group sessions (whom Scott had long since taken to calling the Shuffling Masses), were several steps detached from their emotions by medication and an at-best tenuous hold on reality, it was always going to be a weird session and Scott only went because there was nothing else to do. There was no television in the ward now, hadn't been since the start of the problems outside, and the empty bracket on the wall was a mute reminder of their isolation and relative safety. There were no new newspapers or magazines, and the only books available to read were battered paperbacks that Scott couldn't concentrate on.

Rhodes had pulled the chairs into a circle and the Shuffling Masses were sitting in them, restive. Some of them had dressed, mostly in blue jeans and T-shirts but barefooted, but some like Scott had stayed in their nightwear and it gave the meeting the look of a sleepover party that had somehow gone terribly wrong. No one looked anyone in the eye, and no one looked at where Collister had been when his eyes burst; the place was just beyond the circle, and Scott had noticed that no one even stepped over the newly washed patch of floor but skirted around it when they had to go to that part of the room.

"Well, does anyone have anything they'd like to say?" said Rhodes, looking around hopefully.

""No," said someone; Scott didn't catch who.

"Really?" said Rhodes. "Because I thought there might be a lot to say, really. One of our friends died yesterday. How does that make you feel? Anyone?"

"I didn't like him," said a man Scott thought might be called King or Kinger, something like that anyway, and whose shabby beard had always annoyed him in ways he couldn't explain.

"Well, you can still be sorry he's dead," said Rhodes.

"I'm not," said King-or-Kinger, and then Gillen screamed and rose.

"Mr Gillen," said Rhodes, also rising, but Gillen screamed again, clapping his hands to the sides of his head.

"Shut it up!" he yelped. "Shut it up! Please, oh Jesus, please, shut it up!"

"There's nothing—" Rhodes began, but then stopped as other people in the circle began to nod and speak and agree with Gillen, who screamed again. People around the room were rising, some also beginning to hold their heads and ears. It was as though no one had wanted to admit anything until someone else did, but Gillen had broken the wall and now it was all coming out. Actually, most of the people in the circle *didn't* look well, Scott realized. All around him were pale faces, sweat-slicked skin, haunted, bruised eyes. *What is this,* he wondered? *What's happening?*

Gillen took two steps forward, coming to the centre of the circle and screamed a third time. "Mr Gillen, please," said Rhodes.

Gillen ignored Rhodes, instead shrieking, "No no no, shut up shut up shut up," and took something from his pocket and, with a cry of, "Please no more," thrust it against the side of his head.

There was a noise like someone biting into an apple, a sour little crunch, and then Gillen let out a long sigh. Blood welled, dribbling around the stem of the pencil that now protruded from his ear. Dr Rhodes stepped forward, repeating "Mr Gillen?" his voice halfway between confusion and anger and then Gillen let out a long groan, reached up and yanked on the pencil.

At first, Gillen's fingers slipped because of the blood but then he managed to grip it and pull it free. It came loose with an audible, wet *pop* and he groaned again as blood flooded down the side of his face and over his shoulder. Someone in the circle screamed and Rhodes shouted for the nurses but by then Gillen had swapped the pencil to his other hand and had plunged it into his other ear.

This time, he screamed when it went in.

The noise was less like a crunch and more like a tearing sound this time, and the pencil didn't go in as far. Gillen was trying to force it in further as Rhodes grasped hold of him and pinned his arms to his sides. Two nurses that Scott didn't know ran to help Rhodes and, between them, they manhandled the screaming, bleeding Gillen away.

In the chaos, no one realized at first that a paranoid schizophrenic called Craigie, so muted under medications that most of the time he drooled and stuttered when he spoke, had slumped over in his chair and had, very silently, bled out from every orifice in his body and was sitting, dead, in a widening pool of his own blood.

The ward went into lock-down.

In the next twenty-four hours, six more patients died, two by their own hands. Gillen was, apparently, under heavy sedation in his room and everyone else had been assessed by a nervous-looking Rhodes, although the ward didn't have enough staff to keep everyone displaying the symptoms of what Scott heard Rhodes describe as "extreme auditory hallucinations" under close observation. It didn't have enough staff to cover the everyday duties, not any more, of course; not since the rift and the gas and the chaos. Patients were confined to their rooms, which remained unlocked, and the nurses and auxiliary staff went up and down the corridors and peered in at everyone as often as they could.

Every hour or two, there had been a commotion. It was hard to tell because no one was talking, but Scott thought that it wasn't just self-injury or suicide, but that something else was happening, although what he didn't know. What staff there were ran around trying to get to people in time, to sew them back together or get hearts beating and lungs moving again, but even from within his room Scott could tell that they were only occasionally successful. Carts rattled along the ward, the overhead PA sent out increasingly desperate calls for staff members or equipment or drugs, alarms sounded and then stopped, and people cried and moaned and screamed and shouted. Through it all, Scott sat on his bed and listened and wondered what the fuck was going on, and was thankful that his head seemed clear. He couldn't hear anything, not that he didn't expect to hear anyway; the only odd thing was a continual desire to look in the direction of the sunset, although he had no idea what he was looking for, or why. The only thing he saw, looking out of his window and down into the valley below the hospital, was a distant flock of gasbags flying low, just above the trees. He only knew what they were called because he'd heard an orderly talk about them once, them and something called 'toothfishes'. *Not 'teethfish'*, he remembered, *'toothfishes'*. The toothfishes he was sure he'd seen before, in his visions, attacking a young couple and their newborn baby in Paris. These other creatures, the gasbags, were new. They swooped, and although he couldn't hear them, he imagined they screeched as they moved.

The second day of the lock-down, Scott realized that even the staff were beginning to be affected. They were distracted, no surprise given the circumstances he didn't suppose, but several of them had started rubbing at their ears or temples. He watched, intrigued, for several hours as the staff succumbed to what he had assumed before was some kind of mass hysteria. He'd never heard of anything like this affecting staff before; it was, in its own way, fascinating. Oddly, when the staff looked around as though they'd heard something, it was to the west. Scott didn't suppose it meant anything but still; fascinating.

In the middle of the afternoon one of the nurses, Scott thought her name was Rosie, stopped in the middle of walking quickly up the corridor. She took several slow, hesitant steps and halted again outside Scott's door, turning to him.

"Can't you hear it?" she said, so quietly that Scott had to strain to hear. "It's so terrible. It's so *sad*."

"No," said Scott, "I'm sorry, I can't." That wasn't true, though, not quite. He *had* begun to hear a distant sound, behind everything else, a noise that was wrong, jarringly out of place; it was like a scream distorted through layers of material and metal and dust and bone. It didn't bother him the way it clearly bothered other people but it was annoying, like a low-grade hangover, like toothache throbbing in the middle of his head. It reminded him of how he'd felt in those first few weeks before the thing in the kitchen, of the mild pains and the pressure he had felt behind his eyes and got strangely used to before everything went to shit.

"It's terrible," the nurse said again and then, very calmly lifted her hands and cupped them delicately around her ears. She opened her eyes wide; they were bloodshot, the pupils large and black. When she blinked, tears of blood spilled over her bottom lids and rolled down her pale cheeks, leaving torn red tracks down to her mouth and chin. She opened her mouth and moaned, and her teeth were bloody; the moan dissolved into a bubbling, hacking cough and she dropped to her knees, her head swaying. She spat, an indecently large mass of spittle the colour of cochineal spattering on the floor in front of her. "Oh," she said softly, "my." Blood trickled from between her fingers, from out of her eyes. The front of her uniform was bloodied in the cleft at the top of her legs.

"It's so terrible, so sad," she managed to say, and then collapsed forward, her head striking the hard floor with a wretched crunch. She twitched, blood streaming from her nose and mouth. Scott stood, unsure of what to do. He had no medical training, was wary doing something that might make things worse. He wanted to go to her but couldn't get close without stepping in the increasing pool of blood, which struck him as strangely disrespectful. Instead, he pressed his bed alarm and then started shouting, waiting for someone to come and help him with her.

It was fifteen minutes before anyone arrived, and then they simply loaded the nurse onto a trolley and took her away without a word.

By the end of the third day, the lock-down was over simply because there were no staff to maintain it. The noise on the ward, what he had started to think of as the *real* noise, had dropped to almost nothing and although Scott was enjoying the peace, he was trying not to think about what the silence might mean. No screams, no moans, no shouting, no crash carts or alarms. Nothing.

No one.

Breakfast wasn't delivered, which didn't bother Scott as he hated food first thing, but then neither was lunch, and no one brought him his medications. When he left his room, he found the ward deserted and most of the room doors shut. Some had crosses of surgical tape on them and Scott was reminded of the angel of the Passover story. Walking down the ward, he imagined some vast black thing drifting overhead, reaching down to take those that caught its attention, and couldn't help but look up. There was nothing there; he didn't think there would be, of course, but still.

But still.

The ward doors were locked; that security measure, at least, remained intact. Scott went and sat in the lounge. There were thick burgundy stains on several of the chairs and dried, crusted blood was pooled in the nurses' station. It showed no signs of having been cleaned; the station's door was open and he could have walked in if he'd wanted to.

The noise was still there. It was a little louder, maybe, but still not more than a background hum like flies on the other side of a window, busy battering themselves against the glass.

When Scott tried to listen harder, it seemed to drift away, coming back only when he turned his attention elsewhere. He was hungry, jittery, wanted his medications. Where was Goffin? Rhodes? That nurse whose buttocks moved so sweetly in her uniform and whose breasts bounced when she walked?

Where was everyone?

He wasn't sure how much later it was when he heard them; voices from the other side of the ward doors, from the non-secure public area beyond. They were getting louder and Scott stood, moving to the doors quickly. Through the glass panels he could see further doors, also still closed, and then beyond them the hospital's main corridor. Figures moved rapidly along the passage, coming to a halt before the far doors. They were bulky and oddly shaped, their limbs weirdly stunted.

It was only when they raised their rifles that Scott realized that the figures were soldiers.

II: The Clinic

The MRI scan was bad. Scott had to lie still in a tube while the machine whirred and lights flashed around him like robot boosters launching him into space, and as itches flared and receded across his skin. Morris, the army doctor, had told him they would in that laconic way of his. "You can't move to scratch 'em," he'd said, "so the itches that you never even felt before will come say hello."

Scott had no idea where he was. From the moment the soldiers came through the doors, smashing both sets open rather than trying to deal with the locks, to the point the helicopter landed at their destination, no one told him anything. He had been hustled down the corridor to a black army 'copter waiting on the hospital's helipad, its rotors spinning lazily, thrust in its rear then held at gunpoint as the vehicle lifted off and carried him into the afternoon sun. Only when they had been airborne and moving, if Scott was any judge, very fast for half an hour or so did any of the helicopter's other occupants remove the thick helmets they wore.

They were all wearing strange suits, actually; they looked like old-fashioned diving suits, right down to the headpieces, huge domes of curved glass and steel struts in which the men's faces looked outsized and distorted. The material of the suits shimmered as though made of metal or fish-scales and Scott wondered if a nuclear war had happened without him realizing, if these were some kind of radiation suit; later, he came to realize that he was closer to the truth then than he could ever have imagined.

"What's happening?" he asked as the nearest soldier removed their helmet. It was a woman, her eyes flat and hard. She wore no visible insignia, but Scott knew instinctively that she was the commander of this little jaunt. She looked at him for a few moments and then said, "You don't know?"

"No."

"We need your help." Her accent was lilting Irish. Northern Irish, Scott was sure.

"Why?"

"Because," said the woman, "you're the man who can't hear."

However bad the MRI was, the hearing tests were worse. He was tired, which didn't help, and was being pushed everywhere at gunpoint and no one was talking to him other than Morris, but it was the test that was bad; no, not bad, fucking *awful*. He was strapped into a chair and had headphones placed around his ears and then played a series of sounds; he'd had hearing tests before, of course, but nothing like this. Then he had a set of digital beeps played at him and had been asked to say when he heard them and which side they were loudest on. For this test, though, the sounds were longer, louder, varying in pitch. Towards the end of the test, the noise shifted, became something suddenly agonising, like the metallic grind of the gears of some huge machine that was burning itself out. He screamed.

"Interesting," said Morris, coming around and unstrapping Scott once the noise had finished. Scott tried to stay upright but slumped over, unable to hold himself. His eyes ached, his ears throbbed, his muscles felt weak and uncoordinated. Morris held him upright in the chair and said, "You can be made to hear."

"We don't know what it is," said Morris, "only that it's lethal. We're calling it a sound because in some ways it's acting like noise, but it's not sound, not exactly."

They were sitting in a canteen, as featureless and bland as a room could be, drinking coffee from a machine that had no brand identity upon it. The woman, who Morris had called Natalie, was sitting on a table in the corner of the room listening and watching but saying nothing. Morris had dismissed the guards and removed his own weapon from its holster and placed it on a far table. There was no one else in the room.

"We know it's coming from the Collision, and that it affects people with mental health problems first, possibly because their brains are already open or wired differently or something, and then children and psychics for probably versions of the same reason. Eventually everyone gets hurt by it, even the least imaginative, most stolid of us. It's like it vibrates us at the wrong speed, or in ways we aren't supposed to vibrate, and shakes us to pieces."

"Psychics?" asked Scott, thinking of little old ladies with shawls wrapped around their heads and fairground sideshows telling fortunes.

"Psychics," repeated Morris. "There was a test facility not far from Bern. It..." he said, and then broke off and took a deep breath.

"Terrible things happened there," he said after a moment. "Terrible. Everywhere it touches, terrible things happen. Except to you."

"Why me?"

"We aren't sure, although the tumour may have something to do with it. It's left you with a ... hole in your brain that we think may be a mirror for whatever's making the sound. A tiny rift, or a huge Collision seen from a distance, or compressed. We don't know what it is, just that it's there."

"You said you didn't know what was making the sound."

"We don't, but we have a theory. We think it's coming from something on the other side of the Collision. We're hearing its breathing, or its screaming. It gets worse the closer you get to the rift, of course, and it's weaker by the time it reaches Britain, but it's still lethal."

"And what about me? Where do I come into all of this?"

"That," said Morris flatly, "is what we need to talk about."

III: Somewhere, France.

Scott still didn't know where he was, he hadn't been told, but he was at least out in the open. He dropped a gear, manoeuvring the truck slowly into place and then parked it and turned the engine off. The wind blew dust against the windows with a noise like insects being crushed underfoot; it didn't quite drown the distant wail of what he'd started to think of as the Other Sound, which was louder here.

He climbed down from the cab and walked to the back of the truck where the bicycle was stored, unclipping it and lifting it to the ground. The air smelled of earth and blossom, of spring. Was it spring? He wasn't sure, had lost track of time in the hospital. It was warm, he knew that much, warm and the air was clean and if the world hadn't been ending, it would probably have been a nice day. Lifting his backpack onto his shoulders, Scott climbed onto the bike and began to pedal, his leg muscles aching.

So far, he had parked six trucks, long flatbeds that he had been given a crash course in driving before leaving England, lurching through the gears and trying to control their long, unwieldy bodies. He used a folded map for navigation as the SatNav had gone apeshit the first time he turned it on; this close to the Other Sound, all but the most basic electrical items tended to malfunction. The trucks were stripped back to their essential functions, no radios in their cabs or digital displays in their dashboards. On the rear of each were stacks of lead-covered boxes around three feet tall, cables emerging from the rear of each and joining into a thick, shielded tangle disappearing into the back of the cab. Each also held a huge drum of cable on a spindle.

"We have a plan," Morris had said. "We know it's acting like a sound, even if it isn't one, not technically. The auditory test we carried out on you showed us that even you can be exposed to it if we damp the sound of the rift in your head." When Scott looked confused, Morris had said, "We're fairly sure the hole in your head is producing a kind of damper wave which is negating the effects of the other sound. When we damped your damper wave, you felt the effects."

'Damped my damper wave'?" said Scott.

"It's not an exact analogy," admitted Morris. "You still didn't feel the effect of the other sound to any great degree, but it's the closest we can get to explaining it. We think we can reverse what we did to you, create our own damper wave and hem the other sound back in, keep it contained."

"Like noise reducing earphones?" said Scott, thinking of the earbud things he'd seen people using with their iPods and iPhones.

"Exactly," said Morris. "But there's a problem."

The problem being, of course, that anyone who tried to take in the equipment to set up the damper wave would likely die. The thick suits the soldiers wore, which Morris said set up an electromagnetic field around the wearer, worked only for so long before the Other Sound's strength overrode the protection provided, and Scott was the only person they'd found so far who seemed unaffected. Morris asked if Scott, as a good citizen of the world, would agree to drive in and set up the equipment. All the governments of the world would be grateful, he said. He had glanced at his gun as he said it, his hangdog eyes never registering more than a flicker of emotion. Natalie watched Scott take in Morris's glance and smiled at him. The smile did not reach her eyes.

They wouldn't come ashore, Natalie told him. On the boat, once he had agreed to work with them, she had thawed towards him slightly, although she either ignored or deflected the occasional personal questions he directed towards her. They'd arranged for the trucks to be positioned in a mall car park about twenty miles from the coast, along with rations and equipment. Who had placed the trucks there she had not said; there were footsteps and tyre marks all around the vehicles, and an empty helmet wedged under the front wheel of one of the cabs, its faceplate cracked and its inside surface smeared with dry blood. A clump of blond hair was knotted into the blood, and Scott had rolled the helmet into the weeds at the side of the mall rather than have it near him.

They'd given him maps and a bike and dropped him on a shingle beach and told him, *Good luck*. Natalie, to Scott's complete surprise, had leaned towards him as though to kiss his cheek before she got back into the inflatable dingy, veering away at the last minute, pulling back. "We'll see you in a few days," she said. "If this works, we can try to work out a way of increasing it. If not..." she let her voice trail off, the conclusion unspoken. Then, as though embarrassed by the almost-kiss, she reached out and shook his hand, her palm cool and dry against his.

"See you soon," Scott said.

"We can hope," she replied but she had not looked hopeful. That had been two days ago, and he had seen no one since.

He had managed to position three of the trucks yesterday, and three today; tomorrow, he would bring the last one, which would hold the generator, and then he would have to cycle from truck to truck dragging a huge length of cabling with him to connect them in a massive circle.

Each truck held a hastily constructed tower of lead-covered Marshall speakers and the first time they had told him about them, he had laughed without thinking, imagining some massive rock concert. "They're pre-programmed with the right frequencies, based on the tests we did on you," said Natalie. "Once they're connected to each other and a power source, they should create a strong enough wave to at least partially nullify the sound. We need to contain it, because it's growing."

It was like ripples expanding out from a series of stones dropped in water, thought Scott, remembering the map Natalie had shown him. Here was the line of the Collision marked out as a jaunty red scar, the centre of a series of plotted circles. There was the place where the psychics had died, there was a ski resort, here a French military base where something had happened that had made Natalie's eyes cloud when she touched its space on the map, and here over the sea was the hospital where Scott had been a prisoner. There were so many things on the map that it was impossible to comprehend, spaces containing fields, suburbs, schools, old people's homes, churches, roads, industrial towns and farming villages, Christ knew what else, more and more houses and offices and shops and streets and towns whose names he would never know in regions he would never visit in countries that were disintegrating.

More and more people.

It was dark by the time Scott got back to the mall, its lights appearing on the horizon in a distant glow, hazy and indistinct, spreading wider as he closed in on them. The first time he cycled back, he had enjoyed it, enjoyed the freedom and the sweat and the air blowing through his hair. Now it was simply a chore, one that made his legs drag and his lungs burn. He could make out his tent now and the last truck, the seventh. He was almost back, and this was almost over.

One of Natalie's faceless soldiers had told him how to start the generator mounted on the back of the last truck but someone, Natalie herself perhaps, had also helpfully taped a piece of paper to it with the words PRESS HERE and a large black arrow pointing to a red button set in the machine's front. Below the button, Scott inserted the last of the plugs; most of the morning had been spent cycling from truck to truck, loops of cable unravelling from his shoulder and lying in a line behind him. At each truck, he plugged the end of the cable into the rear of the speaker stack behind the cab and then took the next piece from the drum mounted at the truck's tail end. He had positioned them in a circle with the farmhouse and its outbuildings at its centre, ready to swamp them with the damping wave. The farmhouse was far enough inside the Other Sound's range that coming here would ultimately be fatal for a normal person, but the theory was if he could damp the sound in this one place then people could come here; the journey in would be uncomfortable but once here they would be safe, could remove their cumbersome suits and move freely. The farmhouse would become the forward point of the battle, ever pushing forwards as they damped more and more of the noise.

That was the theory, anyway.

As he cycled, the breeze blew about him and the sun cast Scott's shadow like a beetle behind him and the Other Sound hummed and chittered and wailed. Everything was nearly ready, everything connected, everything simply waiting for him. He had cycled far enough, now. The toothache in his brain nagged at him as he stood in front of the generator.

A red button, large and plastic with a moulded nubbin at its centre. Not much, really; not considering its task. Scott, sweating in the heat and from his exertions, pushed it. It clicked in and there was a rumble as the generator rolled over and then started, and then Scott screamed and screamed and screamed.

It was as though someone had turned the universe up, increasing its volume a thousandfold, a *millionfold*, so that he could hear the shriek of sand grinding against itself and roots questing blindly through the earth and things in pain and growing and contracting and living and dying. He collapsed, first to his knees and then flopping over into the dirt in the shadow of the truck's huge rear wheel. It felt as though every part of him was pulling in opposite directions, as though he was being wrenched and yanked and pushed and compressed all at once. He squeezed his eyes shut, thinking *My damping wave is being damped* and he didn't understand it but he knew that's what was happening and he wondered if Morris or Natalie knew that this would happen and thought they probably did. Or at least, that they probably suspected it.

Scott twitched, managed to jerk and roll over so that he was on his back and staring up into the sky. Against the depthless blue, he saw the oddly beautiful sight of the damper wave and the Other Sound swirling around each other. It was like seeing the shadows of convection patterns in water on the bottom of a swimming pool even when the patterns themselves were invisible, dark edges gliding around each other and Scott was still screaming and his head was throbbing and the rift in his head was expanding, tearing open, and he screamed and screamed and screamed. He heard the sound of something huge and mournful, a bell magnified to almost unbearable proportions, clanging and clanging, saw wavering images of fires burning and buildings torn to pieces and things without name darting through the ruins and he couldn't even hear himself scream any more and he raised his hands to his ears and wished that they would burst and put him out of his misery.

There was a pop from somewhere to his left; insignificant, almost inaudible when set against the sound of his own agonies and the yammering that was all around him, but it was there. Scott rolled his head, saw sparks leap like foamed spittle from one of the speakers on the truck. A second popped, the front rupturing and smoke billowing from it. Another exploded, showering him with the dancing firefly sparks.

Another exploded and then another; a sixth simply whined loudly as black smoke poured from it. Above Scott, the dark ridges in the air were driven back, the Other Sound pressing outwards, driving on. The generator began to buck and jolt, its rhythms becoming choppy and irregular as the Other Sound reached it, surrounded it. There was a series of loud pops and the something in the machine ground down in wheezing steps. The Other Sound rolled forwards, reclaiming the world, sucking away Scott's pain as it went. *My damper wave*, he thought, *undamped*.

After a minute, he sat up and looked towards the anonymous farm buildings. Nothing moved. The air felt heavy, dull with tension and energy and anticipation. The Other Sound paused, roiling at the edge of the clearing. He could almost see it gathering itself, building up, pulsing. In a few moments, he imagined, it would surge forwards, reach towards the mall and beyond that. It might swamp the sea what remained of the world of fragile normality beyond, making its way out into the lives of everyone that it had not already touched.

Instead, with a noise like a boat being dragged up a beach of glass, the Other Sound rolled back, towards the Collision, diminishing. Smoke rose from the torn speakers, other black and grey columns emerging from the other trucks, distant ashen fingers touching at the sky. In the new silence, the world felt raw around him, exhausted and ragged and battered.

It was only the beginning, Scott realized, the first skirmish in a much bigger battle. Whatever had been screaming was holding its breath now, watching, preparing. He dragged up the bicycle and mounted it, ignoring the ache that seemed to stretch like a fresh bruise across all of his flesh. Not really knowing where he was heading but knowing he needed to go, to go *now*, he started cycling.

From the other side of the Collision, inexorable and terrible, something finally broke through....

DOORS
by Paul Pearson

Relief.

It flooded through him, warm and light, a shot of whisky and a hot cup of coffee falling through his body, spreading out to every nerve, every vein, every muscle and tendon, through to the pores of his skin.

For a long time he didn't move, content to sink back into the mattress and let the blankets curl around his body. He squeezed his closed eyelids even tighter, until the tiny muscles began to groan in protest, but he didn't open them. He just lay there, and listened.

Silence.

Relief.

It was like discovering that a missing limb had grown back. It was a joy he'd never expected to have again in his life, and now, all he wanted was to wallow in that feeling, to wrap it tightly around his form like a warm blanket, to live in that space for as long as the world would allow him.

But there would be time later, he decided, and opened his eyes.

The television hadn't worked in weeks, and getting an internet connection in the middle of nowhere had been difficult at the best of times. But the radio still worked, so much like whoever had been living in the house a century earlier, he made breakfast with the BBC world service, the only English-speaking channel left on the air, prattling in the background...

"—the world breathes a sigh of relief as this global phenomenon simply stops, for no apparent reason—"

The frying pan hissed as the first egg splashed against the hot metal, the colours becoming solid in the heat. He picked up the second egg, cracked the shell with a sharp tap of a butterknife and let the contents slide out onto the pan. He sang as he worked, quiet and off-key.

"Will you stay," he mumbled, "in our lover's story..."

"—though countless thousands of people have died and many more have suffered what can only be described as psychotic episodes, those who survive are doing what they can to return to some kind of normality—"

"...if you stay, you won't be sorry..."

He sprinkled some salt onto the eggs, letting the grains sink into the whites before they solidified.

"—much of the UK decimated and society on the brink of collapse, disaster continues to affect the European Union, with France and Switzerland effectively gone, Germany, Austria and Italy devastated and the surrounding nations flooded with refugees, everyone is feeling the economic—"

"...cause we believe in *shit!*" He smelled the smoke first, and was halfway towards the toaster before he saw the grey wisps rising towards the ceiling. The pale lime-green linoleum was cold against his feet as he darted around the island in the middle of the kitchen, sidestepping the stools.

"—more and more people are fleeing for North Africa and the United States—"

The toaster shifted a few inches across the bench top, he pressed the button so hard. A pair of slightly-charred slices of bread jumped into view, with smoke billowing out around them.

"—unconfirmed reports of more strange phenomena sighted around the Collision—"

"Ah! Hot, hot, hot!" He held the toast with his fingertips and moved them, quickly, towards the island. There wasn't a plate ready, so he threw the pieces down on the bench and shook his hands out, trying to cool his fingers.

"—eyewitnesses have described what they call 'monsters' unlike anything we've seen so far."

Listen.

Something about the newsreader's turn of phrase caught his attention. He ignored the toast. He ignored the mild burning sensation in his fingertips.

"While there has been no documented evidence of these new creatures, eyewitnesses from all around the site of the incident have reported seeing dark shapes moving quickly from within the military cordons, either on the ground or in the air."

He snorted a laugh. "But that's ridic—"

Listen.

The instinct was so strong, so sharp, that he obeyed it unthinkingly.

"There have been additional reports of violence in the regions of Europe directly adjacent to the cordons. Of the casualties reported since the time of the incident, a total of sixty-three resulted from causes unknown, though leaked police reports speak of home invasions and wounds reminiscent of animal attacks."

It's not safe out there.

The newsreader paused for a moment, and in the silence, he heard the hissing of eggs cooking in a frypan.

When breakfast was done, the pan and plate and cutlery cleaned up and the smell of burning toast and eggs a faded memory, he sat in the kitchen with a black mug of black coffee clutched in both hands. He stared at the telephone, mounted by the door that led to the living room. Like the television, it hadn't worked in a long time, and he'd been in no condition to seek out a repairman, but seeing it resting on its crook made him think —

It's not safe out there.

But, he reasoned, if it's not safe for me, it's not safe for anyone. We'd all be better off in groups, watching out for one another.

And how would you get in touch with other people?

The telephone didn't work. He realized that he'd need to head into town, four miles away. It was a longish walk, but a short drive.

Not a safe one.

Safety in numbers, he decided. That was the way to go.

And how do you know you can trust these other people? You heard that newsreader. Psychotic episodes.

He sipped the coffee. It was warm, and bitter, but he was too distracted to really taste it. The more he pondered his instinctive reactions, the more he agreed with them. Other people were a liability. There was no guarantee they could help him, that they'd make him any safer, that they wouldn't just take advantage of whatever kindness he might offer.

"It's not safe out there," he said aloud.

The house, he decided, that was where he'd stay. There was food, and generator fuel.

And if they come for what you have?

He thought about that. The house was remote, in the middle of an abandoned farm, miles from the nearest town. People would need to be really desperate to come all that way...

And what would drive them to such desperation? Screaming? Monsters? It's not safe out there.

"No," he muttered, "it's not."

Thump. Thump. Thump.

The vibrations seemed to do a circuit through his body every time he swung the hammer. With every strike, the nail was driven a little further through the board and into the window frame, getting tighter by the moment, until at last the metal spear had been pushed as far as it could go and the flat edge of the hammer struck nothing but wood.

He stepped back to admire the work. No experience with carpentry, and yet the wooden slats were perfectly even and there wasn't enough room between them for the setting sunlight to peek through. Puffing, he wiped sweat from his brow and hair with a gloved hand.

There were still more windows to seal up. A pile of boards were stacked neatly in the middle of the living room, lit up by the orange light pouring through the rest of the windows. The doors had to be boarded up as well. It would take a long time.

"What the hell are you doing?" he whispered, panting, feeling an ache through his forearm right down to the fingertips that curled around the hammer's weight. For a moment, just briefly, it all seemed absurd. What good would it do to seal himself off—?

It's not safe. You're protecting yourself from what's out there.

The house was silent, apart from his heavy breathing. He missed the radio, which hadn't been working since that morning: the batteries needed juice, but he couldn't risk charging them, not now that he had to conserve the generator fuel. There were drums of the stuff in the basement, along with the generator itself, and a pallet of non-perishables, the souvenirs of a family and a life marked by isolation and rank paranoia. He only wished he'd thought to get a gun, a handgun or a big hunting rifle, something he could use on...

What? He shook his head, trying to jog his brain into working again.

Enemies.

No, he didn't think that was it. Probably for hunting, if some decently edible animal wandered onto the property. Besides, he didn't have any enemies.

Not yet. These are dangerous times.

The thought made him shiver, and he didn't think twice about picking up more boards and nails and starting on the next window.

Time passed.

How much, and how quickly, he didn't know. There was no more sunshine, no more starlight and moonlight. There were clocks, powered by batteries that faded and died. There were calendars, with days that he crossed off, but after a while he started to lose track. Was it still yesterday? Had tomorrow begun? One day he ripped them off their walls and hanging hooks and burned them in the kitchen's tiny fireplace, using the heat to boil water for a cup of tea. Afterwards, he couldn't clean the tiny brown stains off the mug, lacking soap and high-pressure water, so he scrubbed at the white ceramic with steel wool until flakes of silver metal covered the kitchen. When he was satisfied with the state of the mug, he set it aside in a rack to dry, and only then noticed where skin had been scraped from his fingertips, leaving raw patches of bright pink.

He learned not to trust his sleeping patterns as a way of telling the time. They were never consistent: sometimes a few hours, sometimes what seemed like entire days. Any semblance of a daily schedule slipped. He slept when he felt sleepy, ate when he felt hungry, and spent the rest of the time bent over a book in a corner of the living room's floor, using candles for light, or else walking the house end to end, checking the windows and doors were still boarded up.

There was a bookshelf in the living room, taller than he was, and comfy green loveseats that looked like they'd been designed specifically for curling up with a book, but he never used them anymore. The fabric stretched around him, the cushions depressed when he sat down. There was no support, just a feeling of being smothered in dark green. Instead he sat on the floor in the corner, resting his back against the edge where two walls met, and read each word on the page individually before moving on. His focus kept sliding, irising in and out. He would sit for hours at a time, picking through the paperbacks in the soft candlelight, until the wick burned too far down and he couldn't see the words on the page.

Those were the times he missed the radio and the television. He missed knowing about the rest of the world, and for all the sparks of terror that flicked through his insides, he was curious about what this rift, or Collision, or whatever it was called, was doing now.

Danger.

That was what his instincts told him, every time his thoughts strayed towards those ideas. Danger. Danger in knowing, danger in trying to find out. Danger in leaving the nice, protected house. Danger in doing anything at all.

But that left nothing but his own imagination. He began to dream of the world outside, and what he saw in those dreamscapes made him wake in cold sweats. He saw people driven mad by screaming, melting and twisting until they became hideous misshapen monsters with long limbs and teeth that seemed too big to fit inside their mouths. He saw them emerge from forests with the blood of animals on the ripped, ill-fitting clothes they'd worn as humans. He saw them crawling, along dirt roads and flat, dusty plains, moving fast like giant spiders. One seemed to bend itself over a barbed wire fence and suddenly the monsters weren't just *somewhere,* they were on his property, coming towards the house, spindly hands breaking through his front door —

That was always when he'd wake, shivering and sweating on damp bed sheets, wishing he'd thought to buy a gun when he'd had the chance.

It had been a long time since he'd fried eggs for breakfast. He peeled back the lid on a tin of spam, cut the pinkish meat into slices as thick as his finger and threw them onto the pan before sticking it onto the rack in the fireplace. The coffee was brewed in cold water using a teapot, stirred clockwise and without touching the rim, just to make things more interesting while he waited for the spam to cook. Minutes went past before the frying pan started sizzling and the pink blobs began to turn a charred brown.

When breakfast was ready, he sat at the bench and ate the cooked spam with his fingers. They still had marks from the steel wool, red scratches that hadn't quite healed, but they didn't hurt as he tore pieces off the larger hunks of spam and pushed them into his mouth, through the tangle of curly hair that had been growing off his face since...

He stopped eating, wiped his fingers on the edge of the bench and touched his beard. The hair was long and thick, enough that he could twirl it in loops around his fingers. Tracing the lines of his jaw, he felt the bushy beard reaching up around the curve of his entire face to meet the locks of oily, stringy hair that hung off his scalp. The hair, he realized as he quickly shook his head back and forth, had grown long enough to rest on his shoulders, even though he could've sworn he'd had it cut short recently.

Recently. That word stuck in his mind.

"How long have I been in here?" he said aloud. His fingers felt greasy from where he'd touched his hair and beard, and he wiped them on the legs of his trousers. The spam on his plate didn't seem appetizing anymore. It was dark, so dark, and he hadn't bothered to light a candle—it'd been *ages* since he'd needed to light a candle to see, and even in the darkness he'd only just noticed, everything was crystal clear, from the outline of the bench and the fireplace to the size and the colour and the craggy shape of the spam pieces.

"Holy shit," he whispered, his heart starting to pound, breaths coming in desperate gasps —

You're as safe as you can be.

He didn't know what that meant.

You are alive, for now. You have food, and a bed. If you went outside, you'd probably die.

"I don't... no —"

Just relax, and eat your food.

Calm seemed to return. His breathing slowed. The beating of his heart was no longer a jackhammer in his chest. Of their own accord, it felt, his fingers reached for more of the spam and slowly brought the pink-brown meat to his lips.

"I'm all right," he breathed, and took a bite.

For now.

Thunk. Thunk. Thu-thunk thunk.

Despite having eaten a second meal only an hour earlier, he wasn't in bed trying to get to sleep. His back was pressed against the corner of the living room, eyes fixed on the words on a page of a book whose name he didn't know, illuminated by a fat candle planted on the top of a brass holder.

Thu-thu-thunk. Thu-thunk.

He wasn't enjoying the experience of reading a book. His eyes kept glazing, and despite reading each individual word he couldn't puzzle out exactly what was supposed to be happening. Reading had once been a great source of comfort and entertainment, before the Collision and the screaming, when there'd been sunlight and fresh food. It was why he had so many books on so many shelves, from years of collecting, of sitting in one of those big plushy loveseats and devouring the stories. Now... They'd become simply words on a page.

Thu-thunk. Thu-thu-thu-thu-thunk thunk.

Before he quite understood what he was doing, he threw the book down on the ground, as hard as he could, hoping the spine would break and the worthless pages would scatter and float around the room. It didn't, simply bouncing once and coming to rest on the green rug, the cover facing upwards. He grabbed the candleholder, stood and walked over to the book, pulling back on his right foot, ready to kick—

"Hello?"

He was paralysed. Confused. He didn't quite understand what the sound was, because even though it resembled someone saying 'hello', there was nobody else around to say it.

"Is anyone still in there?"

The voice was faint, muffled. He followed the sound, into the kitchen, towards the far end and a boarded-up door that had once led to the outside world. When the voice came again, it sounded clear and close, filtering through the miniscule gaps between the wooden slats.

"Look, I don't know if anyone can hear me, but if you can, could you just say something?"

A woman, he realized. For some reason, he pictured her on the other side of the door as being young, maybe in her mid-twenties, with long black hair and wearing a blue coat and hood. The image stuck in his head.

"We know there was a guy living here... well, *before*, but nobody's seen him. Are you there?"

He raised a hand, resting the palm gently on the boards —
Don't.

Recoiling, he shivered.

"Well, if you are there... I came from town. And I wanted
to tell you, whoever you are, that we're all leaving. There's...
there's *something* coming, we don't know what, and half the
town thinks it's just us being paranoid, but we're all leaving.
Going west, to try and find somewhere a bit safer. Somewhere
there's no... No monsters."

He felt the cold chills again, and at the same time a brief
surge of pride at being right, and thinking to guard himself
against whatever these "monsters" supposedly were.

"We're going tomorrow, but I thought we should check on
you, or whoever's here. See if you wanted to come with us.
Safety in numbers, right?"

"Right," he whispered, so soft he could barely hear
himself. He remembered that first day, listening to the radio,
his first instinct to seek out others —

It's a trick. It's a falsehood.

But he could see her, in the mind's eye, a dark-haired girl
in a blue hood. How could she be a trick?

*She's not real. Or she wants what you have. You can't go
outside. You can't let her in. You have to stay here, alone, where it's
safe.*

"Hello?" she called out, louder now. "Please, if there's
anyone there, I'm trying to help!"

Tricks.

What sort of tricks?

"Please come with us. Help us — let us help *you*."

She can't help you.

He wanted to touch the wooden boards again. For all that his instincts were telling him, another human being was just on the other side of the door. So close. He'd been alone for so long, in the dark, doing nothing but surviving and thinking about what lay beyond his walls. She was so close...

Thu-thu-thunk. A sharp rapping on the door. The boards vibrated.

With a deep breath that sat heavy in his chest, he turned and walked through the kitchen, back to the living room, back to the book that lay face-up and intact on the green rug.

Thu-thu-thu-thu-thu-thunk thunk thu-thunk.

Then silence.

You made the right decision.

Perhaps. But it didn't feel like the right decision.

The spindly monster-people were advancing, climbing over fences, crawling through the dirt, right up to the front door, when suddenly the entire world shook and he awoke. The blankets were lying in a heap at the foot of the bed, kicked off during the dream, and a breeze touched his bare chest and turned the beads of sweat into needles of ice. He noticed all these things, that he was awake, and then began to panic as he realized that the world continued to shake around him.

Dust fell from the ceiling rafters. Picture frames and lamps rattled their way off the tables and crashed to the floor, glass exploding in all directions. He leapt out of bed and ran, barefoot, to the window, boarded up so tight that not a speck of light made its way through. Still, desperate to see, to know, he lowered his eye to the thin line between two of the wooden boards and squinted.

Black. Nothing.

It sounded like a hurricane outside, the whistling of an afternoon breeze amplified until it hurt his ears, fast and powerful. Then a breaking, snapping sound, like wood or wire, scattered within the storm. It was so *loud*, he couldn't take it anymore, and he covered his ears and staggered away from the window.

A shard of glass sliced into his heel. He hissed, hopping onto one foot, and gingerly tried to make his way to the bedroom door, skirting the largest pieces. Little pieces, tiny chunks, were too small and too scattered to avoid, but didn't break the skin when he stood on them. It just stung.

He was hyperventilating by the time he reached the door and braced himself against the frame. Lifting the bloody foot as high as possible, he saw the shard still sticking out of the skin, covered in the pumping trickles of blood that continued running down the curve on his heel, before dripping away towards the floor.

"Oh jeez," he breathed, taking hold of the glass shard with a thumb and forefinger.

You can do it.

Closing his eyes, he yanked at the shard and screamed a long, low syllable that drew out into high-pitched wailing. Tears squeezed past the corners of his clenched eyelids.

Yes.

The shard was loose, but still stabbing into his heel. His fingers were wet and slippery.

Again.

With teeth clenched, he pulled. The shard came free with a grunted sob of pain and he slid down the doorframe, coming to rest in a heap on the floor, the bloody piece of glass clutched in his fingers. The floorboards vibrated beneath him, in time with the rest of the house and the storm outside. Breathing became ragged, gasping, mixed with more tears.

Yes.

After a while of lying on the ground and bleeding, he staggered to the kitchen, found the first aid kit and bandaged up the cut. Wherever he went in the house, things shook violently, dislodging dirt and dust from the recesses. Books fell off their shelves, cupboard doors were flung open. Wood creaked as the wind assailed it, pushing, trying to get in.

And then something screamed.

It was almost drowned out by the wind, but he swore he could hear it, a low, screeching sound. It felt unnatural, it made him shiver, it made him clench his teeth and draw his arms close around himself. It sounded like a scream, but not one of fear, and not one like he'd ever heard in his life.

Monsters.

He thought of the girl with dark hair and a blue hood, who probably didn't look anything like that but it was the image in his mind, how he remembered that there were still people outside, perhaps in the middle of this storm of wind and screaming, or perhaps lying dead by the side of the road by now —

They will be fine.

How could he know? It sounded like the world was ending outside.

They left town days ago. They're nowhere near this chaos.

Right, of course. He nodded to himself.

Don't worry about them. Worry about yourself. Worry about tomorrow.

He woke in the living room, curled up on the green rug with a single bed sheet spread across his body. The cut on his foot throbbed.

It was quiet in the house. No more shaking, no more noises. Just books and photo frames and candle holders scattered across the ground, thrown in every direction by the force of the storm. One of the loveseats had tipped onto its side. A painting on the wall had fallen off its hook and slipped behind the bookshelf.

He stood, wrapping the orphaned bed sheet around his mostly-naked form, and limped into the kitchen. The toaster had fallen onto the lino and shattered, and the cupboard and oven doors swung aimlessly open, but seemed to have come through the ordeal intact. The boards remained over the door, covering it entirely, leaving no gaps.

The image returned, unbidden, of a dark-haired woman in a blue hood knocking on the door. And he remembered the sounds of the storm, or whatever it was, battering at the house but not breaking it. How had the rest of the property fared, he wondered? Or the nearby town? *Did* everyone get away before the storm came through, assuming it was a storm and not the monsters that everyone kept talking about?

He had to see.

The urge came over him suddenly, breaking free of whatever logical, sensible prison he'd constructed for it in his mind.

The hammer had gone back into the basement, along with the leftover nails and wooden boards, on a workbench next to the generator that he refused to turn on until it was a *real* emergency. He ran down the stairs, grabbed the tool by its worn wooden handle, glanced at the generator and the drums of fuel sitting beside it, and then ran back up to the kitchen.

The bladed side of the hammer was still too thick, so he smashed it against the edge where two boards met and pushed, wedging through loose splinters, until he had the leverage to pull, to rip the board away, nail and all—

Sunlight.

Warm, bright, like coffee and whisky and sugar in a cocktail he drank through every pore of his skin. It beamed through the gaps in the door and the hole in the tapestry of wooden boards, tiny slivers that felt like liquid gold as he knelt down and let it wash over his face.

NO.

He ignored the instinctive voice: the feel of sunlight was just too good. He picked up the hammer again and ripped away another board, and another, until he could push the door open and climb through the hole, crawling across the dirt driveway. More sunlight, flooding over his body, so much that his eyes, grown too used to seeing in the dark, couldn't make out more than the blurry shape of the house.

Go inside.

"No," he whispered, standing. He was still in his underwear, wrapped in a bed sheet that he used to shade his eyes while he blinked and blinked and blinked, adjusting until he could look out at the surrounding landscape and see...

"What the hell?"

Nothing. Absolutely nothing.

There had been grass, in wide fields that stretched to the horizon, but now it was just brown patches of dirt. There had been trees, scattered about, but they'd been uprooted. Wire fences were gone entirely. Even the abandoned farm had looked full of life compared to what he saw now, a completely blank landscape, so featureless and devoid that he felt something heavy drop into his stomach.

Fear, he realized.

Yes.

He started walking, planning to follow the driveway to the dirt roads that criss-crossed the property. From there, it wouldn't be far into town, maybe a couple of hours, and then he'd see what had happened there, if it'd been stripped bare as well by the storm, or the monsters, or whatever it was —

Return to the house.

No, he thought, letting curiosity drive him forwards. Tiny stones dug into his feet, stinging, but he almost enjoyed the new sensation —

Return to the house, immediately.

No, he repeated, ignoring that survival instinct. What did he need to survive at this point?

GET BACK IN THE HOUSE!

It was so loud, like feedback in his mind, that he collapsed to the dirt and clutched his ears. It was worse than the screaming, worse than anything, and even while he cowered on the ground he had to fight the urge to stand and walk back to the house.

Do it now, before I become angry.

In the midst of the pain and confusion, he heard those words in his mind, and understood them, and realized.

"You're not…" He took deep breaths, feeling the feedback sensation in his mind lessen. "You're not me, are you?"

Get back in the house.

"What are you?"

Do NOT refuse me.

He managed to stand on unsteady feet. "What are you? How are you in my mind? What *are* you?"

I am beyond you. I am beyond the creatures that drove across your land, laying waste to everything except the house where they knew I dwelt.

"You're...? No, it's my house..."

No, it is mine. A dwelling for me and my food.

Food. The word sent chills running through him, even before he'd fully realized what this... this *thing* was talking about. When he did, the chills got worse, a blanket of cold fear that wrapped around his body, engulfing him completely.

"I'm not..."

Yes.

He staggered away from the house, not looking where he was going, just unwilling to take his eyes off the house like it was the thing likely to jump up and attack. "I'm not your food," he muttered, "I'm not your food..."

You are.

"I'm not—"

YOU ARE. Listen. Feel the fear, the despair, let it in. Remember what it felt like, all these months —

"Months?"

— being alone, scared, miserable, feel it, remember, let it in, feel it, feel it, FEED ME you pathetic wretch, and GET BACK IN THE HOUSE!

"No!" he shouted.

Now.

He opened his mouth to shout again, but couldn't. It was like trying to speak with lockjaw, and his feet began to move of their own accord, one step in front of the other, back towards the house.

"Stop..." He managed to force the syllable through clenched teeth.

You are so much. I never saw it until I became like this, so mobile and alive, and so FULL of food. Why does no one see it?

He closed his eyes and sobbed, the salty drops snaking their way down his face as he tried and failed to control his feet, his legs, his arms, anything that could stop him from returning to the house. His back bent and curved, like an invisible hand was pushing against it, and suddenly the feeling of sunlight was gone —

"No," he said, with a fresh wave of tears.

Despair. Good.

It pushed him forward, through the kitchen. "What are you doing?"

You will die here.

"No."

It will take weeks, months, perhaps YEARS, but you will die in agony, in fear, and you will FEED ME.

"I won't."

You will. Every day I feed I become stronger and soon I will be able to control your every move. You are mine. You will do as I want.

"I won't," he repeated.

His knees buckled and he collapsed onto the rug in the living room, bracing himself with his hand to keep from striking his head on the floor.

"I won't," he said again, "I won't, I won't, I won't, I WON'T!"

And suddenly, he was himself again. Feeling flooded through his body, down to the tiny sensations of rug fibres against his fingertips, and he could move, and he didn't waste a moment. He pushed himself up and started to run—

STOP!

—towards the basement stairs, throwing himself down the steps two and three at a time—

I'm in your MIND, you pathetic wretch, YOU CANNOT BE RID OF ME!

"I know," he breathed, leaping the last few stairs and landing in the middle of the basement, in the midst of the metal fuel drums and the generator, sitting idle. He charged towards it, grabbing a chisel off the workbench as he passed it.

I told you to STOP!

He kicked at the generator controls, hitting every button he could. It chugged to life for a moment, sputtered, sparked and died, so he kicked it again and then stabbed at the controls with the chisel. More sparks, more chugging, and then a low rumbling.

...what have you done?

It happened so suddenly that he didn't see it, or hear it, or feel it. One moment he was holding the chisel, and the next he was lying on the ground, the basement ceiling directly ahead and the feeling of heat and pressure pushing at him from all sides. Smoke billowed across his view, and orange light flickered. It hurt to breathe, like something heavy was sitting on his chest.

He laughed as the fire began to spread.

What's so funny?

"I..." He coughed out a mouthful of smoke. "I got you. No eating me as I die slowly. We both go, now, and that's it."

The flames crackled, leaping into view above his head, consuming the wooden rafters that kept the basement standing under the weight of the house. The grey-black smoke started to fog his vision.

Then he heard something, in the back of his mind. Laughter. The most disturbing, psychotic laughter he'd ever heard in his life.

You think you've got me, right? Sweet Moses, it hurts how wrong you are.

And then it was gone. Like a weight had been lifted from his mind, he could think clearly for the first time in longer than he could remember, could see where it had pushed and prodded at his thoughts, kept him isolated, kept him "tender", kept him from going outside, kept him from joining the girl with dark hair and a blue hood.

"Will you stay," he mumbled, "in our lover's story?" He felt smoke or gas or whatever it was seeping into his lungs, affecting his mind, but it didn't stop him from remembering the sounds of smells of cooking eggs on toast. "If you stay, you won't be sorry…"

That was all he thought as the flames closed in.

CLOSURE
by Pete Kempshall

Natalie Murphy couldn't shake the feeling that she'd been too late.

The coded government prefix that had been transmitted to the emergency services with her 911 call had ensured the medics had been on the scene in minutes, but it had been up to her to keep Marta alive until they got there. And for all the first-aid training Nat had received over the years, the creeping conviction remained that she hadn't quite been up to the job.

She crossed the room to the entertainment centre, feeling stray pills crunch beneath her soles like tiny eggs, and popped open the fridge beneath the TV set. First chance she'd had, she'd rinsed her mouth out with water from a glass by the side of the bed, but Nat could still taste vomit, lingering after her attempt to push air into Marta's lungs.

Something stronger, then.

Most of the mini-bar's bottles had been decapitated, drained and discarded around the room, along with a wide and varied selection of replacements from room service. Only a single measure of gin remained on the shelf inside the fridge door, the kind that would be considered cheap anywhere other than in a hotel room. Even in her shattered state of mind, Marta had standards.

Natalie snagged the bottle, and with a sharp twist cracked the seal. She sloshed the perfumed liquid into her mouth, swilling it around her tongue, teeth, gums, then spat the tainted fluid into a plant pot.

The taste was only marginally better than the puke.

The EMTs had pulled the blinds up, exposing the room to the first light it had seen in days, but the enclosed space still reeked of alcohol and anguish. The French doors—clearly unopened for some time—gave a sharp crack as Nat pushed on them, like the seal breaking in an Egyptian tomb. She stumbled out of the miasmic fog and onto the balcony, closed her eyes and let the sun warm her face, grateful to be out in the open.

Someone would have to go through the hotel room and collect Marta's personal effects, but the newly formed International Stabilization Group would want Nat at the hospital. So no, the room clean-up was a task for someone lower down on the command structure. Then again, depending on how this all played out, Nat could soon *be* someone lower down on the command structure. Not that she'd care all that much.

Demotion's the last thing you worry about if you've allowed the only person who can save the world to kill herself.

Marta rested her head against the window. The glass felt cool, soothing against her forehead, and she wished she could somehow transfer the feeling to the red pulsing in her throat. She hadn't expected to wake up, let alone feel any pain, but the tubes that had been forced into her to keep her alive had scraped her throat raw and it still hurt to swallow. Speaking would be out of the question, even if she had anything to say to the people who'd supposedly saved her.

The night outside was deep, and she couldn't see the ground rushing past beneath the helicopter. From the moment she'd awoken in the hospital she'd been kept in the dark, with no more idea where she was headed than she had of who was taking her. Clearly her rescuers considered her to have forfeited the right to decide her own fate the moment she'd popped open those pill bottles. It didn't matter. Wherever they took her now, it wasn't anywhere she wanted to be. She'd fix that, first opportunity she got.

In the distance, a gentle glow suffused the horizon. Sunrise. An abject weariness swept over Marta, like she'd been awake for days instead of unconscious under medical supervision. Wherever in the world she was, her body clock was shot to shit. There was no way to see what time it really was — even if she'd been wearing a watch, her wrists had been velcroed to the arms of her seat.

"Alpha Two-Niner from Facility One."

The crackle of radio drew Marta's gaze towards the cockpit. The voice sounded like it was being shouted into a hurricane, filtered through flame.

The pilot spoke clearly into his headset. "Alpha Two Niner. Go ahead."

"Flare activity is high, repeat high. Recommend engage filters."

"Received." Under the drone of the rotors, Marta heard a faint click. "Filters engaged, starting final approach."

The helicopter rattled closer to the light. Suddenly, as she caught more of the scene outside her window, Marta knew that it wasn't the dawn ahead. Myriad colors danced in the nimbus, an electric rainbow constantly moving, shifting, warping. She groaned and struggled against her bonds with all the meagre strength she could muster.

Anywhere else. Anywhere.

They were taking her to the Collision.

"I'm sorry for your loss." Natalie shifted in her seat. This wasn't anything like her strong suit. "The Collision robbed us of so many good people, I can't imagine what..."

"Why..." The word rasped from Marta's mouth. "Why didn't... let me die?"

"You're a very important person, Professor Maszkowski. With your particular skill set, you're the only person—"

"Left?" Marta croaked.

Natalie reddened. "The ISG... We could have located another expert in the field, yes, but from what we could see the work you did with your husband is decades ahead of the pack. And we need the best."

She paused, trying to read Marta, but the woman's face... Nat had seen more than her share of death, but had never met anyone so empty of life. The pills and booze had been a formality.

"I'm sorry your family passed, I am, and what you tried to do at the hotel, I get it." *God knows, I get it.* "But it might help to think that maybe you survived for a reason." She couldn't tell if the choking sound that came from the professor was grief or scorn.

"Trying to get me... believe in... higher power?"

"If you hadn't been Stateside on that conference, the Collision would have disintegrated you too. Now maybe it's just me, but it seems like we've been given a chance here to make things better."

This time, it was definitely scorn. "Tried to do that. You stopped me."

Under the desk, Murphy's fists clenched. "If there was anything to be done that could bring your husband and daughter back... I'd do whatever it took to help you, make every resource we had available to you. But the best I can do now—the best you can do—is stop what happened to you happening to anyone else."

Marta sat silently.

"You know what?" Natalie said, getting to her feet. "How about I just introduce you to someone? Show you what we have in mind." She held out a hand to the professor, and prayed to God that she'd take it.

Without a word of a lie, Jennifer Brooker could say that this was the single most amazing thing she had ever seen. Nothing in all her experience of neurosurgery could even come close — yet the newcomer's lack of reaction bordered on the comatose. Wasn't the woman supposed to be a professor? Where the hell was her scientific curiosity?

"To be completely honest, we don't even know how the guy's still functioning," Jen declared, barely able to mask her frustration. Using the eraser end of her pencil, she indicated the mass on the MRI, a growth about the size of an orange, squatting malevolently at the back of the cerebellum. "At the moment, the anomaly accounts for the majority of the occipital lobe," she said, choosing her words carefully, "which would normally suggest impairment of visual acuity. Blindness, hallucinations, anything that interferes with sight."

She paused, waited for the professor to take the bait.

The older woman maintained her detached attitude, but asked all the same. "At the moment?"

Professionalism alone prevented Jen punching the air. *Gotcha.*

"At the moment. Take a look at this." She reached down for another transparency and pinned it up on the lightboard next to the first. Lo-fi, but effective—Jen could see Murphy at the back of the room nod approvingly.

The professor's face creased into a frown, the first discernible reaction she'd displayed since she'd entered the room. Jen could see her eyes move to the tag at the top of the new picture, the date stamp indicating that the shot had been taken two weeks before the first MRI.

The mass had clearly moved from the front of the brain to the back.

Marta frowned. "What kind of tumour...?"

"We weren't going to drag you halfway across the planet to look at a brain tumour, Professor Maszkowski." Natalie had sat quietly until now. "That's Doctor Brooker's area."

"It's a rift," Jen chipped in. "The patient has a rift in his head, and I need your help to close it."

To Jen's immense gratification, the professor sat up a little straighter in her chair.

"Go on."

"Thoughts?"

Jen yanked open the filing cabinet drawer and stowed the transparencies back in their folders. Maszkowski had asked for some time alone to examine the data, and Jen had handed over piles of notes, images and data before the professor was packed off somewhere quiet. But despite that sudden surge of interest...

"I'm not convinced. She's a bit... disconnected."

Murphy shrugged. "Hardly surprising, considering. You don't like her."

"Not particularly."

The Irish officer folded her arms, leaned back against the door. "I don't need best buddies. I do need teamwork."

"If it comes to that, you'll get it." Jen paused. "You don't think she might try again?"

"Not if we can keep her busy, give her a purpose."

Jen pushed the drawer with her palm and it clanged shut. "OK. But for the record, I think you should look elsewhere before signing her up."

Marta pored over the papers spread out on the table in front of her. There was something charmingly old school about the research they'd been conducting here. She'd queried the use of low-tech options in the facility, and Murphy had filled her in on the flares of activity from the Collision. The facility had been set up in what was left of France, as close to the rift's edge as was thought safe, but spasms of energy still created massive interference with the electronic equipment around the anomaly. On rare days, Murphy had said, when the rift was particularly active, the laws of physics became little more than guidelines. A kettle would boil at less than 100 degrees, light would bend—in the first days of the operation an engineer had fallen down three flights of stairs because his eyes had told him the step was thirty centimetres further forward than its true position.

Since then they'd taken steps to minimize the inconvenience by shielding the facility and any vehicles approaching it. Now the interference was intermittent, and mostly harmless, but the standing orders were to use low-tech back up where possible, just in case.

So for now, pencil and paper.

From the scans provided by Dr Brooker, it was clear to Marta that the brain anomaly wasn't just moving—it seemed to be in a state of constant flux. Shrinking minutely, then expanding fractionally more, the mass's growth was two steps forward, one step back. Marta thought for a moment, then shuffled through the sheaves of notes until she found the page she was looking for. Yes, the effect was increasing. At the current rate of change, it would consume the patient's cerebellum entirely in…

Wait.

The small office where Murphy had deposited her contained little more than a desk and chair—apparently Marta wasn't to be trusted with anything more until she was fully on board—but mounted on the wall beside the door was a telephone, an old analogue unit with a proper dial. Murphy had told her to call '10' when she was done with the notes, and she'd come and get her.

From talking to the brain surgeon to seeing the MRIs to putting her here with the paperwork… breadcrumbs leading

Marta to work it out for herself. That sly bitch Murphy had known she'd reach this conclusion... and when she did, they'd have her.

She scraped back her chair, crossed to the phone and dialled.

"Professor." Murphy's voice was distorted, hissing down the line.

"The singularities are linked, aren't they? They're expanding in unison."

"They are."

Marta closed her eyes and sucked in a long breath. All of Europe, gone in a year, perhaps two. Africa and the Americas wouldn't be far behind.

So many Alexes. So many Katies.

She exhaled into the receiver. "I'll do it."

Her rubber-soled shoes squeaked with every step on the tiled floor. After three months of visits to the secure wing, the guards were able to identify Marta's walk a full minute before she rounded the corner, and no longer felt the need to leap to attention when she approached. Marta liked that—it made the 'guest suite' feel less like the prison it so plainly was.

"Professor." The shorter of the two warders—Greg, she recalled—swiped a card through a reader by the side of the entrance. The scanner bleeped, burped and flashed a red light at him.

"Sorry," he muttered, and rooted around in his uniform pockets. "One of those days." He withdrew a small key which he slipped into a recessed lock; the mechanical override.

"Thanks," Marta said, tagging on a weary smile of sympathy. She stepped into the room.

Subject Zero's quarters continued the decorative theme of military-prison-by-way-of-surgical-ward, and the composite effect was one Marta still found unsettling. Zero didn't seem to care. He still complained of a constant 'tugging' in his head, like he was being pulled towards the Collision, but Murphy had posited that since he'd been relocated to the rather Spartan suite of rooms, Zero was actually more comfortable. It was as if the man's proximity to the rift was ameliorating his pain, allowing him to relax somewhat.

Marta simply read it as resignation.

She tried hard not to think of the patient as 'Zero', but that had become his default title around the facility. Murphy used the term as a way of maintaining distance, like she expected the guy to keel over and die at any second. The guards, meanwhile, were too low down the chain of command to have been apprised of the man's actual identity, and Jen Brooker saw the patient as little more than a carry case for an interesting cerebellum. Marta, however, had struck up an immediate rapport with the Englishman by dint of the fact that they both had somewhere else they'd rather be.

"Good morning, Scott."

"Prof," the man grunted. Reclined on the simple bunk against the wall, he put down the book he'd been absorbed in and smiled at her. "More needles?"

"Not today," Marta said, her eyes drifting to the book on the bedside table. She'd read it—a potboiling thriller about a high-level religious conspiracy. Early on in their doctor/patient relationship, Scott had explained to her that if he was expected to pop off at short notice, he didn't want to miss the ending of anything he cared about.

"You look like shit." Scott regarded her with concern.

Marta pulled a chair over to the bed. "Well, I'm not here to talk about my problems."

"Maybe you should be." Scott swung his legs off bunk to sit facing her.

"How're your pain levels?"

"About a three."

"That's an improvement."

"Fixing me would be an improvement."

"We're working on it. Want me to sign you out some painkillers?"

"Please."

Marta shuffled in her seat, awkward, and fished a penlight from her pocket. Scott leaned forward, knowing what to expect, and she flicked the beam across his eyes, examining the pupils.

"I thought it'd be the other one today."

"She's tied up with reports," Marta replied. "Be a couple of days."

"Reports. Right."

Marta detected suppressed amusement. "Right." Jen had recently embarked on a libidinous relationship with one of the facility's soldiers: clearly the rumours had reached Scott. So much for high security.

"So, have you seen him again?"

Scott rubbed his temples. "Our friend with one green eye and one blue eye? Oh yeah."

"And was he — ?"

"Killing someone? Yeah I think so. It's hard when I see something that already came through the rift a while back. It gets blurry and I can't work out whether it's happening now or it already happened some time ago." Scott glanced at the book on the table. "Anyway, I don't know why I bother reading thrillers," he said. "All I have to do is close my eyes."

She completed the standard battery of tests—blood pressure, temperature and so on—marked the results on a chart, and stood to go. "Be a bit quiet for you without Dr Brooker, I expect."

"I can live with that."

"I'll be back later with your meds."

Scott gave a wan smile. "Looking forward to it."

"Zero?" The chemist had the permanent air of a man with something better to do, someone for whom even the simplest request was an imposition. His pervasive air of irritation made it clear to Marta that whatever he'd been working on behind the barricades of shelves in the small pharmacy unit was altogether more important than actually providing drugs. In turn, Marta would have much preferred to dispense her own meds, but with a population of around 200, the facility was deemed a community all to itself, and to the decision makers that meant a pharmacy separate from the science research team.

"What can I say?" Marta held up her hands, palm outward. *You got me.*

The pharmacist snorted. "What's his pain level?"

"Eight," Marta said. "Better make it two bottles."

The man disappeared behind a bank of shelves, returned with a pair of translucent brown containers. "You know the drill."

Marta scribbled her signature on the paperwork and the chemist passed her the pills. "Better get these down to him then," she sighed. "The man's hurting."

But the pharmacist had already disappeared back into his sanctuary. "Come back soon."

The lamp was playing up again. What should have been a perfect circle of illumination was brighter on the far side of the desk, like tilting a bowl full of water makes it deeper at one end. Jen groaned. It was late, and she couldn't be bothered to change over to pen and paper this late in the day. She closed her strained eyes, feeling them burn behind the lids. A little earlier than she'd anticipated, but time to call it.

Across the lab, Marta's lamp was displaying the same perverse behavior, but the professor didn't appear to have even noticed. The electrical quirks rarely registered with her — she'd taken to keeping paper notes as a matter of course, something that struck Jen as a dangerous eccentricity. All the project's notes were immediately backed up on redundant servers every time an alteration was made on the datapads, so there was little danger of flare activity wiping out the research. Maszkowski's methods were just asking for a crucial piece of paper to go missing at just the wrong time.

Of course, next to the other problems Jen had noted about her so-called-colleague, that was the least of her worries.

Jen was a hard worker, she knew she put in more hours at the grindstone than was, perhaps, strictly healthy. But Marta... Those first couple of weeks, when Jen would arrive at the lab an hour early, Marta would already be hard at work. And despite her best efforts to outlast the older woman, when it came to who'd quit sooner for the day, it was invariably Jen who blinked first.

And so she'd taken to keeping tabs on the professor. Times and dates and patterns of activity. From what Jen could tell, Marta barely slept, ate only when she arrived at the point where she'd pass out if she didn't, and, Jen was convinced, was taking some kind of stimulants to keep herself propped up.

Now, watching her scribble indecipherable glyphs on a notepad, Jen saw a woman on the edge of a complete, irreversible breakdown. A risk.

Which is why she'd arranged to meet Murphy in half an hour and have Marta pulled from the project.

"That's it for me," Jen declared, standing and stretching. The cracking noise from her neck and shoulders was blissfully sharp. "You should get some rest too."

"I get plenty of rest." Marta didn't even look up.

"You need to take proper breaks." Jen shrugged off her lab coat and hung it on a hook on the back of the door. "It'll do you good to think about something else for a change."

"You think so?" Now Marta was regarding her with a steady, red-eyed look that made Jen shudder oh-so-slightly.

"I'm just saying. Take some time out for yourself, like I do."

"I'm fine. Go."

"Okay." Jen pulled open the door. "Good night then."

She waited until the door had sighed all the way shut, but Marta offered nothing further.

"Find someone else."

"You know I can't do that, Jennifer." Natalie tilted her head back and stared up at the ceiling. She'd seen the cracks developing in Brooker's relationship with Professor Maszkowski, but hadn't deemed them worthy of direct interference until Brooker had requested this… conference.

"She's a danger to herself and the project," Jen ranted. "You don't work with her every day, you don't see it."

"See what?"

"Her mind's not on the job. She drifts off all the time, like she's thinking about—"

"I know exactly what she's thinking about," Murphy interrupted. "You know, for someone who works with brains you don't have much of a grasp of what's going on inside people's heads."

"She's self-medicating!" Jennifer spat. "It's so fucking obvious, a child could see it."

"And?"

Jennifer sat back in her chair, as if she'd been slapped. "And you're not doing anything." A thought popped into her head. "She tried to kill herself before, what if she tries it again, uses the pills?"

"She won't. She thinks she's being clever, sneaking extra drugs out of the pharmacy, but I've got every pill accounted for. Seventy-five per cent of what she's taking is placebo." Natalie couldn't suppress a smug look. "Besides, she's too committed."

"Committed."

"She'd have done anything to save her family, but never had the chance. This project is her shot at... redemption."

Jennifer got to her feet, like a soldier jumping to attention. "With all due respect, that's bullshit. I want it on the record that I'm refusing to work with her."

"Noted. You're fired."

Jen's eyes widened. "Excuse me?"

"Brain surgeons are much easier to come by than physicists of Professor Maszkowski's calibre, and I went to some considerable trouble personally to bring her on board."

Jen gaped at her.

"If anyone is distracted from their work, it's you, Doctor Brooker. I would suggest paying a little less attention to your co-workers and a little more to the project. Do we have an understanding?"

Jennifer lowered her eyes. "Yes."

"Then it's quite late. I suggest you take your own advice and get some rest."

There was a faint flutter and Marta opened her eyes. She'd nodded off at the desk, head lolling onto her chest, and a thin string of drool had escaped her mouth, trailing down to soak into her blouse.

She sat up, the muscles in her back and shoulders protesting, and looked around.

The Collision had destroyed almost everything pertaining to her life. Her sole memento was a single photograph she'd taken with her to the symposium in the States; she'd kept the picture of Alex and Katie in her journal and it had been shipped to the facility with what little else remained of her personal effects. From the moment she'd found it again, tucked in the pages of the book, she'd kept it tacked to the side of her computer screen. Most of her waking hours were spent in the lab, but if she were honest with herself, she'd stuck the picture to the monitor because she didn't want to be alone with it in her quarters.

It appeared that the blue putty holding the picture in place had lost its adhesive power. Unstuck, the rectangle of card now rested face down on the desk.

Marta tugged open her desk drawer and rummaged around at the back. She couldn't—wouldn't—sleep again now.

The pill bottle she withdrew was worryingly light; she'd need more soon. One of the guards had been sneaking her Benzedrine from the outside world, sneaked to him in turn by an enterprising villager. The painkillers didn't seem to be doing the trick at night any more, and the uppers kept her going when sleep eluded her, but while the company pharmacist hadn't caught on to her embezzling the pain meds, he wasn't so self-absorbed as to miss her stealing the bennies too.

She popped off the cap and tapped the rim of the bottle against her palm, depositing three small beige pills into her hand. For a second she thought about putting one back, then recapped the bottle and tossed all three into her mouth.

She cast around for something to wash the tablets down, her eyes drifting across the pages of data over which she'd spent so long.

Perhaps that's all it had ever needed—a dissociated moment of abstract thought from a brain run ragged—but suddenly she saw it.

The pills slowly melted on her tongue, unneeded, as Marta bent over the printouts again, her fatigue banished at a stroke.

The tumour-rift in Scott's head was changing, yes, but the figures over the last couple of weeks suggested … what? Her mind grabbed at the solution with slippery fingers.

She snatched up a pen, flailed for something to write on. Application of the right principles was all it took...

Yes. She could do it. If she could predict the fluctuations in the tumour's size, she could estimate when the breach between realities was at its weakest.

And in that small moment, she could close it.

Marta stared at the tight scribbles on the little white rectangle in front of her. She'd need to talk to Brooker, to confirm that the physiological side was feasible... but yes, she could do it. Much as she hated the idea of using Scott as a guinea pig, she'd always known that was exactly what he was there for. If a practice run could close the rift in his head, they'd be ready to see to its bigger brother.

She glanced at the clock: 3:27AM, she'd been asleep for a while. Fuck it, Jennifer could sacrifice a couple of hours in bed with Chuck Norris — if she was half the scientist she liked to think she was, the brain surgeon would be out of bed and dressed the second she knew the score. Marta had tried phoning the doctor at night before, knew the phone would be off the hook. She'd just have to go and drag the surgeon out of bed.

Dropping her pen on top of her scrawled workings, Marta thumped open the door and set off for the accommodation block.

Brooker's quarters were exactly opposite Marta's own, a ten-minute trip from the lab. Marta made it in six. Her mind had arrived still earlier, picturing Jen's face when she told her... relishing it. She raised her fist to begin pounding on the doctor's door... and stopped.

The door to her own quarters was open.

It was no more than a crack, and yes, there was the chance she'd just not closed it properly when she'd left earlier in the day, but the prickling of hairs on the back of Marta's neck said otherwise.

Someone was in there.

She nudged the door and it eased open without a sound. From where she stood, Marta had a clear line of sight into the suite's living area through to the bedroom, a sight that suffused her with ice.

The girl hadn't changed in the intervening years — shoulder-length brown hair framed a freckled face on the cusp of adolescence. She was no taller, no thinner... She beamed at Marta, as if nothing had happened.

"Hello, Mummy."

"Katie?" The word escaped as little more than a whisper, carried along on an exhalation. Marta took a step towards the girl, stopped as if afraid to close the distance between them, the gulf between life and death. Then she flung her arms around the slight figure. "My little girl," she sobbed, tears streaming down her face. "My little girl."

"It's okay," Katie stressed with a maturity that brought a further lump to her mother's throat.

Marta disengaged from her daughter's embrace, stared at her as if to suck her in through eyes reddened with weeping. "I thought... we all thought..."

"But you knew, right? Deep down."

She's right. Without bodies to bury...

Shakily Marta crossed the room and closed the door. Her legs wobbled as she groped for a chair and allowed herself to sink into it. "Where's Dad?"

"He's okay. He's working really hard to get everyone back again. Just like you."

"I'm not..." Marta fell silent. How could she say it without sounding like she'd given up on them? "The Collision," she theorized, struggling to make the connections, "you were all—"

"Sucked in, yeah. Buildings, too. It's like someone just picked up all the stuff and moved it somewhere else. But Dad's fixing it. He's built a bridge to get everyone back."

Marta breathed slow, hard. "Why didn't he come back too? Is he hurt?"

"No," Katie replied. "But he needs to stay there and work the bridge and he didn't have enough power to send a bunch of people."

"So he sent the only person I'd trust," Marta muttered.

"Yup. Said to say he needs your help."

Marta stared into space. Her fingers were clutching at the arms of her chair, digging into them with the intensity of someone who thought that if she let go, she'd fall off the earth. "What does he need me to do?"

"You have to come back with me."

"That... It can't be done. They sent probes through and they all came back as slag. The animals we put in just—"

"But they weren't using Daddy's bridge," Katie cut in. "We can go back and you can help him make it stronger. That's what he said."

God, we might have closed the rift. Cut them off for good... Marta's fingers dug a little deeper. "How?"

"I don't know, he told me, but I didn't get it. He just said you'll have to trust him and we can all be together again."

The silence lasted no longer than a beat, perhaps two, but it seemed to expand, filling the space between them until the room felt as if it would come apart under the pressure.

"Wait here," Marta said. "There are some things I have to do first."

By the time Marta returned to the lab, the uneven light of her desk lamp had puddled over a different part of her desk, and Dr Jennifer Brooker was sitting beside it, absorbed in the small rectangle of card on which Marta had scribbled her workings. Excitement was plain on the brain surgeon's face, her eyes wide with it.

Sensing another presence in the room, Jen looked up. Her momentary surprise washed from her face like a sand drawing under the tide, to be replaced by irritation. "When were you going to tell me about this? This is —"

"It." Marta interjected. "Everything we've been working towards."

"If this works on Zero…" Jennifer jumped to her feet. "I ran some figures, the next best time to try is in about three hours."

Marta stepped between her and the exit. "Not yet."

Puzzlement creased Jen's face.

"They're still alive," Marta gasped, her own excitement suddenly overcoming her. "The Collision didn't disintegrate everything, it sucked it all through to…"

"To?" Jen's incredulity was clear.

"I don't know. Another reality. But all the people… they're alive, Jen. We can save them. My daughter —"

"Your daughter's gone, Marta. You have to realize —"

"My daughter's *here*. In my quarters. Now!"

Jen tried to look calm. The exhaustion and fragility she had become used to seeing in Marta were now backed by a wildness that, frankly, scared her. All the tests that had been run on the rift… what she was saying wasn't even plausible, let alone possible.

She reached out and gently took Marta's hand in her own. "I know you're hurting, that it's been hard for you. But they're gone, Marta, we can't bring them back."

"But we can, I can prove it to you. We just need to keep the rift open long enough for me to go through and —"

Jennifer backed off, her hand wrenching free. "Go through? You'll be burned to a —"

"Alex is alive, he's over there and he knows how to get everyone back to our side." The words rushed from Marta. "But he needs my help to do it. He sent Katie back to get me."

Jennifer shuffled a little further away. "Okay," she replied, "I believe you. But we can't do this alone. We should…" she reached down to the desk and snagged the phone receiver from its cradle, "…let Murphy know. She'll be very interested to hear what you've found out."

"You think I'm —"

"No, no I don't. I just think that the higher ups should know what we're planning. You're too valuable to just disappear, right?"

Marta's eyes dropped to Jen's hand as she dialled. It was shaking.

She bolted across the room and smashed the receiver from the doctor's hands. It spun through the air, arrested in mid-flight by the short, coiled length of plastic that attached it to the cradle, and snapped back to crack against the side of the desk. The scant seconds it took for Jen to register her shock were all Marta needed to get between her and the door, blocking the exit.

"You can't see it, can you?" Jen panted. "What's happening here, you just can't see it." She circled the room, trying to force enough space to make a run for it. But Marta's movement mirrored hers, cutting off each new avenue as she opened it. "All this time and you still can't put your family to rest, can you?"

"They're still out there!"

"I get it now," Jen continued, sidling to Marta's right. "Now you've found a way to close the rift, you've *got* to let go, *got* to admit that there's no possibility left of them coming back. And you can't, can you?"

"They're alive, all of them. My daughter's here!"

"So why didn't security pick her up? Why didn't she show up on the closed circuit? All those cameras, why — ?"

The portable hard drive crashed into the side of Jen's head, swung with all the force Marta could muster. The surgeon went down like someone had cut the power to her, crumpling to the tiled floor where she twitched for a second or two, then was still.

"Because of the flares, you dumb bitch."

And then Marta was moving, lunging for the workings on the desk. She picked up the card and tucked it into her pocket. Without the figures, there would be no way for Murphy to close the rift before Marta was able to bring everyone back. Once she'd saved her family, *then* they could save the world.

Stepping over the body of her fallen partner, Marta slipped from the room.

"How did she get out of the compound?" Natalie had flung on her rumpled fatigues from the previous day, fastening them so quickly that the buttons were out of alignment.

"We don't know, ma'am." The trooper behind the banks of monitors had the earnest briskness of someone who knew heads were going to roll, and who wanted to make damn sure one of those heads wasn't his.

Murphy sighed deep in her chest, knowing that if anyone was getting crucified for this, it was her. It would be better if Brooker had died from her head wound. As it was, she'd surely be all too keen to fill in the brass about how she'd only warned Murphy a few hours ago that something like this would happen.

Natalie had known, of course, deep down. She missed her son, Calum, more than she could ever articulate, would do anything to be with him again. How much worse would it be for Marta? True, the trick cyclists had given Maszkowski the all-clear to work, so the powers that be had turned as much of a blind eye to her problems as Natalie had. But while they surely knew Marta was a ticking bomb there was no way they'd take any of the blame for this…

"Patch me through to Greyhound One," she snapped.

"Connected."

"Trap One to Greyhound One. ETA?"

The crackling response echoed around the room. "Greyhound One, ETA six minutes."

By the time Dr Brooker had come round and dragged herself to a sentry post, Maszkowski had been long gone, maybe a half-hour head start on her pursuers. That'd put her close to the Collision if she was on foot. If she'd stolen a transport... "Jesus. Pick it up."

"Confirmed."

The door swished open to reveal two soldiers flanking a tired-looking man in a jumpsuit. Murphy nodded towards a smaller office off to the side of the monitor room. "In there, please."

The escorts led their charge towards the office and sat him down at a small table. Natalie joined him, closing the door first to ensure privacy.

"How're you feeling?"

"Had better weeks."

"We've got a problem, Scott. Professor Maszkowski."

Scott sat up a little straighter. "What is it?"

"She's figured out how to cure you. How to close the rift in your head."

"Not getting how that's a problem."

"She's gone AWOL. Taken her notes with her. We think she's going to jump into the Collision."

"Fuck me." Scott thought for a second. "Hang on... *that's* how she's going to close it?"

"I should be so lucky." Natalie exhaled loudly. "She thinks everyone who died in the Collision is still alive, on the other side of the rift. She's gone to get them back."

"How'd she figure that?"

"Her daughter told her."

"But I thought—"

"So did I. I just spoke to Dr Brooker. Maszkowski told her that her little girl came back through the rift to get her. Which is why I sent for you."

"Because if anything came through the rift in the last day, I'd have felt it." Scott rubbed his eyes with the heels of his hands. "Nothing has. Nothing at all."

The brilliance of the thing… from the air, from a distance, Marta had never quite grasped it. Fractured shapes danced in the white light, like shards of glass reflecting and refracting, parting and coming together in constant defiance of the laws of physics. The spectrum split and rainbows danced like sunlight through a waterfall's spray.

"It's beautiful," she murmured.

She withdrew her calculations from her pocket, turned the piece of card over and looked at the picture on the other side of it. Somewhere behind her, an engine roared.

Here they come to save me. Or at the very least, what I know.

As she stowed away the snapshot, she felt a touch at her side. Katie slid cool, firm fingers into her mother's free hand and squeezed.

"I love you, Mummy."

Marta looked down at her daughter and smiled tearfully. "I love you too, sweetheart."

And together, they went into the light.

BLACK WHISPERS
by Trent Zelazny

The dust was like fog, the way it moved, thin streaks and opaque blotches, whirling, gliding, undulating. A kaleidoscope of brown, black and gray, ever changing while remaining the same, filling the night with an arid haze. It made him think of youthful nights in Carrizozo. Dust storms were more common there. Here they were a rare occurrence. Weather-wise, Aislado was usually very calm. Other than chilly winters, it was seventy-five degrees year round.

Mike raised the collar of his jacket. There was no reason to do it other than to do it. The two-lane blacktop was lonesome, desolate. There was unseen nocturnal life, but he was the road's only occupant.

And he trembled. He ached. His teeth tried to chatter but could not quite do it. The quivering made his jaw hurt. He needed a drink.

A hundred yards back was his home. Barely a home. Hardly a house. A rundown, stand-alone studio casita, one room with a bed and a sink and a stove, a tiny bathroom with a lot of broken tile, an ancient television with a coat hanger taped to it, and a baker's dozen of paperbacks. He used to read a lot. He used to read all kinds of things.

That was when Rachel was still alive, back when life gave him things and he gave things back. He did a lot of things back then. He was interested in things and he was interesting to people. He was community driven. Then he became drunkenly driven. So much so that, even the memory, shrouded in thick and fuzzy amber smog, was vividly crystalline. The punch, the crunch, the single cry of pain. The blood that poured from his nose, and the sight of his wife beside him, not moving, not breathing, not being anything other than dead. Mike was drunk and bleeding, and Rachel sat there, jaw slack, eyes rolled, never to climb out of the car on her own. Never to do anything again, nothing but be dead.

He squeezed his eyes shut, opened them. The road was still empty. The dust had settled down. He continued to walk. Another ten minutes and he'd be at El Coyote. Twenty minutes after that he'd be in town, but there was neither reason nor desire to head into town. El Coyote was what he wanted, what he needed. A double shot, a beer, then again, a third time. Get drunk until he passed out and someone drove him home. This is what he did most nights. He didn't have a car. Not anymore. Nor did he want one. He knew what would happen if he had one again. And anyway, they'd revoked his license. In a way he was lucky that's all they did. Vehicular Homicide had been on the table.

He'd lost his license, and he'd lost Rachel. Apparently they'd figured he'd lost enough. And now he walked. He walked the desolate road almost every night. Once a week he walked into town and got whatever groceries he could. He always bought a bottle, too. More than one, if he could. He'd take shots on the way home. The bottles at home now were empty, sucked dry. So he trembled, and walked.

Work was sporadic at best. Odd jobs. Mostly he drank. El Coyote was his best friend second only to booze. Pathetic. He knew it. He knew it and he embraced it. It was his drinking that killed Rachel. It only seemed right that his drinking kill him, too.

He stared down through the night, watched his feet carry him forward. Step after step, like every other night. His feet ached. They burned. They always burned. Without getting used to it, he'd managed to adjust. Foot pain, ouch, son of a bitch, it hurts; okay, now carry on, my wayward son.

He looked up, not to see anything but to uncramp his neck, which throbbed from his downcast posture. The sky was clear but with a minimal speckling of stars. His neck made a popping sound. He cranked his head one way, then the other, tasted the dehydration in his mouth, then squeezed his eyes shut, opened them, blinked several times, then furrowed his brow and blinked some more.

It was to his right. Dull, miniscule, possibly the moon reflecting off of something out there in the desert. He looked back at the sky. The moon was an emaciated scythe sagging low, barely keeping balance on the mountaintops in the opposite direction. It was not reflecting itself that way. It was not creating the soft point, the glowing, pulsing, almost mirage-like thingamajig, flickering out there, in the arid darkness.

He allowed his eyes another frenzied blinking. He drew a breath and held it, let it out. The light was still there, and it was colorful. A rainbow array that diminished, expanded, contracted, protracted. It seemed to shrink and grow while staying the same size. He stepped off the road's shoulder and onto dirt. He walked. The ground was uneven but not too bad. He wanted a drink. He needed a drink, a double shot and a beer, one of each to start the process, another set to calm his nerves. He wanted them, needed them, yet he was too compelled by the shimmering glow, the strange light that seemed to reflect off itself. Like a prism.

Drawing closer, the bending of the light's path crossed and curled in on itself. It refracted and entered itself at different angles. The image was clear enough in his eyes, yet what he saw was infinitely blurred, a rainbow of every possible color one could imagine.

It was a prism, but it was fading. The closer he moved to it, the dimmer it became. Each step he took and the thing darkened itself another shade, almost as though trying to hide. To blend in with the environment, a defense mechanism.

Closer, curiouser, darker, the prism ceased being a prism, and as Mike stepped up and over a large rock, the thing blipped out. Shut off like a television. But it hadn't disappeared. It was still there, right before him. It was almost as tall as he was, and as wide as it was tall. At first he thought a circle, but it was squared off in splayed edges. Like a hexagon, or an octagon. No color anymore, it was solid black. Darker than the night. Completely opaque. Blacker than black. And flat. It stood upright with its splayed corners, flatter than anything he could think of. If the blackness reminded him of anything, it was of shiny black silk, but it was too black for that. Too textureless. Too... something else. His mind ran amok through bafflement, and made a seamless transition into utter curiosity.

He stepped to the right of it, and examined the side. But there was no side. From where he stood there was only the desert night. The black thing was gone. He swayed left and looked back at where the front was. The front was still there, black on black. He returned to his right and the thing was gone. Further to the right, the thing had no back. He could just make out the road he'd been traversing.

Curious experiment, he walked through where the back of the thing should've been. Nothing happened. No tingling sensation, no hot, no cold, just his involuntary trembles from the need to have a drink. He turned around; the thing was there again.

"So what are you?" he asked it.

The black thing stood there, unspeaking, unmoving. Mike couldn't determine if the thing were solid or hollow, at least not by mere sight. A dead television screen, only without the screen.

He nibbled his tongue, bringing the slightest bit of saliva into his mouth. He raised his right hand, extended it forward, but his attempt to touch the thing was pointless. Like when he'd walked through the back of it, there was nothing there, no sensation. Only the sight of his hand disappearing. He quickly drew his hand back. It was still attached to his wrist. It still had all its digits. Whatever this was, this baffling blackness in the middle of nighttime nowhere, it was hollow. Maybe simply a mirage, a sight his rotting brain had conjured. Too much liquor can do that.

No. This wasn't a mind game. He didn't know how he knew this, but he did. The thing before him was real. It was as real as the fact that his wife was dead. It was surreal, but real. Surreal realism. Who said it? What was it? *Reality is the only word in our language that should always be used in quotes.*

This thing was real. Strange, but real.

He stepped forward. He was no more than a foot away from it. Being so close did not alter the thing's appearance in the least. He thought about his hand, how it had disappeared into it, and how nothing had happened. Curiosity, natural to the soul, injected itself into him again, this time with a heavier dosage. He leaned forward, brought his face right up to the thing, then slowly pressed it through.

The only sensation was in his eyes. Oh God! Light! Bright, colorful, blinding light! The prism he had seen, he was in it now. Prismatic patterns of every array. So skewed but so clear. And intense. In all his life he had never felt anything so intense. So beautiful, so bright, so utterly terrifying. A terminal kaleidoscope, shifting, transforming, breathing lifeless breaths, tearing at the roots of his nerves, at the core of his very being. He had not been in it even a second when he yanked his head out.

A moment passed in which all he saw was color. Then white, which dwindled to gray. Charcoal. Then black. The black of the thing. Perfect blackness surrounded by night. Darkened desert muted now, crispness gone, sprayed with smudges. He stepped back and sat on the large rock. He shuddered, flinched, trembled, calmed. The shakes were now merely from the lack of liquor.

He only sat another minute or so, then stood up and made his way back to the road. As he walked, his hand began to itch. A minute later so did his face.

There was conversation when he entered the bar.

"You know what I'm talking about," Renny said. It was

clear he'd already knocked back several. "The rocket weapon. Shit, a rocket launcher, you know what I mean."

"Yeah," Tom, another regular said, "but I promise you, it isn't called a kazoo."

Mike rubbed his forehead, then scratched the back of his hand as he made his way to the corner, where his usual table waited, unoccupied. Not that it much mattered where he sat. He'd sit on the floor so long as they'd serve him, which they would. Mule didn't care. Mule owned and ran the place. He never carded anyone either. There wasn't much in the way of law in the area. There was little need for it. Aislado was a very small town.

"Rum or scotch tonight, Mike?"

Mike placed his hands on the table. The trembling was bad.

"Hit me with one of each," he said. "Doubles."

"Usual chaser?"

"Please."

Mule nodded. The guy didn't bat an eyelash at anything Mike ordered. Two doubles of two different liquors would be no real surprise to anyone who'd known Mike Powers over the last two years. And with what had just happened, it was all the more needed. What had just happened, he didn't want to think about. What he'd do was have his first round, let his nerves settle a bit, give the whole matter two or three minutes consideration, then drink his mind into oblivion. It seemed the logical thing to do.

There were about a dozen people in the bar altogether. Most of them he recognized, a few of them he didn't.

Roger Miller sang "Dang Me" through the stereo. The lighting seemed different than normal. Brighter. Scads of refractive floaters glided on his eyes. He half hoped what he'd seen hadn't caused permanent damage.

Mule placed two generous shots on the table, along with a bottle of Pilsner. He turned away and left without saying a word.

Mike picked up the scotch and downed it. There was no burn, no bite; it went down smooth as water. He set the glass down and lifted the bottle, took a few long pulls on it. A wheeze of relief cascaded down through him, so faint it was hardly a breath at all. He picked up the rum and did the same thing, chased it, then raised his hand and got Mule's attention, gave indication to repeat all three. He finished off the beer as he waited for Mule.

"Well, it ain't a kazoo," Tom told Renny.

Then Mule was back with two glasses and three bottles, one small, two large, one beer, one fifth of rum, one fifth of scotch. Neither fifth was entirely full, but the glasses already had shots poured.

"I can tell it's gonna be one of those nights," Mule said. "I don't wanna keep bouncing back and forth like a goddamn Ping-Pong ball. Pour your own. You're on the honor system." He turned and walked away again.

Mike downed the scotch, used the rum as a chaser, then chased *that* down with beer. This did it; he began to calm. The circuitry of his nervous system stopped oscillating. His hands steadied. His breathing normalized, or became a close facsimile. The dirty-faced clock showed it was a quarter past ten.

Okay, he thought, let's take a look at what happened.

He drank some beer.

You're walking along and you see this thing, like a drop

of rainbow at night, all bright and sparkly. Dumb people are attracted to shiny things, so of course you go over to check it out. And then all the shine is gone. Just a black thing. A make-no-sense black thing, geometrically sound on one side but nonexistent on all the other sides. Stop. Strike that. It didn't have sides; ergo it wasn't geometrically sound. Just a thing.

He scratched his hand. His eyes burned and he squeezed them shut. His eyelids became one mental blackboard, and with a piece of cerebral chalk he drew an octagon on it. Around it he made little wavy lines to designate the desert. The image went from two dimensions to three, became almost as real as when he'd been out there.

Keeping his eyes shut, he found his beer, drank, and continued to stare at the shape his mind's eye had recreated. Within the octagon the black of the blackboard got blacker, deeper. It appeared multi-dimensional without having dimension. Just a thing. A fucking thing in the middle of nowhere. A widget. A whatchamacallit. A shrug and an *I don't know.*

He was aware that Roger Miller had stopped singing. It was the Beatles now. He didn't know what song. He didn't care what song. It might not have even been the Beatles. He didn't care because behind his eyes he was pushing his face into the mental octagon, and he had no choice but to open the box of psychical chalk and take out every conceivable color and enhance each piece with an excessive, high intensity light. Quicker than he could follow, bright lines drew before his eyes. They drew on his eyes, through his eyes. Even now just being a mental image, it was too much to handle. He snapped his eyes open, poured a shot of scotch, drank it.

It still didn't seem real. But it was. He had to buy it. It was a hard sell. As hard as selling ice cream at the North Pole, but the salesman had already taken his money. He had no choice but to take this as fact. Drunk or sober, good or bad, what had happened had happened. He rubbed his eyes, scratched his nose, then scratched his hand again.

"Excuse me?"

The voice was right beside him, right at his table, but for a moment he wasn't sure that it was addressing him. He blinked several times, then looked up. It was a minor form of shock that sluiced through him. The woman standing there was beautiful. Mike would have chalked up her beauty to his own inebriation, but he had yet to achieve even so much as a buzz. She was petite, brunette, eyes like caramel. She wore a loose-fitting flower-printed blouse, and tight jeans that accented her lower curves in a very pleasing way. Why this woman had stopped at Mike's table, he couldn't even venture to guess.

She smiled a little. She almost looked embarrassed.

"Sorry to bother you," she said, "but is your name Mike Powers?"

A low dose of confusion injected into him.

"That depends," he said.

"On what?"

He shrugged. "I dunno. Isn't that what people often say?"

She smiled a bit more, said, "Chloe."

This was a code word, in the sense that the code was the actuality, and the actuality was that the woman standing before him was Chloe Allen. The confusion evaporated. He was surprised to feel his heart beating, and a bit ashamed to be spotted with so much alcohol before him.

"Good God," he said. "Hi. How the hell are you?" He rose

from the table, gave her a hug. She felt nicer than he remembered; of course, it had been almost twenty years, and his memory wasn't what it had once been. He could have been remembering wrong.

"I'm good," she said. She looked at the table, and the bottles upon it. "Am I interrupting something?"

Mike could offer nothing more than a sheepish smile. "Just a useless drinking binge. What—what are you doing here?" He offered her a seat. She took it. Mike only then noticed she was holding a beer of her own.

"Just came here to get away for a week or so," she told him. "Seems like ages since I allowed myself a vacation."

"And you chose Aislado of all places."

"Actually, Cloudcroft." She sipped her beer. "My family used to go there all the time when I was a kid."

"Where are you living these days?" He poured a shot of rum. He was starting to feel better.

"Traded dirt for water," she said. "Been living in Bradenton the past several years."

"Bradenton?"

"Florida."

"Ah." He downed the shot, then picked up and held on to what remained of his beer. "Yeah," he said, "I'd imagine Florida has more water than New Mexico."

"Just a little."

"So what are you doing out in Bradenton, Florida?"

"Being a geek."

"Really? And they pay you for that?"

She laughed. It was a very cute laugh. "Well, actually, yes, in a sense." She sipped her beer again. "I'm an anthropodologist."

"They must pay you well cause that's a long-ass word."

Another little laugh.

"What, exactly, is that?"

"It's a branch of entomology. Bugs and things."

"Wow, so you really are being a geek." He said it with a smile, and his tone was light-hearted. At least he hoped it was. It must have come off the way he intended because she smiled, and this time, rather than a laugh, it was a tiny giggle that escaped her.

"Yes," she said. "I really am being a geek."

Mike scratched his cheek. He rubbed his palm then the back of his hand against his pants leg. He blinked more than usual. The itching was really starting to bug him. He did his best to put it in the back of his mind, and looked at Chloe. It had been a long time. A very long time. There had been a time, way back in high school, when they had been something of an item. A long time ago, back when they both lived in Santa Fe. More than a forever ago.

"What about you?" she said. There was something in her eyes that told him she knew his life had not gone well. He knew that the sight of him on any given day was a rather sad thing to behold. Tonight was no exception.

He told her. He took a shot of rum and told her, took a shot of scotch and told her some more. As he told her, invisible strings tugged Chloe's face into a visage of sympathy. Her eyes seemed to glisten, and the nods she offered every so often exuded compassion.

"So that," he concluded, "is why you see me here in this very coveted fashion."

Moments passed. They were long moments. Mike spent these moments staring at the table. Staring at the table and scratching his hand. The itching had graduated to a mild burning sensation.

Then, "I'm so sorry, Mike."

He shrugged. "I am too, thanks."

He poured another shot. She joined him in one. Then Mike decided if he wanted to remain coherent, he'd lay off the hard stuff a while and stick simply with beer. Mule didn't seem to care any which way.

"Are you here alone?" he asked her.

"Yeah. I spent the day in Carlsbad. Seen this place several times over the years. Finally decided to stop and relax a bit, check it out."

"So it's a random coincidence, us running into each other."

"Or maybe serendipitous."

"Fortuitous."

"Let's just say providential, and leave it at that." She smiled again.

Time ticked off in seconds and minutes. They spoke of old times, and more of the times between then and now. So many years gone by, two completely different paths through life, and yet their connection remained. Time hadn't severed the threads they'd sewn more than a forever ago; there were still strands linked between them.

As they talked, Mike continued to scratch. It was absent-minded scratching, just something he did, until he looked down at his hand and found he'd tore away a strip of skin. Upon seeing it, the sting grew much worse, and he couldn't help wincing.

"You okay?"

Mike, who'd been scratching his hand beneath the table,

brought it aloft for Chloe to see. She cringed at the sight of it. Tiny rivulets of blood cascaded down the sides. Chloe grabbed a napkin and wrapped his hand. Under other circumstances, he would have enjoyed the brief handholding, which *was* brief. But the pain, and even moreso the realization of what he'd done, dominated the moment.

She had him hold the napkin in place as she poured a mouthful worth of scotch into one of the glasses. Then she had him remove the napkin. She poured the scotch over his hand. He winced again. Then she applied a fresh napkin to the wound. Then she squinted at his hand.

"Good God," she said. "That looks like one nasty rash."

"Been bugging my face, too, though not quite as bad."

"Turn your hand this way, into the light." She examined his hand closely, squinted at his face, then looked back at his hand. As she did the invisible strings pulled her expression one way then another, this way, then that. None of these expressions filled him with confidence. He poured a big shot of rum and drank it down.

Eventually she stopped studying and started pondering.

Mike looked at his hand. It looked like someone else's. He began to scratch his brow then ceased, for fear of ripping his own face off. But it itched. It burned. It was annoying as hell. The annoyance bled from mere physical into mental, and what might pass for emotional. He felt like an idiot, only now putting two and two together. He'd had a chalkboard right in front of his eyes and he hadn't been able to do the math.

His hand itched. His right hand. Only his right hand; his right hand and his face. The only two parts of his body that had entered into the black thing. The black nebulous void. He'd experienced no sensation when he'd placed his hand inside it, but this meant nothing. His eyes had seen it. Horrible, frightening bitch of beauty, he'd seen what was inside the thing. The black thing. The rainbow thing. It was the explanation without explanation.

"They look like chigger bites," Chloe said.

"Chigger bites?"

"I've seen enough of them in my time," she told him with a nod.

Mike examined his hand. It still itched like a motherfucker. "But chiggers? Really?"

"That's what it looks like, and I'm the bug geek."

"But, well, I dunno. I thought they only lived in, like, more humid climates, or something."

"Well, that's more common."

"It's dry as hell here."

"Well, they're more common in humid areas, yeah. They require a high level of humidity for survival, but it isn't impossible out here. In fact, it's not even uncommon." She looked at him. What had been moist eyes in her sockets were now inquisitive spears.

Mike sought his mind for a reason as to why he might have these bites. A logical explanation. An explanation that could be easily explained. In other words, a convincing lie.

"You got them on your face, too," she said.

He knew this. He hadn't considered how obvious it might be, however. Now he imagined himself as the Alligator Man in some carnival freak show. How a teen feels when they have some zits. His face and his hand, the only two places, the parts of him he'd stupidly stuck into the blinding, bright, colorful black thing. The black thing which was probably still there. Maybe not, but why would it be there only to not be there?

Mike poured himself some scotch.

"It's too weird," he said.

"What?"

He looked at her. Beautiful. She was even more beautiful than she had been in high school. Her face still carried sobriety, and trustworthiness. Unlike the regulars, unlike himself, Chloe was still a human being. He drank his scotch, crossed his arms and set them on the table.

"Can I tell you something you likely won't believe?"

Trustworthy, no doubt about it now. "Yeah," she said.

He told her about the thing he'd found on his way to the bar. At first he felt like an idiot, like a drunk suffering dementia, conjuring pure insanity, but steadfast that it was fact. But the more he talked about it, the more it became natural, and the more he sounded like someone who wasn't simply talking out of his ass. He drank more scotch when he finished. So much for sticking with beer.

The look Chloe gave him started as the look of someone staring at a car crash. Invisible chisels carved that away, and he watched her face go from doubtful to skeptical to curious.

He began scratching again.

Chloe stood up and walked away. Mike watched her cross to the bar and say something to Mule. Mike prepped himself for being subdued, waking up later in a white room. He watched Mule turn away, then turn back with a bottle of a clear liquor. Likely vodka. He handed it to Chloe, along with a handful of paper napkins. Chloe thanked him and returned to the table.

"You believe the guy doesn't have a first-aid kit?" she said, pouring vodka into a couple of the napkins. "I think that's illegal."

"Aislado doesn't care much about legalities," Mike told her.

"I'm sure that's true. Here." She handed him the doused napkins. "Hold these to your face for a minute."

Mike did. He felt like a fool. His face burned but it was the kind of burn that told him it was doing something. A disinfecting sting, and he cringed beneath the lovely smelling paper-thin gauze.

"What's happening with you?"

Mike knew the voice of Randy Scouse when he heard it.

"Nothing you'd ever understand, Randy."

"How's that?"

It was on the tip of his tongue to tell the entire bar what he'd seen. Instead he let the tip of his tongue touch the vodka-soaked napkins.

Then he said to Chloe: "You think I'm crazy, huh?"

"No," she said. "Drunk, yeah, but not crazy."

He took the napkins from his face, wrapped them around his hand. "I am drunk," he said. "That's all I ever am. I'm a miserable, self-deprecating drunk, and there's a big part of me that likes it that way. There's a certain comfort that comes with living in a pit of despair. But that thing out there, whatever it is, it's there. I dunno what it is, or how it got there or what it's doing, but it's there."

Their table filled with quiet. Some unrecognizable song was playing.

Chloe nodded. "Okay," she said. "Let's go check it out."

"Check what out?" Randy said. He was a big guy, a faux cowboy type, beard and boots.

"Nothing you'd ever understand, Randy."

"That's twice you said that," Randy told him. "You ain't

nothing goddamn special, Powers. Gotta woman sitting with you and now you're some sort of fucking professor."

"No," Mike said, "it's nothing like that."

"So then tell me."

"Why? What does it matter to you?"

"It does," Randy said. "It just does."

Tom was looking at him now. So was Mule and Renny and all the rest of them. He was on the spot, center stage in a theater of drunks and illusions, only tonight the illusions were real. If they weren't, then he'd go home, load up his 357, put it to his head and pull the trigger.

He cursed himself, then without thinking about it, he talked about the black thing.

Incredulous eyes, all of them. Skeptical, scoffing scrutiny, all of it directed at him. He imagined he was now a homeless bum, the Alligator Man who licked the soles of his shoes, and spouted crazy shit, the grassy knoll, Roswell, Paul is dead, a piece of hollow obsidian in the middle of the fucking desert, bug bites, bed bugs, chiggers, rainbows in blackness. He felt like a goddamn moron, and his face started burning again. He lifted the bottle of vodka and poured some on his face, making sure his mouth was open as he did.

"You're out of your fucking mind," Tom said, then turned to Renny. "He's fucking lost it, hasn't he?"

"Three sheets to the wind," Renny said. "I think he finally broke his brain."

"Agreed," said Tom. "And it's a bazooka, by the way. Not a kazoo."

"Bazooka, thank you. You could've said that a long time ago."

"I wish my brain was broken," Mike said. "I've been

sitting here trying to come up with any reason I possibly could to explain what the fuck it is I saw out there, and from every angle I've looked at it, it keeps amounting to the same damn thing. The reason I saw the fucking thing is because the fucking thing was there."

"Was, or is?" Randy asked.

"Was," Mike said. "And maybe is. How the hell would I know? I'm not there anymore."

Chloe seemed to be shrinking in her seat.

Then Mule spoke. First he cleared his throat, then he said, "Mike, you know I've always respected you, but are you listening to yourself? Do you really believe what it is you're fucking saying? Spacemen or something, aliens, whatever the fuck? Some random black square that gives you bug bites, just sitting there in the middle of nowhere?"

"It was more of an octagon, not a square," Mike told him.

"Bat shit," Renny said. "Killing your wife really fucked you up, Powers."

Before Mike could blink he was on his feet. His eyes became daggers and they prodded Renny, dared him to say that again, dared him to say another word.

Renny chewed his lip then looked down. "I'm sorry," he said.

"Look," Chloe said, and her voice helped sever the tension. "Whether true or not, Mike is certain he saw something out there. I don't know about you idiots, but it's certainly piqued my curiosity." She stood up. "I wanna go check it out."

"Who the hell are you, lady?" Randy said.

"I'm an old friend of Mike's," she said. "And in all the years I've known him, he's never made shit up just to make shit up." She reached out and touched Mike's shoulder. "Let's go see what this thing you're talking about is."

It was a short drive. Probably less than a minute. Chloe had a Prius. It was so quiet it was hard to tell if it was even on. Within that minute they spoke.

"Thanks for believing me."

"I don't know if I believe you or not," she said. "But I meant it when I said I know you don't just make shit up. True or not, I believe you saw something out here."

Two cars followed behind them. Renny and Tom were in one of them. Randy and a guy they called Arm, as well as Mule himself, were in the other. Arm used to be a professional crapshooter, then had his arm chopped off at the elbow. Being right-handed, the guys who did it were kind enough to chop off his left arm.

"I'm sure I haven't made a very pleasant impression on you tonight."

"You're fine, Mike. I've known you too long to worry about that."

Through the itching and burning sensation in his face, Mike felt something strange in his cheeks and lips. It was vaguely familiar, then he realized it was the tiny etching of a smile.

He pointed to the left. "There," he said. "There, look, you see it?

"I do," Chloe said, and the car slowed.

It was like when he'd first seen it. A dull, pulsing pocket of rainbow, diminishing, expanding, staying the same size.

"Holy cock-sucking mother of Christ, there's the son of a bitch. Pull over."

She crossed into the oncoming lane, slackened her speed a bit more, and drove a good fifty yards over the desert land before the terrain became too rough for the Prius to handle. The two cars behind them followed, and stopped when she stopped. Everybody climbed out of their respective vehicles. The thing was darker than it had been from the road. For a time not a single one of them could find words.

"The hell is that?" Tom finally said.

Nobody answered. The desert night was silent. Mike stepped forward, then stepped again. He had brought the fifth of vodka with him. He carried it as he walked towards the thing, sipping from it, and applying light splashes to his face.

Chloe, Renny, Tom, Randy, Arm and Mule followed, and the light of the thing continued fading, fading like a dissolve in a movie, like memories do when they're engulfed in liquor. The rainbow shuddered, faded, shaded, and when they all stood before it, it was just a black thing. The black thing, but now it was less of an octagon, slightly more rounded, as though the thing had melted just a little bit.

Mike walked to the side of it—there was no side—around it—it wasn't around—then joined the others back in front of it.

"Told you," he said. "If my brain is broken, so's all of yours."

"I don't believe it," Mule said. "Strap one on and fuck me sideways, just what the hell is it?"

"I dunno," Mike said. "It's a… it's just a thing." He looked at Chloe. "What do you think?"

Chloe shook her head in disbelief. "A thing," she said. "A big, black, shiny thing." She took the vodka from Mike, downed a shot, then passed the bottle back.

"You say the thing is hollow?" Randy said.

"I put my hand through it. I put my head into it." The image of the fractured prism returned to his mind. Staring at the blackness, he could almost make it out. Refracted light, passing obliquely from itself and into itself and into another. He could almost see it; it was almost there, but not quite. If Death could smile, that was how the thing looked. A pure black, empty, incandescent face.

"So what the hell do we do?" Arm said.

"What the hell *can* we do?"

Silence smothered them all again. No more than ten seconds, but it seemed to last an eternity. The thing remained black, opaque, but glowing. The thing didn't make any sense. It hadn't before and it didn't now.

"Well," Randy said, and stooped down. "There's a simple test we can try." He came up. He was holding a rock.

"I dunno if that's a good idea," Mike said.

"Shit. We don't have any other ideas. Step back."

They all did. Like a professional baseball pitcher, Randy flung the rock right into the thing.

Nothing. Not a sound. It didn't make an echoing clink, nor did it land somewhere out in the desert. The thing had seemingly just swallowed it up.

"It's just goddamned nothingness," Mule said.

"No," Renny said. "You know what it is? It's like goddamn Area 51, or something. Remnants of a crashed spacecraft or some shit. Some alien craft probably crashed out here. The Army or Air Force or whoever found it, maybe even captured some surviving occupants, and just like Roswell they've engaged in some sort of a cover up. Only this"—he indicated the black thing—"this was left behind."

"That was a fucking radar-tracking balloon," Tom said.

"The whole Roswell thing was a hoax."

"All right, Tom, fine. What the hell is your explanation?"

Before the argument continued, Chloe said, "Shit."

Everybody looked at her looking at the thing. Then they looked at the thing, and gasped in unison.

Something inside the black thing moved. Something colorless swirled within it, fluid, gliding. And with the swirl there emerged a high-pitched ringing sound, like that of a dog whistle. In the distance coyotes began to howl.

"This can't be good," Chloe said.

Then, like the flick of cigarette ash, a tiny red glow fell from the thing. It disappeared instantly. Mike didn't know if anyone else saw it. It was so small and fast, he wasn't even sure *he'd* seen it. But then he saw it again, and within the dog whistle-like sound rumbled a low murmur, and with the rumble the air suddenly both smelled and tasted metallic.

Another glowing droplet. Then another. They petered out to blackness as quickly as they flashed.

"I don't like this," Arm said. He turned to Randy. "Why the fuck you throw that rock into it?"

"It's like it was giving out blow jobs. I wasn't just gonna stand here staring at the fucking thing."

Then, like fireflies pouring from a salt shaker, dozens of little glowing drops fell out at once. Then dozens more. The thing was a solid black cloud, raining glowing things. Glowing things that disappeared almost as soon as they dropped, and the glowing things got bigger. Most of them were bigger than fireflies now.

Everyone stepped back, eyes riveted to the sight before them. They were the size of large coins, and as the glow vanished little plops sounded. They weren't disappearing.

Their glow was dying out but they were landing on the ground.

"The fuck?" Randy said.

And still the things poured out, plinking and plopping and thudding, some of them now the size of Ping-Pong balls, then baseballs. In their glowing state, the big ones showed Mike and everyone else what they were. A giant lump swelled in Mike's throat as he beheld a particularly large red body, six or eight legs, it looked like; he wasn't entirely sure.

They look like chigger bites, Chloe had said.

Chiggers. Bugs. Mites. That's what they had to be. That's what they were. Glowing mites pouring out, pouring at a steady pace now. Hundreds of them, maybe more, definitely more. The ground was becoming a blur of movement, and everyone continued stepping back, quicker than before, wanting to run but held by their own disbelief.

A rock toppled. There was a thud. Somebody grunted. Mike looked and saw Arm sitting on the ground.

"Shit," he said with a laugh that lacked humor. He braced his right arm to push himself up, and there was a fast blur as one of the mites shot forward, and dug its claws or teeth or whatever into the man's forearm.

With a cry, Arm fell on his back, shaking his arm violently, trying to dislodge the damn thing. It held fast. He slammed his arm against the ground, then again, again, each time harder than the time before, but the mite held on. And then there were more mites on him, big and small, and soon he wore a suit of mites, then his cries gurgled and reverberated with the sound of the swarm. He formed one word, "Help," and then he choked and then he coughed and then his body twitched, and then finally, it stopped moving.

Mike shook his head, and for a split second wondered how everyone, all of them, could simply watch what had just happened. How they could simply stand there and let the man die. He turned and looked at everyone else, but they weren't there. They were at the cars, or headed to them, and sound entered his ears, cussing and screaming sounds.

He heard Chloe call his name. He could just make out the shape of her. Then he looked down. They were everywhere now, swarming the ground, jostling the brush. Yet in all this chaos, they weren't touching him. They weren't doing to him what they'd done to Arm. If anything, they seemed repelled by him.

He gulped down a shot of vodka. It was a very big shot and some squirted from his mouth. The ocean parted where the stream fell. The things skittered away from the fallen booze.

That was odd. Or was it? Coincidence, or...?

He cupped his hand, filled it, and dumped the alcoholic smattering over a clustered swarm. The things scattered away from the inebriant shower at breakneck speed.

"Son of a bitch," he said.

"Mike!" It was Chloe, calling his name in desperation.

The bottle was still mostly full. Mike placed his thumb over the opening, lifted the bottle above his head, turned it, and gave himself a light dousing, keeping his mouth open as he did. The metallic smell was gone; he could only smell vodka. He ran to where Chloe was standing on the hood of the Prius. Thumb still over the opening, he shook the bottle and sprayed her.

"The hell are you doing?"

"They don't like the booze," he said, and sprayed her

again.

Randy's pickup truck revved and backed up. Mike didn't know if anyone was in there with him or not. Then somebody screamed, and as the pickup's headlights switched on and the earth's floor moved, rippled and splashed like insectile ocean waves. Drowning in it was Renny, battered and bloodied. He was crawling along the ground. Or trying to. He seemed to be melting into the ground more than crawling over it. And crying. He was crying and crying and the things were all over his crying face. Then he sunk beneath the surface and didn't reemerge.

Mike spun to Chloe. "Back to the bar," he said.

Chloe, a disheveled mess, dripping with vodka but still with her wits about her, hopped off the hood of the Prius. Mike kicked an exceptionally large mite out into the scrub, then the two of them climbed into the car. The doors closed and she was saying "Jesus Christ, Jesus Christ," over and over like some sort of panic-stricken mantra. Her hands shook but she started the car. The headlights came up and sprayed on the weaving ground.

"Jesus Christ, Jesus Christ."

"Just drive," Mike said. "Drive back to the bar. Get us out of here.

One of the rear doors flung open. The dome light came on and Mule flung himself inside, moaning, whimpering, covered in mites. His flesh was red and pocked and bumpy. Without thinking, Mike doused him in vodka, emptying the bottle. The mites zipped away and hid in the seats, or stopped moving altogether.

"Close the fucking door!"

Weak and twitchy, Mule sat himself upright and pulled

the door shut.

Chloe reversed all the way to the road. On the other side of the road was Randy's pickup. It was upside down. The windows were broken. No one was moving inside the cab. Smoke or steam or a combination rose from the vehicle. And just down the road a spell, someone was running.

Chloe braked alongside him as Mule flung open the back door. Tom climbed in, his head awash with red. "That fucking idiot," he said.

Conway Twitty sang *It's Only Make Believe*. The doors and windows were locked. No one had said a word in nearly half an hour.

Mule was on the floor, conscious but weak. Tom nursed the head wound from when Randy's truck flipped over. His eyes couldn't follow straight. Likely a concussion.

"So what are we gonna do?" someone finally asked.

The exterior of El Coyote had been covered in booze of all kinds. There wasn't a whole lot remaining for anyone to drink. Enough to get everybody good and plastered, but probably only once.

"They mostly seem to be going north," Chloe said. "Maybe a convoy south."

"Have you seen how many are out there now?" Tom said. "They're all around the cars. Shit, you saw what they did to Renny and Arm. Just getting to the cars might be signing our own death warrants."

They were out there, all right. They could see them. The moon had risen and brightened a bit and they could see them out there, scurrying about. Big ones, little ones, it was hard to tell, but they were there. The ground continued moving. It rippled in waves of vermin. They were out there, thousands of them, maybe millions, but they didn't come to El Coyote. Liquor, for whatever reason, and for the time being, seemed a damn good bug repellent.

"So what are we gonna do?" someone else said.

"I dunno," Mike said. "I guess, for now, we're gonna wait."

"Wait?" Tom said. "You saw what they did to Renny. You saw what they did to Arm. We're just gonna wait until everything dries up out there, and they come in here?"

"You just said it yourself. Trying to get to the cars is a suicide mission. And even if we do make it to the cars. Even if we make it safely to the cars and head south, what then? We don't know what's out there. There could be black things like that one all over the fucking place." He turned to Chloe. "You said they're less active in dry places."

"Yeah, that's why heading south crossed my mind. That and they seem to be heading north. But they can still be active in dryness, and this area is very dry."

"Well—"

"*And*, those aren't chiggers or ticks or spiders. They look like them, they look a lot like them, but they're something else. Something else, from that weird black hole, from that… fucking… rip in reality, or whatever the hell it is." She sighed. "I know that sounds crazy when you say it out loud, but what the hell else would you call it? God knows how they got here all the way from France. They're strong out there. They're just going about their business." She looked at Mike, then at the floor. "I don't know *what* the hell to do."

There were nine of them in the bar. They sat in silence, passing around the bottles of the booze that remained, each thinking, thoughts confined to their heads, bodies confined to this rundown middle-of-nowhere bar. Outside was death. They could hear it swishing outside in the night, like black whispers. Whispers whisking through a billion fangs.

Nine of us, Mike thought. *Nine of us. Billions of them.*

The night rolled on and they sat in silence. There was little to say. Mike thought about Rachel. He drank hard and thought hard. He drank and drank but he kept thinking hard. He didn't want to think. He wanted his brain to just shut the hell up.

Eventually he shifted his thinking to slightly more positive things. To life before drinking. Life before Rachel had been killed. He remembered when he'd first met Rachel, then continued traveling back in time and remembered first meeting Chloe, way back in the ninth grade. Life had been simple then. It often seemed hard but it was really very simple. The simple days were over now. Even if all of this ended, if it all suddenly just went away, life would never be simple again. Life begins simple, then it's built out of complication upon complication. But there are always blessings. There are always blessings and you just need to remember to see them, and to count them.

He turned to Chloe. It was a strain, but he was able to smile.

"In spite of everything," he told her, "it's great to see you."

She smiled back. "You too," she said.

He put his arm around her. They snuggled. The radio had been turned off but nobody seemed to notice.

"Remember when we got banned from the mall?"

Chloe giggled. "The hell made you think of that?"

"I dunno."

"You claimed you'd just seen *Teen Wolf*, figured it was okay to surf on the top of my car."

"Yeah. Stupid, I know. But it's a memory now. And kind of a fond one, I might add."

They snuggled a little closer.

"You were so cute back then."

"I'm still cute," he said. "I've just added the alcoholic mystique to the whole thing."

"It's a tragic mystique," Chloe told him. "But an understandable one."

"Well," Mike said. "If I had the chance to do certain things over again, I would. But I don't. No one gets that chance. We weren't given a reset button."

"Another tragic thing," Chloe said. "There are a lot of things I'd do differently, too."

Mike shrugged. They snuggled a bit closer. "No point in regretting things now."

"No, I guess not."

"It's nice being with you."

"Yeah, you too."

"I've missed it."

"So have I."

Mike downed two big gulps of spiced rum. Then he closed his eyes. Behind them he was driving, and his wife was beside him, snuggling him as he drove. They seemed to drive forever, upon an endless road. He drove and drove and drove, but it didn't matter. He wasn't getting anywhere. He heard the tiny clicks and scrapes and he drank and drove another hour. People whimpered now. Some of them blubbered. But nobody bothered to move.

"It's nice being with you," he said again. His voice was a faint and defeated whisper, and he was still driving.

Driving and driving, and the car hadn't moved. He'd never gone anywhere. The road sweeping by was stock footage. A loop of the same scene over and over, and the rustling sounds grew steadily closer. The footage of the road repeated again, and Mike sat motionless in the midst of moving swarming bodies. He could no longer move. He couldn't move a bit. He felt them digging in and taking hold of his flesh, and he kept on driving. He snuggled Rachel as the creatures moved and bit and tore at him. He could hear them in his ears, the sucking sounds they made.

Then he crashed. The punch, the crunch, the single cry of pain. Rachel died. Pain shot into the very center of his being. He tried to pray. His body was dead but his mind continued. He was not a praying man but he still tried to pray. There was nothing else left for him to do. But ensnared in darkened, voiceless malice, his vespers dwindled to blackened whispers.

His very last thought was *Please, let it end.*

COLLISIONS
by Dave Hoskin

Joseph Tern was asleep when the intruder broke in.

He felt no pain as it settled into place, and indeed for the next hour or so, the only hint of its presence were the new images that began slowly blooming inside his head. Joseph's face started to flicker as he dreamed of impossible particles smashing together at fantastic speeds. A voice was saying there's something *moving* in there, something *dark*, and then there was a terrible flash of light. Joseph felt himself being twisted, felt three dimensional space harrowed away in an instant, and then everything stopped making sense.

Hours later, a noise woke him. He opened his eyes and tried to blink.

He couldn't.

His eyes stared at the ceiling, widening as far as they could. His pupils flicked from side to side. Something clumsy was controlling them, like a toddler piloting a 747. His arm began groping spastically, searching for the edge of the bed and then attempting to lever his body upright. His legs kicked and swung. It took Joseph a full minute to realize he wasn't having a fit of some kind, and that's when he started trying to fight back. He sent frantic signals to his arms and legs, but to no avail. It was as if his mind had been unplugged from the rest of his body, and all he could do was sit helplessly as he was hijacked. He could still feel everything—as his body shambled across the room he was painfully aware of the intruder clumsily triggering cramps as it figured out which parts of him to flex and which to relax—but otherwise he was paralyzed.

Suddenly his body lurched to a halt. The cramps receded as the intruder's touch grew lighter, and then his body made a beeline for his wardrobe. His hands threw open the doors and rifled through the shoeboxes on the floor. Their contents were emptied and his face examined the haul. His eyes were stinging now—they still hadn't blinked—and with an absurdly conscious effort he forced his eyelids to close and open up again. Then he refocused on the contents of the shoeboxes, eyes wide with greed.

Trapped inside his own head, Joseph felt the first prickle of an alien emotion. Control was the one thing he prized above all else, and now something had stolen it from him, he was terrified.

He'd never been terrified before.

Even worse, the intruder seemed to know where his most precious things were. Indeed, just as that thought completed itself, his traitorous fingertips touched the first trophy: a curl of red hair tied into a bow. His hands lifted the hair and regarded it, clearly trying to figure out what it represented. Then the hair was tossed aside and the hands returned to the pile. A little more rifling and then... three more curls of hair.

Different colours. Joseph watched his hands as they placed each of the trophies on the floor. They were noticeably more careful, thinking through the significance of their find.

It was just as the intruder clearly figured out what the trophies meant that Joseph heard the noise that had woken him. It was louder now, more insistent.

Someone was knocking at the door of his apartment.

His body jerked around, and flailed toward the kitchen. It yanked out a drawer, pulled out the tray full of knives and forks and found the secret tools hidden underneath. It ran a finger along the edge of Joseph's short blade, and then grabbed some clothes. It never hesitated once. Joseph was still trying to hit the brakes, and still nothing was happening. He felt like a twig borne along on a raging river, and the simple concept of being so completely out of control was pushing him towards hysteria.

The last of the clothes were tugged into place, and his body walked over to the front door. The door shook as the person on the other side knocked again. Joseph's face clumsily pressed itself against the spyhole and he immediately recognized a policeman. He wasn't in uniform and he wore no badge, but Joseph could tell just by the way the guy held himself that he was a cop. Under no circumstances did he want to speak to him, not with his trophies lying out in plain sight...

His hand reached for the door handle.

Joseph threw everything he had at diverting his hand. The fingers twitched a little, shying away from the handle. Then the intruder reasserted control, albeit not as firmly as before. Slowly, fighting against Joseph's efforts, it placed his fingers on the handle, tightened them and twisted. The door pulled open just a fraction and Joseph waited for the cop to stick his foot in the gap.

Nothing happened.

Carefully, Joseph peered out into the corridor. He was just in time to see the cop turning the corner and disappearing down the stairs. He must have been knocking for ages, thought Joseph. He'd delayed the intruder just long enough for him to give up. Good.

His hand lifted the short blade and carefully placed the tip inside Joseph's nose.

Inside his own head, Joseph froze.

He could feel the intruder slowly twisting the blade, was acutely conscious of his breath slipping in and out past the razor-thin obstruction. There was nothing fearful about his breathing — he didn't even have control over *that* — but the *feel* of the weapon inside him was maddening, and somehow he could tell this reaction was pleasing the intruder. He did his best to reassert control, but it was useless, like he was floating in space.

He screamed in frustration.

And as he did, he really *felt* the intruder's presence inside his head for the first time, felt it gorging on his agitation.

Then the blade was pulled from his nose, and his body slipped out the door.

He ran clumsily down the stairs. It didn't take long to catch up to his quarry, and Joseph watched as the cop exited the building and walked out onto the street. There weren't many people around and Joseph felt sure the intruder would halt his pursuit now. With no crowd to hide within, it was dangerous to leave the shelter of the building. However, just as he was thinking that, his body jerked into motion again and began following the cop at a short distance. Joseph was seriously worried now. The best thing about his new life was his anonymity. He liked being able to slip among the sheep unnoticed, and he particularly liked the fact that the police — or what was left of them — had no idea who he was. Now he was apparently doing the best he could to get arrested.

That's when the intruder caught sight of the man walking four steps behind the policeman. Joseph recognized a victim straight away, a runt desperately trying not to be conspicuous. He was keeping pace with the cop, sheltering in his protection.

Like a roller-coaster car tipping over the edge of a precipice, the intruder suddenly lengthened his stride. Joseph's anxiety spiked as he tried to hit the mental brakes. The intruder had his eye on the runt, but Joseph tried frantically to keep the cop in focus, hoping he wouldn't notice what was clearly about to happen.

He felt himself reposition the knife in his hand. He felt his other hand, still slightly clumsy, slipping around the runt's shoulder and placing itself over his mouth. Blessedly, the runt didn't even struggle. He just froze, submitting to the predator, even though help was just a few metres away. As the knife came over his other shoulder, Joseph was buzzing with anticipation, fear and a weird kind of delight. He didn't know if there was anyone behind him, and now he couldn't even see what the cop was doing. He just knew this was going to happen and there was nothing he could do to stop it.

He felt the runt's fingers claw weakly at his arm as the tip of the knife slipped neatly up his nose. He heard himself make a quiet shushing sound, felt the runt's arms fall away, perhaps hoping the gentleness of the sound signified some kind of mercy.

Somewhere inside his own head, Joseph Tern felt the intruder *expand*, felt it feasting on the waves of terror and excitement that coursed through the air like warm, tangy milk.

Then the knife was slammed upward.

The runt fell to the ground like an empty coat.

Joseph's body walked on, casually slipping the knife back up his sleeve.

As he passed the cop, Joseph heard somebody cry out from behind him. He saw the policeman turn around, but Joseph's body kept walking calmly towards the corner. He didn't look back as the crowd gathered to examine the runt, and by the time the shouting started, Joseph Tern had disappeared.

He was standing in the lounge room of his apartment, covered in sweat. He felt wrung out, but for the first time since he'd woke up that morning, something was different. He sent a command to his lips and the sound of his voice almost surprised him when it actually arrived on cue.

"What are you?"

Smug silence. No answer, but he could *feel* that smugness. That sleek self-satisfaction.

"How do you know all this stuff about me? Where I keep everything?"

Again, no answer. Perhaps the intruder had exhausted itself. Joseph looked around his apartment, surveying the mess it had left. He'd need to clean all this up. The intruder's recklessness was even more concerning than the fact it could mentally overpower him. He wasn't egotistical enough to think he couldn't succumb again, and he picked the trophies off the floor and placed them back in the wardrobe. A little more relaxed now, he closed his eyes and spoke again, mostly to prove he still could.

"What are you?"

I'm your conscience.

Joseph's eyes snapped open, startled to get a reply.

There was a knock at the door.

I wonder who that could be.

Another knock. Clearly not going anywhere.

Joseph walked over to the door. Composed himself. Opened the door. Smiled.

The cop smiled back. He didn't even ask to come in, simply walking past Joseph into the apartment. "Good morning, Mr Tern," he said. His voice had a Czech accent, so he was definitely local. The intruder in Joseph's head uncoiled a little as his mind raced. He knew the police were short-handed these days, but this guy was clearly someone to be reckoned with. He could already tell the cop was trying to rattle him, so he determined to play it cool.

"Won't you come in?"

The cop smiled at this. "I'm Sergeant Kladivo. Why do you think I'm here?"

"I presume word's got around: I'm an excellent kisser and still relatively cheap."

Kladivo smiled again. "Are you going to shut that door?"

Joseph did so. He tried to remember if there was anything incriminating lying around the apartment. He knew he was already in trouble, but there must be a reason he wasn't already in handcuffs. His heart-rate slowed and his mind began preparing a strategy...

Sweat broke out on his brow.

He wasn't hot.

Nor was he nervous.

But for some reason now he *looked* nervous... The intruder? Could it *do* that?

He considered wiping the sweat away, but figured that would merely draw attention to it. "So. What can I help you with, Sergeant?"

"Just a couple of questions, but can we start with a cup of tea?"

"Sure." Joseph walked to the kitchen, Kladivo watching him like a hawk.

The short knife was sitting on the kitchen table. Its blade still had the runt's blood all over it.

Joseph immediately stepped between Kladivo and the table so that he couldn't see the knife. He didn't stop moving, and he'd already figured out what he would do: he'd grab the knife and quietly put it in the sink while he filled up the kettle. When the kettle was full he'd leave the tap running and let the water clean the blade without raising any suspicion.

He reached for the knife, his body still blocking Kladivo's view.

His hand closed into a fist, refusing to pick it up.

Joseph stopped. Inwardly his mind began to seethe. The intruder *wanted* him to get caught, or at the very least it wanted him to *worry* about getting caught. That's what it likes, he thought, that's what it feeds on.

He willed himself to go *cold*, choking off the emotions it was feeding on.

His hand uncramped.

Relieved, he grabbed the knife and walked over to the sink. He picked up the kettle, using the action as a cover for him to let go of the knife.

His fingers refused to open.

Stupidly, he flicked his wrist a couple of times. The knife remained stubbornly in his hand. Then Kladivo's voice came from right behind him. "Everything all right, Mr Tern?"

"Sorry. It's my first time making a cup of tea."

"Thought so. You don't use a knife in my experience."

Had he seen the blade yet? The blood? He couldn't have, not in any detail. But if he should peer over Joseph's shoulder...

For just a moment he considered turning around and lashing out. The trouble was that Kladivo had already spotted the knife, and if Joseph had read him correctly, he'd be waiting for exactly this kind of incriminating move. Too risky, particularly when he couldn't trust his own body to do as he commanded. Instead, Joseph tried to open his fist one final time. Nothing. He put down the kettle, defeated. Deep inside his head, he thought he felt the intruder smile.

Joseph raised his other hand and deliberately slid his palm down the edge of the knife. Blood immediately began to trickle down the knife, commingling with the runt's. Joseph carefully flipped the blade over to ensure that he got his blood on both sides, and then he let out a perfectly spontaneous-sounding curse.

"What's wrong, Mr Tern?"

"I've managed to do something really stupid." He held up his bloody hand and Kladivo immediately reacted, looking around the kitchen for a towel. As he did so, Joseph put the knife in the sink. There was no problem letting go of it now, and he quickly turned on the tap and began running water over his wounded hand as well as the knife below. The thing in his head seemed to have withdrawn for now. He didn't know if the pain had driven it off, or whether it was simply waiting for its next opportunity. He'd figure that out later.

Kladivo had returned with a tea-towel and helped Joseph wrap his hand.

"You might have to make your own tea," said Joseph, sitting down at the table. Kladivo nodded slowly and switched on the kettle. As Joseph pointed out the cups and teabags, he quickly took mental inventory of all the other objects in the flat that might incriminate him. All of them were safely hidden for now...

"I need to talk to you about a murder," said Kladivo. Joseph's concentration snapped back into focus. The policeman was leaning against the bench, casually sipping his tea.

"So you weren't serious about the kiss?"

Kladivo smiled, but Joseph could see the steel behind it. He wasn't bantering anymore. "A man was killed nearby, earlier today."

"Really...?"

"And I did a little checking, little bit of reading. Record-keeping's not exactly a priority for the police these days, but I found some really interesting stuff about you. Page-turning stuff." He paused to sip his tea. "There's a girl you used to work with, a Hildy Davenport... From the records it looks like she disappeared a while ago."

"I remember, but I don't see..."

"And she's not the only one. This lab you used to work at... It seems that disappearing under, quote, mysterious circumstances, unquote, seems to be an occupational hazard. Do you remember a Lisa Carrigan?"

Joseph began to tread very carefully. "We were right on the edge of the rift," he explained hastily. "People went missing all the time."

"'All the time'?" Kladivo smiled and took another sip of tea. "Why did you leave Paris, Mr Tern?"

The conversational zig-zags were starting to make Joseph very uncomfortable. "Well, the lab was swallowed up by the Collision. We had to abandon it. I headed east..."

"Trouble seems to have followed you."

"I'm a security guard. That's *my* occupational hazard."

"Not *this* kind of trouble. I'm not talking about the ripped-apart-by-tooth-fish, or death-by-dreadful-scream kind of trouble. I'm talking about the classics. I'm talking old-fashioned, cold-blooded murder."

"I can honestly say I don..." Joseph stopped. He wanted to continue, but he couldn't.

"Yes?" Kladivo stared at him intently. Joseph casually shook his head, as if to indicate he had nothing further to say. He curled his lower lip between his teeth and held it there. Inside his head, Joseph began to worry. He wasn't doing this. With an effort, he managed to reassert himself.

"Sorry, feeling a bit light-headed." He held up his hand for sympathy. "I was saying I honestly don't know what you're implying. I liked Hildy. I was really upset when she disappeared."

"Were you?"

"Of course I was."

"I'll tell you what I think, Mr Tern..."

The intruder took hold of his lip again, curling it back between his teeth. Joseph tried to fight it, but he knew it would only look stranger if he really struggled, and so he finally let it go.

This proved to be a bad decision.

As Kladivo continued to speak, the intruder slowly bit down on Joseph's lip. He felt the pain sharpening until his lip popped just a little, and the taste of blood filled his mouth. Joseph attempted to surreptitiously wipe it away, but the intruder locked his hands at his sides and forced him to stare at Kladivo as the first shoots of blood began oozing down his chin.

Caught up in his monologue, Kladivo didn't immediately notice. More blood oozed from Joseph's mouth. He could feel a large drop hanging precariously on his chin, trembling with his inner tension. Finally it fell with a patter onto the kitchen table. It was a soft sound, but it made Kladivo refocus on Joseph's face and he immediately recoiled.

"Mr Tern...?"

The intruder held Joseph's tongue. He simply stared at Kladivo, the blood steadily dripping from his chin.

Kladivo grabbed another towel and with a minimum of fuss, held it to Joseph's lip. Joseph tried to take the towel from him, but his arms still refused to move. Realizing that Joseph seemed immobilized (and presumably thinking he must be having some kind of mental blackout), Kladivo dabbed at his face. "Are you all right? Can you hear me?"

The intruder let him go. "Sorry...?" Without a better option, Joseph coolly adopted the role of someone coming out of a haze. He took the proffered towel and wiped at his mouth. "You may have to excuse me, Sergeant. I seem to be having a bit of a day."

"Of course, Mr Tern."

Kladivo suddenly turned and walked back through the apartment. It happened so quickly that Joseph was caught off guard and struggled to keep up. Kladivo paused once before he reached the door, stopping for just the briefest of moments, but then he continued as if nothing had happened.

"I'll be in touch," he said, opening the door.

"I'm sorry about..."

But before he could finish, Kladivo was gone.

It took three minutes for Joseph to figure out what had caught the policeman's eye.

There was a tiny spot of blood on the carpet, still fresh.

It must have come from the knife he'd used to kill the runt. But would Kladivo be able to figure that out? After all, Joseph had been bleeding almost from the moment Kladivo had arrived thanks to the fucking intruder...

No. Only in the kitchen.

Kladivo was a watcher. He'd remember the sequence of events and he'd realize this spot of blood couldn't be Joseph's. Maybe he'd *already* figured that out. It wasn't a slam-dunk piece of evidence of course, but with a murder practically on Joseph's front doorstep, it certainly painted a convincing picture. Joseph had seen cops like Kladivo before, the type that just wouldn't let something go. He might be short-handed, but he'd be back, and he'd probably bring some kind of back-up with him. After all, that's what Joseph would do in his place.

"What are we going to do about this?" he said.

No reply.

Joseph didn't bother asking a second time. Instead, he began to attack the flat. Like a machine, he methodically tore through his collection of trophies and set them alight in the sink. It hurt him to do this, but he hadn't got this far by taking unnecessary risks. It was going to be hard enough to deal with a creature like this—there was no need to leave landmines lying around for it to deliberately step on when Kladivo returned.

We.

Joseph didn't stop moving, but he was glad the intruder was talking again. "We what?"

What makes you think we *are in this together?*

"An educated guess. You chose me for a reason."

True. You're not like all the other boys. He felt its hunger spike a little as it said that.

"I'm not from around here."

You came through the Collision?

"I did."

And you're an American?

"I am."

It seems we have more than a few things in common.

Joseph twisted the tap and watched the ashes of his trophies swirl away. "He'll be back soon," he said. "And he'll be bringing back-up." He felt the intruder squirm in delight. "Trust me, that's not a good thing. You're thinking short-term. He's not coming to put me in prison." He paused to let the intruder think about this. He knew it wanted him alive. "I can feel what you need. I can give you that. I can feed you. But you have to start thinking long-term."

Are you negotiating *with me?*

"I'm pointing out that we have... more than a few things in common."

And what's in it for you?

"Let's find out."

Joseph let his mind go *cold* again, a sudden sociopathic blankness. He felt the intruder shrivel under this knock-out punch, but he allowed himself to feel no triumph. Any emotion might feed it again. Instead, he simply began to probe at it, his cold mental fingertips turning it over, trying to understand it. If he could just...

The inside of his head imploded.

All light streaked off into blackness, all bodily sensations bled away.

His consciousness... fell.

No, it wasn't falling it was more *directed* than that. It was being whirled at incredible speeds and...

The essence of who he was smashed into the essence of the intruder.

There was no sound or impact, just a deep vibration at the core of him. For just a moment he could see his apartment again. There were new colours, swarming skins of bubbling particles and enormous *gaps* between every single object.

Then the darkness returned and he was whirled away again.

The intruder was trying to break him apart, to dominate him. Joseph wasn't sure why it had chosen this particular scenario to symbolize its attack, but he was already figuring out how to turn this to his advantage. He'd heard the scientists at the LHC talking about their experiments, about smashing particles together to create something new. If he could just keep himself together, could just work out how to perform the opposite of the intruder's strategy, then all this might just be worth...

Another shattering collision.

But this time... this time Joseph got a *taste* of the intruder. For another eternal moment he saw the quantum world, but he also felt the core of the creature, felt that he'd shaken something loose. A firework of memory sizzled through him. Suddenly Joseph remembered the Wraith Lights were waiting. He remembered staring into the heart of a great machine and seeing something *move*. He remembered pain and prison and the desperate need to be free. Most of all, he remembered why he'd come back through the rift.

Darkness again. Memory cut off. Spiralling off on another circuit.

Joseph could feel himself weakening. He couldn't take much more of this. This wasn't his battleground and this wasn't the way he liked to fight. But if he could figure out how to bend the rules just a little, even turn these memories to his own advantage, then perhaps he might survive.

He could feel the intruder getting closer. It was huge now, suckled on the milk he'd unwillingly fed it. He could tell it was determined to snuff him out. Everything up to this point was just preamble. Now it wanted full possession.

Joseph remembered talking to those scientists at the Collider. He remembered them explaining how a particle could simultaneously be a wave. It hadn't made logical sense at the time, but here in the realm of pure thought, Joseph's consciousness began to change. He imagined himself spreading out, unfurling as he hurtled towards the intruder. He imagined himself getting larger, expanding like an explosion of light...

...And somehow, this time there was no collision. Instead the light wrapped around the intruder like a fist.

Got smaller and smaller.

Disappeared.

Light began to drift back, like fireflies in the dark.

The apartment seeped back into focus as Joseph Tern opened his eyes. He smiled weakly. "That wasn't supposed to happen, was it?"

He breathed in deeply. He could feel the essence of the intruder inside him in a way that it hadn't been before. He wasn't possessed anymore, he was the possessor. The jailer.

He looked around the apartment with weird double vision. He could see how things used to be, but now he could see the gaps as well, could feel where they were. This must be how the intruder saw the world. He reached out his hand and watched the dance of molecules on his fingertips.

I remember...

Joseph smiled at the weakness of the intruder's voice. "What do you remember?"

I remember... who I am now. Sweet Moses, I remember what I'm supposed... to do...

"Good for you."

There was a long silence, and then the intruder said, *I'm going to need your help.*

"Are you *negotiating* with me?"

I am. Because I think you'll need my *help.*

"And why's that?"

There was a knock on the door.

Joseph's head snapped around. He could hear murmurings in the corridor outside. It wasn't just Kladivo this time.

You've got me trapped in here, but without me, I don't think you can get out alive. You need me and you need what I can make you do.

Joseph closed his eyes, and then smiled again. He didn't bother to argue. He could see the logic of the intruder's bargain, and if he was honest with himself, he wanted to see what would happen next. "OK," he said. "I feed you and you let me access your… skills."

Sounds like a plan.

Joseph Tern walked across his lounge room and placed his hand on the door handle. He could feel the vibrating particles beneath his fingers and with just a little effort he suddenly pulled his hand *through* the handle in exactly the same way he'd pulled it through Hildy's hair four years ago.

The sensation was exquisite.

The intruder immediately began to feed on his delight. Joseph smiled, savouring the moment. Then he jerked the door open.

Kladivo stood, his hand still raised to knock. Behind him were three more big guys. None of them looked like cops, so Joseph presumed that Kladivo had deputized them just for this afternoon's work. One carried a knife, and the other two had riot batons. They probably figured that would be enough to subdue just one murder suspect, and any other day they would have been right.

Joseph grabbed Kladivo, and by the time the policeman had opened his mouth to scream, Joseph's fist was already three quarters of the way towards his face. But rather than impacting upon his cheek, Joseph's hand passed between the gaps of Kladivo's face and stopped at the back of his throat where the scream was just being born. He could feel the vibration of the sound and pinched his fingers together savagely. The scream was snuffed out.

Joseph spun the policeman around and threw him against the wall of the corridor. Before any of Kladivo's cohorts could save him, Joseph began to *push*, finding the gaps in the wall and sliding the policeman's squirming body in between them. Just as Kladivo opened his mouth to scream again, Joseph let him go and it was as if the wall *set*. Kladivo instantly choked as his throat filled with plaster and woodchip, and the parts of his body that were still visible shivered as the last of his life spasmed away.

The remaining trio didn't stand a chance. They stood horrified, staring at what Joseph had done, and before any of them could run, he pounced on them.

The first was simply pushed head-first into the wall, disappearing up to his shoulders.

The second tripped and Joseph stepped on his outstretched hand, forcing his hand into the gaps in the floor and effectively anchoring him on the quantum level.

The third threw a punch, but his hand simply passed through the gaps in Joseph's jaw, and by the time he'd gotten over his surprise, Joseph had already reached into his head and with the tiniest flick of his finger popped open a blood vessel. He turned around before the aneurysm had completed its work and smiled at the terrified survivor. He was hauling at his hand like an animal in a trap, begging in Czech. Joseph placed his foot on the man's forehead and pressed down, forcing him backwards onto the carpet. Then he began to push, listening to the sobbing as the man's head slowly began to disappear beneath the surface of the floor, feeling the gaps ease around his body like a snake's jaws.

Then he took his foot away. The sobs cut off like a switch had been thrown.

Joseph breathed out, letting the surge of his emotions come back under control, but still allowing the intruder to feed on the massive discharge of pain, fear and excitement that hung in the air like electricity. He could feel it rearranging itself inside him, its hunger satiated. They'd worked like one organism, their violence co-ordinated, reflexive, artistic. Joseph could tell the intruder was pleased, and both of them knew instinctively that this was just the beginning.

"OK partner," he said. "Maybe now's the time to tell me: what's that thing you're supposed to be doing?"

WHAT LITTLE BOYS ARE MADE OF
by Nicholas Blake

I ask Lilbet when Mommy and Daddy will get home and she just says *soon* like she always says. This makes me cry a little bit until she takes me into the fort we made in my bedroom out of the two chairs and the sheet and we feed Peregrine the Elephant marshmallows and the marshmallows make him sneeze. I laugh and feel better even though it's been ages since Mommy left to try and find out why Daddy had taken two days at the grocery store.

Daddy had gone to the grocery store because the TV said everyone was going because of the Big Hole In The Ground appearing, which has made a lot of people very hungry and want to buy as much food as possible. I don't like the grocery store much because it's very boring and I get scared of the fish at the fish counter staring at me with their eyes and their mouths wide open like they're surprised to see me. I think that's why Mommy was so worried about Daddy being at the grocery store for two days, because of him having to sleep there with those dead fish staring at him with their googly eyes.

"There's nothing to worry about, sweetheart," she kept on saying as she was trying to hug me and Lilbet and put her coat and shoes on and turn the TV off which was showing people talking about the Big Hole again. She also had a lot of things to say to Lilbet which I wasn't meant to hear but Peregrine and me hid behind the couch without them knowing and we heard Mommy telling Lilbet that she'd only be twenty minutes and not to open the door to anyone and that she would phone the house if there were any problems and to look after me and make sure that I was okay. Peregrine was a bit upset because Mommy didn't mention him but I hugged him and whispered that I'd look after him and then he felt better.

After Mommy left, Lilbet stood on a chair and got down the cookie jar and we ate some cookies and then we bounced around on our beds and watched some TV. Then I had a nap on the couch and then Lilbet woke me up and we stared at the door until eventually Lilbet put me to bed and when we woke up the next day Mommy still wasn't home.

Lilbet says it's okay and that Mommy and Daddy will be home "soon", she just says "soon" like she always says.

Twenty minutes is the longest time ever.

There used to be lots of people outside, running around and shouting a lot like in recess at school, but now it's quiet and there's no-one around except for the cats and the people who are so tired they've gone to sleep on the road. Lilbet says I shouldn't stare at them in case I wake them up because then they'll be all grouchy and angry at me so I don't. But I still like looking out the window sometimes.

Today there's a cat standing out in the yard, scratching at the ground and mewing. Lilbet said we are to hide if we see one in case we scare them, because they get scared very easily, but this one is a lot prettier than the other cats so I think I'll draw a picture of it. I'm not sure where my crayons are at first because I thought I left them under the table in the kitchen but then I find them in a drawer all put back in the packet in the right order, like a rainbow. Sometimes Lilbet takes all the crayons and draws an upside down U with them all at once. It's very pretty when she does that. I try to do it now but my hands are too small and I drop some of them so the rainbow looks far too red and there's not enough blue and green and yellow, and it ends up just looking like a big angry face and not like a rainbow, not even a little bit.

I go back to the window and hide behind the curtain, just peeking a tiny bit round the side so I can see the cat but also so it can't see me and get scared and run away. It's hard to draw all its tentacles right because they keep on moving, and the way it drools as it tries to eat the climbing frame makes me giggle a bit, but not too much in case it hears me.

I don't quite have the right green crayon to color in the cat but I do the best I can, and then I go to find Lilbet to show her what I've done. At first she seems upset that the cat may have seen me, but I tell her that I hid and that it had no idea I was there and it wasn't in the least bit scared of me, and she seems better and tells me it's a great drawing but she doesn't understand what the thing in the sky is, even after looking out of the window to check, so I have to tell her how it's meant to be a rainbow but it came out wrong.

"At the end of a rainbow there's always a pot of gold," she tells me.

"What's at the end of the Big Hole in the Ground?" I ask.

"Another country," says Lilbet, "where all the cats came from."

"Is there a Walmart there?" I ask.

Lilbet looks doubtful for a second before saying that there probably is.

"Do you think that's where Mommy and Daddy went, then?"

"I suppose they may have gone to that one instead of the one down the road," Lilbet says, but she's frowning a bit.

I turn the TV on but it's gone away. There used to be people talking about the Big Hole In The Ground, but now there's just some writing I can't read and a beeping sound like a computer which is trying to hum a tune but doesn't remember how it goes. I ask Lilbet what the writing on the TV is saying and she says it's a story about me and Peregrine and she'll tell it me, so I get Peregrine so he can hear it too because if he knew there was a story about him on TV and he missed it he would be very grumpy. So we sit and listen to Lilbet tell us the TV story and it's a good story and then when it's done Lilbet turns off the TV and it's all quiet again.

I'm hungry so I find Lilbet and she goes to see what food there is except there isn't any cookies anymore and there isn't any marshmallows either but she stands on a chair and gets the bread from the cupboard and makes me a peanut butter and jelly sandwich and it's my favourite sandwich and I eat it all. As I'm eating it, Lilbet is getting out some cans of food which you need the special can opener to open. Lilbet tries but it doesn't work because you have to be a grown up to use the can opener but she keeps on trying and it still doesn't work. But Lilbet says it's okay because we don't even want to eat the food in the cans anyway so that's okay and I know it's okay because Lilbet says it's okay so that's good.

BANG! goes the front door. BANG! BANG!

That was three. I quite like the number three, but I wish there would be six. Six is a much better number because it is my favourite number because it is how old I am. Daddy used to laugh at me when I said that, and he'd ask what my favourite number would be when I turned seven, but I'm not sure I want to turn seven because I'm not sure I'll be very good at it. I think I will stay six for a bit longer.

When Mommy and Daddy lived here lots of people would come to the door and Mommy or Daddy would open it and talking would happen. Sometimes it would be Mrs Waxstaff from down the road who I don't like because she has weird eyebrows and her moustache tickles when she kisses you. Or Daddy's friend Uncle Tom who bounces you on his bony knee but it's okay because afterwards he gives you candy.

Now that Mommy and Daddy aren't here anymore we're not supposed to open the door, but not everybody can know that because they still ask to come in.

BANG! goes the front door, again.

The first time someone came to the door after Mommy and Daddy left I asked Lilbet if we should open the door to let them in in case they wanted to hug us and give us candy, but Lilbet said we shouldn't in case it turns out to be Mrs Waxstaff. Lilbet is cleverer than me and thinks of these things.

And anyway, Lilbet pointed out, it was just Mr Mailman at the door, and we shouldn't worry about it.

I asked Lilbet if we could open the door and say hello to him but she said we mustn't because he's allergicked to kids and if he sees us his head will swell up and his eyes will go all red and Mrs Mailman will be cross with us, and she's more scary than three Mrs Waxstaffs all on top of each other.

BANG! BANG!

That's six! The perfect number! No more, Mr Mailman, please. He must know what I'm thinking because it goes all quiet and I peep through the window and watch him skip down the road, swinging his flaky arms in a silly way as he walks.

I promise to hug Peregrine tight tonight in case he's scared of the thought of three Mrs Waxstaffs on top of each other trying to triple kiss him with their eyebrows all wriggling. He gets easily scared, you see.

I want another peanut butter and jelly sandwich but Lilbet won't give me one and says that we have to play a new game and I don't like this new game but Lilbet says we have to play it. She calls it "rat-shuns" and it's stupid and we have to just eat little bits of food and save some food which we want for later. Lilbet says that the peanut butter and jelly sandwiches will taste better if I don't have them every day and then she stands on a chair and puts the bread up high in a cupboard where I can't get to it. Then she finds some crackers in the cupboard and she lets me eat three of them with some cheese from the fridge and it's nice but I really want a sandwich. Then I say that Peregrine hasn't had any and what if he goes hungry so she gives Peregrine a cracker with some cheese on too but when she's not looking I eat it myself and Peregrine looks at me funny and I don't want him looking at me funny so I put him behind the couch for a bit until he forgets I ate his food for him. Then I get him out again and he's forgotten and we're friends again. He forgets things quickly, which is good.

Lilbet is underneath the curtain looking out the window. I get under it too to remind her that she said we weren't to look out of the window.

"I was looking at the smoke," she says. "Do you see it?"

And I do look and yes there is this gray smoke appearing in our yard. Lilbet says it must be coming from a fire and I ask if it's a house burning down and she says no, it'll just be from the people next door having a barbeque. I didn't think the people next door would be having a barbeque because recently all they've wanted to do is lie down in their back yard in funny positions, but Lilbet knows things better than me so I believe her.

The smoke gets bigger and bigger and soon we can hardly see anything outside. We run, giggling, from window to window looking out but it's like there aren't windows any more just sheets of gray paper, though if I screw up my eyes then I can see a little bit of our climbing frame. It looks like a ghost climbing frame for ghost children to play on. I hope I get to be a ghost one day.

Just then I think I see something moving in the smoke and I'm afraid in case it's The Three Headed Mrs Waxstaff Monster, but it turns out to be a tiny fish thing with massive teeth swimming through the air, so that's okay. But then there's a hundred of them and they're heading for the window and Lilbet grabs me and pulls me back and we fall backwards as the fish teeth things hit the window. THUD! THUD! THUD! THUD! THUD! They look confused for a second then swim away through the smoke. I'm crying a bit and Lilbet gives me a big hug and tells me not to be scared because the Toothfishies are only there because we're about to play at being pirates, fierce pirates sailing the piranha infested high seas. Only land lubbers get scared of Toothfishy piranha things, not us, yo ho ho.

And so we hoist the anchor and man the main brace and set sail across the high seas stealing treasure and capturing Peregrine as our prisoner. Captain Lilbet tried to make him walk the plank and be eaten by the flying Toothfishies but he looks sad so I give him a hug instead and he joins our motley crew and Lilbet makes him an eye patch out of some colored paper and an elastic band and we do a lot of yo ho ho-ing which is the sound pirates make, and also Santa, I think.

The next day the smoke goes away and there are no more flying Toothfishies. Lilbet declares our pirating days to be over and we become land lubbers again which means Peregrine has to take off his patch and we're not allowed to do any more yo ho ho-ing any more. I decide I will secretly still say yo ho ho to myself anyway, only quietly so Lilbet can't hear me.

Lilbet says I have to finish eating the crackers today and then I can have a peanut butter and jelly sandwich again tomorrow as a special treat. I really want the peanut butter and jelly sandwich now but I have to eat the crackers because Lilbet said I had to. So I eat the crackers but there's no cheese with them and they taste really dry and I'm still hungry afterwards. Lilbet gives me some of her crackers as well and I eat them too but I'm still hungry and Lilbet tries again to open the cans of food with a knife from the drawer but it doesn't work because the cans are made of super strong metal but she says it's okay and that I can have a sandwich again tomorrow and I look forward to my sandwich. It'll be delicious. It's hard to sleep because I have a hungry in my tummy.

I wake up feeling really tired and I go to find Lilbet but she won't get out of bed she just lies there and tells me to go away. I tell her I'm hungry and she doesn't answer and I tell her again louder and she turns to face the other way and I tell her again much louder and she yells at me to go away and leave her alone. I run away because she's horrid and I hate her and I hate everything especially Peregrine because he's stupid and I take Peregrine and I shout "go away Peregrine leave me alone" and I throw him across the living room and he falls behind the couch and then I sit on the floor and cry a bit and then suddenly the TV turns itself on and there's this horrible screechy noise like when Mommy's in the dentist's chair and hasn't been cleaning her teeth properly.

I try to stop the noise from getting into my ears using my fingers but it's no good it's so loud. Lilbet runs in and turns the TV off and tells me off for turning it on so loud but it wasn't me, it turned itself on! She doesn't believe me and is getting angry at me and I think I'm going to cry again but then there is a ringing sound. The phone is ringing!

Lilbet looks at me and laughs and then she runs to the phone and she picks it up and she puts it to her ear and she says hello into it, and then she has to hold it away from her ear again because there's that screechy sound like from the TV and it's really loud, I can hear it even though I'm on the other side of the room. Then the screech goes and there's some other noise and Lilbet puts the phone to her ear again and her eyes are getting bigger and wider and I think I can hear a person's voice on the end of the phone, a really deep voice, and her eyes are getting wider and wider and she's looking really scared and then the voice sounds like it's laughing and screaming and Lilbet slams the phone down and runs out of the room.

I find her in her bedroom back in bed again and I'm a bit nervous to talk to her so I find Peregrine from behind the couch and he's a bit grumpy so I say sorry to him and then I take him to Lilbet and she gives him a hug and I ask her who it was on the phone and she wipes her face and says that it was Mommy on the phone, and that she and Daddy are going to be home soon, and that they send their love. And then I get in bed with Lilbet and Peregrine and we all have a cuddle and it's nice except the hungry in my tummy is getting bigger.

I hear a strange sound and I don't know what it is and it scares me and it's coming from the kitchen and I look in there and it turns out the strange sound is Lilbet and she's on the floor. In front of her is the bread and it's also on the floor and it's gone all green with mold and she's crying and she sees me and she's crying even more and she's saying she's sorry, she's so sorry, she should have let me have a peanut butter and jelly sandwich before and it's too late now because the bread has gone off. It's all gone green and there's no peanut butter and jelly sandwich for me to eat now and there's no other food now because all the food is gone now apart from what's in the cans and we can't open the cans. She picks up a can and she starts throwing it at the ground and the can dents a bit but it doesn't open and she's still sobbing and she's still throwing the can and it's still not opening and she keeps sobbing more and I get scared and I take the jar of peanut butter and I run and find Peregrine. We go hide in the fort and I eat the peanut butter with my fingers until it's all gone but I'm still so hungry and I want more and I want to watch proper TV which isn't screechy noises and I want Lilbet to stop crying so much and none of those things are happening, none of them are happening not even a little bit.

We're going on a trip outside! I thought we weren't allowed, but it's a special treat, Lilbet says, because I've been such a good boy. I'm really excited and I ask if we can go to the zoo and see the scary animals, but Lilbet says we have to go to the grocery store first, and I get a bit scared but she says that she'll protect me from the dead fish with the googly eyes, so that's okay.

She puts on my coat and hat and gloves and then we put Peregrine's hat on too, and then we wait listening at the front door for ages before she opens it a tiny bit and looks out, and then she makes me stop singing while she listens for something. I don't know what she's listening for because I can't hear anything at all but silence. The silence is really loud. After ages she says that we can go, so we do, and she puts a toy car in the doorway so the door won't close and we can get back inside, which is quite clever really.

It's nice to get to go outside again but it feels a bit weird as though the air is fizzing, like when Daddy takes your sweater off too quickly and it all crackles around your ears. It's all sunny even though there are gray clouds and I get a bit excited and start skipping and at first Lilbet tells me to stop but then she decides to skip too so we skip down the sidewalk towards the grocery store and there's nobody else about at all because they must have got all their bread earlier and already they're inside their houses eating peanut butter and jelly sandwiches.

I tell Lilbet that I can't wait to see Mommy and Daddy again, and she's quiet for a moment before agreeing that they will probably be at the grocery store, but if they're not, someone there may be able to tell us where they've gone to. I ask Lilbet what we're going to buy at the grocery store, and she says that we can't buy anything because we don't have any money, but hopefully they'll let us have some things and Mommy and Daddy will pay them back when they return.

"What if they don't let us take anything without money, though?" I ask Lilbet, and she doesn't say anything and we carry on walking down the sidewalk until we see that there's some kind of lumpy moving thing up ahead.

Lilbet stops and says we have to cross the road, but I want to see what it is so walk forward a bit more, and I see that it's one of those people lying on the road having a sleep, and the moving things are just these two cats. I yell at Lilbet to come closer to see the cats kissing a sleeping person, and Lilbet hurries forward but she's trying to pull me back. Then I see that the sleeping person is someone I know, and then I realize it's Mrs Waxstaff, and she's not sleeping at all, her eyes are wide open, staring, like the googly eyed fish in the grocery store, and now I'm scared, really scared, and the cats stop licking her with the tentacles and they start walking towards Lilbet and me. I'm not sure what to do because I'm not sure I want to play with the cats any more, but then there's this yell and this man runs out of a house and he's waving a baseball bat and the cats turn and look at him and he's yelling at us to run, run as quickly as we can, and we do but we run in different directions, and there's a cat between us and it's mewing and Lilbet is screaming and the man is yelling too and there's more cats appearing and they start leaping at the man and he falls over and the cat in front of me makes a funny sound and spits booger goo at me and I hold Peregrine up over my face and it all goes on Peregrine and Peregrine starts fizzing and I drop him and there's smoke coming from him as he melts away and I start running and running and running and it starts raining really hard but I don't stop even though I don't know where I'm going and I keep running away and when I do stop running I look back there's nobody there it's just an empty street and there's no baseball bat man and there's no cats and there's no Lilbet, there's just me.

I want to go home
    I want to go home
    I want to go home
    But which way is home?
    Lilbet would know if she was here, but she's not.
    But Lilbet said that the people in the road were sleeping and that the cats were afraid of us and that the Toothfishy things were piranhas and that we were pirates hunting for gold and saying yo ho ho and I try saying yo ho ho but it's no fun anymore and there's no point in being a pirate now because I want to go home and pirates don't have a home, they just live on a ship and try to find gold and there isn't any gold here, you only get gold at the end of a rainbow.

And I look up into the rain and there is a big upside-down multicolor grin in the sky and I have nothing else to do but follow it so I do.

Lilbet was wrong about there being a pot of gold at the end of a rainbow, because at the end of a rainbow is our house.

I let myself in and walk quickly to the bedroom, trying to avoid the faces pressed up against the window, all the staring eyes of the sleeping street people watching me. All our neighbors are there, as well as Mrs Waxstaff and Uncle Tom, and the man with the baseball bat. Some have bits of their heads missing, or skin coming off, their hands patting at the glass.

Please don't let Mommy or Daddy be at the windows. Please don't let them be there, I don't want them to be outside, I don't, I want them to be inside, with me. I screw up my eyes tight as I get into my bed and pull the covers over my head to block out the glassy stares but nothing hides me anymore and I can still see them and they can still see me.

I wake as a lady enters my bedroom. She looks a bit like my mom but her clothes are dirty and torn and a lot of her hair is missing and she's trying to clutch me in her arms but I leap out of bed quickly and I back into the corner and I scream, scream at her to leave me alone, to get away from me, and she stops and she stares, and I think she's going to cry, and my sister is there and she's clutching the lady's leg, fighting back tears.

And then the lady stops, and holds out this raggy bit of cloth she has been holding, and she says, "Look, look I found

Peregrine, here he is," and I notice a bit of trunk and an eye in the cloth which is all that is left of him.

No, not him. It. My old toy.

She speaks again, "I found him and I thought it meant that you were gone, but you're not, you're safe, you're here, but we've got to go, I only just managed to get away, they'll be back to look for us soon, we have to leave, we have to move on, quickly, please, my darling, my lovely, my little boy, please..."

And I stare at her and we're silent and then I ask her where my dad is.

She swallows. "He..." She stops. Then tries again. "He'll...catch up with us later, my darling, he'll be with us...later..."

And I look at her eyes, and I look at my sister's eyes, and she isn't looking at me, she can't look at me, and she's crying properly now, silent tears running down her face.

"I don't believe you," I say, and I'm not crying any more, I'm not crying even a little bit.

BEYOND THE SEA
by Dave Hutchinson

The Strongman's goons were in the habit of raiding Sarkozytown in the wee small hours of the morning. They came in out of the pre-dawn gloom on quad-bikes and armoured dune buggies, engines blaring, loudspeakers pumping out death metal and Rodgers and Hammerstein show tunes, rousting residents and setting fire to tents and benders and lean-tos.

It was a tactic as old as human conflict—strike when the enemy is asleep, when their mental and physical alertness is at its lowest, do not give them any opportunity to rest. Unfortunately for the Strongman, Marlowe was savvy to this and had organized Sarkozytown's residents in shifts—some sleeping by day so that they would be alert when the raids came, others standing guard in the daylight. It took some discipline, but the people adored Marlowe. He had led them across the sea, out of harm's way. They would have done anything for him.

The Strongman was certainly strong, but he was not terribly bright. Someone smarter would have hit the refugee encampment at varying times of the day or night, kept the residents off-guard. But the Strongman was wedded to a certain course of behaviour. Some said he had studied military tactics at Sandhurst, and he thought he was being crafty and psychological. He thought he would wear down the foreigners, drive them out of his country. He did not—because he hadn't been in France during the Collision, or Barcelona during the Scream—quite understand just how desperate they were.

So the goons—they wore police combat suits, plastered with sponsor logos, but they were just goons—came in every morning, around four, and every morning their convoy of vehicles roared past the villa and woke the Poor Girl to another day in Hell.

Not that she slept much anyway. The headaches and the visions made sure of that. But sometimes exhaustion built up to a point where she could snatch a couple of dazed hours, although more often than not the dreams woke her if the passing goons did not.

Bringing her here, the demons had hooded her, but her struggles had briefly dislodged it, and she knew that she was in a villa on the edge of the city. She had felt herself being carried, not very gently, down a flight of stairs, so she was definitely in the villa's basement. The room she was in was white. Someone had used an industrial paint sprayer to put down layers of blinding white paint on everything—walls, ceiling, floor, furniture. Light came from ten portable lamps arranged on the floor around the edges of the room, their beams trained on her. The chair she sat on had been ballistic-bolted to the floor. It had been custom-built by welding thick lengths of square-section steel tubing together. Her ankles were bound to the legs with cable-ties, and her wrists to the armrests. Another cable-tie looped around her neck and through the bars of the chair's backrest, holding her upright.

She had been sitting here for many hours. Days, perhaps. The demons would not free her to use the lavatory, so she sat in her own filth. But that was not the worst thing. Not by some considerable distance.

Footsteps on the stairs. A key being turned in the lock. The door opened and the demon-she-could-see stepped through. He looked at her and smiled.

"Shall we have some fun?" he asked.

This time it was the cloth. The demon-she-could-see picked her up and strapped her to a solid dining table, which stood in one corner of the room. She was too weak to struggle. He watched her face as he did up the buckles, jerking them tight against her raw wrists and ankles. Then he laid a cloth over her face. Knowing what was coming, she took a deep breath and held it. She heard him reach under the table for the watering-can, and then she felt the first dribbles of water on the cloth over her face.

"Say yes," he said softly. "Just say yes and I'll stop."

She wasn't going to say yes. She closed her eyes and clenched her fists as the wet cloth moulded itself to her face. After an eternity, she had to release her breath, and when she tried to breathe in again there was no air, only the patient pattering of water against her face, and she started to struggle weakly against the straps.

The demon-she-could-see had done this to her three times now. She thought she might have died the second time, because when she came back to her senses she was sitting in the chair again and her chest felt bruised, as if someone had been giving her CPR. Later, she heard the demon-she-could-not-see muttering angrily, berating its host for going too far. She thought she heard it now, urging him to be careful, be careful, *not too much*...

There was nothing. No air. She felt herself start to convulse against the straps, but it went on and on and there were only the two voices, fading away down a great tunnel. "Say yes...say yes..."

Scott opened his eyes and lay staring up at the stained concrete ceiling of the bunker, waiting for the images to subside. He smelled coffee brewing, and cigarette smoke, and sweat. He heard quiet conversation over on the other side of the room. He checked his watch. Half past nine in the morning.

Finally, he unzipped his sleeping bag and sat up painfully. He'd padded the hard floor with layers of flattened cardboard boxes but it was still rather less comfortable than a spring mattress. He got up, stretched and went over to where two of Natalie's team were crouching around a little catalytic stove, on top of which stood a two-stage metal flask. He nodded good morning to the soldiers, poured himself a mug of coffee from the flask, and walked across to the other side of the room.

Natalie and RSM Spicer were deep in discussion about something. They were sitting on upturned plastic crates and they were examining a sheaf of notes and diagrams and hand-drawn maps spread out on top of a third crate.

"Morning," said Natalie, her Belfast accent always making her sound more cheery first thing in the morning than she usually was. "Sleep well?"

"You are joking, right?" Scott settled himself on the floor and sipped his coffee. He nodded at the documents. "What's that?"

Natalie shook her head tiredly. "Nothing. Something. We don't know, do we, Sarn't Major?"

Spicer was a compact plug of a man with skin tanned the colour of a granary loaf. He had a faint bristle of a moustache, the hands of a watchmaker, the grace of a ballroom dancer and the eyes of a mass murderer. He adored Natalie, and refused to let her out of his sight.

"We don't, Miss," he said in his gentle, weary voice. "Something or nothing. We can't tell any more." Spicer offered him a ration bar, but Scott shook his head. He never liked to eat breakfast.

Scott rubbed his face, felt days and days of stubble under his palm. He couldn't remember the last time he'd managed to have a wash, but it didn't matter because they all smelled the same now. They'd been out in the field for weeks, on what Natalie described as an intelligence-gathering mission, in the course of which they had gathered precious little intelligence but lost four men.

"Can I have a word in private, please?" he asked.

Natalie and Spicer exchanged glances. She gave the merest nod, and Spicer got up and went over to the stove. Natalie looked at Scott and shrugged. "I'm all ears, Mr Fletcher."

Scott thought she looked terrible, right on the ragged edge of exhaustion. As well she might. Of the four men who had died on this mission, they had lost three the day before, to a thing that looked like an old-style English pillar-box, apart from its eight legs, mouth like the gaping maw of a wood chipper, and venom-barbed tail. Only a lucky shot straight down the throat with an RPG had brought it down. It was a miracle they weren't all stark raving mad.

"I think I know where he is," he said.

She sat up a little straighter. No need to ask who he was talking about. "You're sure?"

As sure as I can be. "He's somewhere in North Africa," he said. "In a large town, maybe a city." He paused. "He's got a young girl."

Natalie raised her eyebrows. "A young girl?"

"Maybe thirteen years old. Fourteen at the most. He's torturing her."

She watched his face. "You're sure about this?" she asked again.

He sighed. "He's trying not to inflict permanent damage, but he's *waterboarding* her." He looked into her eyes.

Her expression changed and she sat back a little. "Oh, you're not *serious*," she said quietly.

"She's important to him somehow," he said. "Or important to the thing in his head. Or to both of them, I don't know." He shuddered. The clash of the killer and the phantom had rung out so clearly in Scott's tortured mind that he'd screamed for ten days straight. That had been a year ago, but the memory was still raw. "I know him, Natalie. If she wasn't important he'd be..." He stopped. Looked around the room, the old Cold War bunker outside Toulouse they'd found the night before, defensible against nightmares. Physical ones anyway. He took another sip of coffee. "She's important to him," he said again. He looked at Natalie. "So she's important to *us*."

She never took her eyes off him while she thought about it. Finally, she shook her head. "No," she said. "I'm going to need more than that. You don't know where in North Africa he is. And I have no idea how you know *that*."

That makes two of us. "If I could get closer, maybe..."

"No." She shook her head again, gathered the documents off the crate in front of her, and stood up. "I can't authorize a deployment to North Africa, Mr Fletcher. We already have a mission. Sarn't Major Spicer!" This last with a snap of authority in her voice.

"Miss?" Spicer called from the other side of the bunker.

"We're moving out. Ten minutes."

"Yes, miss."

Natalie looked down at Scott. "Ten minutes," she said, and turned and walked away.

She'd had a name, once upon a time. And logic told her that she'd had a mother and father. But those things were misty, vague. Unreliable memories. Something she saw in a film, maybe.

She'd grown up in an orphanage, where nuns had tried to beat Godliness into her. It hadn't taken. As soon as she was old enough she was climbing the big old pear tree that grew up against the wall of the orphanage, dropping over the other side, and exploring the streets. The shopkeepers and traders and denizens of the *demi-monde* all grew to know her. Poor Girl, they called her. An expression of pity, initially, but eventually it became a badge of honour, a defining of who she was. For she *was* poor. The only thing she had, in the whole world, was Omar.

Maybe he really was her brother. Or at least half-brother—his skin was much darker than hers, there was a look of the North African coast about him, while she was pale and fair and blue-eyed. Such a little beauty, they called her. Whatever. She and Omar had arrived at the orphanage together, ostensible siblings, and she loved him with a fierce pride.

Most of her forays over the wall—each stoutly punished by the Holy Sisters—were for Omar's benefit. She became quite the expert little thief, stealing trinkets to bring back for him. Nothing of great value—stuffed toys, little shiny beads with holograms of cartoon animals at their hearts—but they delighted the little boy and his smile was sunshine that lightened her heart.

For the nuns, though, such excursions were intolerable. The tree was cut down, local shopkeepers and police alerted to watch out for the Poor Girl. She learned to climb the rough stones of the wall itself—the nuns couldn't bring that down—and was brought back, again and again, to face beatings.

Finally, the orphanage authorities reasoned that the only way to bring this madness to an end was to remove the cause of it. If she absconded in order to steal things for her brother, they would remove her brother.

She got wind of the plan one day when she was being more than usually stubborn in class. Sister Anunciata brought her out to the front, told her to hold out her hand, and gave her two sharp, stinging slaps with the wooden ruler she kept about her person for such punishment. She bore the blows silently, without flinching, which enraged the nun.

As the Poor Girl went insolently back to her seat, Sister Anunciata, red-faced with fury, yelled, "You won't be so clever when that little half-caste bastard's gone!"

The Poor Girl paused, for perhaps half a beat, between footsteps, before carrying on back to her desk.

That night, she broke into Mother Superior's office, using a key she had stolen from Sister Maria-Assumpta. She stole four thousand euros from Mother Superior's safe and the spare set of master keys, which she used to enter the boys' dormitory and wake Omar. The little boy was confused and a little weepy when she told him what they were doing—he liked the orphanage—but he trusted her with all the unconditional love of a five-year-old, and, when she was eight years old, she took her brother out into the night and the great wide world.

For the next two days, the team trundled east towards Carcassonne. The countryside here was mostly clear, though they paused to burn out a nest of toothfish that had established itself in an abandoned filling station, and once they saw, far off in the distance, seven gasbags sailing serenely across the Northern sky.

They stopped every ten kilometres to deploy the scientific equipment. They spent an hour taking readings of air quality and composition, radiation, magnetic field strength, soil and vegetation samples, a dozen more tests. Then they moved on.

It was, Scott thought, rather beautiful. The countryside was deserted, save for the occasional farmer too stubborn to flee. Fields and woodland were growing wild; roadways were cracking for lack of maintenance. A huge and very profound silence seemed to have settled over this part of Europe. Had it not been for the need for constant vigilance, and the dreams — of the young girl and other things — it would have been an enormously pleasant time.

On the third day he was standing beside the road during a sampling stop. He was drinking a cup of coffee and eating a granola bar when Natalie climbed down from the command vehicle, looked around for a moment, saw him, and started to march purposely over. Scott finished his granola bar and washed it down with a mouthful of coffee.

Natalie walked right up to him and looked him in the eye and didn't say a word. He stared back at her. After a few moments, she cocked her head to one side and looked past him towards the West. Scott turned. He drained his cup.

Up in the clear, depthless sky were nine little black dots, growing larger moment by moment as they approached.

"I'm very cross with you," Natalie said.

"Yes," said Scott.

"You called Command."

"Yes."

"You asked Sergeant Breillat — who is now Private Breillat, by the way — to contact Command on the comms net and you went over my head."

"Yes."

They could hear the sound of engines in the sky now, a low thrumming. "Well, you got your way, sort of."

He glanced at her. "Sort of?"

"We're being redeployed. One of the research stations has picked up a signal from the Collision." She took a pair of sunglasses from the breast pocket of her jacket and put them on. She crossed her arms.

Scott wasn't surprised. "What kind of signal?"

She shrugged. "Morse code. An SOS. You heard it too, didn't you?"

"Yes."

"And you didn't say anything to me because you want to go after Tern, am I right?"

"We've got to—"

Natalie smiled a thin-lipped smile. "Relax, Scott. Captain Carrigan and his team are going to check it out. Skeleton crews will take the scientists and the vehicles back to base. You, Sarn't Major Spicer, four of the boys and me, are going to Narbonne. We've got control of the civilian airport there. We'll fly to Cairo. You get your wish."

They stood and watched the helicopters approaching, two passenger choppers and seven gunships, all in the colours of the International Stabilization Group.

"Who is Carrigan?" Scott asked at last. The name was familiar.

"He's good. If someone needs rescuing, he'll pull it off. I want you to talk to him before he goes. Tell him everything you know about this beacon."

"Did he lose someone?"

"His wife, yeah. Lisa, I think her name was."

A vision—a memory of a vision—surfaced. An easy smile with crooked teeth. A pretty face with large blue eyes. A twisted scream of agony and disbelief... Scott felt an overwhelming sadness. He quickly changed the subject. "It wasn't Breillat's fault, you know?"

"Oh, I know," said Natalie. "You lied to him. You told him you had some urgent data you needed to discuss with one of the scientists at Command."

"That wasn't really a lie."

"Yes it was. Anyway, I didn't demote him because of that."

"No?"

"No. I demoted him because he didn't bother to tell me about it afterwards. Silly sod."

The money she'd taken from Mother Superior's safe didn't last long. Five months after leaving the orphanage the Poor Girl and Omar were living in a disused shipping container on the edge of Perpignan port near the border with Spain. They shared the container with half a dozen families, Algerians, Moroccans, Tunisians, flotsam from the days when France had found its immigration policy impossible to enforce and had simply given up.

She fed herself and Omar by stealing, and what they had left over they shared with the other families in the container. She felt no moral qualms about this; the alternative was just unthinkable. She ranged far and wide, by day and night, through the streets of the city. She kept her thefts small, stayed light on her feet, and was never once caught.

And then, one bright sunny day, the world changed.

She'd been suffering increasingly severe headaches for some weeks, sometimes so bad that she began to see things that weren't there. Insects, monsters. She dreamed of dead men walking. She dreamed of a hole in the Earth, a dream that left her sick and feverish and unable to leave her rough bed for days.

In the hand-to-mouth world in which they lived, news from the outside world arrived piecemeal or not at all. The first indication that something awful had happened was the sudden influx of refugees from the North and East.

Thousands, tens of thousands, began to arrive in Marseille, fleeing to the coast in the hope of leaving the country. Something in the Poor Girl's head went *click*, like a key turning in a lock. She didn't understand the news that was spreading by word of mouth, but she understood that she and Omar could not stay here. Something awful was coming.

Wracked with pain, she went out onto the streets again, and found panic there. Perpignan was simply unable to cope with the enormous numbers of refugees. With Spain closing the border and everything north of Narbonne apparently *not there any more*, the town was overwhelmed. Food was in short supply, people were sleeping on the pavements surrounded by what belongings they had managed to grab as they left home, gang violence was sweeping the city. The army had been brought in to try and keep the peace, but they had more or less given up; the police were nowhere to be seen. Barely a shop remained unlooted. Walking down one short street she saw four dead bodies, a naked woman crouching in the gutter bawling her eyes out and tearing at her hair, and half a dozen people roasting the body of an Alsatian over a fire built in the upturned bonnet of a car. Gunshots rang out. Somewhere, something was burning; she could smell it in the air.

Down in the port, things were even worse. Every form of water transport was being pressed into service. Ferries, container ships, yachts, pleasure cruisers. All were departing dangerously overloaded with human cargo — it was understood that they would not be returning to pick up more passengers — and sailing South.

It seemed impossible. She had no money to buy passage. She was almost trampled underfoot several times in the crowds desperately pressing their way to the quayside. Disheartened and dispirited, she withdrew.

Back at the cargo container, she found that the other families had vanished, all but one man, a Moroccan named Hassan. Standing beside him was a sad-eyed middle-aged man wearing oil-stained coveralls and a filthy baseball cap.

"This man says he has a boat," Hassan told her. "He says for a price he will take us away from here. You shared your food with us, so we have paid for you and your brother." There was no grand gesture, just a statement of fact. *You helped us; now we help you. That is how the world works.*

"Name's Andrew Marlowe," said the other man in thickly-accented French. "Leaving tonight, if you want to come with us."

And that was how the Poor Girl and Omar went to Africa.

The intruder in Joseph Tern's head wanted the girl unharmed, physically at least, and that posed a number of challenges. His renewed sense of mission bothered Joseph slightly. Not enough to worry him—there was very little in this world that worried Joseph—but enough to put him a little on edge. The intruder had a name, but so far had not bothered to share it with Joseph, which added to his discomfort. If someone is going to live in your mind, Joseph reasoned, he should at least tell you his name.

The intruder was looking for very special individuals who were, at first glance, indistinguishable from everyone else. At first, it had all been rather hit-and-miss and time-consuming. They'd just abducted anyone, which had been amusing but not terribly productive. But over the past year, the intruder had become more in tune with his surroundings. Before finding Joseph, he had been unfocused, moving from host to host, feeding on raw emotion. Just a month ago, the intruder announced that Joseph needed to come here and find a teenage girl with a hole in her head. And here she was. Joseph didn't much care why he was being asked to torture her. He was just told that sedating her would not allow the entity trapped on the other side to migrate through the rift in her head. Joseph assumed the intruder was talking about others like himself, but again did not care enough to ask. Psychoactive drugs wouldn't work either. The intruder said the brain had its own deep defences. He said he had come to the conclusion that the host had to willingly open themselves to possession; they had to *want* to let the entity through and take over their body. Hence the need for Joseph's own special brand of persuasion.

But the girl was proving tough. Tougher than she had any right to be, considering her age. Sleep deprivation, sensory deprivation, waterboarding, a room full of tethered, barking attack dogs, lack of food and water, straightforward threats. Nothing worked. It was, Joseph thought, rather exciting. The intruder could allow Joseph the power to reach into the girl's head and manipulate her mind on a molecular level, but he was withholding that special talent for fear of damaging her and making her an unsuitable host. Joseph was quietly fine with that. Sometimes the conventional techniques could be just as delicious.

They weren't getting results, though. Time for the nuclear option. He let himself out of the front door of the villa and set out across the city.

The heat was a physical thing, a weight that sat down on Scott's shoulders and the top of his head on the short walk from the military transport aircraft to the line of Egyptian Army Hummers sitting on the tarmac where their liaison, Captain Nasser—"No relation," he said without a smile—was waiting for them.

In the air-conditioned cool of the lead Hummer, Nasser turned to them and said, "I am to provide you all support. My government is not happy about this."

"Well I'm not turning cartwheels either, Captain," Natalie told him. "But we're all here now so let's get the job done, eh?"

Nasser stared at her for a moment. Then he sniffed and said, "You search for a girl, yes?"

"Yes." Natalie turned to Scott. "Yes, we are. Aren't we, Mr Fletcher?"

Scott closed his eyes, tried to make the images surface. It wasn't hard. What was difficult was finding the *right* images, the ones that would be of some use...

He opened his eyes. "Does anyone have a pen, please? And some paper?"

Natalie and Nasser exchanged glances. Nasser snapped open the breast pocket of his fatigue jacket and took out a pad and a pencil. He handed them over.

"She's been thinking," Scott said, sketching hurriedly. "She's been thinking about men in uniform. They've got all kinds of insignias. Here." He held the pad up so Nasser could see what he'd drawn.

Nasser gave him a you-have-to-be-kidding-me look. "It is," he said, "the advertising symbol for a soft drink."

"Egyptian?" asked Scott, feeling himself starting to panic.

Nasser shrugged. "Everywhere."

"Okay." Scott started drawing again. "This?"

Nasser pursed his lips. "It is the logo of a multinational pharmaceutical company."

"Right." More sketching. "This."

Nasser looked at the sketch. Looked at Scott. Looked at Natalie. Looked at Scott again. "It is the insignia of the police force of the city of Tunis."

Natalie rubbed her eyes. "Oh, fine," she said.

No one ever found out where Marlowe had got the ship from, but everyone agreed it was a deathtrap, a decrepit old freighter named *Daughter of Neptune*. In any sane world, it would have been in a breaker's yard. But this was not a sane world any longer, and the ship brought them across the sea to Tunisia.

Where the Strongman had recently come to power after an election so rife with ballot rigging on all sides that the international observers had thrown up their hands and gone home. The government tried to stop the refugees from landing, but Marlowe solved that by the simple expedient of cranking *Daughter of Neptune*'s ailing engines way past their danger limit and driving the old ship up onto the beach, where everyone disembarked in a hurry and scattered into the outskirts of Tunis.

Eventually, they drifted together again, and set up camp in the ruins of an abandoned shopping mall, and there, raids by the police notwithstanding, they had managed to eke out a reasonable life ever since.

Until one day, returning to Sarkozytown from a shopping expedition, weighed down with fresh loaves, the Poor Girl had found herself snatched off the street by two demons, bundled into the back of a car, and brought here.

The demon-she-could-see was tall and rangy, of indeterminate age. He wore a stained white linen suit and a white shirt and he smoked small cigars. She had never seen his eyes; he wore mirrored sunglasses, even down here in the basement. But she knew that one of his eyes was green, the other blue. She had seen them in her mind. There was something about him that reminded her of Marlowe, something about the way he carried himself. Some said that Marlowe had once been a soldier, and perhaps the demon-she-could-see had also been in the military.

She could not see the other demon, but she knew it was there, sitting on his shoulder. She'd seen it, seen them both, in her visions, long before she was brought here. The demon-she-could-see was a creature of great evil, but the demon-she-could-not-see was something unutterably *different*. It was sarcastic and sulky; she could hear it muttering and plotting to itself. It wept sometimes. Sometimes she felt it relish being inside the head of a killer, and other times it would strain and struggle to get out. It *wanted*, all the time. Most of all, it wanted her to say yes to a simple question.

There was never any chance of that. If she did, there would be a demon on her shoulder too. It would not be a partnership like the two demons enjoyed. It would mean surrendering complete control. Omar would mean nothing to it; it would make her abandon her brother. So she refused. Through all the hours of sleeplessness, the wet cloths on her face that almost drowned her, the pain in her legs and arms, the sheer terror of it all. She would not break.

She heard the demon-she-could-see coming down the stairs to the basement. As he reached the door she could also hear muffled squealing, as if he had brought a small animal with him.

The door opened and the demon marched in. Under one arm, kicking and screaming, he carried Omar. In his other hand he was holding a long kitchen knife.

"Right," he said, throwing the weeping Omar to the floor and putting a foot on the boy's chest to hold him down. He pointed the knife at her. "Never forget," he told her. "Never forget that this is your fault. All you had to do was say yes, but you were too fucking stubborn. So here we are. You did this." And with that he bent down and started to cut.

The girl's screams were so loud that they were clearly audible to the people standing in the villa's garden.

"Jesus," said Natalie. She turned to Nasser. "Go," she said.

Nasser gave a signal, and the Egyptian Special Forces team stormed the villa. Scott had been provided with a pistol, but he followed orders and hung back as the Egyptians blew the front door off its hinges and poured inside. The Tunisian government would never have agreed to this operation, so Natalie hadn't even bothered to ask. She and her team and Nasser's people had simply flown across the border in stealth helicopters under cover of darkness. The closer they came to Tunis, the stronger Scott's sense of the girl grew, and it was a simple thing to fly over the city until he *knew* where she was, and drop quietly into the villa's grounds.

The villa's interior blinked with the detonation of thunderflashes; there were gunshots, the sound of glass and furniture breaking. Natalie turned to her team and beckoned and they ran into the house.

Inside all was dark and quiet again. The beams of their torches shone through drifting panes of smoke from the thunderflashes.

"Downstairs," Scott said. "She's in the cellar."

Three of Nasser's men went ahead of them down the stairs, barely breaking stride as they broke down the door at the bottom. They burst into the white room beyond, and the first thing Scott saw was the blood. It was everywhere, but mostly on and around the barely-moving form of a little boy on the floor. Beyond him was a weird home-made looking metal chair, and in the chair sat the little girl from his visions, her face almost purple with screaming and crying, twisting her wrists to try and free herself from her restraints. Of Joseph...nothing.

"Ah, bollocks," said Scott, and charged back up the stairs drawing his pistol. "Stay with her!" he called to Natalie.

"Fletcher!" she bellowed after him, but he kept going.

At the top of the stairs he ran straight into Corporal Burton, the team's medic. "Someone's hurt," he said. "Get down there but give me your torch first."

Burton handed over the torch and hurried down the stairs. Scott stepped out into the hallway and stood very still. Nasser's men had searched the villa top to bottom, in a quick and dirty sort of way, and then withdrawn to form a perimeter. The Tunisian authorities would be here soon, and someone had to hold them off until the Egyptian helicopters came around again to pick them up. The villa was silent.

He went from room to room, quietly as he could, shining his torch into corners, looking under furniture, opening cupboards. It wasn't until he reached the second-storey hallway that he felt a *presence* and turned to find Joseph watching him by the shattered window at the end of the corridor.

Joseph took off his sunglasses. One of his eyes was green, the other blue. He regarded Scott levelly, calmly, weighing him up, and Scott had the impression of another presence, somehow occupying the same space as Joseph, doing the same. He lifted the pistol and aimed the muzzle at the centre of Joseph's chest.

The monster smiled and pointed to his head. "My friend says you'd make a good host, too," he said. "An *excellent* host."

"This stops right now," Scott said. "You both have to go back."

"Back there?" Joseph took out a pack of cigarillos and lit one. "I'm having *much* too much fun here. And as for my friend, well, it took a lot of effort for him to get here in the first place." He grinned and exhaled smoke. "Can't see him wanting to go back, can you?"

"Does your friend have a name?" Scott asked, his voice shaking.

"Bosley. His name is Bosley. Nice to meet you, Bosley."

The name rang a bell at the back of Scott's mind. He saw creatures stalking the corridors of the LHC. He saw a man staring into the heart of the Collider. He saw the same man and four others, trapped in hell, trying to find a way out, any way out. He saw the Wraith Lights...

"Step forward," Scott said, the gun wavering. "Away from the window."

"Oh, fuck off. Bosley can see inside your head. He says you won't shoot. And you won't. Bosley's never wrong."

"He is this time," Scott said and fired the gun.

What happened next was a blur. The bullet hit Joseph square in the chest. But there was no blood and the killer didn't even flinch. There was a puff of brick dust from behind him—the bullet had gone right through! Scott fired again, three more times. Joseph just laughed.

"See you later," he said. And with that, Joseph hopped over the windowsill and dropped out of sight. Scott heard gunfire and shouting, but when he ran to the window and looked out the killer was gone.

When Scott came back downstairs, Natalie was standing in the hallway with the girl sobbing in her arms. Burton had brought the little boy up and laid him on the floor and was applying compression bandages to what looked like multiple and very serious knife wounds.

Nasser came in through the front door. "Two of my men are dead," he said.

"Joseph?" said Scott.

"Gone. And the Tunisian police are coming. We have to go."

"That went well, then," Natalie said.

"We've got her," Scott pointed out.

"Yeah." Natalie hugged the girl. "That's something. Eh, sweetheart?"

"Omar," she sobbed. "Omar."

"Your little friend?" Natalie asked. She and Scott looked down at Burton, who could only shrug. "He's going to be fine, sweetheart. You're safe now. Everything's going to be fine now. Isn't it, Mr Fletcher?"

Scott shook his head fractionally.

Natalie sighed. A sudden gust of wind blowing through the smashed door announced the arrival of the helicopters.

"What's your name, love?" she asked the girl.

She thought about it for a moment, as if she had forgotten her own name a long time ago. Then she managed a weak smile. "Thérèse," she whispered.

Natalie hugged her gently. "That's a lovely name. Let's go, eh?"

Scott and Thérèse talked for an hour while sat at the bedside of Omar in the field hospital somewhere in southern Italy. The boy slept soundly, damaged but alive, much like his older sister. Scott's heart went out to her, and he felt a weird pride at her astonishing resolve in the face of sheer terror. He hadn't asked her what had happened to her parents, but it was obvious there was a huge parent-shaped hole in her life.

He gave the Poor Girl a hug, accompanied by the now familiar crackle of an electrical charge that accompanied any physical contact with her, and left her side to speak with Natalie as she entered.

"So, who is she?" Natalie asked, keeping her voice down.

"She's like me," Scott said, talking quietly but unable to contain his excitement. "She has a rift in her head!"

"Well yeah, I guessed that."

"Don't you see what this means? It means I'm not alone! There could be even more of us!"

Natalie's expression didn't change.

"You knew, didn't you?"

"About her? I suspected it. But I've known for a while there were others."

She handed Scott a tattered printout. It was taken from a blog, some hospital worker from the UK by the name of Jess. There was a comment from a Chinese guy called Pang. Scott scanned through the description of his grandmother's behaviour.

"When were you planning on telling me about this Mei-su woman?"

Natalie shrugged. "I don't have to tell you anything."

"But this changes everything! We have to find her."

"We're trying to, but this senile old Chinese granny is proving surprisingly elusive. Besides," she said, nodding towards Thérèse, "now we don't need her."

Scott tried not to feel betrayed. Sometimes he found it easier to believe he was an equal part in this operation, such as it was. But he was an asset, a tool to be exploited by Natalie and the ISG in their mission to close the rift. Thérèse was a tool now too, his backup. They didn't need anyone else like him for the time being. If something happened to Scott, they had a replacement. Suddenly he found himself feeling even more protective of the battered teenager.

"Listen to me very carefully, Miss Murphy," Scott said in his most business-like tone. "You can use me any which way you like as long as our ultimate goal is the same, but leave her alone." He glanced back at Thérèse, who had fallen asleep in her chair by her brother's side. "She's been through enough."

Natalie didn't seem even slightly fazed by his demand. "Better keep yourself alive then, Fletcher," she said.

She left him then. He went over to the sleeping girl, picked her up and carried her over to a nearby bed. He covered her with a blanket and then took her place by Omar's side. Just for today, he didn't resent the hole in his head quite so much as usual.

CAUGHT
by Elise Hattersley

The navigator was screaming incoherently and the medic was still out cold. Higgins was gone, and Carrigan felt sick at the thought of what had happened to him. What could he have done differently? He tried to remember how they'd gotten into this situation and couldn't do it. He remembered setting off, and some jumbled images of their journey into the heart of Europe. Then, nothing.

His head was pounding dully and his beard itched. He scratched it, hating the way it felt under his fingers, and cursed under his breath before turning back to the medic. Van Veen, he reminded himself. Her name was Van Veen. It wouldn't do anybody any good to dehumanize the other crew members, even though it seemed easier that way.

The blood dripping down the side of her face didn't look good, but the shifting light from the Collision, overwhelming in these close quarters, made it hard to tell if it was fresh or old. Old, he hoped. Surely she couldn't have been bleeding steadily for a week?

A week. That was his guess, anyway, based on the beard-growth on his face. Tough to get an accurate gauge; a beard was hardly a reliable timepiece, but it would have to do. He found himself wishing he'd been able to tell them what they were in for, but what else could he have done?

"McGraw!" he shouted, "Shut your face. Jesus!"

McGraw stopped screaming and stared at him quietly, his eyes huge hollows in his face. The silence was enormous, and for a moment Carrigan fancied he could feel their collective fear pressing in on him like a physical weight. He smiled at McGraw, aiming for encouraging and probably falling short by quite a margin.

"What's going on, man?" he asked, and McGraw started weeping quietly. Openly. Carrigan felt his gut twist with pity. Why was he asking? They were trapped, tangled in a web of warm, pulsating grey tentacles next to the Collision. It wasn't the cheeriest situation Carrigan could imagine, and he'd been briefed ahead of time. Again he felt their fear as something tangible, perhaps alive and in this cramped space with them. Something born from his choices. He knew others routinely took out crews without telling them what was going on, but it had never been his way, and it felt like standing out in the cold and watching friends enjoy each other's company inside.

He shivered, shrugged; then shoved the thoughts aside. Panic wouldn't help them, and he could feel it nibbling at his heels. He focused on the sobbing man suspended in front of him. "McGraw?" he asked, gentler now.

McGraw looked up, tears leaving uneven streaks through the smudges of dirt and blood on his face. His eyes seemed huge; hollow gaps in his face with fear glistening up from the depths.

"My head, boss," he whispered. "The burrowing... I can't stand the burrowing."

Then he opened his mouth and howled. For a moment the cave held, and Carrigan heard a confused shout from Scroggins, hanging in his bonds next to McGraw and staring at his neighbour with horror in his eyes. Then reality spun upside-down and turned itself inside-out.

The damp cobbles felt reassuring, familiar, under the thick soles of his boots. The cold air slapped his face; with the beard gone, Carrigan felt more like himself again. For a moment, he maintained a hold over the facts, the urgency of the situation and the things he needed to do to get them out of it. He turned to Scroggins.

"The burrowing? What burrowing? What did you see, Scroggins?"

He felt the question slip from his thoughts even as he asked it, tried to grip it, then let it go.

"It had... It was... His head..."

Scroggins shook his head like a dog shaking off water after a bath.

"What were we talking about?"

Carrigan shrugged one shoulder, annoyed with the lack of professionalism.

"We don't have time to talk, let's *move.*"

They ran through the narrow street, dusty old leather crunching on the debris strewn across the street, heading from an uncertain past into an uncertain future.

He was still weeping when he came to in the cave. McGraw, like Higgins before him, had disappeared. Carrigan fancied he could see the tentacle which had dug its way into his skull, imagining a dark smear of blood. It was hard to be sure. The cave was quiet, even though Van Veen had woken up. Carrigan smiled at her as best he could, and she seemed to take heart despite the puzzlement in her eyes.

"Boss, what the fuck is going on?"

The rift-light pooling in Scroggins's eye sockets reminded him of the boy, and Carrigan shuddered for a moment, pulling uncomfortably against his little cocoon of tentacles. Then he steeled himself for the inevitable.

"We're in a web, folks," he said, trying to impart to his voice the same businesslike quality he always used to discuss a mission. The rift-light, blue changing to purple across Kensington's face, showed nothing but cool professionalism. Scroggins registered a wary puzzlement. He didn't dare look at Van Veen, didn't need to see her horror at the fact that he hadn't informed them properly beforehand. Could telling them have been a better way? Would he ever forgive himself? Had there been a choice at all?

"We're being kept by the riftspider," he said, shouldering his way through his apprehension. "It's… It's complicated."

Kensington nodded. Not a flicker betrayed his inner thoughts; an unsettling quality at first, Carrigan now found it comforting to know the sniper retained his logical coolness.

"Carrigan," Van Veen said, and he wondered if the others heard the angry tremor in her voice. "How long have you known we might end up in this… This stupid situation?"

Carrigan smiled at her. There was nothing genuine or joyful about the smile, nothing friendly even… That was what the Collision had done to him.

When he met Scott Fletcher on the road to Carcassonne, Carrigan was still steeping in fresh loss. Every waking moment was dedicated to her last ones on earth, her own pain and fear, her horror—or his imagining of it—stamped indelibly on his every thought. For the longest time he thought she might have survived; until he came across a man who had worked at the same Paris facility when the Collision expanded and had got out in time. The man had talked about how quick it was and how little she'd suffered, but his haunted eyes told a very different story.

One look at Fletcher's face confirmed that he knew it too; from the moment their eyes met, Carrigan saw an understanding in his face that went beyond the rational.

Fletcher wasn't locked up or kept in handcuffs, but it struck Carrigan that the civilian was still a prisoner. The woman standing next to him had nodded coldly at Carrigan and had removed herself from the vicinity, but she kept a watchful eye on her most highly valued asset in case Carrigan got any ideas. There could be no illusions as to who was in charge here.

As he sat down on a battered metal chair, Fletcher smiled a smile that almost convinced him, and his first words hit Carrigan like a blow.

"Joseph Tern."

Carrigan stared back, forcing down the feeling of being a helpless child faced with an all-knowing adult. He hid the pain that lanced through him on hearing the name of the man who had taken his life and wrung from it all the joy he could. He hid it quickly and, he felt, expertly. But the surprise shone through. He could feel that, too.

Fletcher laughed. From any other man, in any other situation, Carrigan would have taken the name and the laughter in any combination as a signal to start punching. But there was a gentleness in the laughter, and a strangely personal twinge of pain. Carrigan decided to wait. Waiting for others to speak and tell him more than they intended to was how he had made his career; he was good at it. He forced his shoulders to relax.

"I bet you aren't even wondering how I know, are you?"

Carrigan shrugged. "I doubt anyone's too worried about secret-keeping, at this stage of the game. It's not going to patch the rift, is it?"

Fletcher nodded. "I think you're quite right. But nobody showed me a top-secret file and let me fill my boots. I think… You could say I have a special affinity with the Collision."

Those soft eyes found Carrigan's again.

"Lisa's last thought, I don't doubt, was of you."

Carrigan had no memory of standing up; one minute he was listening to Fletcher's voice, the next he was halfway back to the chopper. Fletcher raised placatory hands, and Carrigan stared at the fingers, the nails bitten to nubs. He was disconcerted to notice they were blurry; were there tears in his eyes? Was he on the verge of weeping in front of a stranger?

"Come on, Captain Carrigan, sit down. I'm sorry… I guess the end of the world has done nothing for my social skills. I won't bring her up again."

Carrigan stayed where he was for a moment, breathing in her memory; the colour of her hazelnut hair so bright and clear for a shining second. Then he sat back down, pushing her deeper inside for the time being. Knowing he'd take her back out of her little corner in his mind, later, and probe the size of the wound she'd left like a tongue poking at an angry tooth; helpless to stop, almost relishing the pain even as it destroyed him piece by piece.

But all of that couldn't matter, shouldn't matter right now. He looked at Fletcher, waiting and hoping for something interesting. Something of a distraction.

Anything.

"There's an emergency beacon going off near the Collision edge," Fletcher said.

"That's why I'm here."

"Word is it's some scientists who were presumed dead... And they're claiming they have a way to close the rift."

"Claiming?"

"The head honchos think it's for real... Me, I'm not so sure."

Carrigan nodded, feigning thoughtfulness. He was pretty sure he'd do it, whatever it was. What else was there *to* do?

"I think it's a trap too."

Fletcher didn't reply. He looked away, clearly unsure of what to say.

Carrigan asked, "How far in?"

Fletcher smiled.

"Close enough to touch it."

Carrigan smiled back. "Tell me what you see."

The rest was history.

He faced the accusation in Van Veen's face. He'd known about her crush, but he hadn't been able to talk to her about it. He couldn't figure out how to bring it up, how to explain that he would never care about her the way she wanted him to. She knew, he thought, but people seemed to feel he should be getting over it. Recovering. Carrying on as if all of that had never happened. As if his life hadn't ended almost as soon as the Collision happened. And why would he have that conversation with her at all, when it was much easier not to? She had nothing he needed. Still, he felt ashamed. He could have treated her better, considered her feelings instead of only seeing his own.

"The emergency beacon was a trap. We're in the web of the riftspider, and we're kind of fucked unless we work out where it is and manage to kill it. Are you guys with me?"

"Did you know this would happen?" Van Veen asked, her voice high with... Anger? Self-righteousness? He didn't know and couldn't bring himself to care. It was too late to worry about her feelings now, and he didn't have the time. Might not have the time for much at all, if things carried on the way they were going.

"Yes, of course I did," he said. "I was under pretty strict instructions not to tell anyone until and unless I needed to."

"Damn it, James, this isn't the army any more. You don't get court-martialled for not following orders," she exploded. He was mildly startled by the tears in her eyes; she was so well-known as a level-headed professional.

"Carrigan," he corrected her absently, not liking the feel of her mouth forming his first name. Not liking the fact that she was the one saying it. James didn't exist anymore. Not for her, not for anyone. Her mouth twisted bitterly, and her tears sped up. Was she crying over him?

"The riftspider is all of this," he said, liking the lack of comprehension on her face and the fact that he had the upper hand again. "Every tentacle, every bit of grey... Stuff. Fletcher called it a spider because it has a lot of legs, I guess."

He yanked angrily at a handful of webbing, heard Scroggins gasp when it moved in his hand, tightening itself around his chest.

"And when it burrows into the back of your skull and sucks out whatever the hell it is that it lives on, it gets your thoughts. Your knowledge. Your *plans*."

Her face was a brittle mask now, tears still sluicing across. She was shaking her head, and suddenly he was very angry.

"I couldn't tell you because telling you would get you *killed*," he shouted, suddenly furious. She looked at him, an almost-comical look of surprise on her face. And then she chuckled.

He felt he would never forget the derision in that laugh, the shame he felt when he realized she was laughing at the idea that she was crying over him, over his secret-keeping or his failure to feel the connection she thought they'd shared.

"So it feeds on us?"

Carrigan stared at her, his eyes glued to the trickle of blood sliding down the side of her neck. Fresh, he saw, even in the busy flashing from the Collision. He saw her shaking her head, and heard her grunt softly just before the trickle thickened to a stream.

"Carrigan, I don't have much time. Hurry up!"

"It feeds on us, projecting a shared hallucination it puts together out of memories and thoughts in our heads. That's why I don't have a beard when we're... Dreaming. Because I think of myself as a clean-shaven man, you see?"

The crew nodded, and for a moment the scene seemed normal; how many times had he briefed them just like this? He sighed.

"Then we wake while it sleeps, and when it wakes it chooses a new victim. Van Veen…"

She looked him in the eye. For a moment the world seemed to narrow, focus on the pain in her face. He groped for an apology, a string of words that would make it all right.

"Don't worry about it, Carrigan," she said, and smiled.

The world tilted.

As they rounded the corner, boots clattering off the uneven road surface, his eye caught a blob of white in a pile of grey and black rubble. He turned toward it, feeling the tendons in his neck creak. Something was itching at his brain, déjà-vu scrabbling for purchase in his mind.

The tiny hand was upturned in the road, palm facing the sky as if begging for a mercy that could never come. A smudge of blood dotted the thumb; otherwise, it was clean, as if recently wiped by a loving mother or father. Carrigan felt his stomach flip lazily. He felt revulsion crawl its way up his throat, and for a startling moment he thought he would be sick right there. Then he stuffed the feelings down, wilfully forgot the little hand and the child attached to it, and ran on.

They skidded into a small square, the fountain in the centre dry and filled with dust and dirt. A spatter of blood marked the stone fish in the centre, its mouth ludicrous without the customary water spluttering forth.

Kensington stared at him, that cool professional gaze as familiar as his own boots. His eyes flicked to the other side of the square, and Carrigan followed them. The houses had been pulverized, cobbles melted and twisted in the road. Soot and char were everywhere.

Now the boy will come, he thought, not knowing what he meant but turning toward a cluster of mostly-demolished houses. A smoke-licked piano peered morosely from behind a corner. As if on cue, a keening noise rose from one of the ruins. Fear rose in him like a cold hand, settling around his heart and squeezing. He had no time to consider why he knew what he knew. All he had time for was a here and now that wasn't, strictly speaking, anywhere.

"This is not how I want to die," Kensington said. The fleshy tentacle by his head stroked his hair back from his face, and he recoiled from it, revulsion plain on his face. Carrigan stared at him, remembering all the blood, all the death they'd seen together with the man's composure unfailingly intact. Kensington stared back, all the coolness now gone from his face. The tremor in his voice and the grizzled facial hair made him seem much older than he was, and for the first time Carrigan realized that they were so close to death they could almost smell it. For the first time, he realized it mattered. He nodded, felt his beard scrape his collarbone, and shuddered.

"If I'm not very much mistaken, we have two more chances—including this one—of getting out. So what do we do, Carrigan? How do we kill it?"

Carrigan looked at Scroggins, at the wide-eyed despair on his face, and swallowed. He felt his throat click. Suddenly his friends, his colleagues, his crew had been transformed into a haunting game of Russian roulette.

"We need to find the riftspider and kill it. Its body is somewhere in here, hidden behind one of us."

Kensington smirked. "And how are we killing it? I don't exactly have a million guns on me, mate."

Carrigan smiled back.

"All in good time."

Carrigan hung in his web. For a moment he focused on nothing, letting the tension slip from his muscles. It felt like wasted time, but he knew he needed the chance to gather his wits, get ahead of the panic. He stared into the shifting riftlight, seeing her face for just a moment, the smile trembling on the corners of her lips. He felt the pressure to succeed, and for the first time since meeting Fletcher he felt the weight of human life wasted. He couldn't let his entire crew die for nothing.

"The riftspider's body will be behind one of us; that's how it hides. Look for dark streaks on the tentacles around our heads. Whoever has it behind him may even be able to feel a small bulge behind his neck or head."

Scroggins winced, and Carrigan gave him a worried glance.

"Are you all right?"

Scroggins's grin was both savage and bleak. Carrigan nodded, needing no other confirmation. For a split second, he tried to discern whether the spider had broken the skin yet. Time became something physical, something he couldn't wrestle to the ground but had to, all the same. He looked at the tentacles above Kensington's head, trying to spot an arterial darkening. The riftlight pulsed, rippled, and shifted from green to pink and back again. He couldn't tell what was shadow and what was colour.

He strained his eyes, noticing the way the tentacles slithered lazily across one another, making minute adjustments he couldn't understand. For a second he realised just how enormous the riftspider was, coating the entire cave.

He heard Scroggins begin to scream when the light turned briefly white and he spotted the black streaking above Kensington's head.

Their eyes met as Scroggins's screams turned into shrieks, and Kensington nodded. So calm. Carrigan's face felt wooden, and for a moment he could feel the pulsating tubes feeding him and eliminating his waste. For just that split second, the anaesthetic effect of the creature's saliva was lifted enough to make him see the true horror of his situation. Or was he imagining it, the sensations caused by the knowledge Fletcher had cursed him with? Did it matter?

He blinked, and Scroggins's screaming stopped. Under the bleak French sky, Carrigan clapped the man on the shoulder.

"I'm so sorry, Scrog."

Scroggins's face was blank. For a moment, Carrigan held onto the truth of their situation, his pity for Scroggins like a dull ache behind his sternum. Then they were running, the rhythm of his feet comforting and familiar in the alien landscape of post-Collision France.

The boy seemed to be bleeding from a dozen different places, but Carrigan knew the blood belonged to others. Others who had run, screaming, been crushed by falling bricks or had killed themselves to escape the horror of what was coming. He wondered hollowly what had happened to the boy's parents.

The delicate eyelids looked so fragile. Long, blond eyelashes studded their edges, hung with the tears that leaked steadily from below. Carrigan wasn't great with children's ages; he couldn't even take a guess. The cartoon on the front of the grimy T-shirt was enough to tell him the boy was far too young—but then who was old enough for *this?*

In the back of his mind, a gibbering mantra started up. *Not again, not again, please I can't do this again.* He ignored it. A good soldier can ignore anything, his old man had always said. Carrigan had always felt there were a lot of things people were better off not ignoring, but as he gazed at the keening, weeping child he wasn't so sure.

The opening of the eyes was visible only by the riftlight slipping through. The child opened them just enough to show what lay beyond, stone bubbling and boiling where the light touched it.

"S'il vous plaît," the boy whispered. "S'il vous plaît."

"I'm sorry," Carrigan whispered back. The gunshot chased away the silence.

The blood looked black against the grey of the sky, the small body barely making a sound as it thudded against the crumbling wall. Kensington was pale as a ghost.

"You did the right thing," Carrigan said, but his voice broke. Kensington shrugged and looked away.

There was no peace in the tiny corpse. The face was tense, pain and stress twisting together to show how unpleasant the boy's last moments had been. When Carrigan looked up, Kensington was crying.

Carrigan was still recovering from the shift, gulping at the air. The splatter of blood against the sky, the subtle way in which the boy's face shifted as the exit wound in the back of his head distorted his features; it was all still too fresh. He struggled to pull himself together. Time was so short now. He forced his breathing to slow from angry gasps to a measured, rhythmic beat. Was that pain in his chest panic, or the riftspider's first move towards consuming him?

Kensington's face was almost as grey as the tentacles holding him in the web. Carrigan started worming his fingers along his body, feeling time pressing in on them as he found the zip undoing his jumpsuit. He didn't know who he was talking to, but he found himself muttering quietly, industriously, under his breath.

"Please don't be gone."

Every second stretched to a ridiculous length, and Carrigan felt watched, somehow, as if the riftspider had woken and was witnessing his scrabble for salvation. And laughing. He pushed the feelings away, recognizing their uselessness, but they twisted in his gut as if mocking him.

When his fingers stumbled into the butt of the gun he almost sobbed in relief, fumbling with the holster that strapped it to his side. He pulled it up and looked at Kensington. The other man's outstretched arm stopped him in his tracks.

"What do you think I'm about to do, Kensington?"

"You don't think I'm expecting you to do it?"

There was a strange patience in his eyes. Carrigan frowned.

"You want to do it yourself?"

Kensington scoffed, more incredulous than annoyed.

"What good is that gun going to do me when it's all the way over there in your hands?"

The puzzle pieces fell into place.

"You want to shoot *me*?"

"I can see the darkened tentacles right above you!"

Carrigan leant his head back, looked up at the mass of tubes above his head. He shook his head, tried to clear his eyes, and wished for the steady glow of a lamp. Why had the spider taken his torch, but not his gun?

"It looks clear to me, Kensington. Just... I know this is hard, okay?"

Kensington's look of disbelief almost seemed real.

"You're joking, right?"

Carrigan felt pity stretch his face into a smile. Compassion? Condescension? Was there a difference? He had to harden his heart. He could feel tentacles shifting around him. Was it awake yet? How long would it be before it came for him? Every breath of air against his skin felt like the start of an assault, every second piling up behind him like a tick-tock too many.

A chilling thought occurred to him; what if Kensington was already taken? What if the spider—or rather, the rubbery creature he was calling a spider—had taken control of him and was using him as a puppet?

He stared hard into the man's eyes, but saw nothing unfamiliar there. Only panic and anger.

"Carrigan, give me the gun," he said, and Carrigan was startled to hear the note of reason in that voice. He looked up and tried to memorise the other man, searched for peace in those haunted eyes.

The light painted glittering tracks down Kensington's face. His voice was strangled when he said, "It isn't funny anymore, Carrigan."

Carrigan raised the gun.

There was a moment of utter silence. Kensington stared down the barrel. With horror, Carrigan watched the tears sluice down his face and splash onto the spongy grey skin below. They were absorbed quickly, almost greedily. He raised his eyes to meet Kensington's again.

His mouth opened. To apologize? He didn't know.

Where the blood hit the rift, it sizzled.

He didn't know how long he'd been staring at the Collision. He'd been waiting for the web to either relax in death or starve him slowly. If he got bored, he'd shoot himself, but the gun hung loosely in a breast pocket, unheeded. He didn't really care. Not now.

Then a tentacle slithered across his forehead, slipping across his sweaty brow and pulling him out of his reverie.

He looked back at Kensington. The body had been removed, taken off to wherever the riftspider stored its depleted prey. He hadn't even noticed. All that remained was a hole in the web, blasted all the way down to what seemed to be crumbling brickwork. The light glinted off a nail sticking out of some ancient-looking plaster. It took him a moment to realise that there was no bloated body, no faintly arachnid centre console for the tentacles that surrounded him.

He felt a weak pulse behind his head, nudging him almost playfully.

For a moment he thought he could feel its laughter. Kensington had been right. Where were the dark streaks he had seen above the other man's head? He couldn't find them now, and the rift was cycling through its array of colours more rapidly; it was hard to tell. Had he really seen them? Had they been a trick of the light? Or had he wanted to live so badly he'd imagined them?

He remembered meeting Kensington, the thousands of little moments building and expanding their friendship. The man's gentleness despite an ungentle profession. The eyes full of panic and confusion.

Betrayal.

When he looked back above his head, he could see them; darkened places where the tentacles were almost black. Places he couldn't, wouldn't see before.

Around him, the riftspider pulsated slowly, softly. Awake, he realised. Awake and enjoying itself.

As he stared down the barrel, he smiled softly.

I'll be with you soon, my love.

His beard itched. Was it grey? Had he become the old man he now felt himself to be?

His finger tightened on the trigger, and he closed his eyes as he felt sudden alarm tighten the tentacles around him. A sharp pain in the back of his head announced the arrival of his enemy's understanding. He thought he could hear human voices, but it was too late for that now. Too late to be right, or wrong.

One last time, he thought of her face mid-laugh.

There was nothing but blackness.

Carrigan was okay with that.

The light on the other side of his eyelids was painfully bright, but he opened them anyway. For a heart-stopping moment the girl looked like *his* girl, then his eyes focussed and he saw the grooves bracketing her mouth and the hint of red in her hair.

"They got to you just in time, sugar," the nurse said. "We almost lost you a bunch of times. How are you feeling?"

Carrigan yawned hugely. His hand, coming up to cover his mouth, skidded on cleanly-shaven skin. For a moment he thought that was important, alarm blooming in his gut and rising to his chest. He tried to hold onto it, figure out what he should be doing. For just a moment understanding seemed so close he could almost touch it, then it slipped away.

Carrigan touched his face again and smiled back.

"I'm feeling great."

BASHER
by Jonathan Templar

7/18/2013: Blackwood to Belltown - four miles.
Traction used: Class 450 EMU.
Weather: Sunny and cloudy.

*T*he *train moves slowly past ancient semaphore signals before increasing speed. Isolated farmhouses pass by as we reach 60 mph. Industrial units appear to the left.*

We go into a short cutting, past a signal box and into Belltown station. It has four platforms with some carriage sidings next to the original Victorian station building. On the front of the station buildings are a couple of plaques. I am unable to read them from my vantage point on the train.

We come to a slow stop.

Journey's end.

England 2021

Colin had his eyes closed so he couldn't actually read the journal on his lap. But then he didn't need to read it. He knew it by heart. Every journey, every station and every class of carriage he'd ever ridden. Colin could just close his eyes and he would be back there, could escape at any time onto whichever train he wanted to revisit. There were plenty to choose from. He'd ridden them all, bashed every line in the country up and down, passed through every station on the network and seen everything the railway had to offer.

Or so he had thought until two days ago.

The service station was supposed to be a safe place to rest. Colin had spotted it from the road just as night had begun to fall. He had taken to sleeping inside abandoned cars or underneath bushes if the cover was sufficient. It tended to be cold and dangerous so he only rested when he was on the verge of collapse.

But the station looked a better bet for a good night's sleep than anything he had seen since he had set out. It was derelict, most of the roof had gone and the damage caused by six years of infiltration from the elements was devastating.

But it offered concealment from the night hunters and Colin had found a spot under what might once have been a serving counter that was reasonably dry. He had made himself comfortable, tucked into a can of what was probably supposed to be chilli and flicked through one of his journals in the fading light. Colin had thought he was safe to switch off for a while.

Then the creature arrived.

It had appeared silently, somehow navigating the wreckage of the building without betraying its presence. Or perhaps Colin simply hadn't heard it. He had been absorbed in the memories conjured by his journal, had taken himself back to a warm July day and a comfortable seat by the window as he had noted his observations on the Blackwood to

Belltown line. He could smell the stuffy odour of the carriage, the heady tang of ten thousand travellers ingrained in the luridly colored seat covers that could never overwhelm the faintly acidic tang of electricity that hung over trains and that Colin loved to breathe in. Colin could smell it all, could relive his journeys at leisure. This was how he preferred to exist, walking alone through his own memories.

The first he knew of the creature was when one of its legs appeared inches from his face, if what carried the thing could be described as a leg. It was a long, thin, brittle stalk that tapered to a sharp point. It tapped onto the remains of the linoleum as it moved through the building. Small, sharp hairs quivered along the leg, sensitive to movement, trying to detect his presence. Colin froze, held his breath. The creature circled the room, hooting a vile chorus as it moved.

He couldn't see the entirety of its body but the closest comparison Colin's mind could conjure for this thing was a giraffe, but there were far too many legs, and instead of a trunk it appeared to have some sort of sac, a grey membranous bulk that pulsed and heaved. In its centre was a ferocious maw, sucking and drooling with acrid bile. A throbbing proboscis protruded from the centre and hovered in Colin's line of vision, a long twisting tube of translucent skin that sniffed at the floor and through the air, hunting him. It searched for his scent or the scent of any other flesh that it could consume.

Colin kept still. He knew that whatever smell he gave off these days was likely to be far riper than anything strictly human.

Eventually the proboscis withdrew. With a sound like crisp autumn leaves falling from a tree the thing moved away.

Colin finally breathed out.

He had lived in his basement for over six years.

Not that Colin had been keeping track. A day was a day, all alike, he had no interest in counting them, barely acknowledged their passing.

For Colin, life was a simple matter of routine, and this was exactly how he liked it. Any variation would cause him nothing but distress so the simpler the routine, the better.

And his was very, very simple.

He ate food only to survive, shovelling the contents of random cans into his mouth without ceremony. He used the lights on battery power for just an hour a day, during which time he could check the integrity of the shelter, conduct the brief exercise routine he had perfected to ensure that he stayed at least reasonably fit and perform whatever biological business was required. Once a week he would go upstairs and dispose of his waste, spend a few hours taking in the fresh air and the sunlight.

The rest of the time he would be alone in the dark with his thoughts. This was how he preferred it.

When he had been younger his parents had spent considerable time trying to discover what was 'wrong' with their son. He was tested for every condition imaginable, was relentlessly diagnosed by the latest doctor or psychologist as 'autistic' or 'bi-polar' or one of a hundred other buzz words.

The truth was that Colin simply didn't care for the world as they understood it. He found it ugly, noisy, impossible to comprehend and utterly alienating. He wasn't stupid, he didn't fail to understand the concepts that he was presented with in school, he just refused to engage with any of them.

He didn't see the point. Colin just wanted to be on his own.

The only things he cared for were trains. The simple complexity of the rail network that lined the United Kingdom like a nervous system, the interweaving pattern of tracks that decorated the countryside was the only thing in which he found any beauty.

From the age of eleven to twenty-three all his energies had been devoted to covering the entire network, travelling each and every line in every direction. To *bash* it, cover the whole country point to point. And he *had,* and the memory of those rides, the way the hundreds of individual trips joined together to make one Total Journey, consumed Colin. It sustained him. It kept him alive with its simple, undemanding pleasure when anyone else would have lost their sanity alone in the dark of the basement.

He would have stayed there forever, content in his routine and enriched by his memories.

But then a week ago he had been called by the one thing that could lure him out.

He had decided to avoid the major cities. There was little left of them anyway.

Colin's intention had been to follow the railway lines to the south east coast, his knowledge of the way they spread, each branch line and terminus clear in the map of his mind. But the sheer extent of the damage that the debris from the rift had caused had been greater than he expected. Whole areas of the midlands were simply devastated and any trace of the railways long lost. Anywhere the line passed under a tunnel would have been impossible to traverse anyway. Colin decided to follow the roads, the ugly motorways that took cars, monstrous, pointless cars. They were easier to work around, to bypass where there was danger but rejoin at a later point. His progress had been slow but steady.

The motorways were a carpet of abandoned vehicles left to rust and decay much like their owners, who often still sat behind the wheel, slowly turning to dust. A faint aroma still hung in the air around the wreckage, the smell of death that had faded but never gone away. There had been carnage here, in the open, with the hordes of unprotected travellers trapped and exposed when the things had come through from the rift, the creatures that were barely conceivable until they were eating your face.

Colin had seen what was left of some of those creatures, the occasional body left by the side of the motorway. Slender, bat-like things, leathery wings dried up but still vast, heads that were nothing but circles of teeth, row upon row of sharp incisors that would have ripped and torn their prey to pieces. Colin took a wide path around those carcasses, just in case. Once or twice he passed the remains of larger things, creatures with an anatomy completely alien to anything he had ever seen before. There were colonies of flies feasting on one such corpse that lay across three lanes of the M6, a fleet of vehicles crushed beneath it as if it had just fallen from the sky.

As Colin passed by, thousands of flies rose from the body in a black cloud and the communal hymn sung by their wings nearly burst his ear drums.

Colin's mother had been with him when the rift opened.

She had maintained the shelter in the basement just as her husband had instructed. He had not lived to see Armageddon but he had always known it was coming. He would never have imagined that it could be caused by something other than Russians, though. He had become obsessed with the prospect of a nuclear winter ever since he had seen *The Day After* on television and had worked for years creating the perfect shelter for when the Red Peril finally took their ultimate option.

He had died after suffering a stroke in the bathtub, drowning as his heart gave up on him, racing his lungs to see which would kill him first. But Colin's mother had kept the basement stocked with canned food, 'enough for ten years' she used to say, which proved to be prophetic.

She had lived down there with Colin for a few years at the start, cowering in the dark while the radio told them of the horrors occurring above. Civilisation fell as they feasted on canned spam and recycled water.

His mother hadn't survived the scream.

Colin could screen it out; he had spent his life perfecting the ability to ignore everything that was going on around him so he was perfectly able to manage this as well. But his mother couldn't handle it, had eventually bashed her head repeatedly against the steel door to the basement until her forehead had caved in and her life bled out onto the concrete floor.

Colin had stood over her corpse for hours unsure of quite what he should do.

Eventually he wrapped her in some refuse sacks and carried her upstairs, leaving the body outside the kitchen door, thinking that he might return to bury her in the back garden at some later point.

The next time he had come up to the surface the body had gone. Colin hadn't given it a second thought.

There was very little of London left, and what still stood did so perilously.

Colin skirted the city in as wide an arc as he could but he couldn't avoid staring at the landscape as he passed. What had once been landmarks that dominated the city were now crumbling spires of desolation, stunted towers razed and smouldering and bridges burnt. Smoke still rose in numerous areas, newly lit fires suggesting that there were still people alive somewhere in the city.

As he passed by, Colin could hear things as well, a regular booming beat, like a drum, a deep heavy bass sound that he could feel through his legs and into his chest. He heard gunfire, distant but still disconcerting. He slept underneath a car that night, excruciating discomfort more appealing than the prospect of encountering strangers in the dark.

It wasn't until the following day that Colin stumbled into the other survivors.

Colin had never dreamed. When he slept he had always done so deeply and with a mind empty of distraction.

So when he began to see things in his sleep he was disconcerted to say the least.

The first time it happened it was little more than a flash, an explosion of sound and image that woke him in an instant. He was shocked by the experience, it was as if something had invaded him, forced its way in. It wasn't like Colin to surrender to irrational thoughts, but when it happened again, and the flash was longer and the images began to expand, formed pictures he could almost distinguish, he began to feel unsettled, tiny seeds of terror starting to germinate.

Colin didn't like it. He went about his daily routine trying not to remember, not to think about it in case he made it happen again.

But when he slept, and for the first time in years sleep had not come easily, the images arrived in force and he had no choice but to surrender to them.

He was on a train, the place he most wanted to be, but this was no train he had ridden before. Whatever this was, it was no memory. It was something new, something *fresh*.

It was dark aboard the train, everything was a shadow and any light that entered the carriage was consumed before it had a chance to illuminate. All Colin could distinguish were outlines, wraithlike fellow travellers blurred as if he were squinting at them, their shapes constantly twitching and adjusting as if they were struggling to keep hold of their form.

He looked out the window, and the landscape beyond was impossible to comprehend. The colours were unstable and unlike anything Colin's eyes had ever encountered before. Amorphous structures passed by, giant things that towered inward and shifted and slid as he tried to assimilate them. It made his head spin. Colin wanted to be sick.

The passenger next to him tapped him on the shoulder. Colin turned to look at him and he had no face. Just a wide, grinning mouth with far too many teeth.

Can you feel us, Colin? We ride through all the worlds and all the worlds are the same to us. The bones of the dead are our tracks and we hunt the living. Join with us, Colin. Ride with us! he/it hissed.

And Colin woke up.

He was following the path of a ring road that skirted the city, keeping under cover as much as he could. They must have seen him first, despite his efforts at stealth. Three of them, men, they were prowling through the chaos of abandoned vehicles, scavenging anything still left on decade old corpses. They were young, could only have been infants when the rift opened.

Colin froze as he saw them, scuttling across the rusting framework of cars, the one in front waving a gun as though it were a baton.

'You clean?' the alpha male said in a hoarse voice.

Colin raised his hands, to show that he hadn't got a gun. He seemed to remember that was what you did in these situations.

'*I* said *are you clean*?' the man/boy said again, louder.

'I haven't had a bath for years. I used to wash once a week with rainwater but I've been travelling for a while now —'

'Shut up!' the man/boy swaggered his way over to Colin, his two compatriots lingering behind. Up close he looked distinctly unhealthy. There were boils all over his face, some of them a violent red that hinted at sickness, pus straining to burst. His teeth were brown and loose and his eyes had a milky hue that didn't disguise the madness.

'Last time! Are you clean?' he hissed, fetid breath in Colin's face.

'I don't know,' Colin said.

The boy brought his head closer, moved it up and down Colin's body as if he hadn't been able to see him before now. He sniffed rapidly, tasting Colin's scent.

'He's just a scrub, come out of the woods, yeah?' one of the other boys, who looked no healthier than this one, called over.

The alpha spun back to face Colin, waving the gun.

'You a scrub?' he asked.

'I don't know what that is.'

The man/boy hissed through his rotten teeth and then spat on the floor, a brown glob flecked with blood. 'You ain't clean,' he said. He gestured to the two behind him. 'Let's go, he ain't no scrub, I ain't gonna eat nothing that ain't scrub.'

They swaggered away, moving as though it was something they had little control over.

Colin stood there, his arms still raised above his head, desperately needing to urinate, until the men/boys were out of sight. Then he lowered his hands and half staggered, half ran as fast as he could until his lungs started to ache and his feet were blistering.

The dream had troubled Colin, had threatened to bring disorder to his perfectly ordered world.

He had seen images that his mind struggled to process, that human eyes were not meant to see. But if Colin was nothing else he was rational, he was adept at finding order within chaos. So he focused in on the important thing. There was another train, a *new one*. It was like nothing he had ridden before, it was not a carriage he had ever had the chance to assess and categorize, its course was unlike any he had ever logged in his journals. Throughout one long, long day between his first and second dreams, it plagued him, nagged at him relentlessly.

Wherever it had come from, whatever tracks it followed, he had not bashed it. It was outside his Total Journey. Worse, it made a lie of the Journey, suddenly made it incomplete. That was inconceivable for Colin. The Total Journey was everything to him.

That night he slept but the train did not come in his dreams. Instead it whispered to him, told him where he could find it, where he needed to go if he wanted to ride.

Colin woke in the morning, packed the few things he needed and left his basement for the first time in years.

Kent had often been described as England's garden. That garden had not been tended for a *long* time and was now nothing but wilderness.

And it wasn't only nature that was running wild.

There were dogs, gangs of them, scraggly desperate creatures drooling with hunger and madness, the affinity that they once held with man long since displaced by the impulse to feed, to survive. Colin had seen random packs of them before now but most of them had been timid, their terror of the new world governing their behaviour. But here they were more confident; they had a boldness backed by sheer weight of numbers.

Colin had managed to avoid them till now, had stayed away from the open spaces and crept through the jungle of foliage that surrounded the major roads. His face was a jigsaw of scratches from hedges and brambles that had torn at him as he fought his way through but he had otherwise been unmolested.

It was a signpost that lured him out of the safe places, a blue motorway sign that still hung over the devastation, one that would give him an indication of how far he was from Dover, from his destination. Colin was getting impatient; he wanted this trek across the rubble of England to be over.

Twelve miles. That was better than he had expected. Far better. It could only be midday at the latest, he'd been walking since before dawn but he still felt fine, reckoned that he could cover the rest of the distance by the end of the day if he really put the effort in.

Colin hitched up his shoulder bag. If he didn't stop to eat he might even get there before the sun came down.

The dog growled and Colin realized he hadn't been paying attention. It was ten feet away, an emaciated, feverish creature that bore little relation to man's best friend. Its teeth were bared, the mouth around them raw with disease. This dog wouldn't have to do much damage to Colin for it to be terminal; its saliva would be swimming with death.

And then he saw there were others, three, four, more than that. They crept from their hiding places, the wreckage that had been their larder for years and when the food was exhausted became their sanctuary. One of them alone would be deadly, a dozen and Colin had no chance. They stalked toward him, not working as a team but still cutting him off with their sheer number.

Colin backed away, toward the cover he should never have left. He couldn't outrun them, he could walk all day but he ran like he had two left legs. They would be on him in seconds.

There was nowhere for him to go.

And then a sound like something terrible giving birth while being flushed down a toilet shook the air. A hunting call, a roar of something utterly alien.

The dogs whined, they whimpered, one of them urinated uncontrollably onto the tarmac. As one, the pack dispersed, scampering back into the rusting hollows of long dead cars.

Colin didn't count his blessings; he hurried back into the undergrowth and was instantly swallowed by it, sliding carefully down a verge and away from the open.

Behind him, where the dogs had hunted, he could hear something moving, something vast, crushing whatever it fell upon. Its footsteps shook the trees even at Colin's distance, and what little light reached him was eclipsed by the size of the creature. He only caught a glimpse of it, something reptilian that absorbed the light, asymmetrical and abhorrent, a form that would repel human eyes.

Colin moved on.

The road led all the way into Dover.

As Colin made his way further south it became clear how much damage had been caused by the original Collision. Enough debris had fallen to flatten whole districts in one go, and in places it was difficult to tell what was UK territory that had been destroyed and what was simply a lump of France that had been blasted over the channel to land on its neighbour.

But Dover was surprisingly intact. Perhaps its proximity to the French coast had spared it.

The port, however, was a site of carnage.

Like a child's bedroom that hadn't been cleared for a month, cars and trucks were scattered and overturned on its approach. Closer in, leftovers of what had once been the military; a spread of munitions, jeeps and command posts. A tank lay on its back like an upended beetle, half crushed as if a giant foot had stepped on it. The walkways and gantries that made up the port's infrastructure were twisted and bent by the crossfire.

There was only one cross channel ferry visible in the harbour, partially capsized, the bow of the vessel rising from the water, the dead, rotting tentacle of something bigger still wrapped around it in an embrace, two behemoths of the sea decaying together.

There had been a battle here, and everyone had lost.

The town and the port were silent, not even the sound of a seagull.

Colin was only a few miles from his destination. The channel tunnel was along the coast a few miles in Cheriton. The voice in his dream had said that the train was hunting these shores. If it existed, it was close.

There was a terrible smell hanging over the outskirts of the town. There had been many new smells since Colin had left the basement, most of them foul, but this was worse, something that brought bile to the back of his throat and made his eyes water. Colin covered his mouth with his sleeve, tried not to breathe through his nose to block the odour out. He was partially successful. He didn't vomit, at least.

The smell gradually grew stronger, and Colin caught the first sign of what had made it. As he stumbled down a deserted but relatively undamaged street with his eyes running he saw what he initially thought was some form of structure in the middle of the road.

As he got closer he saw it was a sort of mound, almost like a mole hill. It was steaming, he noticed. The day was reasonably warm, even though there was a crisp sea breeze blowing in, but the mound gave off a mist like breath on a winter's morning. The smell was intense, enough to make Colin recoil. As he passed the mound he realized what it was.

It was excrement. Something had shit this out.

After a decade of living in a basement eating canned food Colin was well used to the odour of his own waste but even he had never come close to anything as foul as this stench. He retched as he walked around it, and his cloudy eyes focused on the contours of the mound, of what it was that constituted the droppings. There were bits and pieces mashed together under the slick coat of digestive acids, the remains of animals. Dogs. Limbs and trunks, bones that had been broken or crushed, clumps of fur wrapped in flesh, bodies that had been churned inside out. That had been chewed and partially digested.

He appreciated now why the dogs he had encountered had been so scared. The pack had become prey.

Colin looked closer; saw that it wasn't only dogs, that there was something that looked like a hoof. A cow, he assumed. Next to the hoof was a hand, a human hand. Almost perfectly preserved, it had once been attached to a woman, he could tell by its slender fingers and the presence of rings, one on the wedding finger, a glistening contrast to the pale dead flesh. Close to the hand was the shape of what looked very much like a human head, clumps of hair still dangling from it. But Colin had seen enough. He continued by, still covering his mouth. Whatever had excreted these remains had done so recently, and he had no desire to be on its menu.

Ten minutes later he found the tracks.

Colin knew tracks, knew his rails, fasteners, sleepers and his ballast. These tracks had none of those things. They were a marble white flecked with twisting veins of black.

The bones of the dead.

The tracks ran in an impossible line, into the distance across the cliff face but back toward the town they seemed to run *through* buildings, as if the tracks had existed first and the structures had been erected on top of them.

Colin wished he had his camera.

He knelt down and put his hand on a track. It was cold, dead, like a fossil, something that had died long ago under the town. There was no tingle underneath his fingers, no trace of vibration. If the train was riding, it was a long way down the track.

Colin sat, crossed his legs. He would wait. He had spent more time than he could calculate waiting for trains.

It was always worth it.

It had been hours, but it might only have been minutes. The sun was dipping behind the cliffs, the light was fading. Colin stared along the bone tracks impassively. The tracks finally began to respond to the freight they carried.

But they didn't vibrate.

They *screamed*.

The train came through the buildings that blocked its path, ghosting through them without a sound. It stopped abruptly, no squeal of breaks, just a sudden, silent halt.

Colin looked upon it with only joy, despite its horror.

It was black, perhaps, but a black that wasn't a colour in itself, was more the absence of any other. Its surface was sleek, curved, a fleshy bullet that glistened as though it had been through the rain, but the moisture was a part of it, like the skin of a slug. Hot steam rose from the train, misting the air.

And still it was silent, pulsing, ominous.

Colin took a few steps toward it, held out a hand to touch the surface. It felt cold under his fingers and he pulled his hand away. He touched it again and it was warm. He put his whole palm flat against it, breathed in time with its regular pulsing contractions.

The last feeble ray of sunshine reached them, and Colin saw that there was a window in the side of the train. Was it a window? It was more like a transparent film, or the lens of an eye. He could see inside, vaguely. There were shapes in there, the shapes of people, only shadows, phantom profiles that sat row upon row looking out at him through invisible eyes. The sun went behind the cliffs for the last time, and the window vanished.

I've been collecting, Colin, the voice of the train whispered inside his head. It was the sound of a thousand sharp spiders scurrying through his thoughts.

I've been collecting people like you. This isn't the end of the line, Colin; this is only the beginning. Mine is a journey that never ends. Oh, I have such sights to show you! Come with me, Colin.

Come ride my tracks.

A door appeared in the side of the train next to Colin. It slithered opened like a sphincter, and a blast of corrupted air from inside the train poured out, the smell of the journey, of all the new and terrible places they could go.

Colin looked back at Dover, at the devastation of the world that he barely knew and had never understood. In his bag, he could feel the weight of his journals, journals that he had believed to be finished, to be a complete history of his travels.

He dropped them to the ground, kicked them away. They were useless now.

Without hesitation Colin stepped onto the train.

The sphincter closed behind him. Without a sound, the train moved off along its dreadful tracks, towards the tunnel, towards the heart of the rift.

And Colin bashed to a whole new level.

Scott Fletcher awoke from a nightmare that didn't end. He was still having it, right now, even though he was awake. He could tell he was awake because his brain was on fire, his ears rang and he felt too weak to rise. He was on a train he'd boarded about an hour ago and now it had stopped; he didn't know where. He peered through the window, which wasn't made of glass but of skin stretched so tight as to be almost translucent. He recognized the Sacré-Cœur Basilica, he was in Paris? Oh God, the pain. It hurt so much he wanted to shoot himself in the head to make it stop, but he didn't have a gun. Why was he here? Why was he waiting?

His ears rang so loudly he couldn't hear anything from the vision. His brain burned like someone had doused it in petrol and set it alight. He was desperate for it to end, but the train kept on waiting and calling. *Calling?* Why did he think it was calling? Who was it waiting for?

Eventually, mercifully, the train started moving again and Scott's vision ended. The pain receded to a thundering roar and he opened his eyes. Thérèse was shaking his arm, concern flooding her petite features.

"I'm OK," Scott assured her, patting her hand. "Go back to your bed."

She did so. She was used to seeing him have one of his visions, and he felt equally powerless when she had one of hers. In the morning he'd tell her all about it, but for now he needed to sleep if he could. He hoped this thumping headache would not persist when he woke.

Scott slept fitfully that night, and dreamed of a train made from skin and muscle and bone...

LEAD US NOT
by Meg Moore

Her grandfather was a prophet, and I was a lifelong atheist, so right away I knew there were going to be problems in the relationship. It didn't help that she, and a whole bunch of others like her, clung on to his every word. But she was pretty, and when she kissed me it tasted like strawberries in summer, so I went along with it.

I pretended to pray when I bowed my head, and I went to church in the little makeshift chapel every Sunday. I said the right things when prompted, and I pretended to hate the right people, and shook my fist in the right show of righteous indignation when Obadiah Bard told us all who was to blame for the way the world had gone to Hell. Whether they saw through me or not at first, I don't know. But I was big and strong, and I came with my own gun, so they let me stay.

Before I met Bard and his little congregation I'd traveled alone. Before that, back in the days when the world was still a decent place to live, I was an exterminator. They put me to work on the rat problem, and I spent a happy couple of years murdering the little bastards, who had somehow managed to quadruple in number even when everything else in the world had died off almost to the point of extinction. They were even hardier than the cockroaches, despite what people used to say.

The things you learn in an apocalypse.

In the end, it made me pretty popular, and Bard even let me marry Susannah. We built a cozy little lean-to up against the main house, where the older folks and the children lived. It used to be a vineyard and even the explosion at the rift hadn't been able to leech the life out of the land there, so we were able to grow a fine little bunch of crops out in the rich earth. Not much in the way of grapes, but a few decent potatoes, some tomatoes, peas and carrots.

It attracted even more rats, of course. But it was good, honest work, so I didn't mind. Every morning I'd go out and set my traps, then in the afternoon I'd go and help with the harvest. Every evening I checked on the traps and burned whatever I'd caught. Everybody gained weight, and said that God had blessed them while I just smiled and thought to myself that these people had got really damned lucky, and it almost seemed that it was possible to be happy.

It was almost possible. But every time things seemed to settle down, Bard would have another one of his visions. There's a plague on the way, he'd say, and a little while later everybody was sick and covered in sores. A month later half of us were buried in a mass grave.

Or he'd announce that he'd seen hordes of insects. Then we'd spend a month holed up inside with whatever crops we'd managed to harvest while giant mites the size of a grown man's fist tried to break in, but Obadiah had seen the weird half-invisible box they came out of and we were prepared, with the building doused in our entire store of potato wine and even the tiniest crack in the walls sealed shut. But that wasn't the thing that pissed me off.

No, what pissed me off was that in between all these visions, which were actually helpful, Bard would come up with his favorite story — the one with the angels.

Typical end of the world bullshit, except it made it harder to think of it as bullshit when he seemed to be right about everything else and the end of the world was pretty much here already. Susannah certainly thought it was real. She hung on to Bard's every word, and when she curled up to me at night she'd get all wistful and talk about how she couldn't wait to see them. Meanwhile there I was thinking to myself how insane it was, looking for an apocalypse when it had already come and gone and we'd managed to survive it.

But Bard wouldn't be happy until we were all dead. He'd been waiting for the end of the world his entire life and, from what I could remember from before the Collision, it wasn't the first time he'd predicted it.

The old man wasn't just any crazy old prophet.

He'd been famous for a while, but until it happened nobody but his followers thought of him as anything but a joke. I know my mates and I had laughed when we saw him on television the month before it happened, babbling about the LHC and how we were all doomed. I'd wondered how an old bastard like that ever managed to get people to listen to a word he had to say.

When I told Susannah that story I left that part out and I pretended I remembered her from the broadcast, which made her smile and kiss me.

You could just see the edge of it from the vineyard, and the sky above. Sometimes I went and watched it after I was done with my work, and wondered how something so horrible could be so beautiful. In my fantasies, which didn't involve the world ending, I imagined me and Susannah telling our grandkids about it. I'd try and put into words how incredible it was, the blues and greens and reds in the midnight sky.

In my fantasies they'd roll their eyes and go off and do more important things. By then it would just be some tragedy from long ago that everyone tried to forget. Susannah and I would go to bed and curl up together where we were comfortable and clean, and remember what it was like to have to starve and sleep in the dirt. Then I'd finally tell her, when we were old and gray, what a load of nonsense I always thought her grandfather's visions had been, and she'd laugh with me and tell me I was right.

Then my fantasies would fade away like dust and there I was, a man surrounded by people who couldn't wait to die. Sometimes in moments like those I felt lonelier than I had been when I was all alone.

It was early summer, in my third year with Bard and Susannah and the others, when she told me she was pregnant.

She cried and fell into my arms when she told me, and I thought to myself how terrible it must have been for a girl like her, who loved life so much but who was certain we were in the last days of living it.

"I don't think there are really angels," I tried to tell her, but as soon as I said it her tears dried up and she pushed me away. I knew I'd said the wrong thing when a little while later, as I went out to pick up the rat traps from the garden, Bard came down to talk to me.

"Susannah told me what you said." He looked furious. It was the first time I realized just how dangerous that man could be. Not because he was cruel, but because he really believed it all. Something cold settled down over me. I forced myself to bite back the things that I wanted to say, and instead shrugged.

"She's pregnant. I said what I thought would calm her down."

"You said," Bard snapped, "that there are no angels. Tell me, do you really believe that?"

What I said next was damned stupid, but I was tired of the lies so I told him what I believed in: in people, and the future, and that the world goes on and on, no matter what happens, because that's just the way things work. And when I was done speaking he gave me one short nod and told me to get out.

I found a small bag waiting for me in my lean-to, and Susannah was gone. The door to the house was barred shut, and nobody would answer even after I pounded at it for an entire night. But I'm certain I saw a pair of bright eyes from behind the curtain. They were wet with tears, and they were only there for an instant before they disappeared.

By the time the sun edged up over the horizon I'd realized it was useless and had gone my way, if only because I knew that Bard was one hell of a shot for a man in his seventies.

I didn't go far, though. For two months I lived as close to the vineyard as I dared. My clothes, which had been neatly filled out, began to sag off of me. Then, when I was about to starve, I got lucky.

Rats are really resilient creatures, you see. I killed thousands, almost eradicated the bastards. Then I was gone for a handful of weeks and they came back tenfold. Not much meat on one, but if you stay down near the water and lay the right traps you can catch a dozen or more in a day. Felt bad about it, at first, until I realized that if I died out there they'd happily gnaw at my corpse without a second thought.

I ate, and I gained weight again, and I waited around in misery, hoping that somehow it'd all work out in the end. When I had a spare moment I'd creep as close to the house as I dared and watch. One time I saw her, with just the faintest hint of a curve on that otherwise rail-thin frame. It was the hardest thing I ever had to do, but I kept quiet and didn't move until she went back inside.

Another month went by, after that. Then one morning, while I was asleep under a blanket of leaves, I heard footsteps. My hand went automatically toward my gun, but it was blown away from my grasp along with three of my fingers. "You haven't gone yet," said Bard.

I screamed and clutched my bloodied hand close to my chest. He watched me patiently while I continued to scream. Then when I stopped he sighed.

"Come on. We'll get something to patch that up."

He took me back to camp and wrapped my hand up himself. He even gave me a handful of aspirin from his own personal supply. As I sat there and wondered where my wife was and what the hell the old man had planned, he cleared his throat. "Sorry about that," he muttered, in a tone of voice that clearly stated he wasn't.

"Where is she?" I asked.

He shook his head and gestured to the pills. I chewed on them without any water and savored the bitter taste. The pain had radiated from my hand all the way up to my shoulder, but I could bear it. In fact, right then it was the only thing that kept me from doing something stupid which, in turn, would have ended up with me dead on the floor and Bard even less repentant about the situation.

"You are not to see my granddaughter; I went for you because it's what God would want me to do. I have so little time left to do good things on this earth. I suppose the Lord just saw fit to give me one last test." As he said this he gave me a sad look and stretched out his empty palms, as if he could fill them with faith and then shove that faith down my throat. He probably would have done so, if he could.

"And what does my wife want?"

"My granddaughter," he said, "Wants to live in peace as long as it's possible to do so. She's been through a nasty shock. You lied about what you were."

"I lied for her."

"You lied. That's all that matters," Bard said. Then he stood up and ushered me out of the small, ramshackle kitchen that nobody had cooked in for years, and back out, where several people had gathered around to watch and listen. The children darted away, as if I were the devil himself in disguise, which is probably what they thought. One of the women, an old friend of Susannah's who'd sung hymns at our wedding, spat in my face. Then I was left to bleed alone and think about what I'd done.

Susannah stayed in the house, but Bard let me move back into the lean-to. There were conditions, though. Every day before I went off to work he came down to me, Bible in hand, and read passages. I'd smile blandly and nod along. He'd ask me if I believed him yet and I'd say "No, sir," and he'd frown and go off and leave me alone. But he was always back the next day.

I hated that man. Then, as time passed, I found it impossible to stay angry. He was interested in my immortal soul, after all. He thought he could save me. I became aware of the fact that he wasn't dangerous, not really; he was just a sad old man who was far more frightened of the world than the world was of him. And in time, my "No, sir," became, "Maybe, sir," and because it seemed to make him happy and it could possibly bring my wife back, I started to say, "Yes, sir".

I was still a liar, but I was a more honest liar now. I had to protect Susannah from the world, and in a way I felt I had to protect Bard from the truth. My hand healed over with fresh skin, and people started to speak to me again. I went to Sunday service in the kitchen of the house and did my best to keep my eyes off of Susannah, and failed, and sometimes she'd turn around and stare at me, and my heart would leap up.

And in the night I would hear the door of my lean-to scrape open and see a faint light. Sometimes she'd lie down next to me, and sometimes she would just peek in and then leave again.

I began to hope that somehow things could get back to the way they were. Then one morning Bard didn't come. I was out in the fields by the time news reached me. He'd had another one of his visions, and everybody was to stop what they were up to and head to the house. I waited until my work was done and it was an hour later before I trudged my way up.

By then everybody was seated out on the wide stretch of grass out front, eyes fixed on the horizon. When I turned and looked myself, I saw why. The multi-colored sky had gone, replaced by a dim white glow. Pearlescent clouds rose up and over the Collision, tinged gold at their edges. Quicksilver swirls of dust rose and fell in the light.

Then I saw them. They seemed to be points of light at first, specks that darted up and down within the clouds. Then one of them got close enough that I could see its outstretched wings.

"Well. Shit," I said.

The gray mountain had been half torn apart in the explosion, so now it rose up like a huge jaw in the earth with hundreds of jagged teeth. That was where Bard said we needed to go, so we packed up everything and left the place that had been our home for so long.

I hardly cared about that. It was just good to be with Susannah again, and it was as if the months behind us had been forgotten. Even Bard didn't seem to mind me much, although he gave me an annoyed look. I expect he'd already decided by then that it wasn't his place to judge me anymore; there were better qualified people around to do the work.

We started our journey in the bright new dawn, made even brighter by the shimmer of that heavenly light.

I still wasn't certain of what to believe, myself, although it was nice to see them so happy. The kids were singing, and some of the people cried. There were about seventy of us, give or take, plus the one my wife was carrying of course. Susannah once told me that when Bard had first set out he'd had over two-hundred followers, but most had died.

Of those who set out for the mountain, several were people like me, who'd found their way to Bard through luck or through rumor of a better way of life. After the first night of our journey most of them had gone. I'd never before considered I wasn't the only one who'd faked his conviction; I was just the only one who'd been stupid enough to say anything.

The abandonment shook their spirits a little bit, but only for a day or two. Then they marched on as if the others had never existed, and continued to do so as night after night more people got up and left.

One night, Susannah woke me. Tears streamed down her face and she clutched me tight. "You can leave if you like, Cal. I won't be angry, I swear. But if you do leave, promise me you'll say goodbye. I don't think I could stand it if you left this world without so much as a . . ."

I kissed her to shut her up. Even after all that time she still tasted like strawberries and sunshine, and I remembered the fantasy I used to have about us and our grandkids. That was the moment it really struck me just how useless fantasies were. After I kissed her I told her that I'd never leave, and I meant it, even though by then I was pretty certain I'd die staying true to my word.

Every night the Collision grew closer, and the sky grew a little brighter. On that night it was practically over our heads, and I could trace shapes in the light like castles in the air. Susannah fell back into a restless sleep but I just watched the shapes and the colors. Then, as I stretched out on the hard ground, I heard a faint squeak. When I turned I could see a pair of bright eyes and a naked tail. The rat stayed there for just a second, then squeaked again and ran off.

In old movies, whenever a ship sank they would show the rats as they ran up from below. It's always a bad sign when you run one way and the rats run another.

As the days passed I watched them, the rats, as they emerged from the underbrush of the forest and went back the way we'd come. But by then it was pointless to argue that this whole thing was stupid and dangerous.

The mountain grew closer, and the rats ran away from it, and the sky continued to glow that unearthly white.

But we never found the angels. They found us.

Their names were Azo and Tenna. Their skin was a deep, rich gold, and it shimmered as they moved. Azo had long black hair that fell almost to his waist, and he wore crimson colored robes that were cut low over a broad, hairless chest. Tenna was slight and fair, with red hair, and he had unusually bright eyes. They were the most beautiful things I think I'd ever seen.

They gave me the creeps.

But I don't think they liked the sight of us any more than we liked the sight of them. Azo seemed to be the superior of the two, and when he went to talk to Bard, Tenna stood with a stern expression on his face in the middle of the encampment with a look that said he'd scream if he even got the slightest bit of dirt from one of us onto his robes.

When Bard came back he told us that they'd been out scouting for survivors, and that there weren't many of us around the rift. Then he told us that they were going to take us with them, to a better place.

My instincts screamed at me to run, but I couldn't. I let them lead me, along with the others, to the base of the mountain where I now saw that several tall crystalline towers stood where just days before there had been nothing. We were ushered into the nearest of the towers, where more angels stripped us of our clothes, all with that same look of disgust on their faces, although I tried to reason with myself that it was probably just pity.

We were a pitiful sight, after all. Better off than most, but there were none of us who didn't have visible bones, and who weren't covered in a fine layer of dirt and sweat. This was in sharp contrast to the room we were in, which was the most beautiful place I'd ever seen. The walls were crystal, and clear. The light that shone through them was broken up into thousands of multicolored streaks of light, which bounced from prism to prism and filled the entire chamber with color. It was an iridescent, fairy tale sort of place. Inside the first tower there was a column, entirely white. I would have thought it was plastic but it felt too solid under my touch. I realized that this inner column was actually hollow as the angels began to usher people in through narrow doors that appeared and disappeared as they approached.

I was freaked, but Susannah couldn't stop smiling, and Bard had this look of perplexed wonder on his face.

The angel that attended me seemed shocked by my absent fingers, and sent another half-dozen of his kind over to investigate. Then I was ushered away from the others, despite my protests, and in through one of the doors in the column.

I entered a small white room where I was instructed to wait; then the door disappeared behind the angel. Literally disappeared, so that there was no way out. I banged on the walls as hard as I could but got no response until several hours later, by my estimate, when Azo came in with a long glass syringe. "Calm yourself," he said. Then he gestured toward a silver grate. I went to stand on it and a faint mist surrounded me. It burned my skin and had a horrible, aseptic smell like bleach and rubbing alcohol. When the spray stopped I was certain a layer of skin had been taken off of me. I was bright pink, and my veins were more visible beneath my flesh. "It's so strange to see a wound like this," he said as he took my hand.

All I was aware of was the fact that I was still naked, and I had been for a while. When I pointed this out to Azo he chuckled, then went to the wall and placed his palm against it. A small slot opened up and some white robes were passed through. "I hope these will suffice?" he said.

"Well. They'll do."

I went to put them on. Then before I was aware that he was about to do anything he grabbed my hand and jabbed the needle in between the knuckles where my fingers used to be. It burned even worse than when they were shot off, and I screamed like hell. Then the white room turned black.

I didn't pass out. Not entirely. Through the haze of pain that swept over me I was aware of being moved. When I started to come back to life my wife was there, with a blank expression on her face. Her hand was on her stomach, which was flat.

"They took her," she said.

"What?"

"They took the baby." Then, as if she hadn't said enough to shock me for one day, she added, "What the hell? Cal, look at your fingers."

There was nothing wrong with them. I had five perfectly ordinary fingers on my right hand, three of which shouldn't have been there.

That was when things started to get a little strange.

"Hello, and welcome to The Nest."

An angel's beautiful face popped up on one of the walls.

"We welcome you, our honored guests, to this refuge in this dark and troubled world."

The angel's face disintegrated into a series of pictures, each more horrible than the next, of my Earth. There was London, which was a disintegrated piece of shit. There was America, on fire. There was Australia, I think, although it was hard to tell if it was really Australia, with all the enormous worms crawling all over the place.

Cue the atmospheric music. Cue the angel's face.

"We have come to take you to a better world. All we ask is that you comply with a few simple rules."

Every damned day, they showed us that. Food appeared and disappeared. The doors would open out into chambers, where we could visit other rooms and see other people. Then there would be a chime, and we'd be instructed to return to our rooms. Then the doors would shut.

Every damned day.

Strangers showed up, puzzled expressions on their faces. The ones that could speak English told us they'd come because of the towers, because of the bright shine of the Collision lights. Others were picked up by the angels, given the same sales pitch we all saw on the walls every day. Some of them were stupid enough that they hadn't yet realized it was all a con.

They'd sit there and talk about their new lives and how great and beautiful everything was going to be, and it made me so sick and angry I wanted to scream.

Every damned day.

"I don't understand. I just don't understand."

Bard sat down on the edge of Susannah's bed. Susannah ran her hand along her flat belly.

"Why can't I come?" he said, as tears leaked from his eyes. "God sent me the visions. But the angels say I can't come."

I wished I could scream. But if I did there'd be an electric jolt, and I'd be out for hours. Learned that the hard way. The angels liked to keep us calm.

One by one they ushered us out for the tests. Some of us came back, but only some of us. I was one of the first to go in.

I was hooked into a little monitor, which one of the angels stared at as the other asked me questions from a small white tablet. And on the monitor they could see flashes, images pulled straight out of my mind. They saw everything: Susannah, and Bard, and the world before, and my vigil outside the vineyard. Then when I was done, they gave me a congratulatory smile and welcomed me to their world. I asked them where my daughter was.

"I'm afraid I can't answer that at this moment," said Avo.

So that was it. I was allowed entrance to heaven, and Bard wasn't, and that freaked the old man out even more than the disembodied voices or the faces on the screen could.

"You're like Moses," I said. "Kind of a bastard thing to do though, isn't it? Make you go through all that work and then lock you out. It's like you planned a party and then you weren't invited."

I'd given up on being nice, by then. But somehow Bard took it as a compliment. "Thank you," he said with tears in his eyes. Then he kissed me on the cheek and went on his way. But Susannah understood. She kept her hand on her belly as she turned to me.

"That was hateful," she hissed.

"Rats in a trap. That's all we are to these guys," I said as I stretched out on my cot and closed my eyes. A few seconds later I heard the mattress creak and felt her curl up beside me. My hand brushed through her hair, and then I just held her as she cried it all out. That happened every day, too, but that I didn't mind. It was all I had left, by then.

"Rats in a trap," I said, as her sobs softened. "They give us this irresistible bait, these crystalline towers. Promises of a better life. And visions of angels."

I'd worked it out by then. It wasn't a pleasant sort of epiphany, unfortunately. I imagine it's the same feeling the rat has when it realizes the cage has closed in on it, and there's no way out.

My fellow rats started to disappear. They'd take us off for more tests, and some would come back and some wouldn't. Some of the ones who still believed took it as a sign they had started to send us over to the better world. I was pretty sure we'd just become too expensive to feed, and wondered what the hell they wanted us for anyway.

Nobody much cared until they came for Bard, though. They came for him, and he said goodbye to Susannah, who cried until she couldn't cry any more. So I decided that overall, I'd had too much of all that. When Avo came for Susannah I bashed his head in until the white walls were spattered with his blood. All I could think after that was how funny it was that angels bled the exact same shade of red that humans did, and they died just as easily. This made me laugh, although my wife didn't seem that happy about it.

Then the shock came and I was paralyzed, and they took me away, still in that dazed darkness that wasn't quite sleep.

When I woke up Tenna was next to me and I was strapped down to a wide white table.

"You really shouldn't have done that," he said.

"Guess not," I responded.

"Well, you've brought this upon yourself. We were planning to put you on the farm, but now you're a liability."

Another shock went through me. It made me tense up, and shiver, and piss myself.

"Are you an angel or an insurance agent?" I asked a few hours later, when I could speak again.

Another shock. Fucker.

"A scientist, actually," he said as the world warped and twisted and colors that I didn't know were colors swam in and out of my field of vision.

A few hours after that I opened my eyes again and Tenna was gone. I lifted my head cautiously, and saw that I wasn't the only one in the room. Bard was across from me, strapped down to a similar bed. Three angels stood around him with long, metal instruments. Blood gushed down his face and onto the collar of his robes as one of the instruments was jammed up his nostrils, and I heard the whirr of a drill as they dug into his temple. Bard's body seized back and forth, and then went still.

I pretended to be paralyzed so I could listen to them talk. It seems that there was something in the old man's brain that they wanted. Something that was far too mysterious for them to leave behind. My guess is it had something to do with the visions he had, although I guess you can't call them visions now, considering where they got us. But they didn't want Bard, himself.

That's when I really started to get it. You see, there's a reason we trap rats. They carry disease. The clean ones, they're great for medical experimentation and all that. And they can be eaten in a pinch, if you can get over your revulsion. But the unclean ones spread disease like crazy, and that's how they saw Bard. Except his was a disease of the mind.

His disease was his religion.

I started to really pay attention, while I was trapped in that room. Imagine my surprise when I figured out that the angels were humans, just like us. They came from Earth, but a different Earth, where a different supercollider in a different country had exploded, and created a different rift.

Their world didn't go to shit like ours though. Actually, from the sounds of it, their Earth was pretty nice. Advanced medicines, advances in technology, and a distinct lack of war and killing that had everything to do with the fact that anybody who disagreed with the vast majority of people were rounded up and used as the rats in the medical experiments that led to all that advanced technology.

This was why they needed us. It seems they'd started to run out of people who disagreed with them, and had run into a little problem. Where were they going to get their lab rats, and their spare skin tissue, and the odd extra organ?

Then, like a miracle, their rift had merged with our Collision, and a pathway was formed between Heaven and Hell.

So the ones who seemed the most compliant, who didn't seem to be in the mood to rebel anytime soon, would be kept in farms as breeding stock. The others would be chopped up for parts.

I wasn't really angry about the whole situation, though. Not until they told me they planned to blow up the planet.

"Otherwise we risk your humans finding the rift and coming through, and that could be dangerous," he said. "Our people don't really know how to fight."

How right he was. As he spoke I watched Bard get up from his operating table, one of the tools they'd used to slice up his brain in hand, and dig it deep into Tenna's neck. As the angel bled out Bard unstrapped me from my table — then he went back to being a gibbering mess. Poor old man. I really did feel sorry for him.

It seems that that infirmary room wasn't built to electrify the air the way the holding rooms were, which seemed to leave them at a loss until the acid spray turned on at full blast from the spigots overheard. I started to burn, and Bard started to scream. Then pushed beyond my breaking point, and left without any capacity to care what else happened next, I sat down on the floor and let it wash down over me. By the time it stopped I had started to bleed from every pore.

But Bard was all right. He was bright pink from the initial blast, but nowhere near as damaged as I was. "Do you really want what's inside his brain that much?" I said out loud. They had to be listening. When they didn't respond I grabbed him by the hair and forced his head back down toward the floor. "I'll bash it out right now if you don't say something."

Another long pause. Then a face flickered up on the wall.

"Don't."

Bard started to cry.

"Why not?"

The face twisted up, as if the angel wanted to smile but had forgotten how. "We'll give her to you. Your wife. That is what you want, isn't it?"

"Sure. So we can all die together," I mused.

But actually it didn't sound like that bad of an idea, I thought, as the words rolled off my tongue.

They gave me Susannah, and she kissed me one last time, and it was sweet like strawberries and sunshine. They took us away from the crystalline towers, and the angels, and we lived at the base of the mountain in a little makeshift lean-to against the side of the ridge. We ate rats and berries, and made love to each other beneath the golden glow of light that filtered down from above the Collision.

Then, we waited for the end of the world.

It was like the vineyard again, except this time I knew better than to hope. There wasn't going to be an after—a time when it all got better. And there wasn't a heaven to go to, either. So we lived in the moment, me and my wife, and I dreamed of the stories I would have told my daughter about the rift and all the colors, if we had lived in another world.

Then one morning, as the bright winter sun filtered down through the white and gold, we saw the towers begin to shrink and compact. They folded up and turned and began to float down towards the gaping chasm of the rift—all but two. I told Susannah that was it, it was the end. And I suppose I should have stayed there, so we could be together for it. But I couldn't help but get one last glimpse at the creatures that were supposed to have been humanity's salvation.

The nearest tower was still and silent. All the doors were open, now, and it was easy to ascend to the top. There, in a narrow cockpit, sat Bard, next to an angel with a solemn look on its face.

"I had a vision," he said.

"I know. Come on, quiet now," I told him.

Then his eyes met mine. "We're going to stop it. The destroyer of worlds." I stared into his eyes, which were as clear as they used to be for just a fragment of a second. Then drool leaked out from his lips and his eyes rolled back into his scalp.

I had thought that the angel was dead, but as I moved forward she turned and looked up at me.

I suppose I shouldn't have been surprised to see Susannah's eyes. They'd been able to grow three fingers out of nowhere, after all; it probably wasn't too difficult to grow a sixteen-year old girl from a fully formed fetus. And I'm sure they knew that Bard would never kill someone who looked so much like her, even in that addled state. I would have thought she was a clone if it weren't for the curve of her jaw, which was just like mine, or the dark chestnut color of her hair.

"They let me watch him," she said. "They told me not to listen to what he said, but I couldn't help it. His words were so lovely. He thought I was an angel."

"You are." A repulsive, beautiful angel, just like the others. But I couldn't hate her, no matter how much I wanted to, because when she smiled it was just frightened enough, just human enough, that I fell in love with her despite what she was. "You're a real angel," I said, and I meant it.

"No. Not a real one, anyway." She faltered, and then she began to undo the restraints that held her back to the chair. She moved over to Bard and placed her hand on his forehead. "He had a lot of visions. When they damaged the prefrontal cortex it took away the ability to suppress them. They told me not to listen, but they sounded so wonderful. He talked about this little house, and fields full of tangled vines, and he called me Susannah. I'm not her, I don't think. But I look like her. I saw, on the machines. I watched his life, and I saw everything."

The machines that they'd used to see my life—she'd used them on Bard. My wonderful, clever little girl. I thought for just a moment that perhaps there were really such things as miracles, and that perhaps I had been witness to one just then. After all, the daughter I thought was dead had just been resurrected. Perhaps it was possible that she held the secrets to the world's salvation in that stern, beautiful face.

"Do you know how to stop that bomb?" I asked. She shook her head and continued to brush her hands along Bard's scalp.

"It can't be stopped. But you can turn it around. Send it back through the rift. I would go, but I think he needs me. And the other one, the one who looks like me."

I thought about telling her the story, like I had in my fantasies, but there was no time. Susannah would have to be the one. I thought of the world, and about the fact that my little girl was going to get a chance to live in it, and for the first time in a long while I felt the weight lift from my chest.

"It's all right. I'll go. There's no reason for me to stick around, anyway. I've sort of overstayed my welcome."

So she told me how. Then she left with her grandfather, and I told her where to meet her mother, and I made my way to the second tower.

As I sit here and descend down through the darkness, I can see the other world. It's as bright and beautiful as I imagined it would be. The buildings rise like glass into a golden sky, and people fly on broad white, mechanical wings. But it's not home, and given the choice I'm glad it's them and not me. Because my world may be broken, it may be ashes, but humans are resilient, like rats. We'll rebuild and make it better. If they did it, we can too. And we'll do a better job of it than they did.

The countdown beeps. And for some reason, I say a prayer as I wait for the end of the world.

Scott Fletcher could tell that Natalie wanted to kill something.

"Damn it!" she hissed under her breath, quiet enough that if anything were around that wanted to kill them they'd be safe enough, loud enough for Scott to know she really meant it.

It was too late. They were miles away when they saw the thin white column lift up from the cover of the trees and glide soundlessly into the chasm. Then Scott's mind began to slip and he saw a tall broad man, behind the wide glass screen of that far-off tower. There was just a glimpse of gold light through all the darkness, and then he was gone along with the vision.

Scott had seen them come through—the people in white. They had seemed normal. Not bloodthirsty monsters, anyway.

He had almost hoped that maybe they could be the ones to save the human race, but he was wrong.

"We could have made it through. We could have seen what was on the other side..." Natalie was beginning to stammer.

"I told you not to get your hopes up. We didn't even know it was possible to pass through without ending up as crispy fried human."

She slumped down next to Scott on the porch of the old, abandoned house they had found. There were still signs that people had been there, not too long before. One could always smell it, the remnants of life. It was a foul, strange, distinctly human smell, and the air was thick with it. Scott wondered if the other people living there had managed to get away. He hoped they had.

"We can get through. All we need is something like those towers, something that can protect us. And if we can pass through, we might be able to close it."

An hour later, there was a bright flash of light, and then the Collision was back as it had been before.

THE LAST CEO
by Jordan Ellinger

I watched from the 50-yard line of the stadium as the Demon Queen slowly covered Joseph in mucus. She dwarfed him easily, caressing him with dark tentacles like a mother stroking a favorite child. Gelatinous, semi-transparent snot darkened Joseph's sun-bleached army fatigues, globules dangling from the bill of his Dodgers cap.

Another man would have already screamed away his vocal cords, but Joseph's peculiar form of psychosis held him as steady as a rock. I could see his eyes follow the birthing appendage as it unfolded from the Queen's body and stretched out towards him. He wasn't afraid or panicked or any kind of emotion. His features were as blank as the day we met.

I'd been hiding under a toppled billboard on Fifth Avenue, sheltered from the gasbags by an advertisement for a giant man-purse from Ricky Soza's spring collection.

Monica was nearby. I heard her fluttering breath as she pulled her leg away from a ray of sunshine. I found her shoulder in the darkness, stroked it, and her breathing quieted.

A few feet away, a tentacle methodically snuffled the sidewalk, smelling for us. It brushed the blasted concrete as delicately as a landing mosquito, working its way towards us.

I knew better than to run for it. Twenty, maybe thirty feet above us, a demon hovered, puffing out methane and hydrogen as it maintained its altitude, a mockery of the zeppelins that had once plied the New York skyline. Ricky Soza's billboard was the only thing keeping us alive. If we bolted—if we made a dash for the bodega across the street—its tentacles would strike with the speed of an anemone snatching a passing fish and pull us into its razor-filled maw.

I felt in my pocket for something to use to defend us and touched the rough, papery edge of a flare I'd rescued from a construction site's first aid kit. I also had a bowie knife tucked into my belt, but that wouldn't be much use against the gasbags. The flare, I imagined, could be thrown into its gullet and maybe ignite whatever gasses were keeping it aloft. Cold comfort, but my hand tightened on the flare as I watched the tentacle slithering its way over to our hiding spot.

I heard gravel shift as Monica pressed close to me. Nothing but skin and bones wrapped in a green US Marines T-shirt and baggy cargo pants several sizes too large. Streaks of road dirt smeared her face, but I could never fail to see the beauty underneath. Lucky we got along too—she was the only living being I'd seen for weeks.

"It's gone," she whispered in a soft voice.

I looked out into the street. No tentacle. "Oh shit."

My knife was in my hands before I knew it, but I was too late. A high-pitched whine echoed from outside and then there were tentacles all around us, whipping black tubes blocking out the light. Monica was pulled away from me and out into the street. I followed, swinging my knife before me, hand clutched tightly on the flare. I reached out for Monica but a tentacle whipped around my heel. I had a brief image of a gray blob against an equally grey sky and Monica's face twisting in fear as she was hauled upwards towards a frightening small snapping mouth. I hacked at the tentacle on my ankle, but it jerked me backwards and I was under the billboard again, sliding towards the other side. My wrist banged against something hard and my hand spasmed open. I'd lost the flare.

In the old days, men in my position might have said their prayers. Me, I knew better. I just hoped the demon wouldn't hurt Monica much before I could put her out of her misery with my knife.

I think I heard the sound of Joseph's .45 over the sound of my own screams. I must have—the damn thing always went off like a howitzer. But at the time all I knew was that suddenly the tentacle around my leg went slack and Monica hit the ground hard, but rolling. The demon impacted a few seconds later like someone had thrown a sack of potatoes out of a fifth story window.

Joseph Tern had found us.

He stood with one foot balanced on a lump of busted concrete, gun barrel bleeding smoke. Joseph could have been ex-military—army fatigues, mirrored aviator glasses, pants tucked into combat boots. A Cigarillo jutted out from between thin lips rimmed by shadowy facial hair. He approached, and I smelled Old Spice and a whiff of B.O.

"Bosley says you owe me one," he said.

If I'd expected a friendly hand to help me to my feet, it never came. "Bosley's right," I said with a grunt and went to check on Monica.

"Who's Bosley?" she mouthed to me when I got close. I shrugged. Curiosity was a good sign. People with broken legs and crushed ribs usually have more pressing things to worry about than the identity of a stranger.

"Keep still," I told her. She had some burns from tentacle mucus on her arms and back. I did my best to scrape the gooey substance off with a piece of discarded cardboard, and then gave her a couple of Tylenol-3s from our precious supply to dull the pain. My ankle was a little burnt, but it held my weight. I retrieved my flare and then walked over to Joseph. He'd been inspecting his kill, getting a real good look at it. He stood as I approached.

"My name's Jamie, and this is Monica."

I hadn't realized Monica'd followed me until she asked a question with her customary lack of tact. "Who's Bosley?"

Joseph didn't blink an eye, and I realize now that he must have gotten this question dozens of times before. "Why don't you ask him yourself?"

It took me exactly thirty seconds of looking around like an idiot before I figured out that Joseph was cracked. It wasn't uncommon to find a nutter out here in the concrete wilderness. I once ran across a man in a crumpled velvet suit who tried to sell me a Miata off a used car lot. For pocket lint. Turned out he'd been raiding the trays at every coin-op for miles and had a ball of the stuff in the back that he'd shaped like a gasbag. Thing was, he was terrified of gasbags. Every time he found a new stash of lint, he'd add it to the pile, screaming like an eight-year-old girl the whole time.

In my experience, insanity has no predefined career path. The mind goes to a lot of strange places when it's broken, and it looked like Joseph's had created himself a friend to talk to. I remember being charmed more than scared.

After he saved our lives, it seemed natural that we should travel together, and when I suggested that to Joseph, he shrugged and said, "Bosley says you might make good bait."

The word "bait" terrified me, but after a couple of weeks of luring gasbags into position so Joseph could bring 'em down with a well-placed shot, I began feeling pretty good about myself. Joseph had explained in colloquial terms that the gasbags had no reproductive organs. According to him, that meant that whatever bio-weapons division, alien invasion, or occult sorcerer had released them into the world had only made a limited number. After all, they were nearly invincible. Injure them and they just puffed up and headed for the stratosphere until they healed up. In fact, I'd never seen a single gasbag corpse until that day when Joseph killed one in front of me. Not a single body. If their numbers were limited—though it might take twenty years of running bait and downing gasbags—we might clear out enough of them to make a difference.

Turned out that the gasbags had four vestigial nodules, one at each point of the compass, and a smaller, bumpier appendage where the gasbags' central helium chamber tapered to a point. It was this bumpier appendage that Joseph would take out with surgical precision—armed only with a handgun — from sixty or even eighty feet away. The man's aim was incredible.

Weeks after we met — even after I'd run bait for him and we'd killed a half-dozen methane munchers — I still didn't quite know what to make of him. He had this intangible "fuck you" aura out to a distance of about three feet. When he spoke to you, he seemed to stare right through you from behind the sunglasses, and he answered questions mechanically.

I'd heard that sociopaths work like that — no real emotions, just clever trickery. But Joseph didn't quite check that box on the old mental health forms. He had emotions, he just didn't know what to make of 'em. Once, when we were clearing rotting cardboard out of the lee of an underpass, looking for some place to sleep where the gasbags wouldn't grab us, we came across two bodies. A young golden retriever mutt, hair as clean as a beauty queen's except where blood from a tear in its side had scabbed and tangled it. Joseph froze when he saw it, a length of cardboard disintegrating in his hand. I stood quietly to the side as he bent and slowly lifted the body. Underneath was a tiny, more fragile form. A kitten, calico maybe, a couple of months old at best. The body draped limply in Joseph's hand, every bone crushed, most of its insides visible through a hole in its stomach, probably from the same strike that had killed the mutt.

Joseph began weeping openly. He held the body in the palm of his hand and stroked the kitten with the top of his finger. I'd seen Monica cry a million times, but seeing Joseph with tears rolling down his cheeks was about as surprising as waking up on the Moon.

Other times, he looked at you like he was just two heartbeats from breaking a hole in your smile with the butt of his gun. Once, I awoke from a deep sleep in the dead of night to find his hands wrapped around my neck. His grip was soft but firm, and I felt the rough edges of his thumbnails on my wind pipe. He had one green eye and one blue, and he stared at me with a gaze that was both dead and terrifying. After a time, he released me and returned to his own bedroll.

Though I didn't sleep for the rest of the night, and lightly for weeks afterwards, we never left. I'd learned to live with death a long time ago, and I preferred Joseph to the gasbags. He couldn't be all bad, I told myself. He was actively killing the demons after all, and, well, the enemy of my enemy, right?

Monica never saw it that way, but then she was always smarter than me. Joseph was fire, we both knew that, but where I saw a foundry, she saw a burning tenement. Worse, she wanted to prove to me that she was right, and the only way she could think to do was to pour gasoline on the conflagration.

We'd entered a new area of the city in the pursuit of an Indian man Joseph said he was looking for. I sensed there was something more he wasn't telling us, but didn't press him for it. Monica sensed it too, and she'd never developed my sense of restraint. She began to simmer as we passed squat white buildings that huddled against each other in a natural corridor that reminded me of nothing more than the hallway in a hospital. Before the infestation, this area had been home to trendy stores and boutiques—we passed a giant navy blue Gap sign that had rusted off its moorings and shattered on the sidewalk. Now, it was abandoned. Signs of decay were everywhere—even the buildings themselves were starting to fall apart. Crumbling stucco littered the sidewalks exposing a web of rusted silver chicken wire and black weatherproofing underneath. In a few years, the whole area would crumble into heaps of broken concrete punctuated by clusters of weeds.

We came across a cracked egg—a small brick building that had once housed a family of survivors. Like many eggs, the only windows were tiny and boarded up, and the door had been reinforced. It might have been a bar or nightclub in another age, but someone had turned it into a fortress.

Didn't matter in the end.

Fortresses are obvious from the air, and the gasbags homed in on them. It looked like they'd taken this one apart brick by brick. Globs of red mud spattered the sidewalk—all that remained of bricks that the gasbags had melted with their tentacle mucus. There'd be a hole in the roof through which the gasbags had pulled their victims before devouring them like little old ladies popping crumpets at a tea party.

I knew that Monica had survived an attack like the one that had taken this building apart a couple of weeks before I met her. As we passed, I looked at her sidelong, thinking that she might want to act tough in front of Joseph, and she did for a couple of minutes. Then she started to tremble, so I held open a wing of my trench coat and wrapped her into me when she came. Her arm slipped around my waist and her cheek was warm against my chest.

Eggs didn't make me nervous. I'd spent a few years after the end of the world growing up with the People Beneath the Streets, or PBSers for short. Life down there was a hellish existence for a nine-year-old. Almost no food—just mushrooms and mold and whatever you could scrounge from the surface. What little illumination there was came from shafts of light lancing into the slime and muck from gratings above. Gasbags camped at every manhole cover, waiting for that inevitable dash for food.

I left them when I was old enough to realize how futile that kind of existence could be. Humankind just wasn't built to live underground. On the surface, there was food. Grocery stores had been picked clean years—sometimes nearly a decade—ago, but wild plants had taken over, even in the heart of what used to be the concrete jungle. You could usually find a blackberry bush growing out of a chain-linked fence, or even kill a feral dog or cat if you were lucky, and cook the meat. I'd given up trying to remember the world that wasn't anymore and started trying to survive in the world that was left.

Cracked eggs were usually decent places to find grub, but this one had long since been picked clean by scavengers. Nothing but a pile of damp flyers in the corner.

"Goddamn Fixers," said Joseph peeling loose a flyer from the top of the pile. It was a recruitment brochure, but one that was obviously designed to work through fear rather than patriotism. It was covered by pictures of various demons, mostly canine looking—pit bulls, with maybe a Scraper tossed in for good measure.

"Who're the Fixers?" I asked, curious.

Monica looked out from my trench coat, then sighed and in a hopeless voice, said: "Probably another group of end-of-the-world cultists that the Good Lord put on this Earth to torment us."

Joseph gave her a sharp look. "Bosley says that God doesn't exist."

"Bosley don't know shit."

My hand, which had been resting lightly on Monica's shoulder, tightened like a vice. If you ever need a shot of adrenaline, try picking a fight with a psychotic killer's imaginary friend.

"Ow, you're hurting me." Monica pushed her way out of my coat. I lunged for her, but she shook me loose again. "No, this is bullshit Jamie. We've been tiptoeing around this psycho for weeks, and for what? I was less afraid when it was just us and the gasbags. Christ, we actually seek them out now. Bait? It's all bullshit!" She turned on him, a woman with the emaciated frame of a small girl, stringy red hair full of road grime, a dozen cuts and scrapes half healed over, standing before a man twice her size.

"Ants! Fucking ants!" Her laugh was harsh, cruel, and a little insane. "Ants don't have sex organs either! They've got a queen. Pumping little ant babies out by the millions."

She gulped in a breath and came at him again, spittle flying out of her mouth. "You thought you were making a difference, killing one gasbag at a time? Somewhere out there is a Bitch Queen spitting out demon babies ten million at a time."

He just looked at her with those dead eyes, then pulled the .45 out of the holster in the small of his back and put it to her forehead.

My instincts kicked in and I leapt at him. The world was shitty enough with Monica in it; I wasn't going to live without her. Maybe I had a plan to pull the gun out of his hand, or maybe I thought he'd shoot me instead of her. All he did was shift his weight to the side and pistol-whip me as I went by.

I came to and saw him standing over me, silhouetted by the sun, his grey eyes looking down at me from the shadow of his baseball cap. He pointed the .45 at me, puffed out his cheeks and made the sound of a gunshot, like an eight year old might make in a game of cowboys and Indians. "Bang," he said calmly. "You're dead."

And I mighta been, if it weren't for the Fixer that stepped into my line of sight and nuzzled the mouth of his AK-47 up against the back of Joseph's skull. All nice and friendly like.

His name was Timmons. At the time, I figured he was a good guy, because he let me sit on the curb and puke my guts up into a storm drain undisturbed. Coming down from an adrenaline high is about as fun as a heaping spoonful of kick in the face. Combine that with the blow I took from Joseph, and I wasn't in good shape.

Timmons was typical for a Fixer. Slim, average looking, dressed in a grey three-piece banker's suit. Yeah, I'm not kidding. There were four of them in the party that found us, all rugged military-looking men, and all of them were dressed in three-piece suits and wingtips. Actors from a Men's Warehouse billboard bearing hulking assault rifles, scanning shadows, moving with military precision. Their headquarters was in the last place in the world I would expect.

They took us to Rogers Centre.

We passed huge billboards of football players from the Toronto Argonauts churning up the gridiron and anonymous Blue Jays batting home runs. Next to these were banks of box offices, now boarded up and sporting gaudy pink flyers streaked with greenish-brown mildew. We entered via the hotel, across the parkway from where lines of taxicabs once waited to ferry guests to and from Pearson's International. Dozens, if not hundreds of moldering sofas were heaped against what must once have been the Renaissance's plate-glass entryway. Our guides went right to a small opening in the sofas and guided us through a twisting maze until we came to a doorway and a small silver turnstile that clicked as we passed through it.

The air inside the hotel reeked of stale water and fertilizer, and we passed row after row of hydroponic gardens. Young children, faces shadowed by the light, looked up at us with eyedroppers in their hands, pruning shears momentarily forgotten in the presence of strangers.

The stink reminded me a little of the PBSers, but the Fixers were way more advanced. Somewhere in the distance, I could hear the rumble of a diesel generator, probably the repurposed backup generator for the stadium. The general level of health was very good; faces were clear of the kind of skin diseases that plagued the PBSers. Hair, though greasy, had none of the straw-like texture that signaled scurvy, indicating that these people had access to a source of vitamin C. After months of trudging lonely streets, Rogers Centre was Shangri-La.

We passed through the concourse and up two flights of wide stairs. On the third floor, we entered the skybox area and passed a row of doors with various corporate sponsors on them-Air Canada, Coca Cola, Ontario Hydro. Finally, we arrived at a door that was flanked by two large men in black suits and ties. They appeared to have a length of white string attached to the inside of their right ears, which draped over their shoulders and hung down their backs, not, apparently, attached to anything at all. Fancy gold lettering proclaimed this the "owner's box." Our "guides" exchanged greetings with the guards and we were led inside.

The room was full of people in suits, men and women both. The quiet buzz of conversation hung in the air. Monica nudged me, indicating with a glance the long snack table that ran along a side wall. This, perhaps, was the greatest sign of opulence I had ever seen. Aluminum bowls sat in some kind of greenery, each overflowing with everything from vegetables to some kind of meat that looked like chicken but was almost certainly rat. The sheer quantity of food was impressive, but the real show of power was the ice that cradled each bowl. Any civilization that could make ice in the mid-summer humidity of Toronto had moved beyond the needs of sheer survival.

After years of living on the streets and fighting for our daily bread, the sight of so much food nearly brought me to tears.

I pictured settling here with Monica. I'd pass whatever tests they set for outsiders to join them—hell, if they were cultists, I'd convert. We'd start low, maybe as hydroponic farmers. I'd even take shifts with their scouting parties—Lord knows I knew the city well enough. Perhaps, eventually, we'd be given our own three-piece suits and be allowed into the Owner's Box, with its table of opulence. I'd peck at it delicately, because by then I'd have forgotten the grinding pain of hunger.

"Something's not right here," whispered Monica. She'd fallen back with me, letting Joseph—our show of force—walk ahead of us. "What is a society this advanced doing in the middle of the thickest concentration of gasbags we've ever seen?"

"The gasbags can't get them here," I hissed back. "They're too well entrenched."

Monica was about to respond, but a booming voice emerged from the crowd.

"Timmons! What *have* you brought us?"

We'd been carefully and deliberately ignored until then, but now a hush swept over the gathered crowd, and people began moving out of our way. As they did, I saw who had originated the question.

His name was Irwin Fischer, and he was the leader of the Fixers. Though the rest of the room looked like a banker's convention, he was conspicuous in his casual attire. He wore a blue-collared shirt over which he'd tied an angora sweater so that the sleeves hung loosely down his chest. Immaculately-pressed khaki pants clung to thin hips. Later, he'd pass close by and I'd smell the cloying scent of men's cologne.

His throne was the skeleton of a stripped down Porsche 911 Turbo that sat in the middle of the Owner's Box. In the seat next to him, as if she was out for a Sunday drive, was his trophy wife. I never did get to learn her name, but I felt an upwelling of pity for her. Her hair was straw blonde, and her cheeks were pale and sunken in, so much so that I could very nearly count her teeth, though her mouth was closed. She wore a flimsy blue sundress, which contained a deep chest and a skeletal frame. She was a living mockery of billboard models advertising the latest fall fashions.

"Jamie. Good Lord," Monica had seen her too. I found her hand and held it tightly. Her palms were smooth, soft, and clean, and when my fingers slipped between hers, I felt her pulse against mine. That was the last time I ever held her hand.

Our captor, Timmons, clicked his wingtips together. "We found them in Zeta sector. They were heading in this direction, so we followed them for several blocks, moving in only when it looked like the big one was going to kill this man and his woman."

Fischer smiled, an expression about as natural as lips on a chicken. As he came towards us the crowd parted—no one dared get within two feet of him. He looked at us like we were cardboard cut-outs. In his mind, there was only one guy in the room, and he was wearing Irwin Fischer's shoes.

"And what," he asked of me, "is your name?"

"Jamie, my Lord." I was shit-scared, but the rational part of me—the part that had been eyeing the snack bar since the moment we entered the room—that part of me wanted to calm the fuck down so we could get something to eat. "And this is Monica. Our friend's name is Joseph, sir, and while it must have looked like something more serious from where your man was standing, we were merely having a disagreement."

Timmons's expression was military in its stoniness. He stepped forward, pulling Joseph's .45 out of his rear waistband. "The big one was aiming this at the other one's head."

Fischer whistled between his teeth and took the weapon, hefting it in his hand to test the weight. He wrapped his hand around the butt, and as his finger found the trigger the temperature in the room dropped about twenty degrees. "This is, um, quite the weapon, Jamie. It would have taken your head clean off. Still might, if I gave it back to your friend, wouldn't it?"

The menace that flowed from the man at that point was physical. I should have grabbed Monica and made a run for the streets, but like a drowning man clutching a life raft, I tried to convince myself that there was some way we could stay. Just keep the hell out of Fischer's way in some hydroponics lab or the generator room, lose ourselves in anonymity. I *wanted* to get the hell out of there. But I stayed. And I would pay for that mistake. "Go ahead," I said, as casually as I could, "Joseph and I were just playing around, right Joseph?"

Joseph was standing rigidly, but from my angle I could see that, behind those aviator glasses, his gaze was following his weapon. "Bosley says you should give me back my gun."

I winced. Nothing like ingratiating yourselves with your host by advertising that you're a nut job.

Fischer's eyes peaked with interest, and he stepped in front of Joseph. Looking alarmed that his King was in harm's way, Timmons made as if to move closer, but Fischer waved him off. "Who's Bosley?" he asked.

Joseph smiled. "Why don't you ask him yourself?"

The silence lasted about three weeks.

Fischer ran his fingers along the top of the gun, bumping up against the sight and then traveling back down towards the hammer. He paused.

"The Fixers," he said, magnanimously, "are a revenue generating company. We're operating in the black, always have been. Morale is high and profits are soaring."

"Profits are soaring," echoed the crowd reverently.

Fischer's posture changed, and he crossed his arms so that the tip of the .45 tapped against his hip. "Whatever dispute you had between you is hereby resolved. We don't have room for Prima Donnas. There is no "I" in team."

A voice suddenly called out from the somewhere in the crowd, "Ask them about the Scrapers!"

Fischer's eyes narrowed and Timmons scanned the crowd to see if he could spot whoever spoke out of turn, but came up empty.

"We would all like to fact-find our competition, but our guests are tired and hungry." He turned to them. "Please, make yourselves comfortable. I have a stocked sushi bar. Please avail yourselves."

He turned to walk away, but Monica interrupted. "How do you keep the gasbags away?" Her tone was surgical and abrupt; that was just her way. My breath caught. Luckily, the question seemed to bounce off Fischer.

"We'll give you the tour after dinner," he said as he opened the door of his Porsche. "I'm sure all of your questions will be answered then." The slamming of the Porsche door was final, and though we could plainly see him through the windshield, clearly, he was done with us for the moment.

"Sushi," as I understood it from reading the menus of the various Japanese restaurants that we'd passed, consisted mainly of raw fish—sometimes chicken or beef—usually wrapped in seaweed. This was nothing of the sort. Limp vegetables, heavily salted, interspersed with chucks of rat meat. It was a one star meal, but that still made it three stars better than what we'd eaten on the streets.

We ate our fill, chewing rubbery meat with gusto. Food can be pretty scarce, especially in the more picked-over areas. None of us was going to look a gift horse in the mouth.

Still, I worried about Joseph. Despite telling Fischer that there was nothing between the two of us, I remembered staring down the muzzle of his .45 and that little childish death noise he'd made. Still, the way Fischer'd made love to Joseph's gun had proven he was psychotic, and while I was sure that Joseph was also a refugee from the straitjacket police, I thought I had his insanity mapped out. Fischer was the devil I didn't know.

"Look, Joseph," I said, trying to make nice, "what happened before...Monica was out of line."

He grunted, and pressed a chuck of rat flesh into his mouth. He chewed, then chipmunked a mouthful into his cheek. "Fend for yourselves."

I retreated to where Monica was standing with a small ornamental china plate filled with chunks of carrot.

"I think we're on our own, honey. Joseph's the lesser of two evils, but I think the operative word there is evil. Fischer... maybe he can be reasoned with."

"How does he keep the gasbags away, Jamie?" Monica didn't look like she'd eaten much. She'd always been the brains to my brawn, and her brain was churning up all kinds of dangerous scenarios for us. Out there, I'd only watched the skies to keep a demon from taking my head off. Monica, she was watching the gasbags as much as they were watching us. As we moved through the city, she'd figured out their paths, knew where they were thickest and where they were thinnest. She'd figured out that they all seemed to come from one direction: Rogers Centre.

"I'm worried they have something planned for us. He didn't ask us where we were from, where we've been, or if there are any more of us. Shouldn't he have asked how long we intend to stay? We could be just passing through for all he knows."

Now that was a telling point. I glanced around at the other party guests, but they seemed to be studiously ignoring us. I quietly stuffed my pockets with vegetables.

"Ladies and gentlemen!" Fischer's sudden outburst made me jump guiltily. He'd once again left his throne to walk amongst the people. "As you know, times are tough. We are currently living in the deepest recession the world has ever seen. And yet, in this time of cutbacks, the Fixers are growing! Witness our three latest acquisitions!"

There was muted clapping from the crowd of suits.

"Profits are soaring," he proclaimed.

"Profits are soaring!" they echoed.

"We are about to induct three new assets into our portfolio. Our corporate balance sheet is strong."

Timmons materialized at my side. "You're coming with us. Don't make a fuss." He patted his rifle. That he needed to threaten us at all made me want to grab Monica and run screaming in the other direction. For now, though, we needed to play it cool. Wait until no one was watching and then duck out a side door.

We walked down the hall, flanked by Timmons and his three goons. Fischer led us, having left his queen chained to the Porsche. No one stared. People went about their daily business with eyes downcast. Perhaps word of our passage had flown before us, because this time the hallways were much less crowded.

We passed into one of the sub-floors and then down a huge concrete passageway. Ahead of us, I saw the dimly lit field, and I allowed myself to imagine that we were a football team walking onto the field to the acclaim of cheering fans. But there were no fans on the field; instead, we were moving towards the Demon Queen.

She waited for us on the 50-yard line. A huge grey mass of bloated flesh covered in a pox of fine silver fur, she looked like a whale carcass after twenty days on the beach. She had no visible eyes, just tentacles that doubled as feelers, which persistently swept the ground around her. Though a body that size must have needed a frightening amount of nutrition each day to stay alive, she had no visible orifice through which to eat, see, or smell.

"My God, Jamie. My God." Monica latched onto my arm. Timmons, who marched nearby, shifted uneasily at the sudden movement and clutched his AK-47 a little tighter. We were prisoners, I had no illusions about that, but Timmons was acting like we had nothing to lose, and that was scary. I thought suddenly of the protein requirements of Her Ladyship, but as quickly as the thought occurred to me, I discarded it. There was no way they'd feed us to the Queen. First of all, we were too insignificant to satiate the hunger of a beast that size. Secondly, transients like us couldn't be a reliable food source. There weren't many of us left.

An ugly rut carved through the field seemed to mark a safe distance from the Queen. A podium sat close by, topped by a blocky microphone, and next to that stood a retractable screen.

With the ease of routine, Fischer slipped behind the podium, while Timmons went over to an ancient projector and flipped a switch. The projector lit up, and a bunch of images flashed onto the screen. At the bottom right corner sat a small rectangular logo that read "PowerPoint".

Fischer waited patiently for the third slide before he began to speak. This slide had a black and white picture of "The City of the Future" with blocky capital letters that spelled out Alien Invasion.

"Many years ago, our world faced a catastrophe of epic proportions. Invasion. The Scrapers came."

The projected slide disintegrated, another left in its wake. A brightly lit lab with a half dissected wolf on an operating table. I'd heard of Scrapers before, even seen one or two of the crazy beasts slinking around in the sewers. But the gasbags were everywhere. They were the cause of all this destruction, not some egg-laying wolf.

But Fischer didn't seem to know what was obvious to anyone who spent more than an hour outside in the gasbag schmorgasboard. He continued: "Able to reproduce in vast numbers and with ten times the immune system of the common rat, they quickly swept through the city, laying their eggs on the bottom of mass transit vehicles, hiding in the holds of salt water tankers. Civilization—," and here he paused to wait for the next slide that depicted the world I'd grown up in, all busted up buildings and crumbling roads. "— was in ruins.

"The scientists of the time had dealt with invasion before." A grainy black and white video of dozens of rabbits hopping towards a farm, then to a sea floor matted so thickly with mussels it was impossible to see anything else. Fischer spoke when the video spliced to a lake lost beneath a sea of lilies. "Water hyacinth clogged much of Lake Victoria, killing native fish and endangering local fishermen but it was controlled. It. Was. Controlled. They discovered that taming the weed was as easy as introducing a predator into the lake to prune it back. In this case, a small South American beetle. Elsewhere, moths to eat prickly pears, cane toads to eat sugar cane parasites—biological control of invasive species was a well understood science. So it was only natural for the world to turn to another species to control the Scrapers. A predator."

I was miles behind him, but Monica had already figured it out. One moment she was watching that shitty slideshow with the rest of us and the next she was drawing four neat little red lines on Fischer's face with her nails and screaming hysterically. Confused and terrified, I tried to pull her off him; my rational mind—still two city blocks behind Monica—couldn't understand why the hell she was so upset. I was rewarded with a rifle butt to the spine.

It took me three tries to get off my belly. The ground kept sliding out from under me, and my vision was mostly green and grey lines with shadowy, pissed off figures running in all directions.

They'd shoved Monica over the rut while my wits unscrambled. One of the Demon Queen's tentacles struck as quick as lightning, a large black protrusion snaking around her ankles, then tightening painfully. Once it had her, another tentacle brushed that stinging mucus all up and down her. I stumbled towards Monica, but my legs wouldn't work right and I fell, my weight landing awkwardly on my face and upper chest. I'd fought every gasbag from Toronto to Lake Superior to keep her safe and here, I had finally failed her.

She turned towards me as the birthing tentacle unfolded. Lips moved. "It's not your fault. I love you."

I leapt at her again, but this time there were three sets of strong hands to restrain me, closing around my shoulders and wrists like manacles.

She screamed when the birthing tentacle began sliding up her leg. I felt rage, I felt fear. I'd always thought that when the chips were down I'd turn into some kind of superman and smash everything in sight until I had my Monica, but scream and claw as I might I couldn't get an inch closer to her.

Just as the birthing tentacle plunged into Monica's chest, Joseph lit up a Cigarillo. Its acrid cherry smoke burnt my nostrils. Fischer flipped a silver Zippo closed and Joseph took a long pull, watching Monica with a killer's stare. My eyes burnt, my jaw tightened, and my balls clenched. My Monica was being turned into one of them and he was having a smoke.

She'd stopped screaming by now, or rather, her scream had faded into a burping gurgle. Her skin had lost all its color and gone gray and rotted. She swelled, her face expanding like rotting cottage cheese, her breasts popping loose and inflating until they were, in turn, absorbed by the swelling ovoid of her torso.

Above us, great machinery groaned to life as hundreds of tons of roof slid open. A shaft of sunlight pierced the sky, cutting a green swath into the field, and then expanded. I heard the sound of ripping paper and a long shrieking wail and then fireworks began going off all around us.

They were beautiful. Magenta, and green, and red, the most striking colors I'd seen in twenty years of walking our fading world. Hovering just above the roof opening, several gasbags retreated, obviously scared off by the light or the noise.

Monica wasn't Monica any more.

Her head, arms, and legs had retreated so far into her body that they were just five lumpy stumps like I'd seen on countless gasbag corpses but never recognized. The Queen's umbilical cord pulled free from what used to be Monica's chest, and a new navel ripped open, spewing out long black ropes of intestine that began to twitch and quest hungrily for prey. A particularly low firework exploded nearby and the Monica Demon retreated into the air. In a few seconds, she had floated over the lip of the roof and was gone.

Fischer closed his eyes, threw back his head, and shuddered. Like he just came. Up in the owner's box there was smattering of applause. They loved him, or at least the cult of personality he'd made up for them. Fischer had created a world where his insanity was admired. Here, he could flaunt his terrible illness, and his elite didn't see how wrong it all was. The blind were being led by the naked.

After a few seconds, his eyes rolled open and he smiled thinly at Joseph. "You're next."

I expected to see some kind of fear in Joseph, even the kind of fear a five-year-old feels when confronted by the schoolyard bully, but his eyes were frighteningly dead. He fought, but his motions were mechanical, as if he didn't care enough to do more than go through the motions.

All of a sudden he made a lunge for his .45. Fischer had tucked it into the waistband of his trousers like the macho dick that he was, and Joseph just homed in on it. Everyone always goes for the gun at this juncture, and Timmons saw him coming. The butt of his rifle knocked the Cigarillo out of Joseph's mouth along with a couple of lower incisors.

They had to wrestle him into position, but the Queen did the rest. Once that big black protrusion had him, a bulldozer couldn't have gotten him loose. The Queen painted him with mucus and then that terrible appendage unfolded.

Joseph stood perfectly still. The birthing appendage plunged towards him, sinking a foot into his chest. It was only then that he showed fear. The sight of his own blood must have reminded him of his mortality. He screamed.

"Bosley, help me!"

Then he began to change. But not like Monica. Something was there in that stadium with us, helping him, guiding his transformation. Tentacles burst not from his abdomen, but from the sides of his face. The Queen's birthing tentacle snapped under rapidly forming, interlocking skin plates. Joseph didn't flinch. His skin greyed and swelled, but the growth was carefully managed.

"Bosley" was helping him.

It was this more than anything that broke me. After Monica changed, I had stayed sane only long enough to see Joseph die. And now that was being taken from me.

I retreated.

The world smeared until those around me lost all trace of humanity, becoming only vague blue and grey blurs. As they moved, their faces left trails in the air.

The only thing in focus was the cherry red glow of Joseph's discarded Cigarillo burning at my feet. I reached into my pocket and pulled out the broken flare, retrieved the Cigarillo, touched it to the tip, and melted half of Timmons's face.

I have never been so calm in my life. I was cool as a cucumber. I squeezed the trigger of Joseph's .45 as I was still pulling it out of the Fischer's waistband. The gunshot sent his cock and most of his bowels into the Astroturf. Three more shots rang out and three more smears dissolved rapidly into the air, followed by faint thumps, as somewhere far away bodies hit the ground. I'd always been a good shot, but that day I couldn't miss.

I was enraged, and though Fisher was breathing his last, five more shots hit him dead in the face. That's how many it took to kill him. One two three four five. Just like that. By the time I was done with him, Joseph was gone.

I left the stadium through the athletes' locker room, blowing a rusty padlock off the back door with Joseph's .45. I left the roof open, and without Fischer's goons to set off the fireworks, it wouldn't be long before the gasbags came back. For all I know there aren't any Fixers left.

Me, I had to go find Monica. I just couldn't leave her like that. I'd killed plenty of gasbags with Joseph. All you had to do was shoot them in the bumpy nodule that I now knew was a vestigial human head. I would do that for Monica.

The only problem was that all the gasbags looked alike. I brought down four or five, looking for some difference between them, a scar, or ear piercing, or anything that might help me identify which one of them was my Monica. At last, I decided to kill them all.

I found a boy hiding in a US Postal service mailbox he'd cut a hole in. I taught him how to run bait, and together we spent many weeks bringing down the demons.

It's hard to feel anything anymore. The boy, I think he's scared of me. And he has reason to be.

Last night, in the dying moments of the day—while I was thinking of nothing at all—something happened that scared me more than the thought of never finding Monica.

Last night, Bosley came to me.

TWITCHERS
by Richard Wright

*O*bservations, Day...

I have lost track of the days. Quelle surprise.

I will say it is day eleventy hundred. I saw nothing until the afternoon, by which time I was cramping in my shoulders from the effort of keeping the field glasses raised. I never dare lower them, for fear of missing something notable.

Today's wonder was in the sky, a dusky ochre this afternoon. Even at full magnification it was only an outline, but it was bloated, gaseous. I saw similar beasts, long ago. The gas thing flew against the gale as though the day was still, and it was a child's balloon, carelessly released.

It has been years since I saw a balloon. Marie used to love them. I shall try to find one amid the detritus in the attic. A balloon would cheer her up.

A couple of hours later a man staggered by, so close to the hide that I almost cried out. He did not see me. Nothing sees me, in the hide. He was a ragged, desperate thing. His eyes were on the sky, and he stumbled along on shredded shoes and bloodied feet. Even though it was out of sight, I am certain he pursued the gas thing. He looked relentless, and made me afraid for Marie. I hoped she had not crossed his path.

Natalie Murphy shoved the pistol into her son's mouth and pulled the trigger, trying to be dispassionate as the back of his head was punched open. A year since she had last seen Calum in the riot-torn city centre of Belfast, and now she was forced to kill him, over and over. It wasn't fair.

Stepping over the twisted monkey corpse that somehow wore her son's face, gun raised, she swept the wilderness.

"Right side clear," she called. There was no response, and she turned back to the Armoured Personnel Carrier. Mark's body lay beside the driver's door. He had been killed before he had the chance to close it, and only the attacking creature's weight had slammed it shut. They had almost lost the cargo.

Wary, she stepped around the back of the vehicle, boots sinking into the mud. George was on his back in the road, flak jacket shredded, organs scattered. His dead face looked puzzled. No sign of Harry or William. Nat banged the side of the vehicle. "Clear. Open up."

The door slid open, and she clambered in. Scott, the cargo, looked at her with a resignation that made it clear he had seen the others go down. "They took Harry alive."

"William?"

"I don't know. Are we going after them?"

Nat answered by sliding into the driver's seat and starting the engine.

Scott rubbed his temples, but didn't argue.

Observations, Day Eleventy-three.

I stayed on an hour later tonight. My body clock has attuned to its schedule. The charnel house screams of its approach is a comfort, marking a distinct unit of time since last I heard it, and the nauseous light spilling from its windows is like the smile of an old friend.

A few weeks ago, I abandoned the comforts of the hide. I scurried across the blasted landscape, and found what I sought. I wrote, long ago, that from a distance they looked like impossibly long bones. I believed I was being poetic, but that is what they are — cold, dead bones. That infernal engine travels on tracks made of bone.

Little wonder Claude was so captivated by them. The train has never spoken to me, has so far refrained from stopping to offer me passage. I wonder often what it saw in Claude that it does not see in the rest of us. Perhaps the children are at fault. Tonight, when it passed, I raised a hand to acknowledge it, but as ever I received no response.

The train plunged headlong into la Fracture, fearless as ever. Hattie will not be pleased that I have, in venturing out to examine the bones, recorded something new. I'm looking forward to telling her.

Sweat dripped down Nat's back as the heat inside the APC inched higher. The fog around the car was the colour of vapourized cat vomit, and highly toxic. Last time they had seen it, three men died. Now, the vents were closed and the aircon off. *Fool me once,* she thought, but couldn't remember how the rest of the saying went. It reminded her of a dead president from a long ago time, when all she had to worry about was not dying in pointless wars.

"Who was the boy?" Scott was sat in the back. Nat said nothing. "There are things out here that can wear faces from our memories. You know that, but you still pulled us over, made the others go with you to check. Was it someone you lost?"

"I don't know." Accepting that she might never know whether or not Calum was still alive made something tighten in her chest.

"After all this time, you're still an enigma, Miss Murphy. You're Irish, right?"

Nat nodded.

"A soldier? The others talked among themselves, but not so much to you."

Nat checked the GPS. The screen flickered on and off every few minutes. When it came back on, it never showed them in quite the place they should have been from the previous reading. "Once." It had been the navy, but having lived most of her life with classified markings on her file, she wasn't about to start delivering her life story now.

"Today? Always meant to ask how you ended up in charge."

"I'm a freelance. A consultant. Every country can distrust me in equal measure."

Scott laughed. "Oh, very good. I suppose I'm a consultant too."

"A scientist."

"You know that's not true. I work with scientists, and they work on me." He chuckled. "I'm an expert, I suppose."

"On the Collision?"

There was a pause, and when Nat looked in the mirror, Scott was rubbing his temples with tired hands.

"Hardly. I don't know any more about the rift than you do."

"What then?"

"Horrors. I'm an expert in horrors."

Observations, Day Eleventy-seven

The train, if that is the correct word for it, is the key. I told the others at tonight's meeting, and they were thrilled by my observations, just as they were furious not to have deduced it themselves. It's churlish, I suppose, to take my pleasures in their discomfort, but needs must in difficult times.

Yet it is one thing to know what is required, and another entirely to implement it. We do not know where to begin, and so must be patient. A solution must present itself. God would not be so cruel as to make us watch for so many years, only to reward us with a solution we are unable to engineer.

I will wait for an answer to come to me.

Nat jerked in her seat as the APC crashed over a fissure in the road. Swearing issued from the rear. "Little warning next time?"

"Should have buckled up." She kept her voice lazy, but her throat was dry. She hadn't seen the fissure, because she was half asleep at the wheel. It was early evening, and she had been driving for fourteen straight hours. It was their eighth day on the move. Once upon a time they would have been there and back two or three times over by now, but with the heart of Europe a twisted, lawless place, that had changed. The strain of continual concentration had exhausted her, and she was endangering the mission by pushing on. If they were not so close she would have pulled over to rest hours ago. She had never respected her expert, but after so many years she knew to trust his instincts. If he believed that this journey might lead to some revelation that would let them fight back, then she did too.

The GPS was useless now, but instinct insisted they were...

There. Not two hundred metres away. A shape, looming in the darkness. A tiny flicker of light. "Something ahead." Her cargo slid into the seat beside her a second later. Nat pointed, and Scott stared. After a moment, he stiffened.

"That's *got* to be it."

Hope and relief smashed through her. If they'd found it, they were halfway home. With a grunt of frustration, she realized the road was sweeping them away from the tantalizing light. "Buckle up. We're taking the direct route." Twisting the wheel, she crashed the APC through the overgrown bushes bordering what remained of the road, sending misshapen branches flying.

The big farmhouse was disappointing in its ordinariness, a rustic, two storey building built more than a century before. The light came from a downstairs window, a flickering candle or lantern. A low fence, recently painted, marked off a front yard. Anger surged through Nat. The Collision was barely five miles away, and had hurled madness far across the world. Nothing so close to it had any right to look as humble as that painted fence, so she let the APC crash over it. It didn't make her feel any better.

Braking, she killed the engine and waited, lights still on. The front door opened. An old man stepped out, shielding his eyes with one hand, holding an ancient shotgun in the other. The man's leathered face showed no fear, only irritation. In his sixties somewhere, he was in robust health, a far cry from the terrified refugees they had imagined rescuing.

Killing the headlights, she let the man see them. The old boy's eyes widened and he grinned with genuine joy.

"Wait here." She drew her pistol and Scott nodded.

Nat stepped out, closing the door behind her. Locks clicked. Keeping hold of her gun, she raised both hands above her head, giving the stranger a chance to examine her military fatigues. She tried to remember how to say something useful in French. Nothing came. "Sorry about the fence," she said instead.

The man laughed. "No matter." His accent was thick, but his English excellent. "Small price, against the pleasure of a new face."

Nat waggled her gun hand. "Do I need this?"

The man propped his shotgun against the wall. "I don't even know if that thing still works. It's been years since I used it. My name is Michel Lisle, and whatever might have brought you this way, you are welcome at my home.

Holstering her pistol, Nat gave a thumbs up to the APC. "Pleased to meet you, Mr Lisle. My name is Natalie Murphy. My colleague is Scott Fletcher."

The passenger door slammed shut and Scott appeared from around the side of the vehicle. He gave Michel a distracted nod, but his attention was on something else. Natalie was faintly aware of the distant sound of a bell ringing.

"May I ask why you are here?" Michel said.

"Of course. We want to know why the hell you're still alive."

They sat at a long, well-used dining table. It was easy to imagine a big family crowded round it, feasting on game and supping wine. With just her and Scott there, it was a lonely place. She smelled furniture polish and it made her heady for home. Three heavy iron candlesticks were spaced along the table, the bare light from the burning wicks both comforting and deceptive. The vicinity of the Collision was the very edge of madness, and it was wrong to feel safe.

Scott rolled his shoulders, easing out the stiffness of the journey. "Not quite what I was expecting."

"You said there would be secrets here, that anything surviving this close to the edge would show us something new."

"Give me a chance. For all I know, he ignores the Collision, and it ignores him right back. Powerful stuff, belief."

The door to the kitchen creaked open, and the aroma of fresh coffee swamped them. Nat's mouth watered. "Sorry to have kept you," Michel said. "We have no power here. Our water is heated over the fire."

There was a framed picture on the wall. Michel, a decade or two younger, with a woman and a child. Almost certainly a daughter and grandchild. The kid was laughing in the photograph. She hoped Calum had found some cause to laugh since she left him.

"We're grateful," Scott said, as Michel poured steaming measures into three chipped cups. "It's been a long road."

"Oui, I imagine. There's so much you must have seen. If I could collect just some of your observations before the others arrive, it would be something of a coup."

Tension creeped along Nat's spine. "Your family are joining us?"

"Non, there is but myself and my granddaughter Marie here."

She nodded at the photograph. "You had a daughter?" Scott winced, and she knew the question was too blunt. Michel gazed at the picture with such an instant swell of love, he had to avert his eyes.

"Yvette did not survive the first months after la Fracture. I have raised Marie. She is out hunting with her friends. They roam ever further in search of meat and fish for our little community. I worry for her, but I am too old for such adventuring myself."

Nat glanced at the antiquated shotgun, now propped beneath the curtained window. Outside, the wind howled and reality raged. "They go out in this? How? What do they use?"

Michel frowned, candlelight deepening the lines on his face. Then he chuckled. "That is why you have come? You imagine we have... what, Madame? Arcane methods of countering this chaos? Unheard-of technologies with which we walk unchallenged here? You see my home. We have nothing for your armies and governments. Marie hunts in the oldest ways."

She leaned forward on her elbows, seeking deceit. Whatever secrets kept these people alive, she would take them by force if necessary. "We lost people to get here," she said. "Trained people. We all chose to get in that crate outside, because the world is being torn to shit by that hole out there. Don't tell me they died so we can learn how to make candles and set snares."

Michel shrugged a hopeless apology. "Your crate is magnificent," he said, trying to change the subject. "I drove trucks once. Does it drive like a truck?"

"Give me something to take home, and I'll let you drive it round the fucking block."

"It could be something they're not aware of," Scott said, voice quiet. "Something environmental, maybe genetic. You didn't expect us to find the answer over our first cup of coffee."

"*I want to go.*" Nat seethed. "I want to see my son." She turned back to Michel. "You know what we've lived with out there? Riots." She blinked back tears, thinking of Belfast. "Diseases nobody understands. Creatures that shouldn't exist. Millions dead. That's what my boy gets to live in, if he can survive long enough. We need something to stop it."

Michel shuffled to a shelf, and pulled a thick notebook down from it. "Oui. They may not trouble me here, but I know the monsters. I have my notes."

Scott joined him. "May I?"

"Mais oui, of course."

The consultant pulled back the cover, angling the first page to the weak candlelight. "Diary?"

"At first, monsieur. Now it is a log of my sightings. I have a hide not far from here. I watch the things that go by, and record them. We all do, my friends and I."

"You're... what? Rift-watchers?"

"Peter, he is from England, he calls us twitchers."

Scott laughed. "They used to call bird-watchers that, back when people had hobbies."

"Oui! A hobby, that is the word. We have little else. This is our entertainment."

There was a knock at the front door. Nat was on her feet, gun drawn, before she realized she'd moved.

Michel flapped his hands. "Madame, non, the Twitchers! Tonight is our weekly meeting, and I am host. You will disgrace me!"

Behind the old man, Scott had his hands raised. She saw the sense of it. The more people they talked to, the more information they would seize. She holstered the gun. "I'm sorry, Mr Lisle. I won't cause any trouble. Will you allow us to join you?"

Reassured, Michel nodded and vanished into the hallway to welcome his guests.

On the very edge of the catastrophe that was destroying the world, Nat shared dinner with the Twitchers. It should have been a hushed, doomed affair. Instead, it was almost raucous. Scott had gestured her aside as the two newcomers were ushered in. "They've been here a long time. They've found ways to cope."

She understood, but it didn't help. People survived these days with a deep sense of constant urgency. Whether their concerns were for the future of the planet, or just how to survive another day, they responded to the rift.

The Twitchers barely considered it an inconvenience.

They dined by candlelight, on a thick chicken broth Michel had prepared the day before and reheated over the kitchen fire. Red wine flowed. Peter apologized. "Should be white, I suppose. No way to chill it properly though. Besides, you know the French and their reds. Drink it with anything, the heathens."

His wife Hattie gave his arm a playful slap. "Peter! Not in Michel's home." They were British ex-pats, who had moved across the channel in their forties, more than two decades ago, searching for a better life.

"This is what we found," said Peter with a wink. "Living the dream..."

Nat nodded at Peter's generous belly. Where Hattie was a trim old lady, Peter could do little to disguise a battle with indulgence. "It must be a constant hardship."

"Ha! As you say. Still, living simply doesn't mean not living well."

"The young ones bring back plenty from their hunting trips," Hattie said. "We grow our own herbs and veg."

"And there are more barrels of wine ageing in abandoned cellars and vineyards round here than we could drink in a lifetime."

Hattie sniffed. "*Some* of us consider that a challenge."

At Nat's side, Scott was on his fourth glass of wine, having responded to her suggestion that they keep their wits about them with weary pity. He was talking to Michel. "Good broth," he said. "You keep your own chickens?"

Michel cackled. "Lots of things taste like chicken, monsieur."

Nat ate no more of the broth.

When all had taken their fill, conversation turned to the purpose of the meeting. Hattie and Peter pulled out notebooks thick enough to match Michel's own. They had their own hide, spending their afternoons there with a flask of soup and a pair of telescopes, somehow safe from the terrors around them. Every week, they met Michel to compare notes, argue, and claim small victories over one another.

"It looked like a unicorn," Hattie was insisting, her fingers resting beneath an entry in her book.

Michel shook his head. "So now we live in a land of fairy tales, Madame? Did you see the little singing dwarfs also?"

Hattie stiffened, and Peter put an arm around her. "Steady on. I saw it too."

"A unicorn?"

"Well, that's just what we called it. Had a big spike on its... well, I think it was the head. Massive big bugger, so it was. Two foot, easy, like a unicorn. Except it had a mouth. The horn, I mean. The beast had a mouth as well, but so did the horn. Like it was a separate creature."

Hattie nodded, bolstered by the support. "And what can you offer this week?"

Michel flushed, pouring more wine to cover his embarrassment. "It has been disappointing. The train, of course, but this time..."

"Train?" Scott straightened up. "You've seen it here?"

They all looked at him. "Mais oui, monsieur," said Michel. "Often. You have missed it by a day."

Nat scanned their eager faces. This was something, and she thought she had heard it before. "What train?"

"There's a train thing," Scott mumbled, rubbing his temples. "Reports from all over about it. I've seen it. Sort of seen it. In my head."

Michel leaned forward. "I do not know how far it goes, only that it leaves and returns regularly."

"Where does it... park? Rest? Live." Nat sighed. "Whatever it does here, where does it do it?"

"It does not stop. It passes, en route to the rift. Enters, and comes out some days later."

Scott was fascinated. "You have proof?"

Michel snorted. "If our word is not enough, monsieur, I have recorded each passing." He nodded at his notebook, now on the table before him.

"If it has a routine... Nat, this could be what we came for."

"Does it tell us what's keeping these people alive?"

"It's more important than that."

Peter laughed, delighted. "Well then, you'll love this. Tell them about Claude, Michel."

Michel sighed. "Claude boarded the train some time ago. He said it was calling to him, so he climbed aboard."

Scott frowned. "Why would it choose him?"

"Why would it not? Such a mind, Claude had! I could listen to him talk of the wonders in this universe for hours! And he loved order, he loved to find patterns..." Michel trailed off.

Nat placed a hand on Michel's arm. "Where did the train take him?"

"It took him into la Fracture."

Scott's mouth dropped open.

Nat was baffled. "It took him *into* the rift?"

Scott nodded, dazed. "The implications..."

There was a single, heavy thud at the front door.

Nat and Scott turned to look. When she turned back the Twitchers were staring at her, like children caught stealing sweets. The candles flickered between them, like the dying light of the world.

Peter coughed and looked down at his hands.

Michel laughed, but it failed to convince. "The young ones," he said, rising and disappearing into the hallway.

"Grandchildren," Peter confirmed, still uncomfortable. Hattie was staring at her plate, pushing food around.

"Yours too," Nat said, and it wasn't a question.

Peter jerked. "Michel told you?"

"His daughter died. He raised his granddaughter."

"Ah." He was relieved. "Yes. Our son and daughter-in-law too. Early days of the rift, you see, before things settled down."

Natalie glanced at the curtains. "This is settled?"

"They left us two kids to raise, Derek and Isobel. That'll be them back from foraging."

"I look forward to meeting them."

Peter fumbled, not sure what to say, and Harriet stepped in. "I doubt they'll come in. Must be shattered, poor things."

"Tomorrow, then."

"Perhaps."

They waited in silence as they heard the front door close. Scott had put his glass to one side.

Michel came back in from the kitchen instead of the hall, and Nat saw blood on his hands. From the day's catch, she guessed.

"Well," Peter said, rising, "we should go and catch up with the kids. Hope you folks will excuse us?"

"I could give you all a ride, if you like," said Nat, knowing she would be refused.

"Good of you, but no," said Harriet. "We like the walk. At our age, you take your exercise where you find it."

"Of course."

Bundling their overcoats on, muttering thanks for the meal, they fled the farmhouse in something close to what Nat recognized as terror.

Michel excused himself soon after. All he gave in answer to Nat's insistent questions about Marie was that the girl had retired to her basement room. They were invited to eat and drink all they wished, and bed down on the sofas at the back of the room to escape the APC for a night. Nat and Scott nodded politely, allowing him to leave.

"What do you...?"

She raised a hand. When she heard the creak of ancient bed springs upstairs, she nodded. Scott began again, voice quiet. "What do you make of it?"

"We're not safe here."

"That's a bit much, isn't it? One old man and a girl?"

"Who they don't want us to speak to."

Scott refilled his glass, and sank into one of the couches, taking Michel's diary with him. "So they're hiding something. Doesn't mean they're going to slit our throats in the night."

Nat eyed the other couch, imagining how good it would feel to sink into it. Too good, she decided, and stayed on her dining chair. "People with secrets try to protect them."

Scott shrugged, opening the book. "Forget about it. I'm more interested in this."

"Will it tell us where Joseph Tern is?"

He rolled his eyes. "I told you what I saw, Miss Murphy. Joseph was absorbed by the gasbag queen. Bosley saved him, I think, and then dispersed."

"Dispersed?"

"Ceased to be. Kicked the bucket."

"You sure?"

"I get this stuff in a jumble, but as sure as I can be, yes."

"And Joseph?"

"Is alive... More than that, I have no idea."

Natalie shifted on the wooden chair. "So why are you so interested in that book?"

Rubbing his temple with one hand, Scott sighed. "Well I have to keep reading to be sure, but it looks like the train leaves the rift on the morning of every fifth day. That same night it returns. In my head, I've see the train come through the rift at five distinct locations. It could be on a five day cycle. I won't be sure until I've read more. It's difficult to explain why it's important."

"Put the wine down and try."

Scott looked at his glass. "I get headaches. You know that. Sometimes a drink helps. Look, the train comes out of the rift. Fair enough, all sorts of things do. But the train *also* goes back in. How many other things have we seen do that? And if it took a passenger...? Christ, that changes everything. That gives us hope."

"It's not what we came here for."

"You don't know that. Let me look around and then you get me home safe. This is the job you gave me, Miss Murphy. Let me get it done." Turning back to the book, squinting in the poor light, he left Nat to her thoughts.

Half an hour later, Scott dropped into a drunken sleep, head back and mouth open. By then, she knew what she had to do. Whatever Scott thought he had found in that book, it wasn't the mission men had died for. Something kept these people safe. Something that might make her son safe too.

Marie had the secret. She was the one who hunted during the day, while Michel cowered in his hide. She knew something.

Rising from the chair, she eased out the cramps in her legs, drawing her pistol. The candles guttered, making shadows dance. Nat stalked to the hallway, pausing at the bottom of the stairs. There was no sound from the upper floor, and she slipped into the night.

A wind was up, but not one she could feel on her skin. It was as though the darkness was made out of particles. She could see it swirl and rush about. Some sort of rift effect. It was nauseating.

Marie had not entered the house. No words had been exchanged when Michel met her at the door, and only one set of footsteps had retreated down the hall. If Michel was telling the truth, and Marie's bedroom was some sort of cellar conversion, there had to be...

She saw the storm doors to the cellar, and made her way toward them. When she leaned down to pull a handle, it rose easily. She put it down again. There had been no light from the crack, and she clipped a slender flashlight attachment to the barrel of her pistol.

She lifted the right storm door all the way back, senses alert for movement or noise. "Hello," she called, voice low. "Can I talk to you?" Silence. Nothing felt right.

There were no stairs or ladder. It was an eight foot drop to what looked in the dim starlight to be a bare earth floor.

She stepped forward, gun to her breast, and dropped down. Letting the impact fold through her knees and ankles, she pushed off into a single fast roll, coming up in a crouch. It wasn't silent, but it was close.

The roll had taken her beyond the patch of faint light filtering through the door, into near total darkness. Her landing had confirmed the bare earth beneath her, and now she felt the space. This wasn't some cellar converted long ago into a bedroom. It was just a cellar, big and empty.

Something scraped. Flicking the flashlight on, she began a slow sweep of the room at waist height, searching for the source of that single sound.

Brick supports for the house above. A row of packing crates stacked four high and running the length of the far wall. Dirt and dust on the pocked floor. The space ran two thirds the length of the house. Marie might live in the other third, with an entrance further round the building. Switching the flashlight off, she stepped back into the square of dim light, readying herself for a leap and grab.

Why was the floor pock-marked? She switched the light back on. There were dozens of holes at her feet, old and new, as though Michel regularly took a pick axe to the ground. Tracing the light across the rest of the floor, she found the same evidence. Holes over holes, shallower than where she stood, but there wasn't an inch of floor unmarked.

Another scrape, and reflex pulled her gun hand to the source. The row of crates. Not against the wall at all, but a few feet into the room. Horrible suspicions dawned in her. The old bastard made his granddaughter *live* there.

She approached the crates with care, light before her. "Hello?" There was no way to guess what condition Marie might be in, forced to live so, and she kept her voice gentle, as though lulling her Calum to sleep.

One end of the row of crates ran to the adjacent wall. They ended halfway into the room. The corridor created would be the sort of place a child might play for hours, the perfect den.

Marie would be a young woman by now.

Another scrape, and then another. Furtive, nervous noises. She wished she could dim the flashlight on the gun. It speared the darkness like a weapon.

She paused at the end crate. "Don't be frightened. I'm going to help you."

Nat stepped into the semi-room between the crates and the wall, shining the light to the end. The moist stench of meat hit her far too late.

A creature rose from a nest of old clothes and teddy bears. It had no skin over its oozing red muscles, and when they twitched she caught glimpses of organs underneath. Instead of feet, the creature's four legs ended with wicked blades of naked bone, makers of the countless divots in the cellar floor. Its jaws made her think of some ungodly bear. Drool dripped from between its teeth. It growled.

Nat's finger began to squeeze the trigger, and then she saw the eyes. They were human. Terrified. "Marie?"

A scared young woman, warped and powerful, who might not have seen a new human face for years.

Having broken into her home, Nat was pointing a gun in her face. "No," she said, raising her other hand in offer of reassurance. "I don't..."

Marie sprang past her, faster than she looked. Before Nat understood what had happened she was kneeling on the ground, her guts sliced open by one of her dagger feet. An impossible cold flushed through the rest of her body.

"...want to hurt..." she said, and everything went black.

When she woke, it was with instant recall of what had happened. She tried to bring her gun up. It didn't work, because her hands were taped together behind her back.

She was in the rear of the APC, and a jolt told her they were bouncing over rough ground. Pain fisted her guts, and cold nausea flooded her. Leaning to one side, she retched. Nothing came up. Hot tears streamed down her face. She was belted into a seat against the wall, and the only illumination came from the scarlet floor lighting running down the aisle. Enough to give troops something to see by, but not enough to be visible through the tinted windows.

Hattie sat opposite her, also belted in. The under-lighting turned her into a witch. Nat guessed Michel and Peter were up front, one of them driving.

Scott was on the floor, back against the rear doors. His hands were also taped behind him, and his ankles bound together. A silver strip of duct tape had been slapped over his mouth, and his eyes bulged with fear.

"Are you all right, dear?" Hattie kept her distance while she asked. Smart woman.

"Dying," she forced out between dry heaves. "You?"

"Not dying," she confirmed with an embarrassed smile. "Hold on. You'll make it."

Nat's brow furrowed. She had been torn open. Somebody had tried to wrap bandages around her, but she was cold to the core. Though she hurt, she knew she didn't hurt *enough*. With an effort that made her whine, she pulled herself properly upright. The sweat on her face had turned to ice.

"She didn't mean anything by it," said Hattie. "She was defending herself. You had a gun."

"Tried to...explain..." The APC went over another bump, and the pain made her bite her tongue.

"Oh, you realized then? That's a shame. She doesn't understand English, I'm afraid."

Nat wanted to laugh. She was dying because the monster that killed her wasn't bilingual. "How..."

"Some sort of yellow fog. It spared us coffin-dodgers, killed the younger adults, and changed the children. It wasn't like Jekyll and Hyde, nothing like that. It's taken years.

They're still changing now. Inside though, it's still the children."

Trapped in mutating bodies, scared and in pain, kept like pets so they could bring home dinner for their grandparents. "Monsters..."

"That's what we expect. People like you, making judgements. Just because they don't look human." Hattie grimaced. "This can't be their world any more."

Nat knew where they were going, and groaned.

"We've watched the things from the Collision for years. It's a place where being different from everything else is the norm. That's where our grandchildren should be." She shrugged. "We may as well go too. Whatever that fog was, it marked us somehow. All these wondrous, deadly things, and they've never given us a second glance."

Scott was shaking his head, moaning. Hattie shushed him. "We'll be fine. Like the train. A big, closed, vehicle. That's what it takes to get through, but once it had Claude it never stopped for the rest of us. We were so glad when you brought us an alternative. That's why Michel insisted you come too. In there, you might not die after all."

Nat saw the diary on the floor beside Scott, and it shamed her. She had been wrong. There were no answers to be had from these people, only bright shades of mutation and madness. Somewhere, Calum cowered, waiting for mummy, and nothing she had done would make him safer. Scott had known, had seen something in the book, and Nat had barely listened.

She bid her boy a silent farewell, wrapping it in as much love as she had, and sending it winging home to Belfast. She tried to imagine him somehow receiving it, knowing that though she was lost, she was still a part of him.

Resting her head back against the seat, she felt the vibrations of the engine dragging them closer to hell. "Nearly there," Peter called back to them. He sounded cheerful.

Hattie glanced at her seatbelt. Nat's hand went to her own, and she gritted her teeth. Raising both feet, tearing in two all over again, she kicked out. Her boots met Hattie's face, and things cracked there. Blood flew in black splashes as the old woman's head bounced back against the seat, and slumped against her bony chest. She didn't make a sound.

With white shock dousing her, Nat unclipped her belt and tried to stand. There was no feeling in her legs, and all she could do was aim her collapse so that she slumped next to Scott. Her bandages splashed.

Not good enough. Jerking, she swivelled to face the doors. Light like hot piss flooded the APC through the windshield. They were nearly there.

She eyed the door release, drew herself back, and smashed her head against it.

The doors popped open as she fell back. Scott dropped into the night, eyes wide, and bounced out of sight. Nat pulled herself back up, the APC spinning around her. Blood poured into her left eye as she shuffled towards the diary. If she could knock it clear, Scott might find it, and survive to do something with it.

"Here we go!" Peter sang the words. The APC bounced hard, doing Nat's job for her and sending the book flying into the night. Exhausted, she readied herself to follow. One push. There wasn't much chance that she would survive her wounds, but it was better than no chance at all.

Red flashed before her, and it wasn't more blood in her eye. A huge weight crashed into her through the doors, throwing her back along the aisle. Daggers of pitted bone stabbed and crunched through her shoulders, out the other side and into the metal floor, pinning her. Pain hit her so hard, in so many new ways, that she forgot how to scream.

Marie's furious, childish eyes stared into her own. She had been following them, and though she had not seen her hurt Hattie, she had worked it out. Two more like her, Derek and Isobel, bounded into the back of the APC beside her.

The light thickened like glue, Michel and Peter howled, and the rift took them all.

LOST SOULS
by Steven Savile & Steve Lockley

Paris. The Eiffel Tower, the *Arc d'Triomph* and the noise of traffic. His head was spinning. He was tired, having forced himself to stay awake through the night, on guard, on edge, and he was hungry. Cities are all different, different streets and walkways, different dark places, different atmospheres and dangers, and yet they are all the same in so many ways.

This city though, this one *was* different. His skin crawled. He knew that there was no traffic; he wasn't blind. The noise was only in his head.

Scott was not sure why he was here; the pull of the Collision was hard to resist. He just followed his feet. He knew that there were others like him out there; he could feel a *buzz* in the air like electricity chasing down the pylons. It threatened danger.

He had lost count of the number of days it had taken him to make it this far. Too many, was the answer. He skirted the worst of the devastation but there was no escaping the fact that Paris was a city of ghosts, figurative ones and literal ones. The lucky ones who had lived and worked on these old boulevards had long since made their escape. The unlucky ones... well, they were gone, too.

Looming large ahead of him, the Tower cast its twisted shadow over the city.

All roads didn't lead to Rome any more.

Now they converged on the Tower.

There was no point in searching street by street for survivors; all he needed to do was go to the Tower and wait, they would come to him, drawn there by the forces of the Collision.

He looked up at the sky.

The bell would sound again soon, like a weird sort of clockwork only he could predict. He knew it was coming. He knew within a few minutes when it was going to sound.

He walked on.

As the Tower grew larger, the once beautiful landmark was so utterly damaged and twisted it was almost unrecognizable—just like so much of the city.

Scott looked back over his shoulder.

He couldn't have said why, it was nothing more than a prickle of hairs at the back of his neck, a sudden stirring of trouble, but he was *sure* he was being followed. He stopped a couple of times, seemingly to check something in a broken window, looking at the reflection of the street behind him, hoping to catch sight of his tail, but every time he did there was no one there. Before long he started to doubt himself. Maybe he wasn't being followed, maybe he was just paranoid, maybe being alone so long had started to get to him, or hell, even if there was someone back there, maybe they just happened to be heading in the same direction?

But if that was the case, given the deserted streets, that meant that they were connected, didn't it?

Walk on. Walk on. With hope in your heart the old song said, didn't it? Fuck it, there was no hope left. But he couldn't stop walking.

The bell of the basilica rang out loud and clear across the ruined city.

A flock of birds were startled into the air by the jarring sound. Only they weren't birds, Scott realised, even if he didn't know what they were.

The ringing continued, one long single note, that only ceased when he saw someone, a shadow, leaning against one of the twisted struts of the old Tower, half-bathed in shadow, half-bathed in light. The figure was split in two, as though the rift ran straight through their flesh.

He started to run towards them, not looking as he stepped out in to the middle of the wide boulevard. He didn't need to. There were no cars, so no one was going to run him down. It was funny how quickly old habits, instincts, died. How quickly you adjusted.

As he reached the central reservation a sharp sudden *tingling* swelled inside his head. He felt its echo deep inside his chest. He knew that it was the stranger's doing. Was the stranger reacting to his proximity in the same way? Probably.

The two of them approached each other like reflections in a mirror.

"Scott!" The voice was female. It didn't just break the spell binding them together it shattered it. He knew the voice, but it was out of place. It shouldn't have been here.

He turned to see Thérèse running towards him.

Thérèse?

Here?

Why?

The Poor Girl should have been safe and a long way from this wretched fucking place.

Had she given the soldiers the slip and made her way here on her own?

Had she sensed his presence? It wasn't impossible, was it? He felt others out there. He couldn't be the only one. There was nothing slow or cautious about the way she ran towards him with her arms open wide. He swept her up in an embrace, spun her around and dumped her back down on her feet.

"It really is you? I wasn't sure." Relief was written all over her face.

"It's me. Where is your brother?" Scott asked.

"Omar's safe," she assured him. "I left him with Mr Spicer and the other soldiers. There was no need to bring him here. I didn't want to put him in danger. I came alone. Where is Natalie?"

"Somewhere else, somewhere safe," Scott lied. It was easy to lie. Once upon a time a lie like that, just to make thinks easier, would have felt wrong. But lying was second nature to a survivor.

The stranger held out a hand in greeting. He'd closed the gap in the few seconds Scott had felt vaguely like a normal guy. "I think we might be the same," he said, awkwardly, like he might have approached a girl at a bar before all this had happened. And in a way maybe it was a bit like trying to chat up a stranger. "My name is Rajesh."

Scott took his hand. He felt the energy crackle between them. Every inch of his skin burned, just for a moment, as though it was about to boil away from the meat of his hand. They released their grasp without a word, but both of them looked down at their hands, so it was obvious Rajesh had felt it, too. "Scott," he said.

"Thérèse" she said.

"Have you seen anyone else?"

Rajesh did that little head roll. It was so very Indian. He could almost hear him shrug. "Yes, yes. Some. Two. Two others. Mei-su, she's," he tapped his temple. Scott saw the little woman lurking in the shadows. She looked like a kindly grandmother. "She doesn't speak much. Only ever asking about her grandson. Every time it's the same, have you seen him, have you seen him. And complaining about the voices. They've been getting worse since she arrived here. Do you see things too? And hear voices?"

Scott knew that feeling; the desire to know if someone else was experiencing the same feelings, the changes, visions, and of course those damned voices. He nodded.

"You said *two* others?" Scott said.

"Obadiah Bard. He's a preacher. He believes his visions are a gift from God. His God not mine," Rajesh said dismissively. "He can't just talk to me, he has to preach at me. He insists that all of the things I have seen are proof that my God is false. He cannot see that there is no proof—or difference. That he is the one who is wrong has never even crossed his mind.

"Or that both Gods are the same," Scott said, but that was territory he really didn't want to get into.

There was something *bad* here too, he could feel it along with the Collision in mind. It was there, a presence, a danger, on the edge of his mind, pushing, probing, testing the limits of his strength. There was safety in numbers—or at least he hoped there was.

Scott heard Obadiah before he saw him.

He was holding out a well-thumbed copy of the Bible, brandishing it like a sword; this was his weapon of choice. Scott doubted it would be effective against whatever it was they were going to have to face. Gods seldom were.

"Unbelievers!" Obadiah cried out the moment he caught sight of Scott and Thérèse.

Scott had seen far too many men like Obadiah when casually flicking through TV channels. All spit and vinegar and lies to massage money from the gullible. He would have loved to have a remote control right here, right now to banish the preacher to some other channel.

"God has spoken to me! He has shown me wonderful things! Wonderful wonderful things! Sights beyond man's imagination! I have seen the light and the way! The Second Coming is at hand! Now is the time to repent! Repent! Open yourself to the Lord. Repent and accept Jesus Christ as your Saviour! Will you join hands with me and pray?"

"I'd rather disappear into the fucking rift," Scott muttered, but Obadiah didn't hear him. He was caught up in his evangelizing. He was almost raving. Scott had no idea of what the stranger had been through to push him so far over the edge, and he had no idea what he might be capable of. Come to that, he had no idea what any of them might be capable of.

"The Angel brought me to this place. The Angel with Susannah's face. This is my destiny! I must spread the Word.

It is my mission to rid the world of evil, and this is the place, right here, right now, this where I must start. It is foretold!" He looked right at Scott, seeming to see right into the depths of his fractured soul. "I need people to share my work. I *know* you have seen the strange and beautiful things that God has shown me. You are marked. Join with me. Walk forever by my side! We will carry the word to the four corners of the world. We will bring salvation to the masses." He fell silent and he stared into the near distance.

Scott turned to see what he was looking at. He needn't have bothered. Even before he could focus, he knew who it was. There was something unmistakeable about the man, an aura that marked him out as different. He was not one of those suffering from the strange rifts that existed inside their heads. And yet something had touched him and marked him out. Something dark. Different.

Thérèse let out a scream as she recognized Joseph Tern.

Finding them all together was more than Joseph could reasonably have hoped for. He had dogged the Indian's man's footsteps forever, following him over land and sea from the other side of the world. It had been an exercise in restraint not to strike at Rajesh along the way. He had had plenty of opportunities since leaving Toronto, but it was all part of his patient long game. He had suspected they would all come to this place, drawn here by the Collision. He knew they would be unable to resist its relentless pull. Now he could orchestrate the grand chorus. Now he could dictate the music of the spheres. Now he could assume control.

The preacher spouted the same claptrap about the divine he had heard babbling from mad men's mouths all along the road. That made him dangerous; he was a man who believed in something. Better your enemy believed in nothing. All but the preacher backed away as he approached. They knew he should be feared. Only the fool of a preacher thought he was invincible. He stood in Joseph's way, presenting an easy target.

The other four of them backed away, and kept on backing away until they were perilously close to one of the legs of the Tower.

"Don't you fear me little man?" Joseph called. It was a fair question.

"I have nothing to fear with the Lord on my side. You do not scare me, Joseph Tern. Kneel before me and let me lay my hands upon your head and drive your demons out. Let me heal you. Let me cleanse this world of evil."

"If only it were that easy," Joseph said wryly. When he thought about it, he realised it would be amusing to humour the little man, let him exorcise his fantasies and break his faith all at once. He dropped to one knee and lowered his head as though in benediction.

The preacher laid his hand on Joseph's head.

The words continued to spew from his mouth. Joseph tuned them out. He didn't care about the ravings of one lunatic over another.

"In the name of Our Father I cast these demons out! In the name of the Father...."

Joseph looked up at the preacher and smiled. Now this, this was funny. He saw the fear on the preacher's face as he realized he was powerless. It was priceless.

"... the Son," his speech grew slurred. One side of his face fell slack as Joseph rose slowly to his feet again. The preacher's hand fell to his side, fingers fluttering like dying birds. It was the killer's turn to perform the laying on of hands.

Instead of drawing the demons out, Joseph's fingers stretched and pressed on the man's skull — and into the man's skull. When Bosley was with him, he could have reached into the preacher's head with ease. Without him, Joseph was forced to do it the messy way.

"... and the Holy Ghost," the preacher mumbled, all strength gone from his voice.

Every muscle lost its connection with his brain.

It would have been a mercy to end it quickly.

Joseph was anything but merciful.

He felt his fingertips sink in deeper, pressing through flesh and the bone until his nails reached the soft and yielding mass inside. He twisted his hand slowly, turning his fingers and slicing his nails through the preacher's skull until the bones fractured and fell away in chips, and leaving the slick membranous surface of his brain exposed. Joseph cast aside the unwanted crown of bone, and the mask of skin and hair. He stared down into the mini rift within the preacher's head, marvelling at the white light dividing the hemispheres.

He reached inside with one hand.

The preacher's eyes were still open, but no longer focussed.

At last his victim gave out a single, ear-splitting scream. The sound, so utterly forlorn and without hope, echoed through the empty Champ de Mars.

It was the most joyous sound Joseph had ever heard.

He plunged his hand into the rift.

The world turned bright sizzling white for a single shocking moment, and Joseph felt pain like he had never known before. It eclipsed the agony of his 'birth' into this damned world. Every nerve ending was aflame. Every single sinew corded and tightened, thrumming, until the muscles bonded to them shrieked with pain. His brain expanded like a planet going supernova, until it no longer felt like his brain, and there was no way on this or any other world that it could all stay trapped within his head.

He was still Joseph Tern.

But he was something else.

Something MORE.

Something that took his shape. Wore it. Something that retained his memories. But something that was so much more than a man.

Even as he revelled in this new strength, he felt the nerve-shredding pain of the rift as it exploded with a burst of white light. And then there was NOTHING.

Joseph withdrew his hand.

It was little more than a stump of flesh and bone cauterized with the heat.

He screamed his outrage and agony but there were only four people left to hear, and they were running for their lives.

He dumped the preacher's lifeless corpse on the ground and howled again.

It did nothing to drive the pain away.

The Earth rumbled; buildings shook and debris fell to the ground.

The Earth groaned; dust billowed up from the detritus of civilization.

The Earth sighed; there was no one left to sigh with it.

The Tower swayed sickeningly as the metal struts struggled to counter the incredible forces at work. The Collision blazed brighter than sunshine, brighter than tomorrow, the smoke and heat turning the sky black and red. The waves of the Collision rippled outwards, expanding and expanding like shockwaves, until they reached and swarmed around the foot of the Eiffel Tower. It stopped there, even as the enormous weight of the Tower heaved and *screeched*, the rivets holding it together howling against the strain exerted on them.

Things were changing. Fast.

It was becoming increasingly unstable. Threatening to let something else through.

Something *big*.

Scott knew what it was even if he didn't know *what* it was. It was inside their heads. It was connected to the Collision. The five of them had somehow kept the balance. But now there were four. A tether that barely kept the effects of the Collision in place had snapped. Five anchor points became four. How many did it need to be effective? Four? Three? One? There was strength in numbers. But was their number strong enough?

Mid-step it hit Scott, driving him down to his knees. Beside him, Thérèse and Mei-Su fell. Rajesh was on his back, clutching at his skull. Joseph Tern stood, head thrown back, arms open wide, as all four of them were scorched by the same vision—an image so *powerful* seared the sanity from their minds momentarily. It was a creature. No. More than one. It was infinite. It contained multitudes. And its multitudes radiated pure rank malevolence. It was there... waiting... on the other side of the Collision.

To stare into those blazing white eyes was to stare into Death.

And they knew it. Their purpose. The thing.

The rifts in their heads weren't merely holding the Collision open; they were holding that thing, the beast of multitudes, back. While they lived, whatever those things were, they could not pass through.

Every fibre of Scott's being felt their *need*. It was unlike any hunger he had ever experienced. They were voracious. Starving. They existed to feed. And they had a hunger for the planet. And once the gestalt had started to feed, there would be nothing to stop it until it had consumed all of reality. Every star. Every dream.

Lux mentis lux orbis.

Light of the mind, light of the world.

Lux ex tenebris.

Light from darkness.

In the beginning God created the heaven and the earth.

And the earth was without form, and void; and darkness was upon the face of the deep. And the Spirit of God moved upon the face of the waters.

And God said, let there be light: and there was light.

And God saw the light, that it was good: and God divided the light from the darkness.

And God called the light Day, and the darkness he called Night. And the evening and the morning were the first day.

The divided darkness, the thing hidden behind the light was waiting.

The Light of Death.

Lux Necris. The Wraith Light.

Scott was the first to recover. He looked up to see that Joseph had abandoned the preacher and was coming after them.

Scott's first instinct was to take them into the Tower; there was nowhere else to hide from the killer. It was too open here, too exposed. They needed to find a place where they could defend themselves, even if it was only buying a few more minutes. It was time, and time was precious.

He had no idea if he could rely on the others; the Chinese woman, Mei-su, looked as though she was barely holding it together, and Rajesh didn't exactly look like prize fighting material. Thérèse, at least, was resourceful. Scrappy. That might come in handy.

But it would take more than fists to fight Joseph. It would take guile.

The man was in agony. There was no missing that. His pain meant this was the time to strike. But how?

Scott took a tentative step forward.

The killer turned his gaze towards him.

There was something *different* about Tern.

He was a changed man.

As Scott stared, he saw something beneath his skin shift, as though the bones were changing shape; making him a new face. He watched in horror as they reformed. Scott struggled to understand what he was seeing. After all of the strange and bizarre sights nothing should have come as a surprise. Limbs grew longer, fingers extended until Tern's one good arm was twice its natural size. Wild tendrils grew from the stump at the end of his damaged arm. His jaw dislocated, bones cracking, until his mouth was more than twice its size, like some huge devourer, and Tern tossed his head back to loose another howl.

This time it was not of pain.

This time it was a warning.

He was coming for them.

"Inside," Scott yelled at the others.

Choice was gone. Now it was all about surviving any way possible. Tern had already taken Obadiah. They needed to move fast if they didn't want to provide his next meal. Scott risked a glance away from the thing, relieved to see the others were already moving. Thérèse was helping the Chinese woman, though helping wasn't quite the right word. Mei-su stood stubbornly rooted to the spot while Thérèse bullied her towards safety. Rajesh had said the old woman was teetering on the edge of madness. Now she was falling. If she didn't get a grip, and fast, she would put the rest of them in danger.

"Joseph?" Scott called, doing his best to stay calm. Sounds were coming from the creature. He had no idea if Tern could hear him, if he was even in there anymore. But he had to try and reach him. "You've got to fight it, Joseph! Cling on to who you are! Remember! You have to fight! Remember your face! Your name! You can control it! "

The creature let out a pitiful mewling sound. It lasted less than a second before being replaced by a guttural vibration. Scott felt it resonate all the way through him. He couldn't wait another second. It was now or never, and never wasn't an option. Scott turned and started running towards the Tower, yelling for Rajesh to hold the door open for him, even as the Indian yelled back, "RUN!"

Tern—or the thing he had become—was already on his heels.

Then Scott was through the door.

They forced the door closed behind them, slamming the bolt into place. It wasn't going to hold Tern back. Not when he could slice through the top of a man's head with a fingernail.

Joseph hit the door hard, with all of his weight. The door bulged inwards, straining against the frame. The glass bowed under the pressure. It did not break. But it would.

"Run!" Scott screamed at the others. They were beginning to make their way up a flight of stairs as Joseph slammed his face against the glass, smearing it with blood and spittle as he scraped his teeth across the surface. The incisors gouged grooves in the reinforced glass.

There was nothing Scott could do.

He ran up the stairs after the others, barking, "Move!" to hurry them up.

He hadn't even made it a dozen steps up the staircase before the desperate sound of something scraping *deep* in the glass grew so loud the noise itself could have shattered it. He didn't look back. Scott ran blind, focussing on the heels he chased up the staircase. As they turned sharply it became obvious they'd come into one of the access stairways that led up to the small observation platform built into the structure. They emerged into an open stair that rose up one of the Tower's buckled legs.

There was nowhere left to run.

In the near distance Scott could see the effects of the Collision clearer than he had before. He felt the warm breeze of its aftershocks on his face. He looked out through the iron bands of the Tower's frame, all the way down to the ground.

They were already too far up to risk jumping. There was no way that Mei Su would be able to climb down the iron frame, either. Options were running out fast. Scott glanced up. He could see the tip on the Tower arcing over him as though it were the neck of some great iron bird no longer capable of supporting its head. There was something metaphorical about that, he was sure, but he wasn't going to try and work it out.

"Demon take us!" Mei-su mewled. It was the first time Scott had heard her voice. Without Thérèse holding onto her there was no telling what she was capable of as the panic gripped her. It wouldn't have taken a lot to launch herself from the platform.

Joseph emerged from around the final twist of the staircase.

His mouth was bleeding heavily. He didn't care. Or more truthfully the thing inside him didn't. Joseph Tern had no control.

"Listen to me, Joseph," Scott said, measuring each word carefully. He could only hope that the conclusions he had drawn from his visions were close to right. "Bosley's gone, hasn't he? Bosley's gone and you miss him. It's only natural. He was inside your head. He was there all the time. He was more than just a voice, wasn't he? He granted you gifts, powers. I shot you. I shot you four times, and the bullets just punched straight through. They didn't stop you. They didn't even slow you down. I saw you kill people, pushing them through solid walls. You want that back and there's a way to get it back... Bosley or at least someone just like him. I can help you if that's what you want."

There was a flicker in his eyes, just for a moment, the endless second between clanging footsteps on the iron stairs, when he stopped moving towards them.

The tendrils growing from his damaged arm no longer writhed; Scott hoped that meant Joseph had gained some ascendancy for a moment, taking back control of his body.

As though proving the point he slowly began to return to his former shape; his jaw clicked back into place, his hand shrank and the grotesque tendrils withered and withdrew. It wasn't some perfect salvation though, his limbs remained out of proportion to the rest of his body, a reminder that the thing was still inside him, even if it was no longer in control.

Joseph struggled to speak. His bloody mouth moved, chewing through the words.

Scott said, "I know what you were hoping to find when you put your hand in Obadiah's head."

"Think you are so clever don't you?" Joseph raged.

"No. But I have opened my mind. That's all you need to do. Open your mind. Will you do that?"

"If you are trying to trick me I will kill you. All of you."

"It's no trick." He glanced at the three others huddled together behind him. He could try to hold Joseph at bay, but where could they go? Nowhere. Any path through the mangled metalwork was only delaying the inevitable. This was their only hope.

Scott turned to the others. "We have to relax our minds, let go and let them through."

"NO!" Rajesh shouted. "Nonono! Do not let it through! The thing… on the other side. You saw what it can do… If we let it in, it will push us aside and take our bodies. I won't be a prisoner in my own head!"

"You don't have a choice, Rajesh. If you don't, you won't have any mind left to relax." It was Mei-su a moment of lucidity arriving at just the right time. "That thing will open up your brain pan and take it, just as it took the preacher's."

Up until that moment, Scott had been concerned that Mei-su might not be able to co-operate, that she would be the anchor that dragged them down, but she understood. That gave him hope—just a fleeting moment of it, but that was worse than no hope at all.

Joseph advanced towards them.

Scott held a hand up, though it could hardly keep the killer back

"Be smart, Joseph," Scott urged. "You didn't manage to pull one of them through Obadiah's rift and you won't get what you want by killing us."

"Won't I?"

"You know you won't. Just think about it for a moment. We can give you what you want," Scott promised. As though sensing his betrayal, the Tower lurched alarmingly beneath them. Time was running out.

"Then do it. Do it now or die." Joseph Tern sneered. "Or do it now and die. I don't care. You will die here. That is all that matters. DO IT!"

They formed a circle and held hands.

Mei-su stood to Scott's right. Her calloused hand pressed into his. Rajesh stood to his left. His grip was tighter than the old woman's. He was barely controlling his fear. Scott wanted to say, "Don't bother being scared, if this goes wrong we'll all be dead in seconds," but the time for talking was done. He gave a Thérèse weak smile, then closed his eyes and emptied his mind, thinking of nothing in particular beyond the simple act of opening his mind up. He felt the nearness of the thing that lurked back there, in the dark light, the multitude, and welcomed it, letting it come to the fore and slowly begin to take control of his mind and body.

There was a high-pitched scream. It sounded like pigs being slaughtered. Scott couldn't help himself. In that one horrible sound he heard another scream, this one from the farmhouse where Natalie had sent him with the sound dampening equipment. That scream had been the world tearing apart. How could he ever forget?

They came screaming out of the rifts inside their heads, rushing back to the world they left a decade ago. Scott tried to brace himself but the onslaught of the multitude was immense and agonizing. It went beyond a single human soul. The multitude were the world devourers. They were infinite, but at their core four souls burned brighter than anything else —

the essential *beings* of the men who had been trapped at ground zero when the Large Hadron Collider had blown. A name swam into Scott's mind. Lauren. It was Lauren. She had been one of the technicians at the LHC facility when it had all gone wrong and her soul had been sucked through the rift within the Collider into... hell. He could feel Lauren's terror: he caught flashes of sensory memory, the sucking void, the howling, the shrieking winds, the overwhelming, hellish heat. Lux mentis lux orbis — *light of the mind, light of the world* — Lux ex tenebris — *Light from darkness* — Lux Necris — *the Light of Death* lit the way, and then Lauren broke through, into his mind, reclaiming her place in this world.

Lauren could not have hoped for a more subservient host than Scott. The others, Brunner and the other two technicians, came back to claim the others gathered around in the circle.

Scott heard the screams again, but was only vaguely aware that they were his own as he gave himself to the soul that was taking control of his body.

He didn't trust them.

He hated them.

They were all that was wrong with the world.

But he missed Bosley.

There was a Bosley shaped-space inside his soul and it was rapidly becoming a huge suckling pit that threatened to collapse in on itself and take everything that Joseph Tern had ever been and could ever be with it.

Without Bosley he was not simply incomplete, he was broken. He wasn't Joseph Tern, either. Bosley might have saved him from being transformed into a gasbag, but the cost to Joseph had been huge. Bosley was gone, and he was different. He knew he had to fight that difference, but knowing and doing were two different things.

Joseph heard Scott's voice.

He didn't have control of a single muscle in his body.

It cut through the void into his core, resonating through every muscle and fibre – such a simple thing, a name – but on hearing his true name Joseph had been able to wrest control of his body from that thing. Even if only for a moment.

He tried to relax but the tension was coiled in each straining muscle. He watched as the others joined hands.

He heard the threat come out of his mouth… if they failed to give him what he needed he would do unto them the same as he had done to the preacher. It was all very Biblical. The preacher would have approved, if he hadn't already died a miserable death.

Joseph willed Bosley to return, calling out into the rift.

He felt the Collision expand and contract, as though it were a living, breathing thing. It made the very stuff of the world around him move.

It wasn't just voices now. He saw shapes screaming, writhing and twisting and gyring from the Collision. All of them swarming in the direction of the Tower.

Four of them came; four streaks of light and colour, each one forming a glow around the four people standing on the platform. They engulfed them. And then in that last moment, were absorbed into them.

Joseph knew who they were in an instant, without the need for voices. They were Bosley's friends. He couldn't stop the smile from playing across his ruined mouth.

"It's me," he said to the blank, slack-jawed faces as they turned to look at him. "It's good to have you back."

There was no change in their expressions.

No noises passed their lips.

"It's Bosley," he lied. Could they tell? Could they sense the emptiness where Bosley had been? "I've been waiting for you for

such a very very long time to share the wonders of the flesh. Taste the fear in the minds of the bodies you possess, enjoy the concerns and neuroses. Feed my friends! Feed!"

He knew that they would be tentative to begin with; it was only natural. It would take time for them to find control, and then it would be overwhelming — too much, too fast, too soon, making it impossible to savour the tastes and sensations. That would come in time. And then they would feed as though on the most exquisite delicacies. "And when you are bored with the bland flavours of the wretched skin-suits you are wearing, then come to me and savour the tastes I have to offer!"

He spread his arms wide, welcoming them.

"Feed on me, my friends!" He opened his mind as wide as his arms.

And they did.

The release was sudden.

One moment Scott had control of his body, and the next every muscle seemed out of reach. He couldn't put the pain into thought — at least not a coherent one. It felt as though every torment known to man was being inflicted upon him.

He felt the voracious soul that had taken control of him — the corrupted thing that once upon a time had been human — and knew it wouldn't stop taking until Scott had nothing left to give.

And then it left as quickly as it had come.

Joseph stood before him, locked in ecstasy.

It had worked far better than he dared hope.

Scott suspected that bringing the lost souls back to this world wasn't going to be the hardest part of the plan. The risk had always been in whether they would move on from the 'doorways' into Joseph. The rifts in their heads had acted as a magnet of sorts, drawing the lost souls through the Collision. They were doors, but Joseph was far more than that. Joseph offered them a *home,* taking them all in so they could be together again, some spiritual, metaphysical gestalt.

There wasn't a moment to lose though. Joseph was in obvious agony. His hands were no longer thrown wide. He clutched at his temples. He had his head thrown back and was locked in the throes of a silent endless scream. One mind was not made to harbour five souls. There wasn't room in there for four extra. He was quite literally trying to hold his mind together with the sheer strength of will. It couldn't last.

Scott launched himself at Joseph, taking advantage of the moment.

He hit the killer hard, driving him back with every ounce of strength he possessed, praying that Joseph would not realize what was happening to him. Scott put his head down and drove on with all of his weight, his feet scrabbling and slipping on the uneven platform. If he had to go over the side with Tern to stop him, then so be it. He'd already realized there were fates worse than death.

He felt the impact pound the air out of Joseph Tern's lungs, but the muscles were relaxed, unresisting. He staggered back, and together they were locked in the parody of some lover's embrace, a twisted tango, the last in this beautiful city, and then Tern's foot caught in the metalwork. Momentum carried them forward. Joseph, locked in the ecstasy of possession, didn't try to free his foot. He didn't even seem aware that it was trapped, even as Scott's weight took him back, bending his leg at an impossible angle.

Behind him, rippling and shimmering, and waiting hungrily to welcome them, the rift opened wider and wider. It was a stark slice of light that sliced across the tarmac of the road, through the wonderful white granite of the arch, and the trees lining the boulevard. It was like a glittering blade carving into the world.

Joseph's eyes flared open, horror in them as he realized what was happening, but it was too late for him to help himself, he was falling into the rift.

Scott couldn't understand why he wasn't falling too, but then he saw that Rajesh had grabbed ahold of him before he could go over the broken railing.

He watched, horrified and fascinated as Tern fell—it was unlike any fall he'd ever witnessed. Tern almost seemed to be flying, falling in slow motion, his arms pin-wheeling, flapping frantically, and seeming to turn to smoke. Then the smoke blackened. And then the black burst into brilliant flame as Joseph Tern was swallowed by the rift. His corpse would turn to ash, and then scatter through the howling winds of the void, but the blackness in his soul, and the four aspects of the multitude that had crawled out to fill him? Would they burn? If they didn't, did that mean that as long as the rift remained open they would come looking for a way back into the world?

Would he ever be able to sleep again?

Would he be forced to lie awake at night, one eye open, unable to look away from the shadows, dreading what might lurk in there?

"Close your minds," he screamed, not knowing *how* to do that. Not for sure. Not for certain. "Think of happy times. Think of joy! Think of sex! Of Life! Think of being alive and how fucking WONDERFUL it is! Just find something and focus on it. Don't let them back in!"

Whatever their personal ideas of happiness were, it must have worked, because the light seemed to dim but the tear in the Earth didn't appear to be healing itself.

Scott felt a dramatic shift as the Tower buckled. Another baleful scream was torn from the metal as the millions of rivets began to fail. The Tower was coming apart, unable to withstand the forces at work now.

Scott leaned against the railing, gasping. He couldn't believe it was over, that they'd done it.

But of course it wasn't over.

Not as long as the rift was open.

The Tower shook with the rift's wrath, twisting further and further away from true. A great crack opened up in the platform, running the width of the Tower and cutting them off from the stairs. Another great shudder went through the Tower.

"You OK?" Rajesh asked, placing a hand on Scott's shoulder. Adrenalin hammered through his system. There was no way of knowing if he was okay. He was still standing. That would have to do. Rajesh was trembling. They had just killed a man—it would have been stranger if he hadn't been trembling.

So Scott nodded.

Thérèse and Mei-su held onto each other for comfort. The Chinese woman looked as though she had no comfort left to give.

"Where now?" asked Thérèse, staring at the gulf that had opened up in the platform.

The answer was, of course, down, but why did they think that he had the answers to everything? Just because he had the Twitchers' book, didn't mean he had the answers. Sure, the book had helped him get his visions into some sort of order, but there were no answers there. It wasn't a cheat sheet.

""We follow the rails," Scott said, pointing down. Rajesh leaned over the edge, but it was Thérèse who saw the bones that ran in the direction of the bridge, and across it.

"Where do they go?" Thérèse asked.

"If I'm right, the Sacre Coeur," he told her, pointing towards the church on the hill. "The train that rides those rails comes into Paris once every five days. It leaves in the morning and returns at night, meaning it passes the basilica twice a day. It's all in here." He tapped the notebook, cutting off any further debate. "I'd never have worked out the pattern between the train and the bell ringing without the book, but it's there. Trust me, we need to follow the tracks."

But first they had to navigate the broken platform, which was no mean feat. With a run up, he could jump the gap—it wasn't that wide, it was the fall that made it feel so much more daunting. Mei-su however wouldn't have made the jump, so they were forced to jury rig a harness from junk they found in one of the maintenance cupboards. It wasn't graceful, but it worked.

They headed down.

It was possible to see the white line running from the Collision, through the dirty streets, to the church on the hill, and maybe beyond.

Scott knew what it was, even if he didn't really *believe* it.

He pulled the book out of his pocket, running his fingers over notes and sketches again, still hoping to find more information hidden in there despite the fact he'd read it backwards and forwards.

He didn't say anything to the others; there was no point alarming them.

He led them until they reached the white line and they could all see it for what it was.

"Bones," Thérèse said, "It's made of bones."

Scott nodded.

"You knew?"

Scott nodded again.

"There's a train," Scott said. It was time to tell them what he knew. He licked his parched lips, knowing it was going to sound insane. "A train of bones; of flesh and muscle, driven by blood pumping under extreme pressure. In some ways it is alive."

He didn't know what he'd expected—shock maybe, but there was no sign of that on any of their faces. It wasn't just that nothing surprised them any more, though. Yes, they had already seen things that no one should ever be made to see, but he realized, looking at their acceptance that they'd seen the Nightmare Train in their visions, too. So instead of wasting time pretending they hadn't, Scott just said, "The tracks cross the Seine at Pont de l'Alma. It's the only surviving bridge into the city."

They walked a winding path through the rubble and decay.

Mei-su struggled to keep pace with them, but she showed no sign of wanting to stop.

They all wanted desperately to get to wherever they needed to be.

It was as simple as that. That was what their lives had become.

Scott wasn't sure if they realized what he intended, but surely they must understand that they needed to close the Collision, even if doing that would almost certainly cost them their lives because the rifts inside their heads were the only thing keeping it open.

It wasn't as though they could have the rifts surgically removed.

Scott knelt beside the bone tracks, feeling the ground for any tell-tale vibrations.

There was no way of knowing how old the bones were or where they had come from. His mind raced with questions. Were they the recent dead or robbed from the graveyards and ossuaries across the city? Who built this macabre structure? There were no answers to these questions in the book. Scott was beginning to think he would never know the truth.

Scott was right about one thing: the bone-tracks ran past the doors of the glorious old Sacre Coeur. It had taken them hours to reach the Basilica. They had been forced to navigate the streets by broken landmarks. The light was starting to fade. Countless boulevards were blocked—and not just by rubble. They'd had to skirt around swarms of toothfish and other horrific abominations along the way. When they were lucky, they got to walk between the tracks, the shortest possible route to where they needed to be. When they weren't they had to take their lives in their hands and risk the predators. None of that mattered now they were here. The beautiful domes of the church appeared intact, and remarkably free of damage in fact.

The doors were closed.

Thérèse ran ahead and hammered on them, but no one came.

She traced her fingers along one of the great gouges in the wood.

Scott saw them too but could only begin to imagine what kind of creature could have caused the damage. There had to be someone inside but banging on the door wasn't rousing them. Refuse bags were piled up outside the church. Seeing them bundled up felt wrong. Rubbish wasn't the stuff of true faith. Scott chuckled mirthlessly. He was drawn to the bags as though they were the answer.

They were.

He didn't need to lift them to see that they were new. The church itself may have escaped the destruction but the terrain around it was distressed.

Mei-su hurled a rock at the door.

The sound of the bang echoed all around them.

As it faded away they heard movement from inside and slowly bolts were drawn back. The door opened a fraction. After a moment it opened wider and a sallow-faced man stepped out. He seemed cautious, afraid of the light, "We don't get many visitors," he said. It was more of a grunt than a sentence.

"We seek sanctuary," Scott said, not saying from what.

The man ran a finger along the gouge in the door, much as Thérèse had a few moments earlier. Perhaps he knew?

"It's been a long time since we have had any new additions to our community, but you are of course welcome. My name is Fournier." He spoke with a thick French accent. Once they were inside, he seemed eager to close the door and slam the bolts and braces back into place.

Suspicious faces followed them from the shadows and alcoves as they walked into the Basilica; despite the mask of shadows Scott could see they were full of fear and inquisitiveness in equal measure. It didn't take him long to realize that an entirely new society had risen within the walls. He saw children born after the Collision, raised down here. Entire families huddled together in the old prayer chambers. Who knew how many had taken refuge within the church and its catacombs? Hundreds? More.

The man motioned to the people who had gathered together with a ragtag collection of possessions. "The bell brought them all here. It's safe inside. Safer than outside. But the bell doesn't just attract survivors."

Scott saw the familiar fear in his eyes. They all had that look. It was the effect of seeing the strange and terrifying things that had come through the Collision.

"The bell didn't bring us, we found our own way," Mei-su said.

"We saw the door," Rajesh said, before the man could express his curiosity. "What happened?"

"Three nights ago a great beast clawed at it. We feared the worst. Surely it must only be a matter of time before our sanctuary falls, but," he shrugged, at a loss to explain the workings of the no-longer mundane world, "It left. It seems that power," he looked up at the ceiling, as though God or whatever power he was invoking, lived up there, "can be a powerful ally. It's not the first time we've had something come to the door.

"So why ring the bell? Therese asked. "Why draw attention to yourselves?"

Scott answered for him: "Because you're protecting someone here, aren't you?"

"I don't know what you mean."

"It's the only answer that makes any kind of sense. There's a connection between the bell ringing and the train leaving the Collision. In my visions I've seen the train waiting outside the Basilica doors, waiting, calling, and I've always wondered what it was waiting for. The answer has to be someone. It's waiting for someone."

"Why would you think that?"

"Because you're the one who rings the bell. You are protecting that someone. Tell me I'm wrong."

"I could deny it."

"You could, but you would be lying."

"Let's just say it's true, that I am protecting someone, why would I give them up to you?"

"Because we are not the creature that keeps returning to your door."

"And that would be reason enough for you?"

"No, but it would be the truth. Tell me I'm wrong, that's all you have to do. Tell me I'm wrong and we'll turn around and leave you to your secrets."

Fournier didn't. Instead he gestured towards the altar where a woman stood with her daughter.

"This is Helena. She was born on the day of the Collision." Fournier said as the girl came down the three short steps to the aisle. "She is a gifted child, smarter than all of us, though she says little. She will lead us all to salvation."

"She is a prophet?"

"No, she will close the rift."

And in a way she might just do that, Scott realized. "The train comes every fifth day, morning and in the evening. When it does, it calls to the girl. She fights you, doesn't she? She fights you for all she's worth, desperate to break free."

"She does," Fournier agreed.

"And you ring the bell and the spell is broken. She stops being a danger to others and herself and the train moves on." Fournier said nothing. "But tonight she *must* board the train," Scott continued. "The next time the train comes, she must ride the rails. There's no other way this can end. You have to let her board the train."

"Why should I believe you? You're a stranger here. You come in spouting answers to things you couldn't possibly know. Give me one good reason why I shouldn't just cast you out."

Scott looked at him. "Because we're part of it. All of us. La Fracture runs through our heads. We understand it better than anyone because we are the rift."

"And that's supposed to make me feel better how, exactly? This thing threatens life as we know it, and you tell me you're made of the same stuff?"

"Not made of, a conduit. We need to close the valves — the mini-rifts — inside us, and we can close the Collision."

"And Helena boarding the train is the key to this?"

Scott nodded.

Fournier nodded once, grimly determined. He glanced up at an old wooden clock mounted above an archway.

"Time," Scott said. "That's what so much of this is all about." he pulled the notebook from his pocket finding the sequence of numbers that related to the train. "It's approaching, isn't it?"

Fournier consulted his watch, but he didn't need it or the great wall-mounted clock to tell him what he already knew. Even inside these thick walls they could all hear the terrible wails, the cries and the screams of living wheels on bone track. The Nightmare Train was coming.

"Five minutes," the Frenchman said nervously.

"We should wait outside," Scott said.

"You're leaving with her?" asked Fournier.

"Yes, we're going together to the end of the line," Scott said.

"No."

Scott looked around to see where the objection had come from. It wasn't Fournier. "You cannot walk in here and take my daughter," Helena's mother said. "I don't care what you say, she's special, the Chosen. One day she will close the rift."

"Today is that day," Scott said.

"No. This is a trick. You are one of them. You said so yourself. They are inside you. You speak with the voice of the multitude. You mean to kill Helena so that the rift remains open forever."

"Believe me, if we could do it without your girl, we would, but the train won't stop for us. It wants her. So if we are going to travel through the rift, we need her help."

"So we let her stop the train, you get on and go your merry way. And my girl stays here. With me."

"She's safe here," another woman said, joining them.

"Ordinarily, perhaps. But this is no ordinary day. I don't know what I can do to make you believe me, not in the two minutes I've got to convince you. But I need you to trust me. There's something on the other side, something hiding in the darkness behind the blinding light and it's trying to come through. All of Earth will burn and everyone here along with it. The world eaters will come, and everything will be wiped out." He dropped to one knee, holding out his hands to Helena. "I need you to trust me, okay?" He tapped his temple as he said, "I saw the day you were born. I saw it through the rift in my head. I saw your mommy carry you towards the hospital just minutes after you were born." He looked at the woman, who regarded him with a mix of fear and loathing and something else. What was it? Hope? "Your clothes were covered in blood, weren't they? You were desperately weak, and in the chaos when all you could think about was getting to the hospital you were attacked." She raised her hand to her mouth. "You were stumbling along the rift edge when a swarm of toothfish came, drawn by the blood on your clothes. Do I need to say more to convince you? Do you need me to tell you how they tore through the crowds of fleeing people and cornered you and baby? Do I need to remind you how your husband sacrificed himself? No, I didn't think so. I'm not looking to hurt your daughter. I need her help. We all do."

"I want to help you," Helena said, taking his hands.

"This could be a one-way ticket for all of us," Scott told her, looking into her bright wide eyes.

"All journeys are one way," the girl told him.

Perhaps she was the wisest of them all, after all, Scott thought as the shuddering of the walls announced the Bone Train's arrival.

It was waiting for them when they stepped outside.

Muscle stretched across bone, sinews pulled tight and tatters of flesh binding it all in place.

A door slid aside and invited them in.

Mei-su did not hesitate, neither did Rajesh. They clambered aboard. "This is it," the Indian said, disappearing into the carriage.

Thérèse took one last look around before placing a foot on the long rail of bone that acted as a step and followed him in.

Scott stepped aside to allow Helena to board ahead of him. Her hands trembled noticeably as she touched the structure. The meat of the Bone Train moved and shifted beneath her touch as the girl pulled herself onto the train.

She reached out a hand for Scott.

He took it, and climbed onto the train.

He wanted to say something; some rousing words of heroism. Something to tide them over to journey's end.

Scott said nothing.

The door slid back into place with a wet, meaty, *thunk*, and the walls began to move — in and out, in and out, like the wet innards of a ribcage as the body breathed. The movement grew faster and faster, in and out, in and out, until the train began to glide forward, slowly at first then starting to pick up speed, the world in motion.

They held onto the structure and each other as the Nightmare Train rattled over the uneven tracks of ivory bone, building up a head of steam as it hurtled towards the Collision.

The pain inside his head raged now, making it impossible to think.

Closer and closer, the wheels of bone bouncing and juddering on the femurs and tibias and fibulas laid out across the ground.

They were in the right place.

For the first time since the Collision opened, they were in the right place, and the right place was a train hurtling towards oblivion.

Scott clutched the Twitchers' book with one hand and Helena's hand with the other. Thérèse curled her arm around his and drew herself close for comfort. Rajesh did his best to hold Mei-Su upright. The five of them, hardly heroes, filled with uncertainty.

Scott had no idea if this was going to work, if the rift would close, if they would be alive five minutes from now.

Still, they had to try.

Humanity had to survive.

And as they approached the edge, hurtling along the bones towards the abyss, a single bright burning image overpowered all else: he saw the things hiding in the darkness, the multitude, the infinite, the devourers of dead worlds.

They were waiting; hiding behind the light.

The Wraith Lights were waiting...

KEEP CALM AND CARRY ON
PART FOUR
by David N. Smith and Violet Addison

Jess
OLD CALENDAR: Monday, 1ˢᵗ March, 2027.
NEW PARISIAN CALENDAR: 1ˢᵗ Day, 2ⁿᵈ Quarter, Year TWO.
07:15am CEST

I am alive.

Nobody could be more surprised by this than I am.

When the lights of London went out, I was just twenty-four years old, far from the reach of my family, terrified and traumatized beyond belief. I ran. Hell, we all ran.

I spent the first two years with Mike and Laura. They looked after me. They kept me sane. They became the most important people in my world. Then I lost them.

We became separated.

Our camp was over-run by giant red mites—chiggers we call them back home—that poured from this weird prism object. We ran for our lives, fleeing in different directions. The tidal wave of bugs was massive, over-running all of our pre-planned rendezvous points. Our carefully laid back-up plans were worth nothing.

It was such an avoidable mistake, but once it was done, there was no undoing it. Back then there was no easy way to find people, if you lost them, that was it, you were on your own.

I still wonder what happened to them.

For the sake of my own sanity, I choose to believe that they escaped from the mites and that they're still out there somewhere, fighting to stay alive.

I was lucky. With my nursing background, I was a much sought-after commodity; every group of survivors was in need of medical help. So I was always able to find a warm place to sleep and a few scraps of food to eat: just enough to stay alive. I know many others were a lot less fortunate.

Everything changed in May 2025.

There are stories.

Many stories.

The most common story is that of a man called Joseph, who chose to throw himself into the Collision, his noble sacrifice somehow ending the evil that mankind had brought upon itself.

We don't know if this story is true, but it has helped many people come to terms with the ten years of terror that we have suffered, and so the story has been told and retold around the camp fires of many survivors, until most consider it to be fact.

For the last year and a half, since the rift closed, I have been working as the chief medical officer in King Harry's First Infantry Battalion. We have successfully purged most of the monstrosities from the shores of Britain, and have now relocated to the continent, where we have united with survivors in Paris in order to deal with the terrors that are still roaming the French countryside.

But this is not just an errand of mercy. We have a mission, and yesterday we completed one of our key objectives: we reactivated all four reactors at Paluel nuclear power station, and successfully restored the electricity supply to Northern France and South-East England.

We attempted this at various power stations in Britain, but found that all the reactors had been completely shut down. It must have been one of the last orders given by British government, to avoid a nuclear catastrophe, which possibly explains why the power went off so suddenly all those years ago. It's good to know, right at the end, they managed to get something right. Meanwhile, here in France, there was no time for them to give the shut-down order, meaning it's been relatively simple to reactivate the reactors, we're just lucky none of them went into melt-down in the meantime.

Now we have electric lights again.

We have heating again.

But more importantly, the internet is back.

It seems that overnight we have dragged ourselves out of the stone-age, and into something that vaguely resembles the world we once knew.

Most of the communications infrastructure has survived the disaster intact, meaning that we now have a life line to the rest of world.

This is my first internet post in twelve years.

I'm not the girl I was. I'm now thirty-six years old. I can shoot a toothfish at twenty feet, debone it and make stew from its brain; it tastes awful, but it'll keep you alive if there's nothing else to eat. I can bring down a gasbag too, though we haven't seen many of them in a while. I can also strip and reassemble my own P226 handgun.

I have a daughter.

Naomi is six and half. She never knew the world before the Collision. She doesn't know how much we lost. Right now, she is playing with an electric light switch, mesmerized by the light, as to her it seems like magic. She is smiling.

So we wait, hopeful of the future, keen to hear what other voices may be out there.

Over time, we expect to hear from almost every corner of the globe, as we doubt there is a country in the world where there aren't survivors. I am of course hoping to hear from my missing friends, but more than anything else, I am desperate for news of my family in the USA.

It's been a decade since I've seen them, but I love and miss them more than ever.

My daughter has never even met them.

My brother…

My father…

My mother…

Are you alive?

CONTRIBUTORS

Violet Addison was first published through Big Finish's 'Doctor Who: How The Doctor Changed My Life' writing competition. She has also co-written short stories for Obverse Book's 'Faction Paradox' range and the Doctor Who Information Network fanzine, 'Myth Makers.' She's currently planning on writing her first novel later in 2012, but there's a fair chance she'll just end up surfing the internet instead.

Nicholas Blake is known within Doctor Who fandom as editor/co-writer of the awkwardly titled fanzine 'Planet of the Ming Mongs', and outside of Doctor Who fandom for not very much at all, not even a little bit. He currently works for the libraries at Nottingham University and believes all soft toys are real, especially the ones shaped like elephants.

Carolyn Edwards is a freelance artist, based in the UK. She has been working professionally since 2000 and has been a regular face at Doctor Who and Sci-Fi Conventions all over the UK, also Los Angeles, selling and exhibiting original paintings, prints and greetings cards.

Her work has appeared extensively in Fanzines, books, theatre posters and magazines. Since beginning work as a sketch card artist for Strictly Ink 2007, and then Topps in 2008, Carolyn has scaled down Convention appearances to spend more time on sketch cards, portrait commissions and other projects. Her works are in private collections all over the world.

Carolyn doesn't have much spare time as a full-time mum/artist, but when she can, she loves running, rollerblading and playing the violin, guitar and piano.

http://www.carolynedwards.blogspot.com
http://timedancer.deviantart.com/
https://www.facebook.com/SpiritedPortraits

Jordan Ellinger is a recent first place winner in the Writers of the Future Contest and is a Clarion West graduate. His work can be seen in "AE - The Canadian Speculative Fiction Review", and the anthologies "Time in a Bottle" and "Warhammer: The Gotrek and Felix Anthology". In 2012, he partnered with award-winning illustrator Luke Eidenschink to produce the graphic novel "The Seven". In his spare time, he helms Every Day Publishing, publisher of Every Day Fiction, Every Day Poets, Flash Fiction Chronicles, and Raygun Revival.

Jonathan Green is a writer of speculative fiction, with more than forty books to his name. Well known for his contributions to the Fighting Fantasy range of adventure gamebooks, and numerous Black Library publications, he has also written fiction for such diverse properties as Doctor Who, Star Wars: The Clone Wars, Sonic the Hedgehog, Teenage Mutant Ninja Turtles, and Moshi Monsters.

He is the creator of the Pax Britannia series for Abaddon Books and, to date, has written eight novels set within this steampunk universe. He currently divides his time between

West London and rural Wiltshire. To find out more about his current projects visit http://www.jonathangreenauthor.com

Kelly Hale is the author of several short stories, a play, a novella, some overwrought poetry, a co-authored TV tie-in novel of the Doctor Who variety, and her own book, "Erasing Sherlock" that languished out of print for two years but is now available on Amazon Kindle. She lives in a crazy little place called Stumptown—jewel of the Pacific Northwest— where the streets are paved with espresso beans and the garbage recycles itself. She is the mother of a grown-up son/comedian, and a grown-up daughter/sailor/mother of two. Make of that what you will.

Elise Hattersley works in commercial collections by day, and fights crime and injustice by night. With the aid of her husband and their two sons, she aims to rid the world of supervillainy such as that perpetrated by their family cat. She has lived in the North-West of England since 2005 and expects to start understanding what people are saying any day now. Her greatest fear is that an army of hyper-intelligent crabs will find its way to her secret lair, not because of what it might do once it gets there but because a crustacean invasion would be a deeply unpleasant discovery to make first thing in the morning.

Dave Hoskin is a writer living in Melbourne. His fiction has appeared in Doctor Who - Short Trips: Transmissions, Bernice Summerfield: Something Changed, Faction Paradox: A Romance in Twelve Parts, Tales of the City and Midnight Echo. His non-fiction has appeared in The Big Issue, Metro,

Australian Book Review and Overland. His favourite colour is jam, his favourite band is world peace, and his favourite pastime is talking about himself in the third person.

Dave Hutchinson was born in Sheffield in 1960. He's the author of five collections of short stories and one novel, editor of two anthologies of science fiction and fantasy and co-editor of a third. His novella 'The Push,' published by NewCon Press, was shortlisted for the BSFA short fiction award in 2010, and his short story 'The Incredible Exploding Man,' published in the anthology Solaris Rising, was longlisted for the same award in 2012. A former journalist, he lives in London with his wife and several cats.

Pete Kempshall is a writer and editor living in Perth, Western Australia. Despite first being published as a sci-fi writer, he has become better known for his horror stories—World's Collider marks a return to his original genre, and to the prospect of people being able to read his stories without thinking he's a little bit wrong in the head. Pete has been nominated for a variety of awards—including the Australian Shadows, Aurealis and Ditmar Award for Best New Talent—and blogs about his writing projects at www.tyrannyoftheblankpage.blogspot.com.

Steve Lockley holds the record for the most consecutive nominations for the British Fantasy Award, has approaching 100 short stories in print, and is the co-author with Steven Savile of the Sally Reardon Supernatural Mysteries series, that began with Of Time and Dust, and includes Missing, Deadlines and Out of Season. Lockley and Savile are currently working on an Arkham Horror novel together, which features Harry Houdini and a young Dennis Wheatley as the unlikely heroes...

Megan N. Moore is a writer and artist based out of North Texas. After publishing several non-fiction pieces for a variety of blogs and websites, this is her first published work of fiction. She is currently in her senior year at Texas Women's University and originally hails from the small town of Midlothian, just a few miles away from the site of the cancelled Superconducting Super Collider.

James Moran wrote the films Severance, Cockneys Vs Zombies, and Tower Block, and has written episodes of Doctor Who, Torchwood, Spooks, Primeval, Crusoe, and Spooks: Code 9. He also wrote the "TARDIS" episode of the Doctor Who Adventure Games, several short stories, a Highlander audio play for Big Finish, and the Streamy Award nominated web series Girl Number 9, which was screened on the US FEARnet website and Australian TV. He likes watching documentaries about things that explode, and can be found on twitter.com/jamesmoran

Paul Pearson is a new writer from Australia, a self-proclaimed geek, a Browncoat, a podcaster, a time traveller, a legend, a lunatic, a Hufflepuff, a book ninja, a zombie pimp, a devious romantic, a Magnificent Bastard and a serial liar. He majored in Creative Writing at the University of Wollongong and graduated in 2011 with a Bachelor of Creative Arts (with Distinction). When not working on fiction, Paul writes online reviews and is a co-host and/or audio engineer for several podcasts.

Aaron Rosenberg is an award-winning, bestselling novelist, children's book author, and game designer. His novels include No Small Bills and For This Is Hell, the Dread Remora space-opera series, and the O.C.L.T. supernatural thriller series, plus novels for Star Trek, Warhammer, WarCraft, and Eureka. His children's books include Bandslam: The Novel, books for iCarly, PowerPuff Girls, and Transformers Animated, and the original series Pete and Penny's Pizza Puzzles. His RPG work includes Asylum, Spookshow, the Origins Award-winning Gamemastering Secrets, The Supernatural Roleplaying Game, Warhammer Fantasy Roleplay, and The Deryni Roleplaying Game. You can visit him online at http://www.gryphonrose.com or follow him on Twitter @gryphonrose.

Richard Salter is a British writer and editor based just outside Toronto, Canada. He has sold over twenty short stories to various anthologies, including tales in Solaris Rising: The New Solaris Book of Science Fiction, Warhammer: Gotrek & Felix The Anthology, Horror For Good, Phobophobia and Machine of Death 2. He previously edited the Doctor Who Short Trips anthology Transmissions for Big Finish. His website can be found at http://www.richardsalter.com and you can follow him on Twitter @chababug

Steven Savile has written 20 books for various media properties including Doctor Who, Torchwood, Stargate, Warhammer, Slaine and Primeval. Shadow of the Jaguar, which was a #1 bestseller in the UK in 2008, and sold over half a million books worldwide. 2010 saw the release of his first non-fiction book, Fantastic TV, charting 50 years of science fiction television in the UK and US. He is the co-creator of Monster Town, recently bought by Sony Entertainment to develop for cable TV in the US (with Adam Fierro, Dexter, The Shield, 24, Walking Dead, as show-runner) and his novels have been translated into 9 languages, including German, French, Italian, and Spanish. Silver, his debut thriller, was released in January 2010 from Variance, in the US, It reached #2 on the e-book bestseller list of Amazon UK and spent over 100 days in the top 100, having sold 50,000 copies since Feb 1st 2011. Steve also wrote the storyline for Electronic Arts' Battlefield 3. He has been runner up in the British fantasy award, and won the Writers of the Future Award and the Scribe Award for best Media Tie-In in 2010. His most recent novels, Each Ember's Ghost and Dark Water: Risen 2 are both released in August 2012.

David N. Smith won Big Finish's 'Bernice Summerfield' short story writing competition in 2006. He went on to write a story for the 'Doctor Who' Short Trips range, which was later reprinted in a best-of anthology. He has also co-written a 'Faction Paradox' short story for Obverse Books. He's written a handful of corporate training videos, but people tend to be less interested in these as they involve considerably fewer dragons, pirates or aliens. Full details can be found on his website — http://www.davenevsmith.co.uk — if he's found time to update it.

Jonathan Templar has written horrible things for a plethora of publishers including Smart Rhino, Siren's Call, Wicked East Press and Rymfire Books. His recent stories include 'The Meat Man' for Cutting Block Press's charitable anthology Horror for Good and the forthcoming novella 'The Angel of Shadwell'.

Jonathan can be found hiding from the sunlight at www.jonathantemplar.com.

Lukas Thelin is a self-taught digital media illustrator from the north of Sweden, currently living in Stockholm. Since starting out as a freelance artist in 2000, his work has included covers and illustrations for various role playing games, a collectible card game called, a comic book for a museum exhibition, and a book of stories of animal lore as told by elders from Sweden's indigenous Saami people. His art has been featured in every issue of the gaming magazine Fenix, since its start in 2004.

Simon Kurt Unsworth was born in Manchester in 1972 on a night when, despite increasingly desperate research, he can find no evidence of mysterious signs or portents. He currently lives on a hill in the north of England with his wife and child awaiting the coming flood, where he writes essentially grumpy fiction (for which pursuit he was nominated for a 2008 World Fantasy Award for Best Short Story). He is tall, grouchier than he should be and the owner of a wide selection of garish shirts. His work has been published in a number of critically acclaimed anthologies, including At Ease with the Dead, Shades of Darkness, Exotic Gothic 3, Gaslight Grotesque, Never Again and Lovecraft Unbound. He has also appeared in four Mammoth Book of Best New Horror anthologies: 19, 21, 22 and 23, and also The Very Best of Best New Horror. His first collection of short stories, Lost Places, was released by the Ash Tree Press in 2010 and his second, Quiet Houses, from Dark Continents Publishing in 2011. He has a further collection, Strange Gateways, due out from PS Publishing in 2012 and his as-yet-unnamed collection will launch the Spectral Press Spectral Signature Editions imprint in 2013, so at some point he needs to write those stories.

Richard Wright is an author of strange, dark fictions, currently living in India with his wife and daughter. In the sixteen years since writing his first novel Cuckoo, his short stories have appeared widely in the US and UK press, most recently in anthologies including Dark Faith, and Wildthyme In Purple. In 2010, Shroud Publishing released his novella Hiram Grange and the Nymphs of Krakow, and his second novel Thy Fearful Symmetry will be released in August 2012. You can find him spending too much time online at http://www.richardwright.org, http://www.facebook.com/richardwrightauthor, and on Twitter as @richard_wright.

Trent Zelazny is the Nightmare Award-winning author of To Sleep Gently, Fractal Despondency, Shadowboxer, The Day the Leash Gave Way and Other Stories, Destination Unknown, A Crack in Melancholy Time, and Butterfly Potion. His novel, Too Late to Call Texas, will be released this fall.

He was born in Santa Fe, New Mexico, has lived in California, Oregon, Arizona, and Florida. He also loves NBA basketball.

Also available from

Printed in Great Britain
by Amazon.co.uk, Ltd.,
Marston Gate.